SAVAGE

NATE TEMPLE SERIES BOOK 15

SHAYNE SILVERS

ARGENTO PUBLISHING

CONTENTS

Shayne Silvers

Savage

Nate Temple Series Book 14

A TempleVerse Series

ISBN: 978-1-947709-42-3

© 2021, Shayne Silvers / Argento Publishing, LLC

info@shaynesilvers.com

THE NATE TEMPLE SERIES—A WARNING

Nate Temple starts out with everything most people could ever wish for—money, magic, and notoriety. He's a local celebrity in St. Louis, Missouri—even if the fact that he's a wizard is still a secret to the world at large.

Nate is also a bit of a...well, let's call a spade a spade. He can be a mouthy, smart-assed jerk. Like the infamous Sherlock Holmes, I specifically chose to give Nate glaring character flaws to overcome rather than making him a chivalrous Good Samaritan. He's a black hat wizard, an anti-hero—and you are now his partner in crime. He is going to make a *ton* of mistakes. And like a buddy cop movie, you are more than welcome to yell, laugh and curse at your new partner as you ride along together through the deadly streets of St. Louis.

Despite Nate's flaws, there's also something *endearing* about him...You soon catch whispers of a firm moral code buried deep under all his snark and arrogance. A diamond waiting to be polished. And you, the esteemed reader, will soon find yourself laughing at things you really shouldn't be laughing at. It's part of Nate's charm. Call it his magic...

So don't take yourself, or any of the characters in my world, too seriously. Life is too short for that nonsense.

Get ready to cringe, cackle, cry, curse, and—ultimately—*cheer* on this snarky wizard as he battles or befriends angels, demons, myths, gods, shifters, vampires and many other flavors of dangerous supernatural beings.

DON'T FORGET!

DON'T FORGET! VIP's get early access to all sorts of Temple-Verse goodies, including signed copies, private giveaways, and advance notice of future projects. AND A FREE NOVELLA! Click the image or join here: www.shaynesilvers.com/l/219800

FOLLOW AND LIKE:

Shayne's FACEBOOK PAGE:

www.shaynesilvers.com/l/38602

I try to respond to all messages, so don't hesitate to drop me a line. Not interacting with readers is the biggest travesty that most authors can make. Let me fix that.

CHAPTER 1

The dark shadows reached out to me, sinister and foreboding, as a maniacal cackle echoed through the ancient halls of the austere castle. My linen pants were baggy enough to ease my movements —an obvious choice for my mission. I'd opted for no shirt, relying on the magical runes and spells I'd painted over my chest and arms that granted me enhanced stealth and silence. I risked a quick, careful glance into the gloomy hallway beyond, shifting the feathered headdress I wore so that my vision was unobstructed. The long cape of feathers trailed down my back, tingling with magical power that gave me a heady, euphoric sensation. It was paramount that I escaped this hellhole with the powerful shamanistic artifact before the enemy caught me.

The future depended on it.

I gripped my only weapon in my left hand—a sleek compact bow. Well, my other weapons were always at my disposal, but attack magic in this place would set off alarms and ruin my chances of escaping with my prize. The bow and arrow were silent and sneaky. I was down to three arrows, having exhausted the rest of my quiver taking out patrolling guards on my way into this cursed place.

A loud *crack-crack-crack* erupted from the shadows and a trio of bullets careened off the wall a few inches from my face. I reeled back on reflex, sucking in a breath. Shit! I'd been spotted. Stealth was no longer an option and standing still was death in this cursed place. I bolted out into the open, racing as fast as I could. My leather moccasins whisper-slapped against the cold marble floor as I ran, risking everything to escape with my prize. I was so close to safety that I could no longer entertain caution.

Do or die.

I dropped to my ass and slid beneath a long wooden table just as more bullets ricocheted past my ear, hammering into the ancient furniture. I grinned wolfishly at the near misses, chuckling under my breath at the flood of adrenaline that coursed through my veins as I nimbly danced the line between life and death. I cleared the table but bumped into a chair, knocking it over with a loud crash. I heard a triumphant shout behind me as the noise helped my hunter locate me. I shambled to my feet and lobbed a small burst of magic at the ground, creating a dense cloud of thick fog that filled the room, hopefully masking my precise location.

No alarms went off at my subtle use of magic and I let out a breath of relief.

I heard a muttered curse that let me know I had succeeded. Rather than pausing to gloat, I took off again, aiming for the grand staircase ahead. At the base of those stairs was safety and my only escape. Air rushed through my lungs as I poured on the speed, faster than I'd ever moved before. My muscles strained and screamed, burning like fire, but it was a pleasant, victorious source of pain, and I realized I was grinning from ear-to-ear at my approaching triumph.

I heard the sounds of pursuit behind me as my hunter caught onto my ruse, spotting my mad dash to freedom where my thievery would be rewarded.

More bullets cracked through the halls, zipping past me like a swarm of bees. I zigged and zagged, bobbing and weaving as I ran, careful to make sure the ancient Native American headdress didn't fall off in my haste. If I lost that, this whole thing would have been for nothing. I would never get a second chance to steal it for my Armory. It wasn't simply a headband with feathers. No. This was the real deal with feathers trailing down to my lower back like a hoodie with no jacket or sleeves. I couldn't wait to get it to Grimm Tech for further study.

The hallway opened out onto the wide, open-air balcony overlooking the floor below. Priceless paintings hung from the walls, featuring the grim visages of generations of the royal bloodline of this thieving wizard family. My victim was an asshole, so I felt no regrets. Robbing a thief was virtuous.

All around me was more proof of the family's centuries of success as robber barons. The banister overlooking the floor below was made of rich carved and polished white wood, the metal posts supporting the banister were hand forged with painstaking detail and gold filigree, and the floors of swirling marble had been imported from Europe hundreds of years ago. Stolen, most likely—just as everything else here had been. Ornate wooden statues of deadly, winged, nightmarish beasts lined the halls like I was racing through a museum of antiquities.

Some of them had come to life and now sported arrows in their sides, necks, and foreheads from my earlier trek through the halls. I'd been able to kill them from a distance without raising an alarm, but the moment I'd grabbed the fabled headdress, the top hunter in this temple had been too experienced for me to avoid.

One of the beastly guards turned to look at me and I let loose with two arrows in quick succession, not slowing down in the slightest. One arrow struck it in the eye but the other went wild, sailing over the open railing to the floor below. The beast didn't make a sound as it died. I paid no more attention to the rich surroundings because I'd seen all of it on my painstakingly slow, stealthy invasion to acquiring the coveted headdress. All that mattered now was my escape. I refused to die here. The world was relying on me for the upcoming Omega War. I leapt into the air and planted my ass on the railing to more speedily descend the wide elegant staircase. I slid down the railing in a blur, the feathers of my headdress whipping and cracking behind me as if cheering me on.

I hefted my legs up at the end of my ride so that I didn't spill out onto the base of the stairs in a tumbling crash. My moccasins struck the marble as lightly as a deer leaping a bush to flee a pack of ravenous, bloodthirsty wolves. But a sudden flare of light ahead drew me up short. I lifted my bow, nocked an arrow, and drew down as I shuffled laterally in hopes it would make me a harder target for my foe, who had somehow managed to materialize *ahead* of me. Damn this place!

My hunter stood at the end of a shadowy hallway, exactly where I needed to go to safely open up my Gateway out of this cursed temple. The figure slowly advanced, emerging from the shadows. Her heels struck the rich marble floor with the resounding thud of wood, followed by a metallic chiming sound. Cowboy boots. Made of ink-black leather, and spurs. My eyes trailed up from the boots and were rewarded with the darkest of temptations because this cowgirl wore skin-tight booty shorts. As alluring as it was, I knew it was only one of the many deadly weapons in her arse...

Arsenal, I corrected, mentally dousing myself with a bucket of cold water.

The black leather gun-belt crookedly hanging off her hips sported two gleaming revolvers.

But she had two other cannons aimed my way and the safeties were obviously off—because she wore no shirt. Her hands hung loosely at her sides, ready to draw down on her revolvers and end my adventure for good. She wore a black cowboy hat that shaded her face, but her dual-colored eyes—one green and one blue—sparkled in the ambient light. She held a clove cigarette in one hand and slowly lifted it to her lips to take a dramatic puff.

"I got you now," the sheriff drawled, exhaling a cloud of the sweet licorice smoke into the air between us.

"You're a daisy if you do," I murmured back, struggling to focus on the danger she represented rather than the cup size of her assault rifles. I managed to focus, barely, feeling the blood coursing through my veins in anticipation of the fight ahead.

"Say *when*," the sheriff murmured in a lazy drawl. The corner of her lips curled up in a taunting smirk as she mirrored my movements, side-stepping in a slow, steady shuffle. *Click-clack, scrape. Click-clack, scrape.*

I stared into those eyes, feeling the dance of death creeping up over me. Freedom was just beyond the sheriff. We continued circling each other, glacially slow, like two stray cats in an alley.

I released my arrow between steps, hoping to catch her off guard. She leaned to the side, impossibly fast, dodging the arrow as she drew a revolver and fired. It struck me in the arm with a flash of searing pain and I recoiled instinctively, gritting my teeth. I was out of arrows, so I dropped my bow to the ground and clutched my throbbing, wounded arm.

She aimed the pistol at me, thumbed back the hammer, and then pulled the trigger. The gun clicked on an empty chamber and she slowly lowered it to her side before dropping it to the ground. The air was tense. Was her other gun loaded or was it also empty?

"You gonna' do something, or just stand there and bleed?" she asked, taking another puff of her clove cigarette.

Rather than continue on with the Tombstone references, I smirked. "Oh, I'm gonna do something, honey," I drawled, calling up my magic. No need to hold back now. I was already caught, and you had to cheat like a bastard to win like a king. "I reckon I ain't got no reason to be discreet no longer, sheriff—"

A faint fluttering sound whispered to life behind me, and my mouth clicked shut as my instincts kicked on. My senses exploded like a fire doused with oil and my playful demeanor evaporated. My sense of smell instantly latched onto the thick, cloying scent of fresh, lush vegetation and my skin pebbled at the sudden proximity of lethal magic directly behind me. Almost forgotten memories of old battles and swarming enemies took over, superimposed over my current surroundings. I growled and spun to face the new threat, feeling as if a great leviathan had taken over my body.

My Wild Side. My Fae instincts.

The land of do or die, win or lose, dominate or be dominated.

And Wylde Fae never lost a fight.

CHAPTER 2

I lifted my hand and snapped my fingers, tapping into my Fae magic. An orb of darkness promptly swallowed us, extinguishing all light and leaving our surroundings in perfect darkness. The unseen Fae assassin disappeared like a popped bubble at my sudden reaction, sensing its chances at success had just been doomed to failure.

I growled furiously at the creature's lack of bravery. The phantom taste of roasted fairy meat tickled my tongue as I recalled sitting before a campfire with Talon after a successful and rewarding hunt in the deepest, darkest forests of Fae. More than anything, I wanted to taste that victory—drink that blood and chew that savory meat—again! It had been so long! But the would-be assassin had fled like a fucking coward.

Rage took me over. A cup full to overflowing without an enemy to douse my fury.

I felt the instant a pressure orb was conceived behind me—the initial flare of creation in a placenta of danger that would promptly mature and be birthed as a dense, concussive blast of some foreign power intent upon harming me. My instincts took over in that gestational fraction of time and I dove to the side, rolling clear just as the power screamed into the world of life, birthed by a sharp *bang*.

I was already moving through the darkness as more baby *bangs* were delivered into my world. I counted them. *Sextuplet baby bangs*, I thought to myself as I cloaked my mad sprint in perfect silence, commanding the stone floor to swallow the impact sounds of my fleet feet. *Time to conquer the banging mother.*

The darkness was my element. Even though I could not see my surroundings, I was one with the stygian void because the darkness was mine, Grammaried into existence by the will of Wylde, the manling king. So I could feel everything the shadows touched, where they touched—and it was all *mine*.

The shadows silently whispered to my ears, telling me where the banging mother was. That, and the cloying smell of licorice smoke, led me to her like a beacon. I exploded out of the void of darkness like a leviathan from the depths and tackled her hard enough to elicit a stunned grunt as I caught her entirely off guard, knocking her from her feet. I flashed out with one hand to cradle the back of her head, knowing how easy it was for a fragile egg to crack upon solid ground. I didn't want to kill her. I wanted to *conquer* her. To show her I held no fear of her strange powers.

I batted something from her hand and heard it skitter across the room as we hit the ground. My knuckles, still cupping the back of her head, burned with fire as my skin squealed across the stone before we finally came to a halt. My foe furiously bucked and hissed, fighting to call upon some strange well of deep inner ability. I marveled at the uniqueness of this foreign energy, knowing it was alien and not of Fae like mine. As formidable as it was, I suffocated it with barely a thought, imprisoning it with midnight shadows and ephemeral bars of willpower. A mad grin split my cheeks as she let out an astonished grunt of terror at how swiftly I had cleaved her powers from her reach. As easily as stealing candy from a babe.

I straddled her tightly, trapping her with my thighs and enjoying my victory as she wildly bucked her hips, struggling and fighting against me in a futile attempt at freedom. I used one hand to pin both of her wrists above her head, stretching her out below me as I loomed over my prey, in complete control of the situation.

She continued to fight, refusing to submit, and I felt my heart begin to race with excitement. She was a fighter. I *loved* fighters. I snarled back at her, adjusting the darkness with a thought so that I could finally see my prey and she could finally see her conqueror. I kept the rest of our surroundings dark, leaving us in a cocoon of nothingness. I wanted her to see the manling who had bested her. Whatever this creature was, I was captivated by her tenacity to never give up.

Her bare breasts heaved beneath my chest and I was momentarily bewitched by her mystifying, dual-colored eyes. For a heartbeat, they were wild around the edges, and then I saw a flash of recognition in them that abruptly morphed into a look of baffled confusion. As quickly as that, she ceased fighting, blinking up at me.

"Whatever it was is gone. It's okay," she whispered reassuringly, as if she thought I was frightened. I studied the banging mother, wondering what type of creature she was and what her strange power had been. She licked her lips nervously. "Are you feeling okay, Nate?" she murmured uneasily.

The name sent a sharp flash of pain through my temples and I gritted my teeth. "Wylde!" I snarled, squeezing her wrists in warning. My tone caused her to purse her lips. I panted, glaring down at her.

"Okay. Role playing," she murmured.

I didn't know what that meant. Her pupils slowly dilated, and those mystical eyes began to sparkle with an inner light, making them glitter like polished jewels.

And I loved sparkly treasures. I wanted them for myself. I was Wylde. I took what I wanted, and I never let a threat go unchallenged. I was still panting, staring down at her, content to let her know that I had won and that she had lost. No more blood needed to be shed. As we locked eyes, I realized that something within her had changed. Perhaps the sound of my name upon her ears had struck her speechless. Maybe she had heard stories of my might. My legend. Whatever had caused her body language to change, I could tell by the look in her eyes that she suddenly accepted my authority.

Fully.

As I stared into her soul, I began to feel a strange kinship.

I had so summarily squashed her powers that her opinion of me had changed. She began struggling again but in an entirely different manner than before. She was no longer fighting to break free but to get *closer* to me. In fact, she suddenly seemed to crave my domination more than *anything*.

Whatever she'd heard in my voice had completely turned her into my play-thing—as she should be. She sucked in her lower lip, biting it as a soft whimper escaped her throat. "Take me," she begged in a breathless rasp.

"To the victor go the spoils," I growled, slowly lowering my mouth to hers, eager to explore this unexpected treasure chest of desire. The scent of her raw lust suddenly filled my nostrils and I felt myself drowning in this bewitching vixen's eyes.

"Please," she croaked. Her hips writhed beneath mine and I felt a blooming heat building beneath the thin fabric covering her inner thighs. I growled, gripping her wrists tightly as my arm shook with pent up antici-pation. She cried out breathlessly, begging me again and again and again. My very bones seemed to creak and groan, and I feared she might be breaking me from within, although I sensed no power of hers clouding my mind.

I wanted her to *try* to break me, though.

It was a delirious, heady sensation that I'd never personally experi-enced before.

Curiosity took over my suspicion and I felt my guard dropping like falling rain as my free hand began awkwardly, furiously fumbling at her waist. I could have used my magic, but I wanted this to be raw. Primal.

And I could see in her eyes that she wanted the savage looming over her. She demanded it. This was a new experience for both of us warriors. And new experiences were never to be wasted, for the one cold truth all warriors lived by was final and unrelenting—we might die tomorrow, so seize the moment.

I wanted to get my hands dirty with this creature and I felt a surge of frustration that one of my hands was currently preoccupied with pinning her arms above her head. I wanted her hands there, but I wanted my hands free to explore and touch every inch of this creature's feverish flesh. Although I couldn't quite explain what I wanted to do, some phantom animal instinct within me knew exactly what it wanted and how to accom-plish it. I needed to fully feel this strange euphoria, to drown in the new sensations dwarfing me, even though they were seeming to cloud my usually rational, simple mind.

I let out a husky laugh as I discovered the solution to my frustration. With a thought, I used my magic to pin her hands above her head, finally freeing up my hands. The wild creature railed against the invisible bonds, but not because she wanted to escape—because I could see that she wanted her hands free to claw my back as I took her. Her shoulders arched back as her chest strained upwards, craving the contact of my flesh against hers.

She let out a long moan as the tips of her breasts brushed against my own sweat-slicked torso, and I immediately bit the inside of my cheeks hard enough to draw blood as that brief contact between our chests sent waves of deep, primal hunger throughout my entire body.

I could hardly breathe as her impatience threatened to overwhelm me, flooding me with a violent need to become one with her. I fumbled at the fabric covering her hips, my frustration mounting. With an impatient snarl, I ripped the fabric in half like I was peeling open a ripe fruit. She cried out in breathless abandon as the shackles of her torment were shredded and the dark air kissed her hot, sweat-soaked flesh. Something felt incredibly familiar about this maddening encounter yet impossibly foreign at the same time. Why? What was this mind-breaking flood of desire within me? Why had I not known that the act of mating was such a rush?

If I had known before that this ritual was so all-encompassing, I would have lived for nothing else but to fuck. To sip and sup only insomuch as it would give me the energy to fuck *again*.

Fuck, I thought to myself, the word touching the base of my neck like an icy finger. *Where had that word come from?*

I was no beast in the field hoping to continue my bloodline with mewling babes. But this was different. Whatever I was feeling had no place in procreation. This was the ultimate conquest, and I knew, suddenly, why the concept had remained so elusive to me.

Because I had never met a creature worthy of *being* conquered. I knew, in some strange manner, that she was conquering me as well. That we were both voluntarily walking into a prison of pleasure that was worthy of our incarceration. I'd seen plenty of beautiful women in my adventures through Fae and I had even once considered mating, but it had been a casual, absent, fleeting thought. Beauty had stirred little in my loins. This wild creature beneath me, however, was entirely unique.

This was the granting of our selfish desires to each other for the sole reason of giving and getting pleasure. This was a different form of magic that I had never experienced before. A maddening, intoxicating, unbelievably powerful magic.

This was a victory neither of us warriors could accomplish alone. A song that could only be sung in a duet, our bodies and voices echoing each other in a raw, deafening crescendo that could no longer be stopped or silenced. This was a forest fire, and our only solace was to burn together.

I felt my mind breaking, shattering, exploding, and reforming again as a long, croaking, crying laughter echoed throughout my soul, vibrating my bones like wind chimes in a thunderstorm.

A strange, feathered cloak draped over us like curtains, casting us in privacy. I lowered my lips to her neck and trailed my tongue up her throat. My mouth immediately salivated at the savory taste of her frustration. She shuddered, hissing and straining to press her neck closer to my mouth but my magical restraints over her wrists prevented her from getting closer. I chuckled hoarsely and nipped her earlobe with my teeth, causing her to cry out and squirm like a crazed animal. I knew I was almost as mad with desire as she was and that I could no longer permit myself to simply *taste*. I needed to *feast*. To gorge.

To that effect, I hastily tugged down my own pants before slapping my palms back into the stone floor on either side of her chest so that I hovered over her. She wrapped her legs around my back, scraping her boots against my skin as she struggled to pull me closer. With painstaking slowness, I fought against her wishes, slowly lowering my hips until I only just pressed against her.

She let out an agonized gasp as I teased her wet, eager—

A large, white, scaly, clawed foot stepped into my peripheral vision a few feet away and I snarled out a hoarse, territorial growl as my fingers instinctively clenched, sinking into and shattering the marble floor beneath my palms like it was made of powder.

The furious creature beneath me hadn't noticed the invasion of our privacy and whimpered in raw, unfiltered rage at my endless teasing. In a flash of power, she somehow snapped free of my magical restraints and grabbed my hips to pull me fully into her. Her claws sank into my back hard enough to draw blood and I fought back on reflex, my muscles locking rigid to prevent her.

I panted hoarsely, fighting against the desperate woman as my eyes rose from the newcomer's clawed foot to assess the level of danger interrupting us, but we were still enshrouded in the darkness of my earlier magic. Perhaps it hadn't actually seen us.

With a thought, I banished the shadows and my eyes fell upon a tall, white-scaled, lizard warrior looming over us. He wasn't looking at us, but instead at a black hat on the floor a few paces away. He scooped it up with a seemingly satisfied grunt and set it on his head with a practiced gesture.

"That's where my cowboy hat went," he murmured in a thoughtful tone.

The woman beneath me let out a startled shriek of horror.

The white lizard's eyes finally shifted our way. "You two are very, very loud, Master Temple," it said in a perfectly understandable and entirely judgmental tone.

CHAPTER 3

I felt a wash of dizziness slam into me and I fell back on my ass, blinking wildly as the room spun. I frantically tried to cover my lap with my hands. I panted hoarsely, jerking my head from side-to-side to process my strange surroundings as two realities waged within my mind. Wylde and...someone else.

"Fucking Carl," I finally croaked, the phrase whispering past my confusion like a distant birdsong. With that, the real world came crashing back and I felt two entirely different kinds of headaches hit me with hammers of hatred. One in my temples and the other down low in my family jewels. "What the *hell*?" I wheezed, shifting my hips in an effort to alleviate the low-level ache I felt building in my unhappy sapphires.

The Elder pursed his lizard lips, clutching a bundle of white fabric under one arm. "Your old butler would not approve of public mating," he said. "We need to hire a new butler," he suggested, indicating me and the savage creature I had been playing with.

Kára. Not a *creature* I had conquered in Fae. Fucking *Kára*. Or, rather, *not-fucking* Kára.

She lay on the ground between us, completely unashamed despite her blatant nudity. She stared up at the ceiling with an almost dazed look on her face, breathing heavily.

I was *Nate*, not *Wylde*. Losing my grip on reality had never happened before. Well, not since I'd successfully adopted my inner alter ego. The rest of my bizarre personality shift came into focus and my eyes widened in embarrassment. Sex was one thing I now knew very well with my Valkyrie, Kára, but my Fae side taking complete control over me? That was insanely alarming.

Carl extended his arm to reveal two fluffy white robes. He tossed one to me and I hurriedly slung it around my shoulders, grateful to cover myself up. I carefully tugged my pants back up underneath the robe and let out a sigh. Carl tipped his cowboy hat at Kára in a polite gesture. "Lady Valkyrie," he said, holding out a similar robe for her.

Kára did not get up from the floor. Instead, she slowly shifted her attention to the Elder as if she couldn't quite yet focus her eyes properly. She let out a long sigh and then shakily lifted one hand to give him a weak salute before letting her arm fall limply to the tile. "Where are my clove cigarillos?" she murmured absently, blindly patting her hand on the floor as if searching for the licorice cigarillo she'd been smoking before I tackled her. "I need a smoke, not a robe."

"Thank you, Carl. We were kind of in the middle of something," I said, blushing. "And we would like to finish."

"Even better idea than the smoke," Kára agreed with a soft laugh, waving her hand at Carl in a dismissive wave. "Please fuck off so we can fuck on."

His gaze drifted to the couch and he tasted the air again with his tongue. I glanced that way to see that one of the two airsoft pistols she'd been wielding during our game was poking out from beneath the furniture. "Cowboys and Indians again?" he asked curiously, absently draping Kára's robe over his forearm.

One thing he did *not* do was catch the rather obvious hint that he wasn't welcome right now.

"Shamans and sheriffs," I corrected, resigned to the fact that it was more effective to answer his questions if I wanted him to leave. I pointed at the plastic bow and the suction cup arrows I'd been using. Some of them still stuck to a few of the Guardian statues. "Way cooler." I remembered Kára nailing me with one of the plastic BB's and glanced down to find a small welt on my arm. Lucky shot.

Carl glanced at me with a strange look. "Is that why she is naked? Again?"

Kára smirked. "I was wearing shorts before someone ripped them in half," she said, eyeing me with a feral grin. "Rawr!"

I shrugged, having no complaints, or regrets. Carl studied me again with that strange look. "Is that why you're wearing a pretty feather scarf wrapped around your head? A mating habit?"

Kára burst out laughing. "I meant to tell you that your illusion spell winked out when he caught us."

I let out a curse, tugging the feather boa off my head and tossing it to the side. "It's a powerful Native American headdress," I argued firmly.

Kára finally sat up and gave me a mischievous wink as she took the robe from Carl. My blood was still up, despite the Elder's interruption. I mentally sacrificed a goat at the altar of fornication. Kára tied the robe around her waist and then slowly rose to her feet while doing her utmost to bend at the hips.

"That is bad for your back, Mistress Kára," Carl suggested. "Bend at the knees."

"Shut up, Carl," I growled, watching the show. "Some things are worth the risk."

Kára laughed, scooping up the feather boa from the ground and wrapping it around her neck. "Valkyries can bend at the hips all they want, Carl," she said. She did look much better in the boa than I probably had.

Carl frowned longingly at the accessory, not realizing he held one of his claws outstretched as if to take it.

I grinned, shaking my head. "There are plenty more boas in my mother's closet, Carl," I said, climbing to my feet. "Even some red ones. *If* you tell me why you found it so important to interrupt us."

He grinned happily. "Yesss!" he hissed. "The Randulfs are waiting downstairs."

Someone cleared their throat from down the hall, and I whipped my head around to see Gunnar leaning against the hallway wall; his side was to us, and his face was averted so as not to leer. "Don't worry," the beefy alpha werewolf of St. Louis said, pointing a finger up at his eyepatch. "You're on my bad side."

Kára burst out laughing.

"Not *ours*," a pubescent boy's voice hooted from farther down the hall, cracking mid-sentence. I saw Ashley shoving Calvin and Makayla, their tow-headed teens, back out of view, attempting to shield them from the very adult situation that was now not going down at the base of the stairs.

Ashley wasn't very successful with Calvin, who kept popping his head around her to ogle us with wide, inquisitive eyes, but Makayla was staring up at the rafters of Chateau Falco, her head cocked slightly as if listening to something only she could hear. Gunnar and Ashley were grinning and shaking their heads.

Werewolves saw nothing strange about being naked in front of others, and the new parents were working very hard with their brand-new teenagers in an attempt to catch them up on everything they'd missed over their skipped childhood.

Like their wizard Godfather caught in the act of laying the sword to a Valkyrie. Well, failing to do so.

"I thought Carl died searching for you since we arrived twenty minutes ago," Gunnar grouched.

Kára laughed harder. "Hey, kids!" She flashed the Randulfs a bright smile as if nothing embarrassing had happened.

"Fucking Carl!" I muttered angrily. "You could have led with that announcement."

He folded his arms. "Maybe a *butler* would have," he said in an entirely too snooty tone.

I narrowed my eyes at him for good measure, even though he wasn't wrong. I did need a new butler. We had been eating delivery food for the last few weeks since the events at Mt. Olympus. "Okay, peeping were-wolves. Shoo! Or no presents tonight—"

Calvin and Makayla both disappeared the moment I said the word presents, and I smiled smugly at the fading sound of their racing feet echoing through the halls.

Gunnar sighed, turning his back on us. "Hurry up or we're opening all the presents downstairs."

We waited for the last of the werewolves to leave and then let out twin sighs.

Kára turned to me with a hungry look in her eyes, licking her lips as she gripped one end of the feather boa in each hand, sliding it back and forth across the back of her neck. "Later, I want you to explain whatever the hell *that* identity crisis was all about," she said, waggling her fingers at me from head-to-toe, obviously referring to my Wild Side taking over during our game. "I thought you were trying out role-playing."

Our smiles slipped at exactly the same moment, remembering what had triggered my reaction. "Shit," I hissed. Carl's interruption, immediately followed up with the Randulf family arriving, had shoved the strange occurrence into the back of my mind. Our eyes darted to the spot across the room where I'd heard the strange fluttering sound during our game. A thick ivory envelope with a silver wax seal sat on the marble floor. I eyed it suspiciously.

"It was that wave of power that triggered you, wasn't it?" Kára whispered, suddenly holding a gleaming bearded axe in one hand as she glared at the envelope. For some reason, it didn't look out of place on the dainty robe-wearing blonde. "I felt something, too, but I forgot about it after you got me all riled up."

I recalled sensing a presence behind me and then it fleeing the moment I noticed it—which had subconsciously permitted my Wild Side to take the wheel of the bus. Something from Fae had dropped by.

That was why Wylde had so instinctively taken over. Someone from Fae had delivered some mail.

Carl stormed past us and scooped up the envelope between two claws. He sniffed it for a long moment and then lowered it to his side, staring at us. "It is not dangerous, but it is from Fae. It smells familiar." I approached the Elder, holding out my hand for him to give it to me. He shook his head firmly and pointed at Kára. "Give me the boa."

She grinned, shaking her head at the Elder. "Fine, Gollum." She whipped off the boa and held it out to him. When he reached for it, she yanked it back and whipped him in the snout with the tip. She grinned toothily but he snatched it away with a territorial hiss before she could whip him again.

Then, boa firmly in hand, he finally handed me the envelope. He flung the scarf around his shoulders and began tugging on either end of the boa to slide it across the back of his neck like Kára had been doing—forever ruining the fantasy I had of a naked Kára toying with one when we regained our privacy.

"Fucking Carl," I muttered, glancing down at the envelope in my fingers. It was much thicker than I had surmised from across the room, feeling more like card stock. On closer inspection, the paper was covered in rich green and blue veins and felt more like dried skin than paper. The veins even looked realistic. I felt a shiver roll down my spine.

It was addressed simply to *Wylde*.

I sensed no power, poisons, spells, or danger from it, but it did smell vaguely familiar like Carl had said.

It smelled like Fae.

Why had my instincts so rapidly taken over upon sensing it? A fae of some kind had broken through the wards of my mansion and...delivered a letter? Why? And *how* had they managed to pass my wards?

Kára leaned into me, wrapping her arms around my waist and resting her chin on my shoulder as she studied it. I scratched at my scruffy chin with a pensive frown. I let out a frustrated sigh. "I think our Yulemas is about to get a whole lot more interesting," I said, thinking about the small party I was hosting in a week for my closest friends.

"Open it!" Kára urged, squeezing me.

I opened the envelope without fanfare. Kára let out an almost disappointed breath, sounding as if she'd expected a swarm of pixies to jump out. Instead, I pulled out a folded letter that was as heavy and translucent as glass even though it was no thicker than paper. I slipped the envelope into the pocket of my robe and then unfolded the letter.

I held it up towards one of the distant windows so I could read the words on the clear page.

Wylde,

Your presence is immediately requested at Camelot. I appreciate the suits you gifted me, but they are not my size, so I will need you to return them for me before it's too late and your receipt expires.

Merry Yulemas.

Alex

I frowned pensively. He was obviously talking about the Knightmares, but why did he want me to collect them? They were currently occupied with the mentally broken Knights of the Round Table. They were no longer the chivalrous blokes from the fairy tales. They were bloodthirsty killers, restrained by an unbreakable cord previously used to contain the giant wolf, Fenrir—the Godkiller destined to kill Thor in Ragnarok.

That obviously wasn't going to happen the way everyone had expected. Plot twist.

It was apparently urgent, so something must have changed.

I sniffed the letter with a frown, trying to call upon Wylde in hopes he might pinpoint why it smelled familiar. Was I simply smelling Alex? Wylde was apparently protesting our partnership as a consequence of Carl's interruption of my intimate moment with Kára because he didn't offer me any sudden epiphanies.

Kára snorted and recoiled from me with a grimace. "Did you just sniff it? What if an ogre wiped his butt with it?"

"Ogre ass is an aphrodisiac," I said in a suggestive tone as I pinched *her* ass. She squawked and hopped away from me. I took a deeper sniff of the letter, even extending my tongue as if to taste it.

Kára gagged, laughing as she swatted it out of my hand. The letter hit the ground and burst into a bright cloud of yellow butterflies. Kára froze in alarm, but nothing dangerous happened. A slow smile split across her cheeks as the butterflies twirled around her in a small, beautiful tornado. Two even landed on her eyebrows, slowly flapping their wings. Then the butterflies faded away like smoke. Carl paid us no mind, still toying with his feather boa.

Kára let out a disappointed sigh. "That would have been a great picture," she said with a frown.

I tapped the corner of my eye. "I got it right here," I said with a smile. I couldn't help feeling leery about the letter and it's beautiful, short-lived nature, but nothing terrible had happened. Just a small act of beauty. But why had such innocent words required self-destruction? And how had it bypassed my wards? Who did Alex know in Fae who could make magic like that? Did he even have any other citizens yet or was he just hanging out with Talon and the nine remaining Knightmares? We had killed three of the original twelve, but I'd only managed to cure two of those sets of armor of their curse. Talon had adopted one and the other was up for grabs. So, ten sets were still cursed by Mordred, and nine of those still held bodies that had to be restrained.

I had repeatedly put off talk of curing the ten sets, knowing how taxing such an endeavor would be and how weak it would leave me afterwards.

How easy of a target I would become after wasting all my magic in the attempt.

Maybe I was reading too much into the letter. Perhaps it was simply an invitation for a much-needed getaway for Kára and me. I could show her my old stomping grounds as Wylde. And I now had a few other things to show her regarding my Wild Side, thanks to this morning's adventures. And most of Fae was uninhabited, so privacy would be simple to find. One of the dozens of magical glades or waterfalls where we could really raise a ruckus and have some genuine romance.

Fae was beginning to sound more and more fun by the second—

A chime made Carl jump and spin in a full circle. Then he realized it was the security tablet for Chateau Falco, announcing a call from the Gates. It was tucked into his belt. He didn't even hesitate in handing it to Kára instead of me.

She stared down at it for a few seconds, watching the security camera feed. "Yes?" she asked.

"Delivery for Nate Temple," a woman's voice replied. "It requires his signature."

Kára assessed the camera, tapping the screen suspiciously. I saw a brown box truck and a red-haired girl chewing gum behind the driver's seat. She had a tall, gangly passenger sitting next to her, looking like he might weigh all of one-hundred-pounds. Finally, she nodded, and then pressed a button. "Come on up." She sighed and then tucked the tablet against her belly as she met my eyes. "End of our game," she said with a sad sigh.

I would have to apply experimental cryogenic ministrations to my testicles, because there was only unpleasant unhappiness in my immediate future.

"Maaaaaaiil time!" Carl belted out in a singsong tone. "That's the second one today!"

I jumped at the unexpected shout, spinning to stare at him. "You've seen *Blue's Clues*?"

He nodded proudly, ignoring Kára's fit of laughter. "I must learn to understand the smaller humans," he said, pointing a claw over his shoulder to indicate where Calvin and Makayla had been a few minutes ago. "And dogs. Blue's Clues seemed most appropriate," he said matter of factly.

I studied him for a few moments, frowning. His relationship with the two teens was...curious, tense, and concerning. Carl always kept a safe distance from the two children, like they might be contagious, but Makayla was the one he seemed truly terrified of. Maybe he thought he might accidentally break them. I shrugged, running my fingers through my hair.

Kára winked at me before skipping up the stairs. "I'm getting changed into something more appropriate."

I scowled at her skillful act of throwing me to the wolves, knowing I needed to sign for the inbound delivery and that I couldn't get changed yet.

I sighed. "Let's go," I told Carl, turning to head to the front door.

CHAPTER 4

I walked into Chateau Falco's expansive foyer. My eyes instantly darted to the long table against the wall. It was teeming with a dozen Yulemas presents all wrapped in the same shiny black paper and gaudy silver ribbons. Gifts for the upcoming secret Santa gift exchange I was hosting. I'd invited my closest friends and we had agreed to mail or use a private courier to deliver everything here ahead of time in an effort to mask the identity of each gift-giver from the others. Naturally, I had attempted to cheat, but Kára had so far kept me honest by threatening to withhold her amorous affections if she caught me breaking the rules.

Keyword *caught*. But Carl was a snitch when it came to Kára, so I'd begrudgingly remained honest.

That, and she managed the security cameras at Chateau Falco, so Big Sister was always watching.

Normally, Chateau Falco was teeming with werewolves, dragons and students from Shift—my wayward school of orphans, who were also highly aggressive, frequently traumatized, exotic shifters from all corners of the world—since I had negotiated giving them a weekly lecture on magic and wizards in exchange for their labor efforts to keep the mansion in tip-top shape. My old butler, Dean—or Odin, the Allfather of the Aesir pantheon in Asgard—had not returned to his old duties since revealing his true identity. At times, I felt a cold shiver creep down my spine to know that a god had been making me breakfast and washing my underwear for a few decades. Turned out Santa really was always watching and knew if you'd been naughty or nice.

He'd had a crew of trusted workers for the mansion, but I'd been hesitant on rehiring anyone with a reference from Odin. I needed employees who were loyal to me, not plants or spies for the Aesir gods. With Kára whisking into my life so abruptly, I'd yet to invest any real effort into replacing the staff for Chateau Falco. Health insurance and very probable PTSD from the frequent attacks and battles ruled out hiring any Regulars, so for now I preferred to take advantage of the Shift students.

But I'd sent them all away for a week off so they could get some vacation time during the holidays.

It had nothing to do with the fact that I wanted no witnesses to see all the many, many ways we found to dance on the figurative grave of my years-long relationship with abstinence. No one needed to see what we did to each other in our pursuit of pleasure and recapturing the years together that we'd lost. We had spent many nights just walking and talking, choosing neglected areas of the house to share a romantic meal or drinks. To put it bluntly, we went on a lot of first dates together, all within the walls of Chateau Falco, exploring and adventuring as often as we relaxed and appreciated each other's company in silence, or watched old movies together.

The fact that we boinked like coked-out rabbits had nothing to do with me sending everyone away for a week.

Not at all.

I was doing it for the kids. They needed time off.

"And Master Temple wanted to get off," I admitted with a shit-eating grin.

I frowned, noticing two straw Yule Goats perched on top of the mountain of black presents. As Yulemas tradition dictated, the straw had been woven together and bound in red ribbons. They hadn't been there yesterday, but Carl had mentioned another delivery truck arriving earlier today.

I saw Gunnar standing off to the side, frowning at the straw goats. "I hope those aren't for me," he murmured to Ashley.

She swatted his arm. "What if Nate got them for you?" she asked, noticing my arrival.

Gunnar grunted, glancing over his shoulder at me. "Then I want him to have time to think harder about what to buy his best friend for Yulemas," he grumbled. "Holiday decorations are the worst gift ever. Here, have this thing that you won't be able to use for another year."

Ashley folded her arms and began tapping her foot in a universal warning sign. "And if *I* got them for you?"

His eye widened and he suddenly looked anxious. "They are amazing. Very thoughtful and considerate," he said in a cautious tone, sounding as if he was asking her a question.

She sniffed pointedly and turned away from him to walk into the sitting room adjacent to the foyer. I heard Calvin speaking to Makayla in a suspicious whisper, but he cut off as Mama Randulf entered.

I rolled my eyes, shaking my head at Gunnar. "Smooth, man." I eyed the straw goats. "But I agree with you," I whispered in a softer tone. "Lame as hell."

"Werewolves have excellent hearing!" Ashley called out from the other room.

I flashed Gunnar a guilty grin, shrugging. He let out a resigned sigh and walked into the sitting room to appease her.

I walked up to the huge wooden door and opened it. Chilly air hit me in the face like a wet slap and I shuddered, cinching my robe tighter. A tall, gaunt young man in a long puffy coat stood a polite distance from the door holding a small, plain cardboard box. At first, I'd almost mistaken him for one of the pillars holding up the porte-cochère. His bizarre height and his scarecrow-like frame caused him to sway at each gust of wind, reminding me of the wobbly man inflatables outside most used car dealerships. He had short spiky hair and acne. If he decided to grow his hair out, he'd be flirting with seven feet.

His coworker was the driver I'd seen on Kára's tablet. She was young and pretty with fiery red, jaw-length hair, and her pale cheeks sported a bajillion freckles. In any other company, she would have looked to be of average height, but in the shadow of her coworker she came across as an Oompa Loompa assistant. She held an electronic signature pad. They both smiled at me, but the giant looked shy and awkward when he did it.

"Good morning," I said. "Sorry about the wait. Heard you needed a signature."

The woman did a little curtsy and flashed me an even brighter smile as she approached, holding out her pad. "If you could just sign here, Master Temple."

"Two of you?" I asked absently.

She nodded as she came to a bouncy stop like this was cheerleading tryouts. "Holiday seasons are insane. I was tasked with training the new guy, so I make him carry the boxes," she said with a grin, pointing a thumb back at the human lightning rod. I managed to keep my snark in check, not wanting to pick on the new kid. "I can't believe we got a delivery for the famous Nate Temple." She suddenly blushed. "Sorry. *Master* Temple," she corrected with an impish giggle as she lowered her eyes in flirty embarrassment, obviously angling for a higher tip. "Don't mind Jimmy. He usually talks way less than this, but I think he's shell-shocked. He's a big fan of yours." Jimmy's face turned beet-red. "Me, too, you know. My name is Yetta," she said, batting her eyelashes.

I smiled back at her, imagining Kára's opinion on poaching. She was probably watching me right now, laughing her ass off. Or sharpening her trident as she stared at Yetta on the security tablet.

Jimmy murmured something vaguely affirmative, looking embarrassed as all hell that she'd called him out in front of his apparent hero.

"Nice to meet you, Jimmy," I said, hoping to get this little shit-show over with.

I heard a car horn honk in the near distance, and I frowned, my eyes drifting towards the sound. But their big brown delivery truck was in the way. It was parked crookedly for an easier exit, shielding my view of the entrance gates at the end of the drive, so I couldn't see the source of the honking. I turned back to the delivery duo. "What's going on out there?"

Yetta shrugged, lowering her signature pad as she glanced at the truck blocking our view. "News crews, I think. Four of the shameless bastards are lurking outside the Great Wall of Falco," she said with a giggle. "We had to drive through them to get in. I felt like a celebrity, but I'm sure you're used to it by now. Are you hosting a party or something?" she asked, turning back to me with a curious grin. "Maybe we will be on the news, Jimmy!" she chirped, flashing a smile at her colleague. He nodded sheepishly, still holding the box out for me even though he hadn't summoned up the courage to actually approach my orbit.

Was he really that nervous to meet me? "It's no big deal, guys. I'm a citizen of St. Louis just like everyone else. And I'm not hosting a party," I lied, frowning thoughtfully. "I sent everyone home for the holidays," I added, fearing Yetta might blab something to the contrary to the press on her way back out. It wasn't uncommon for reporters or journalists to loiter outside my gates. Whenever they needed something juicy for their articles, they often tried to fill it by vilifying the local billionaire with some sordid rumor and a clickbait headline. "Just a nice quiet holiday for me," I assured her, wanting nothing more than to get back inside. Robes were not conducive to Missouri winters.

She laughed and extended the signature pad my way. "Well, don't let us keep you, Master Temple."

I swiftly signed the tablet, handed it back to Yetta, and then turned to Jimmy with a patient but expectant look. The giant scarecrow trainee suddenly realized that in his starstruck daze he had neglected to actually do the delivery part of his delivery job. His face reddened and he abruptly shambled forward in a clumsy rush that almost made me instinctively cry out *TIMBER!* and dive for cover as if he was a falling tree.

He was about two paces away and already extending the package when I heard a rapid *clackety-clack* sound from the open doorway behind me, moving as fast and loud as a smoky diesel locomotive over warped railroad tracks.

Before I could react, something slammed into the backs of my knees— and the base of my dangly bits— whipping my feet out from under me. I landed on my ass with a yelp of pain that shot up my freshly bruised—now beyond ripened—blue balls, and then through my tailbone and into my molars. The testicular explosion hurt so bad that I lost the ability to see. I blindly sat up and sucked in a breath, struggling not to vomit or break out into tears as waves of pain rolled through my pelvic region like a struck gong at a Tibetan monastery.

I realized that I hadn't actually lost my vision but that I had instinctively closed my eyes in shock. I opened them an instant later, only to suddenly find that my nose was less than a foot away from a giant, hairy, horny goat's asshole.

My mind momentarily shattered and time abruptly ceased to exist, leaving me in a barren universe of groinal pain, abject terror, and maddening confusion. I thought I heard the familiar startup sound of my first desktop computer in 1996 as it worked to establish an internet connection via dial-up modem.

I stared, horrified, into that dark road to perdition, that puckering, fleshy black hole of chaos, wondering what life decisions had led me to this moment. Was this the start of the Omega War or the end? A distant part of my brain slapped me upside the head, jostling me back to the present like an unexpected bucket of ice dumped over my head.

My peripheral vision suddenly expanded, and I realized that almost no time had passed. My brain functions had sped up in response to my sudden trauma, buying me time. I accepted the impossible fact that I was mere inches away from a goat's anus and that the creature must have tried to slip through the space between my legs before its horns had accidentally clipped my nuts and struck the backs of my knees.

I recoiled in disgust, scooting back a foot just as the goat's tail stiffened and the beast ejected a handful of hellish pebbles my way. Delivery Jimmy stared at the demon goat, his arms shaking as he held the package out for me. This was the moment Jimmy realized that delivering Christmas gifts was a decidedly deadly career path, and that his high school guidance counselor, Dr. Karen, had deceived him.

Then the mastiff-sized goat bleated at the poor man. "Yulemas is the season for slaying!" it screamed, startling the hell out of all of us. And then it leapt into the air impossibly fast, aiming for the startled Jimmy's package —the box, not *that* package. I gagged, scooting back a few more inches from the goat's noxious, steaming shit raisins, trying to understand what the hell was going on, and where the giant talking goat had come from.

I looked up in time to see the goat simply swallow the package—and Jimmy's forearms—in a sickening, crunching chomp that I felt in the very marrow of my own bones. My eyes bulged in disbelief.

Scratch that. Giant, talking, man-eating goat.

The goat's momentum and bone structure served as a battering ram as it slammed into Jimmy's chest hard enough to crack his collarbone like kindling and they both went flying into the truck ten paces away. They struck hard enough to rock the vehicle sideways on two wheels but not hard enough to knock it entirely over. I heard a ton of boxes crashing to the floor within the van. Jimmy lifted up his two gushing stumps, squealing and screaming like a stuck pig, his eyes wide with agony and fear.

Then fire and sparks began spraying from Jimmy's stumps as he unleashed wild magic, unable to control himself in his panic. My skin pebbled and my heart skipped a beat. Jimmy was a wizard.

The man-eating goat had landed lightly on his feet, but rather than finishing off what he'd started, he abruptly took off at a dead sprint away from the mayhem he'd created, bleating furiously. "Bring it on, bitches! You think I'm afraid of a little indigestion!"

"The fuck?" I hissed, jumping to my feet as I spun to face Yetta. I was almost entirely sure that even *my* insurance would not cover a rogue goat attack that resulted in a double amputee. But the fact that Jimmy had been a wizard was setting off all sorts of alarm bells in my mind. I held up my hands, hoping to forestall her panic at seeing magic for the first time, but then I froze, noticing the murderous twinkle in her eyes.

She snarled and punched a button on her tablet. The fleeing goat exploded in a concussive blast that sent up a geyser of flame, dirt, gravel, and bloody goat parts. The package had been a fucking *bomb*?! The shock-wave of force made me stumble and caused my ears to pop. The world was eerily quiet as the goat's head landed on the hood of the van, facing me.

I swear to god it was smiling, and I was pretty sure I knew exactly who it had been, given the circumstances. But I didn't have time to worry about demonic, kamikaze goats from Asgard.

Yetta was no longer a bubbly cheerleader. She flung down her tablet and turned to me, lifting her suddenly glowing hands. "Time to die, Temple!" she hissed.

Another fucking wizard. Well, wasn't this just dandy.

CHAPTER 5

Two wizards delivering an explosive package to me during Christmas season was not the cleverest attack I'd ever encountered, but it wasn't the stupidest either.

But for Yetta to believe she could take on Master Nate Temple all by herself?

Fuck that.

An explosion of fabric behind me announced the arrival of Gunnar and Ashley in their hulking bipedal werewolf forms. They snarled warningly, but didn't advance, and I could hear them struggling to hold back two teenaged someones also wanting to defend me from the assassination attempt.

"I got this, Gunnar," I snarled, flinging up a quick shield between me and Yetta. "Keep them back."

I cast a quick glance at the still screaming Jimmy. He was thrashing back and forth on the ground in a pool of his own blood, still wildly flinging sparks with his bloody stumps. I focused my attention back on Yetta, narrowing my eyes at the red-headed wizard and wondering why she hadn't attacked me yet. Probably concerned with the four werewolves wrestling each other in my doorway. "Whoever sent you two wanted you dead, toots. If they cared about you, they would have sent more—"

The back doors of the truck sprang open and a stream of annoyed, slightly bruised and dazed wizards began stumbling out one-by-one like clowns out of a circus car.

Me and my goddamned mouth. The werewolves began fighting even louder and I could tell Calvin and Makayla were dangerously close to earning a time-out from their parents. *How many times have I told you not to kill and eat wizard delivery assassins? Go to your room for fifteen minutes and think about what you did!*

The truck almost rolling over on the death squad had messed with their coordination because they were clinging to each other and swaying back and forth, struggling to clear their heads.

Yetta tried to use the distraction to get in a cheap shot, but I angled my shield right as she unleashed her fiery blast. It struck with enough force to actually surprise me. She was not a schmuck wizard at all. But neither was I. Her fire rebounded off my shield in an explosion of wet sparks and careened into the first wizard out of the truck, splattering him with lava-like goop. He screamed loud enough to un-pop my ears, but his immolation didn't deter his other pals from continuing to exit the vehicle.

Assassins. Motherfucking wizard assassins. Close to a dozen of them.

I called up my old faithful whip of white ice and lashed out at Yetta's leg, instantly freezing it at the knee. A blur of white scales and red feathers flew past me and skidded to a halt right in front of her face. Carl, still wearing my mother's boa, slammed both of his claws into the center of her chest and promptly tore her in half like he was peeling a banana. Her two halves toppled like wet trees on either side of him and the Elder turned to face the onslaught of wizards. His white scales glistened with blood as he drew two daggers and grinned. "I love mail time," he hissed, licking some of the blood off his ridged lips.

I yanked back my ice whip—and some of Yetta's knee—and cracked it in the air as I called up my fire whip in my other hand. Magic flooded through my veins and I felt a wave of energy roll down my forearms as adrenaline rushed through me. I risked a quick glance back to see that Gunnar and Ashley had succeeded in ushering their kids back into the foyer. I let out a breath of relief and turned back to Carl. "We need one of them alive, Carl."

"Define *alive*," he replied, flicking his tongue out at the air.

I did not expect a second berserker goat to sneak past the feuding werewolves, but neither did the wizards.

Another massive goat *clackety-clacked* past me, nimbly leapt into the air and slammed all four hoofs into the back door of the truck. It slammed shut with a sickening meaty crunch and an explosion of gore. A severed head and a few limbs went spinning into the air as the door dismembered a few of the slower moving wizards still in the back of the vehicle. The goat landed as lightly as a cat and began hopping about excitedly. He wore a vest over his back that read *Emotional Support Goat*.

He juked back and forth as he bleated jarring taunts at the stunned wizards. "Suck on a hairy dwarf-nipple, you feckless twats!" The goat somehow hacked up a loogie and spit it at one of the wizards, hitting him in the freaking eye. The wizard let out a curse before slapping a palm to his eye. The other wizards stared at the demon goat, Carl, and then me with anger, fear, and concern, hesitating to make the first move without Yetta to command them. At least I assumed she had been the boss, because they looked pretty fucking disorganized after her abrupt demise.

"Did you just spit on the wizard?" Carl asked, baffled.

That? That had been the most important question Carl could come up with, given the bizarre arrival of the magical talking goat?

The goat bleated. "I like to spit on pussies before I eat them," he snarled before cackling like a psychopath.

"Wow. There are kids reading this book, man," I muttered under my breath, shaking my head.

The goat had no concern for parental advisory warnings. "Don't just stand there. HIT ME!" he shrieked, and then he lowered his head and barreled into the legs of the visually impaired wizard, shattering his kneecaps on impact. The man bellowed out a scream, but it was promptly replaced by grunts and gasps as the goat began stomping on him with all four hooves.

A squat, baldheaded wizard finally had enough and kicked the goat off his trampled, kneecapped friend. Then he let loose a blast of fire that immediately set the goat ablaze as rapidly as if it was an oil-soaked torch.

The goat never lost his balance and laughed as he erupted in flames.

"Feel the burn! Oh yeah! Give it to me again! Harder! Hotter!" he shrieked. Every wizard stared at the scene in horrified disbelief.

Including me. The phrase *glutton for punishment* had just been redefined, the old definition silenced with a ball-gag and whipped on the ass with a leather paddle. *That's Mistress Merriam Webster, to you, slave. Lick my spine!*

The bald wizard's face paled with sudden anxiety to find that his attack hadn't seemed to harm the horned beast. He lifted up a shaking hand and this time let loose a steady stream of fire like he was wielding a flamethrower. The fire splashed over the goat like napalm and the psycho began laughing even harder and louder than before.

I shot Carl a meaningful look, realizing that all the wizards were still transfixed by the burning farm animal. He grinned and nodded. I flung out my ice whip and struck the bald man's neck, freezing it on contact. His blast of fire ceased, and he clutched at his throat with wide eyes, panicking and choking as he found his throat suddenly frozen solid.

The relentless goat bleated, exhaling clouds of smoke. "My flesh is crackling, and I LOVE IT!" he screamed. Then he ducked his head low and barreled through the surviving wizards like a fiery meteor, bowling them over like pins at the end of a lane, and lighting them up in the process. I gagged at the smell of burning meat even as the fucking sadomasochist goat belted out another hoarse, choking laugh that would fuel my nightmares for decades. "Strike! I'm on fire, boys!"

The suicidal, sadomasochist goat began swinging his massive horns back and forth, stabbing and impaling the scrambling wizards. Carl and I dove into the fray, killing and dismembering indiscriminately. They were so flummoxed by the crazy goat that they didn't stand a chance. I got lost in the violence, feeling a strange sense of tranquility wash over me as instincts took control of my motions. I grinned at Carl as we squared off against the last two wizards, finding joy in the simplicity of war. My foe fell and I let out a faint breath of disappointment that it had to end so soon. Carl buried his dagger under the soft palate of the last wizard so hard that the tip erupted out of his forehead.

Only then did I remember that I had needed one of them alive for interrogation. I cursed, realizing I was too late. I suppressed the cold shudder that rolled down the back of my neck as I surveyed the pile of eight steaming, blood-soaked bodies surrounding us. I wasn't concerned about my capacity for violence—I'd come to accept that darker part of me in recent years. But the fact that I had so thoroughly enjoyed it, even losing myself to the siren song of murder, gave me great concern.

I couldn't risk opening myself up to the Carnage. I had to be careful to not forget empathy or else I might one day end up like Zeus.

I again heard honking in the distance, and let out a panicked curse, having forgotten all about the news crews outside the gates. Had Yetta been telling me the truth about them or were they actually more vans of killer wizards? Regardless, I had a horror show of murder on my front porch if any of them managed to get a camera over my security wall. Or a freaking drone.

Luckily, most of the violence had happened on this side of the truck so none of the chaos had been visible from the distant gates. Still, the explosion might draw the wrong kind of attention and earn me a visit from the police. If they came up here to investigate, they would find a whole lot of blood, dead bodies, and—

The charred, hairless goat stumbled out from behind the truck and I almost let loose a blast of fire on reflex, not realizing he'd survived. He met my eyes. Half his face was burned to the bone and his eye socket was a black, smoking hole. The other eye was milk-white, but he could apparently still see me with it. "Merry Yulemas," he croaked. "See you soon," he said with a horrific smile. And then he collapsed.

Carl studied the goat with an impressed grunt. "That was incredibly considerate of him."

I flicked my eyes back and forth between the charred goat and the second goat's head that was still sitting on the hood of the truck. I was entirely sure I knew who they had been, even though I had no explanation for what they were doing here or how they had gotten here. But my concern for curious reporters shoved all my goat theories into the recesses of my mind.

Kára burst out the front door with a deadly snarl and skidded to a halt beside me, her dual-colored eyes whipping back and forth in search of threats. She had changed into jeans, a tank top, and a leather jacket, and she wore the small backpack where she stored her bug-out bag of techy stuff. She cursed and turned to face me. "According to the tablet, the gate controller is broken, and I saw reporters milling about outside the wall," she said.

Carl nodded. "I shall go kill them all for you," he said, taking a step towards the gates.

CHAPTER 6

Kára grabbed the Elder's arm and shook her head. "No, Carl. They have cameras. If anyone gets to kill them, it will be me."

"Hey, Corleone family," I said, raising my hand. "How about we hide the current incriminating evidence prior to discussing murdering the witnesses."

Kára shrugged. "We could always do both. They might have caught something on camera, so it's probably wise to go out there and have a nice long chat."

Carl abruptly spun around and ran back into the house without a word. I frowned at Kára, but she shrugged. He came back two seconds later with a basket. He began scooping up body parts and tossing them inside like a macabre version of picking berries, humming an oddly jubilant song under his breath.

Kára eyed the scorched goat and the severed goat head on the hood of the truck with a suspicious frown and then shook her head—which basically confirmed my assumption on their identities. But she was right. Now wasn't the time. "We need to clean this up. Now," she said.

I nodded, scanning the mayhem. No amount of hoses would wash away this much blood, and it was winter so it was too cold to risk turning them on anyway.

She pointed at something on the ground. One of Yetta's halves gripped a cell phone in her hand. She approached it like it was a poisonous serpent, bent down, and then plucked it from the dead fingers. Her face paled about two seconds later and she swore, tapping the screen a few times. She rose to her feet, panting nervously as she met my eyes.

"It was recording," she whispered, her voice shaking. "Video. I need to check if it was uploaded to the cloud before her associates get their hands on it."

My stomach did an uncomfortable little flip-flop, followed by a double-gainer. "She was making a video of the attack?" I hissed. "Why the *fuck* would a wizard want to record a magic battle?" I demanded, realizing it had no doubt caught Gunnar and Ashley in their werewolf forms standing in my doorway. Possibly Carl ripping her in half. Not to mention talking kamikaze goats.

Jesus Odin Christ.

Kára pursed her lips at my question. "Evidence."

I shuddered. "Fuck. She was trying to get dirt on me? Either that or they needed proof of my death if they were successful. They did try to deliver a bomb," I said, pointing at the distant crater where the goat had exploded. "That damned goat saved my life."

She nodded, not sidetracked by my mention of the goat. "The more sinister question is what if she *hadn't* wanted video proof of your death. What if she had been live streaming it to the *internet*," she whispered. "She wasn't, but what if?"

My eyebrows almost climbed off my skull at the thought. "A wizard wouldn't do that. She'd have to be insane," I croaked. "With a video like that..." I mused, "at the very *least* I would go to jail for murder."

"And at the worst, the world would see you using magic to *kill*..." she grimaced at the murder scene, "a delivery woman and her coworkers. Average Joes. With the right editing, they could have cut and spliced this video to tell any story they wanted."

I shook my head in disbelief, feeling the overwhelming need to release some pent-up frustration. "Please stop collecting severed limbs, Carl!" I snapped, glaring at the Elder. "That evidence needs to be *destroyed*."

He stiffened as if I'd slapped him. Then he slowly set down his basket, looking hurt.

Kára shot me a stern look and slowly shook her head. Great. Now I was the bad guy.

"Sorry for snapping at you. Just make sure you destroy those. Quickly. You need to get back inside in case one of those reporters catches a shot of you."

"If you stay, I stay," he said in a firm tone. "I want to know how the straw goats came to life," he said, scratching a long claw at his chin. "The ones that arrived this morning."

Kára and I turned to gawk at him. "The Yule Goat presents turned into the real goats?" I asked, frowning. I raked a hand through my hair at Carl's inadvertent confirmation of their identities. I turned to Kára. "Why would Thor's goats show up at Chateau Falco disguised as Yule Goats? I killed their boss and Alex humiliated them in a fight. Yet they show up now, unannounced, to save my life?"

Kára licked her lips nervously, a troubled look on her face. "I...don't know, but I don't like it. Those two are psychopaths and sadists."

Carl watched us intently, looking very interested to learn that the goats had belonged to Thor.

I grunted, recalling the excitement they had displayed while enduring pain. And their increasingly creative, foul-mouthed taunts. "You're telling me." I took a deep breath and almost doubled over as it strained some unknown muscle in my meat satchel.

"What's wrong?" Kára gasped. "Are you hurt?" she asked, patting me up and down in an effort to check for injuries.

"Master Temple got head from a goat," Carl told her.

I hissed, swatting at him. "Head...*butt*!" I snapped. "Not..." I gestured vaguely, "the other thing. That's called Bestiality."

Carl cocked his head thoughtfully. "There were no Beasts involved when the goat gave you head and butt," he said, scratching at his chin. "Ruin is up in his treehouse," he said, pointing up at the giant white tree dominating the grounds.

Kára was literally biting on her fist to prevent herself from bursting into laughter.

I let out a resigned sigh. "Not better, Carl. Try again."

"Master Temple took a goat to the balls like a champion. It was inspiring," Carl said, sagely, dipping his chin at me.

I let out a strained laugh, nodding. "He's not wrong," I admitted. "Friendly fire, I guess. I'm fine, but I think our day just went to hell. Again," I said, recalling the letter from Alex.

Kára tried to bite back a smile of amusement, but she wasn't very good at it. "No more shamans and sheriffs," she said.

"Well, we might still get the sheriffs if any of those reporters are worth their salt," I said, jerking my chin towards the gates to Chateau Falco.

She nodded grimly, glancing down at the phone in her hands. "I need to take care of this." Then her eyes swept the scene before us. "But first, we need to wrap this up." She glanced at Carl. "Finish cleaning this mess," she amended, because Carl was a very literal person and might go grab some Saran Wrap.

I realized I was staring at the truck and that a sickening feeling was worming through my stomach. "Crap. The reporters saw this truck enter the grounds. They have to see it leave or else one of them might start asking questions. We can always blame the explosion on a firework of some kind."

Kára shot me a dry look. "A big-ass, military grade firework, maybe."

"Go see if you can get the truck started. Hopefully it wasn't damaged too badly during the fight." Kára nodded and jogged over to the driver's side. She turned the key, and I heard the truck roar to life. I motioned for her to turn the truck around and get it out of the way of the piles of bloody bodies. She did, making sure to still establish a wall for any ambitious reporters with long lenses on their cameras. She frowned at me as her fingers impatiently drummed against the steering wheel.

"Step back," I told Carl. "I have an idea."

I called upon my magic and opened a Gateway on the far side of the driveway. It opened up onto a desert landscape on the other side of the globe. Kára frowned at me, opening her mouth to ask what I was doing.

I opened a second Gateway between us and the truck, and a river of water roared out of it like a waterfall—because it actually was from a waterfall in New York—and slammed into the nightmarish scene. The bodies tumbled across my driveway and poured through the first Gateway into the desert. I let it go for a few more seconds to make sure it washed away as much blood as possible and then I closed the waterfall Gateway.

Carl stared at me thoughtfully, still clutching his basket of arms, heads, and legs. He then calmly walked up to the remaining Gateway and tossed it through. I released my magic and the portal winked closed. My knees immediately wobbled at the sudden expenditure of energy. I hadn't been expecting to fight today and it was safe to say that my nutrition had been lagging lately as I spent all my recent time lounging about with Kára—a constant source of energy depletion, for obvious reasons. Summing it up, I'd just run a marathon after fasting for a few days.

Kára urgently motioned for me to hop into the truck. "Let's go!" she hissed. She was wearing a black baseball cap in an attempt to hide her blonde hair, but I knew it wouldn't be enough. Yetta had fiery red hair and Jimmy had been a giant scarecrow. We needed an illusion.

I turned to Carl. "Tell the Randulfs we will be back very soon. We have to get rid of the evidence."

Carl nodded, lifting up a giant hairy goat leg. "Good. I have time to cook. Kid. It's what's for dinner."

I grimaced at his bastardization of the beef industry's slogan as well as the poor choice of words in saying he was cooking a kid tonight. Kára gave a warning honk of the horn, saving me the headache. "Okay, Carl. Keep everyone inside." He nodded and jogged back into the house, closing the door behind him. I hopped into the truck and glanced at Kára, shaking my head.

I felt a smile creep over my cheeks as an idea came to mind, thanks to Carl, of all people.

Ruin, I called out in my mind, hoping Falco's baby Beast really was home, and not gallivanting about in Fae with Talon and Alex. He was a free spirit these days, but he usually returned to the treehouse in the colossal, white-scaled tree in front of the mansion.

Master Temple, Ruin replied in a sleepy tone. *You won a great battle. I didn't want to get involved without your express permission.*

I let out a breath of relief. *I'm so glad you're here, Ruin. Can you swamp the property in fog, wind and icy rain? I want to obscure visibility and deter anyone from looking too closely at us or our truck as we leave.*

Ruin chuckled through our bond. *Gladly. Anything else?*

I thought about it. *Keep an eye on the property. The assassins broke the gate on their way in and I don't know if they have reinforcements waiting.*

Ruin wasted no time at all. A crack of lightning shook the house and the sky outside slowly darkened as icy raindrops began pelting the grounds. They struck the windshield in a soothing staccato and wind whistled over the roof and shutters of Chateau Falco, groaning and moaning in a truly grim freak storm. Heh. Thankfully, Missouri weather was fickle like that, so no one would think anything strange about it.

Kára eyed me with a smirk. "Your doing?"

I shrugged nonchalantly. "I am very impressive."

She kissed me on the cheek. "Well played. Thank Ruin for me," she said in a tone so sweet it was practically dripping.

I scowled at her ability to pierce through my bluster. "I get credit for thinking of it, at least. Let's Bonnie and Clyde this shit!" She shifted the truck into gear, and we rambled down the driveway through the fog and pouring rain, leaving the safest place in the city behind us. "Try and get a casual look at the keypad for the security gates," I said.

"You should keep a close eye on the reporters when we pass through. Just in case they aren't reporters at all. They could be reinforcements."

My eyes widened and I sat up straight in my seat, not speaking.

Kára glanced at me sidelong. "You did think of that possibility, right? Before you convinced me to drive through overwhelming numbers of alleged reporters? That it might be a trap?"

"Of course, I considered that possibility," I snapped, folding my arms. "I'm a professional wizard."

Kára sighed. "We should have brought Carl as backup. Stuffed him in the back." She thought about it for a few seconds. "Okay. Maybe not. They will likely also have cameras, so no overt magic."

"Maybe it will be an uneventful drive," I said.

Kára glanced at me sidelong again. "You're still wearing your robe and moccasins, and your face is painted with fake Shaman runes."

I felt my cheeks heat up. "You know what? Fuck this day. It's the worst."

CHAPTER 7

We drove through the security gate without a second army of wizards attacking us. Kára pursed her lips angrily when she saw the sliced wires sticking out from the gate's electronic keypad. The reporters started to swarm the truck, but the fog rolled out with us, concealing the fact that the drivers had changed but still allowing them to see enough to believe no one exciting was inside. That, and the fact that Kára barely slowed down, deterred the reporters from trying too hard to get to us.

We broke through to freedom and made our way towards the city, agreeing that abandoning the truck in an urban or commercial area would be less suspicious than the suburbs where nosy grandmas watched their streets like hawks. We remained silent as we drove, thinking over the afternoon's bizarre series of unfortunate events. In the fifteen-minute drive, I came up with exactly no answers.

I finally turned to look at her, not bothering to hide my frustration. "Wizards," I muttered. "If the Academy had put out a hit on me, they would have sent Justices with an official accusation or something. More pomp and ceremony than *Time to die, Temple!*" The Justices were the Academy's enforcement arm. The top tier battle wizards entrusted with keeping our world separate from the Regulars, and policing rogue wizards who

took a more pragmatic approach to things like theft, murder, and accumu-
lating power. The Justices were not squeamish and they scored high on the
zealot scale, but their intentions were good. Unfortunately, they had read
the ancient sophist, Thrasymachus, a few too many times, and believed
that *might was right*, and *justice is nothing other than the advantage of the
stronger.*

Yikes.

"Those guys were strong," I continued, "but not strong enough to have
a good chance at success." Kára clucked, lifting up a finger to remind me.
"Unless their intent wasn't to kill but incriminate me," I said, agreeing with
her unspoken point. "It's almost certain that the Masters are involved in
this, pulling their invisible strings to see what happens." Kára nodded
soberly. "Or do you think they were mercs? Like that contract on me a
while back for a billion dollars. Maybe it's increased?"

Kára shrugged, pursing her lips. "I could call Niko and see if she's
heard anything. If it's black ops, she might know something. Or at least
know someone who might know something."

I nodded eagerly. I hadn't even thought about Niko, the wizard assassin
who had briefly wanted to kill me unless I convinced her I wasn't an evil
overlord. I'd completely forgotten about her friendship with Kára, but that
was forgivable. A lot had happened since then. "Do that. See what she
knows about anything going on in the world today. Apparently, we are
remarkably ill-informed."

She flashed me a warm, reassuring smile. It was hungry and anticipa-
tory. "To times of war. Skal!"

I found myself grinning back at her, infected by her confidence. I was
still somewhat concerned about the distant part of me that felt just as
eager for war as my two bunker buddies often did. I was still a little put off
at how swiftly I had adapted to battle against the delivery assassins—how
cold and merciless I had felt. Like I was justified to do anything I wanted.

Aphrodite had warned me about the Carnage, that it was a common
malady among gods when their heads got too big for their own good. But I
wasn't a god. I was a godkiller. Did that make me *more* susceptible to influ-
ence, or less? I let out a sigh, shaking my head.

Perhaps I'd spent too long in Chateau Falco with Kára while the pot of
war out in the real world had continued to simmer, and it seemed like

everything boiled over the moment I opened the door. All I'd wanted was a little rest and relaxation with Kára. Was that too much to ask?

I grimaced unhappily, suspecting I already knew the answer. Yes, it was too much to ask.

For the Catalyst, anyway. The man who would start or end the Omega War against the mysterious Masters. The shadowy group of boogeymen didn't take off for the Christmas holidays, obviously. Instead, they had capitalized on my hiatus to great effect. It hadn't slipped my mind that the Masters were very likely involved in this attack—directly or indirectly— but chasing after them directly would be futile because I didn't know who any of them were. They were puppet masters, using others to do their dirty work. I needed a loose thread to tug, first. One of my mother's cheerful life lessons popped into my head: *Wake when everyone else sleeps, work when everyone else plays, and relax in luxury when everyone else works themselves into the grave.*

With an annoyed sigh, I climbed out of my seat and made my way into the back of the truck, hoping to find some clues. Maybe a scrapbook titled *Masterplan to Kill Nate Temple.* Hell, it would be kind of cool to find a dossier on me, discovering what the gossip said about me and whether or not they knew all the things I'd really done over the years.

A tumble of packages had spilled over the floor, but many had been strapped down onto pallets, partitioning the truck into little sections. I made my way closer to the back, stepping around a wall of boxes, not finding anything particularly interesting.

I sucked in a breath of surprise to see a dead body staring up at me with glassy eyes. His head was twisted at an impossible angle, courtesy of the assassin wizards. I let out a nervous sigh and scrutinized him warily.

The original driver of the truck, judging by the employee badge hanging from his lanyard and the universally familiar brown uniform of collared button-up and khaki shorts with sturdy boots. He even wore a stocking cap, and only professional mailmen wore shorts with a stocking cap in winter. I realized that I had completely overlooked the fact that Yetta and Jimmy had not been wearing the standard uniforms like this guy. "Jeff Stevens," I murmured under my breath. He was in his mid-forties, and I would have pegged him as retired military if I had to guess. One who had earned a small gut in retirement but was still hard as nails. He was surrounded by boxes that had been knocked free in the fight at Chateau Falco. I nudged a few out of the way to see if he had a tablet or a clipboard with his manifest or some other identifying information for me to use so I didn't have to resort to opening every box.

Instead, I almost pissed my pants to find two *more* bodies.

I stared, blinking rapidly in disbelief. Because one of them was a wizard-fucking Justice, wearing the dreadfully familiar silver mask that marked his esteemed title.

Even worse, the Justice had a gaping hole in his chest and the floor was sticky with congealed blood. The wound was a few inches in diameter and looked like it went entirely through his chest cavity.

The second man was in his thirties, close to my age, with wavy blonde hair like a surfer bro. His harsh cheekbones looked sharp enough to cut, and he even had a broad jawline with a cleft chin. It was one of those faces that any girl would immediately swoon over. Except it had been beaten to hell like he'd been pummeled to death for information. He had a deep purple bruise on his jaw and his jacket was scorched and burned—

His chest rose in a shallow breath, and I stumbled back in shock, almost tripping over Jeff's boot and falling on my ass before I caught myself on the tied-down pallet of packages.

He was still alive!

Shit shit shit! I raked my fingers through my hair, gathering my composure and dialing back the panic. *The facts*, I told myself.

The Justice and the surfer both wore black suits with black collared shirts, sans ties, and they wore matching metal bands on their wrists— cuffs, I recognized quite well. They blocked the wearer from using magic. Nowhere near as powerful as the Titan Thorns I had recently worn, but they would do the trick for any wizard in the world. I'd required Titan Thorns because wizard powers were only one of the many tools in my arsenal.

The two wizards weren't chained together or restrained in any other way.

"We have a problem," I called out to Kára, staring at the unconscious wizard.

"What?" she asked, glancing back.

"Two dead bodies. One is the delivery guy. The real one. Jeff Stevens."

Kára waited a few seconds for me to elaborate on mystery man number two. "Is the other body one of the wizards from the attack?"

I checked the Justice's body, searching for any hint he might have been in command of the other assassins. Where they had been dressed in casual street clothes, this one wore an expensive suit and a rich overcoat. "Maybe," I said, dubiously. "But it doesn't look like it. Even worse, he's an Academy Justice—"

Kára swerved and let out a curse, sending me tumbling into the body. My hand slipped into the gaping hole in his chest and I gagged as it sunk down to the wrist. The body was still lukewarm. I panicked, yanking my hand out and trying to ignore the wet squelching sound. "Oh, god. It's under my fingernails. I'm going to vomit." I hurriedly began wiping it off on his coat, muttering under my breath as I tried to avoid staring at his gaping wound.

Kára glanced back with an apologetic look on her face. "Sorry! But did you just say an Academy Justice? Like, the heaviest fucking hitters from the Academy?"

I grimaced. "Yeah. Looks like they murdered him. This definitely wasn't from us or Thor's goats. He was bound with magic nullification shackles, so he was obviously their prisoner." I glanced over at the surviving wizard, finding it impossible to dismiss the similar suit, albeit a much cheaper quality. "Even worse-worse, it looks like the Justice had an apprentice, but he's *not* dead."

Kára slammed on the brakes, sending me tumbling into the front seat. I headbutted the console and groaned as stars exploded across my vision. Kára grabbed me by the robe and hoisted me up to her face. "We have to kill him."

I blinked dazedly, trying to shake off the mild concussion. "He might know something. He's been beaten to hell and his mentor was murdered. He obviously wasn't working with the assassins."

"I'm not a fan of coincidences," she argued.

My head cleared enough to see that we were parked under a dark underpass in a shady part of downtown St. Louis. I saw the Arch in the distance, and it was flickering red and blue from the ongoing police presence investigating the scene below. The scene Prometheus had caused when he'd crashed into it a few weeks ago.

That was one of the main reasons I'd kept a low profile lately. Most of St. Louis had bought into the story that the event had been a terrorist attack and the National Guard had been called in to patrol the streets. There wasn't necessarily a curfew, but there was kind of a curfew. If you wandered the streets outside after dark there was a very good chance the cops would harass you with dozens of questions.

So, the city was eerily quiet now. Even though it wasn't yet dusk, it was close.

Kára plucked a thick, brown canvas jacket off a hanger behind the driver's seat and shoved it into my hands. "Put this on. Our plan to abandon the truck here just went to hell. If it has dead bodies inside, and someone later links it to the one sent to your house, you'll have to deal with the police on top of everything else." She glanced up at the strobing Arch in the distance and grimaced. "You're going to have to torch it. Better yet, blow it up so they can't find anything in the rubble."

Sure. Blow up a truck. What's the worst that could happen?

I eyed Jeff Stevens' body with a regretful sigh. An innocent bystander just doing his job. Damn it.

CHAPTER 8

I shrugged into the coat, motioning her to follow me into the back and away from the giant windshield. "Blow up a huge delivery truck in a city swarming with armed, panicked police and National Guard soldiers. Splendid." I let out a sigh. "You're right, but this is turning into a shit-show," I said, pointing out the bodies for Kára. I glanced down at the dead Justice and then his apprentice, making sure he wasn't about to wake.

Technically, it was *possible* that this wizard had been one of the assassins, even though he was wearing cuffs and a similar suit to the bona fide Justice. I crouched down and carefully fingered the collar, checking the label. I grunted. Not cheap, but not nearly as expensive as the Justice's expertly tailored, high-quality suit. His shoes were something easily bought off a moderately priced shelf, but they were scuffed and worn upon closer scrutiny. As a whole, it looked like an Academy-expensed suit that was chosen on a strict budget. Respectable but not the same as the upper echelon price tags a Justice's suit would demand. Nice enough to be seen beside the Justice without embarrassing him, but not nice enough to presume equal status as his mentor.

Definitely not like the street clothes the assassins had worn.

"We can't kill the wizard. He's the only one who might have answers," I finally said, staring at his shackles.

"Good idea," Kára said with a thoughtful nod. "We will torture and interrogate him." She slipped past me and the bodies and sat down on a low stack of boxes near the van's back door. "We have a few minutes and I really need to deal with this phone while we have some down time."

With that, she opened up her backpack and pulled out some wires and a compact laptop. She fired it up and plugged Yetta's phone into it. Within seconds, her fingers were flying across the keyboard and she was opening dozens of applications and webpages on the computer, occasionally lifting the phone to type something there as well.

I shuddered. Chasing down that recorded video was more important than anything else currently on my plate. If someone got their hands on that video, they could easily blackmail me on multiple felony counts, let alone the fact that it would make me the scapegoat for single-handedly letting the Freaks out of the closet to the world at large. I would become a pariah overnight, sending the Regulars and the Freaks of the world into a frenzy.

I crouched over the unconscious wizard and began searching his pockets, careful not to wake him. I saw no magical tracking devices or anything concerning. I also saw no wallet or phone. He did have a small Moleskine journal and a cheap pen in his inner pocket, as if to take notes from his mentor. I cracked it open to see a date written on the first page, and then nothing. The date was three days ago, and the rest of the notebook was empty. I frowned, tapping the journal into my palm as I studied the wizard. Had he and his boss been abducted on his first day as an apprentice? Damn.

The Justice's pockets were equally bare, but I did find a pair of unmarked Tiny Balls. I clenched my jaw angrily, furious to see that they were using my goods from Grimm Tech. I pocketed them and continued searching him but came up with nothing helpful. Then again, Justices didn't need toys. On that note, I plucked off his silver mask. It shifted from solid metal to a seemingly quicksilver hanky as it detached from his skin. I pocketed it with a shudder, telling myself that it wasn't really liquid. It was just over-caffeinated silk and twitched of its own accord.

He had short white hair and a white, scruffy beard. His face was a visage of violence, telling a long, illustrious story of many, many years as a

Justice. He looked like he should have retired a century ago. Despite his obvious age, he was like an oak tree, only getting stronger and more resilient as the years failed to beat him down. This was a hard motherfucker. Not one of the new-age, elitist wizards. This guy made cereal out of gravel and whisky after smoking a stogey every morning when he woke up at five on the dot—no alarm clock.

The gang of wizards had kidnapped an apparently notorious Justice and his apprentice—possibly three days ago. Then they'd beaten the hell out of the apprentice and killed the Justice. They must have caught him off-guard. So, the assassins hadn't been part of the Academy. Mercenaries. And they likely had more associates lying in wait.

Powerful friends. Like the Masters.

"Pass me your phone," I told Kára. "We should get pictures of these three." She didn't even look as she extended one hand behind her to give me her phone. I took it and snapped a few pictures of the Regular delivery guy first. Then I moved to Justice Whisky-for-blood. Finally, I moved to the unconscious wizard, even though we planned on taking him with us. I winced, noticing that his ankle looked swollen as all hell, bulging over his dress shoe and straining the laces. Broken or sprained? I found a duffel bag full of electronics and nudged it open with my moccasin. "Electronic artifacts," I murmured to the technomancer Valkyrie.

She glanced over with a frown. Then she smiled, looking relieved. "Ah. Looks like they were going to upload their video here after they escaped. That's a relief. But I'm still going to burn the bridges behind us. Her phone was linked to a cloud account, and I have no way of knowing if someone out there has remote access. Almost done. Prep the asset for exfil."

I blinked at her. Then I rolled my eyes. "I don't speak *Call of Duty* because I have a girlfriend. Hurry up with your make-up blog post, and I'll get the unconscious guy ready to leave with us."

Kára chuckled. "This girlfriend would pwn you, noob."

I shook my head, having no idea what she'd just said.

I attempted to arrange the facts of the day into some semblance of helpful information.

Thor's Goats had been sent to Falco in disguise. They had then leapt into action to protect me from assassins.

A gang of wizard assassins had tried to bomb me, get me on video killing someone or using magic, and then they had resorted to murder after their first two plans had failed spectacularly.

The Masters were giddily pulling their puppet strings.

Alex wanted me to come to Fae, and it had something to do with the Knightmares.

In summation, after a few weeks of relative silence, a storm had struck my city out of a clear blue sky.

From shamans and sheriffs to assassins, goats, Knightmares, a dead Justice, and his brand spanking new apprentice. But why had the Academy sent a Justice to St. Louis? They knew better than to stick their noses into my territory. I had made that fact abundantly clear in recent years, and I had an understanding with G-Ma, the Grandmaster of the Academy.

Maybe the Justice had been hunting down these mercenaries and had gotten too close. He did have two Tiny Balls that they hadn't taken away from him, and they'd seen fit to transport the bodies with them to my house this morning. Their drama could have even originated somewhere else before spilling over into St. Louis. If I was a mercenary trying to kill Nate Temple, I probably wouldn't have staged it here either. Especially not with the increased police presence and the city on high alert.

I had no delusions that the Justice had been working to keep me safe. No way. Which meant two different things had happened. They'd attracted the attention of this Justice for some reason, and they also wanted to set me up, at best, or kill me. But...why? Hopefully, Niko knew something when Kára called her.

"We're good," Kára finally said with a breath of relief, unplugging the phone. "I hacked her cloud storage account, removed the video, deleted it on every cache available, and then planted a few malicious viruses in the account that will destroy any other potentially connected devices the next time any of the other shared users communicate with the account." She closed her laptop and slipped it into her backpack. "Three other users had access to the account but they were all under dummy names so I couldn't find anything useful on them when I scanned the dark web. Likely expensive burners," she said, waving the stolen phone at me like I understood half of what she'd just said.

"Well, you took long enough," I finally said, failing to bite back a grin. Before she could hit me, I pointed at the unconscious wizard. "Looks like he might have sprained his ankle or something. We'll have to carry him."

She pursed her lips. "Or you could just make a Gateway right here and we could toss him through to Chateau Falco."

I pointed a thumb at the dead Justice. "With one of these guys dead, it's possible more will come to town looking for him. I have a feeling he was a big fucking deal. He's got to be a few hundred years old, and in a fair fight as a wizard, I can honestly admit that I wouldn't want to duel him." Kára's eyes widened and she assessed the dead Justice with a wary frown. "Opening a Gateway anywhere near here would leave a possible trail of magical bread crumbs. I'm not even happy about having to use fire here, but there is no other way to make sure all incriminating evidence is destroyed so the *cops* don't find it." I lifted my hands like I was balancing a scale. "Use natural fire so the Justices can't track us, and we risk the cops finding something in the charred remains." I shot a significant glance at Jeff, the delivery guy. As much as I hated it, I couldn't use magic to get him out of here and make sure someone found him. "Use magic to ensure all evidence is destroyed for the police, and risk Justices tracking us or at least jumping to the immediate conclusion that it's related to the most notorious wizard in town. Their enemy. Me."

Kára frowned, thinking. "The National Guard is out there. If they hear of an explosion and find evidence linking to you, they could send the fucking military to Chateau Falco."

I nodded. "I think that's the worst outcome. It's unlikely any snooping Justices could link wizard's fire to me. Sure, they'll try, but I can't be responsible for any and every use of magic in St. Louis. For all they know, it could have been their own guys," I said, pointing at the dead Justice and the injured wizard. "Fire is almost impossible to trace."

Kára nodded and hefted her backpack over her shoulders. "How far do we need to walk before you can use a Gateway safely?" She asked.

"As far as possible."

She let out a resigned breath and then popped the back door open a few inches so she could make sure the coast was clear. "We're good," she murmured, opening the door wide. "Let's hurry." A flurry of thick snow was now tumbling through the air and I smiled in relief. That would provide excellent cover for our escape.

She hopped out of the truck and motioned for me to hurry.

CHAPTER 9

I grabbed the sleeping wizard by the good ankle and dragged him towards the back of the truck. Then I hopped out and the two of us hurriedly and awkwardly manhandled him into a semi-standing position with one arm wrapped over each of our shoulders. He hung between us, deadweight, but at least he wasn't too heavy. He did whimper as some of his weight settled on his injured ankle.

Hopefully it didn't wake him up during our brisk trek through the darkening streets of St. Louis or he might raise a ruckus and draw attention we absolutely did not want.

Kára and I hustled as fast as possible, dragging the poor bastard between us. When we made it about one hundred yards, I swept our surroundings for any possible witnesses. Thankfully, this was a part of town that most normal people avoided during the best of times. I turned to face the distant truck and called up a huge fireball, aiming for the fuel tank. I unleashed it, growing it larger and larger, hotter and hotter, as it screamed across the pavement. It struck the truck in a wash of flame that was immediately followed by a concussive blast that almost took my breath away.

Kára and I hurriedly shuffled away, slipping around a corner to enter a dark alley full of old car rims, spilled trash, and a vehicle on cinder blocks that had been stripped for parts. As we moved, I kept a close eye on the wizard, wanting to know the moment he woke up. He was no danger to us with his bracelets on, but the first moments of regaining consciousness would be the best opportunity for me to observe his immediate reaction to his current situation.

It might give me a clue to his true identity and intentions. What he'd been doing in that truck with a dead Justice and almost a dozen assassin wizards. But he didn't even stir. We made it a few blocks, pausing at each intersection to make sure we wouldn't be spotted by cruising cars or possible security cameras on some of the mostly vacant buildings and warehouses.

"You picked a damned good spot," I told Kára, shaking my head. "I haven't seen a soul."

She glanced over at me, eyeing the wizard before speaking. "What the hell is this all about, Nate?"

I called up a tiny bit of magic to muffle the wizard's ears in the event he woke up and attempted to fake remaining unconscious in order to over-hear our conversation. It was possible that he was semi-aware of nearby conversations—like those people waking up from comas in hospitals who could recall snippets of conversation from their doctors or family members. Confident his ears were plugged, I answered.

"To be honest, I'm surprised I wasn't attacked sooner. I was beginning to feel forgotten."

"This is serious, Nate. What if the Academy decides that *you* killed that Justice?"

I grunted. "That's one reason I wanted to keep this one *alive*," I said. "We'll have to ensure he tells the truth to his bosses. Hell, we don't even *know* the truth yet. He might have been involved with them, for all we know. In that case, we have a bargaining chip with the Academy to reveal a dirty Justice on their payroll." I shrugged. "I'm more concerned about the gods, not punk ass wizards. Like the goats. Which one of our Asgardian friends sent them?"

She clenched her jaw, looking determined. "I can get some answers on that. We might not know who, but you're right about the Secret Santa address. Asgard."

I nodded. "And I've got a bad feeling about Fae. Alex could have easily visited Chateau Falco himself. Why send a self-destructing letter with a cryptic message and address it to Wylde rather than Nate? Something must be wrong. Sending a mysterious letter is not his style." I let out a frustrated sigh. "And what about the timing of the assassins? Them trying to catch me on video is an escalation I never thought I'd see from a fellow Freak. We might be enemies, but we all lose if the truth comes out." Kára clenched her fist hard enough to crack her knuckles. "So, we figure out who wants to take me down this time and proceed from there."

Sirens began screaming in the near distance, racing towards the source of the explosion I'd created.

I grimaced. "Shit. Their response times have improved. I hope my fire was hot enough..."

Kára nodded. "I hope we're far enough away from the blast that you can make a Gateway," she said. "Because now would be a really good time."

"Probably not, but we don't really have a choice if we don't want to get caught here."

I ripped open a Gateway to my father's office and we hurried through.

Kára unceremoniously dropped the wizard onto the floor. He banged his head into the leg of the table and let out a faint whimper. "Whoops," she said absently. She shifted into her full Valkyrie armor and stared down at the stirring wizard in a way that would give him an instant nightmare.

I flung off the delivery jacket since it was covered in snow, and flung it on the chair behind the desk. I stared out the massive window behind my father's desk, watching the approaching dusk through the storm Ruin had created. It had turned to snow, blanketing Chateau Falco in thick layers of white. On the inside, I felt a different storm brewing on the horizon.

My weeks of lazing about were coming to a thunderous end, it seemed.

The wizard groaned behind me and I let out a tired sigh as I turned to face him. He blinked groggily, his bright green eyes taking a few moments to come into focus.

He noticed the gleaming armor of the Valkyrie first, and abruptly let out a startled squeak, backing away from her. I cleared my throat and his head spun on a swivel.

His eyes bulged upon seeing me, obviously recognizing the Academy's most hated wizard.

"Hey, Bub," I said.

His face paled in confusion and he licked his lips nervously. "Ah, shit," he croaked. "I am *so* fired."

Kára crouched down before him and gripped him by his stupid, perfect chin, turning his head to face her. She flashed him a truly menacing, eager smile. "Funny. I suggested fire as well," she said in a napalm-sweet tone.

He stared into her dual-colored eyes and began to tremble.

I cleared my throat before speaking in a loud tone. It wasn't necessary, but it made me feel more secure and it came across foreboding as all hell. "Falco! Lock the house down from all entrances and exits. No one in or out. We have a visitor who will be staying here indefinitely."

The house purred in response and I smiled at the raw fear on the wizard's face as his eyes darted to the rafters and walls and he started panting in short, panicked breaths.

Then I made my way towards him, slowly walking heel-to-toe and staring into his eyes. "The weather outside is frightful," I sang in a low, sinister tone. I flung a small fireball at the stacked wood in the fireplace. It roared to life, hissing and popping. "And fire is so delightful," I continued with a wicked, menacing grin, holding a second ball of fire to hover over my palm between us. "Let it grow, let it grow, let it grow," I sang as I made the fire in my hand and fireplace grow larger, hotter, and louder until he tried to lean away from me.

Which was when Kára gripped him by the hair, keeping his head in place. "Welcome to the worst day of your life, wizard," Kára said warmly.

"Merry Yulemas," I said, staring at the firelight flickering in his green eyes. "I hope you're not on the naughty list."

"I do," Kára said, slowly drawing a long, gleaming dagger from her hip. "I *really* do..."

He stared at us with more confusion than fear, although he had plenty of that. "Did Jasper make it?"

I studied him in silence, trying to get a read on his thoughts. To learn his tells and motivations. He was an Academy pawn at best, of middling power. Much weaker than the assassins I had battled. That didn't mean much, but it was a piece of the puzzle. So, if I was in his shoes, what would I do in his current situation?

Whether he was one of the assassins or a member of the Academy, I was his enemy. Hence the threats I'd started out with. Knock him back on his heels and see what spilled out.

"Sit down," I told him, pointing at one of the leather chairs.

He narrowed his eyes. "No. Fuck you. And your dirty-ass robe, and stupid face-paint," he added, puffing out his cheeks. "I won't tell you a thing."

I arched an eyebrow. Well. I hadn't anticipated this reaction. And I'd completely forgotten about the goddamned robe and face-paint. Here Kára was, wearing a beautiful set of armor with a fancy dagger, and I looked like a goddamned lunatic. I tried to keep my angry face on, but I burst out laughing at the ridiculousness of it all, shaking my head as it bubbled out of me. I wiped at my eyes with one hand—my clean one, since the other still had pieces of Justice under the fingernails. I slipped that one out of view, not wanting to distract the strangely defiant wizard.

"Yeah. Today kind of got ahead of me," I admitted. "What with assassins and then you," I added with a wave of my wrist. "But seriously, sit down. It's almost impossible to take you seriously with you posing like a dog," I said, eyeing his all-fours position. "And the werewolves downstairs might think you're inviting something you really don't want to invite," I added meaningfully, arching an eyebrow.

Rather than waiting for him to comply, Kára picked him up by the back of the shirt and tossed him into the chair as if he weighed nothing. He landed with a grunt and a yelp as his ankle struck the base of the chair. Kára sheathed her dagger and then brushed her hands together with a satisfied sniff. She sat down on the couch to his right and watched him, forcing him to split his attention in two different directions between me and the Valkyrie. He clutched at his ankle and sharply untied his shoelace. He instantly let out a breath of relief.

"Yeah, that's not happening," Kára warned as he reached for his shoe to take it off.

He froze, grimaced, and then leaned back in the chair rather stiffly, obviously in pain. I waited for him to muster through it for a few moments, and then I cleared my throat, pointedly. "I didn't seek you out, pal. I don't know who you are or why you're here, and I sure as hell don't know what the fuck it has to do with me. So, how about we start with names. My name is Nate Temple, but I think you already knew that." The man nodded warily. I pointed a thumb at the couch. "That is Kára, a Valkyrie bodyguard from Asgard. She tries to keep things from overly annoying me. So, bro, I'm sincerely asking you not to do anything that overly annoys me. For your own sake. Tell me your name, please, and then tell me why you're ruining my day."

He assessed me, seeming to weigh his chances at surviving this encounter, and trying to determine whether or not I was lying. Which meant he knew something juicy that he didn't want to share.

"Aiden. Aiden Maxon," he finally said. "You should have just killed me."

CHAPTER 10

I drummed my fingers across the armrest, trying to unpack that little
nugget of insanity and self-loathing. I shrugged. "I don't see any
immediate reason to do so, unless you're here to kill me?" I
suggested, fishing.

He snorted. "What? I don't even know how the fuck I got here."

I glanced at Kára but she just shrugged. "You asked about Jasper," I
said, turning back to him. "Who is that?"

Aiden grew still, licking his lips. "I literally can't tell if you're fucking
with me right now," he said, speaking very slowly.

I shrugged. "It seems we're on the same page then. I'll go first. My day
started like this," I said, gesturing at my robe and face-paint, "minding my
own business with Kára. Then a delivery truck showed up and a bunch of
wizards tried to kill me. I'm trying to determine if you are an incredibly
convincing ally of theirs or not."

He opened his mouth wordlessly, looking baffled. "What does any of
that have to do with me? How did I get here? And where is Jasper?"

Kára leaned forward. "I hate to say it, but I think he's actually telling
the truth," she murmured, sounding surprised.

I pursed my lips, shaking my head. "I'm not buying it. He has said
nothing of value to explain his involvement. I know plenty of fine actors,

but I'm going to need some kind of proof before I trust you." I leaned forward. "I know you work for the Academy. And I know they'd probably prefer me dead. So, how about you start explaining how you're not here to accomplish that goal for them. And then convince me you're not with the assassins who tried to kill me this afternoon. Either way I see it, Aiden, you're part of a team of wizards who would very much like me dead." I leaned back in my chair, and gestured for him to tell me his story. "Make it very convincing, Aiden. I've entertained this headache long enough. Right now, you are a problem for multiple reasons, and I haven't heard a single word to make me think otherwise."

"Tell us about the Justice," Kára suggested, blindly flipping her dagger into the air in a single rotation and catching it by the tip, over and over again.

Aiden closed his eyes and murmured a prayer under his breath. It wasn't like he had much of a choice. "Jasper Griffin," he finally said, watching my reaction as if fearing an outburst or an instant death threat. After a few moments, he narrowed his eyes suspiciously. Then he turned to Kára, a ghost of a smile crossing his cheeks as if he thought we were teasing him. Seeing our blank stares, he grunted. "You're kidding me. Jasper Griffin. He's the most notorious Justice ever. He's a goddamned legend."

I shrugged, inwardly pleased to learn that my instinctive assessment of the old man had been accurate. "What makes him so special?" I asked, curiously. I'd squared off against the Grandmaster and a whole bunch of Justices, but I had never heard of this guy.

Aiden shrugged. "He's the acquisitions guy, the rogue wizard hunter they send when no one else has a chance. I think he's caught and killed over two hundred dark wizards. Even the Grandmaster doesn't order him around—she respects him."

I scoffed. "I have literally never heard of him, and I've squared off against the Grandmaster directly. I've also tangled with a lot of Justices, and his name has never come up."

He nodded. "He's a wanderer, not part of the typical operations or politics of the Academy. That's why I worshipped him as a child. He didn't have to do all the ass-kissing and scheming like everyone else. He went off and did his own thing, only returning to drop off a fugitive or some recovered artifact. He would speak to no one but the Grandmaster, and then he would leave again."

I pursed my lips, glancing at Kára. She shrugged. "A ghost I can't verify is your primary proof that you're not a danger to me? The very Justice the Academy would have sent after me—their favorite wizard to hate for the last five years—to put me in my place? *He's* your alibi?"

Aiden shrugged, looking frustrated. "I'm not a Justice, so I can't answer that. But I do know that he only hunts down wizards *he* deems dangerous. He is not a dog on the leash of the Grandmaster. He picks his own targets." He shot me a desperate look. "And I swear on my power that he never once mentioned your name."

I took a measure of his power and frowned. "No offense, but you're hardly worth the trouble," I muttered. "Middling at best. What the fuck are you doing working with the greatest Justice in the world?"

Aiden fidgeted with the cuffs on his wrist, looking hurt at my scathing comment. Suck it up, I thought to myself. "Jasper returned once a year to offer a ride-along to a Justice recruit. He held a selection process and chose his favorite candidate. The other Justices had no say in the matter, so there was no politicking. He would take them out for a few days, showing them what life as a Justice was like and teaching them some of his hard-learned lessons." He met my eyes, shaking his head. "The recruits who get that experience have been some of the only Justices I liked at the Academy. I've applied for that opportunity for fifteen years and never gotten accepted. Until this time," he said, looking miserable. "Maybe my persistence? There's not much else about me that's impressive, as you pointed out. Other than me despising authority and the bureaucracy plaguing the Academy. It's corrupt as hell."

I pondered his story, paying close attention to his face and body language, but I was picking up on nothing deceptive or elusive. Even though I wanted to distrust him, my mind was voting against me. But I kept my face blank, not letting him see any of that.

"So, Aiden Maxon," I said, choosing my words very carefully. "Let's say I buy all of that. If he takes these candidates on educational ride-alongs, how in the hell did you end up at *my* door in a delivery truck full of rogue wizards, beaten to hell, and your legendary mentor dead? That hardly seems like a job he would have taken an apprentice on."

Aiden's face broke as if he'd just taken a blow to the gut upon hearing the Justice was dead. I gave him a few moments and watched as he took calming breaths, gathering his resolve. Then he grimaced, brushing a strand of blonde hair back from his forehead. "That's not how any of it started," he explained, his eyes growing distant as he reimagined it all in his mind. "Our first hunt had gone well. I'd held my own against a reckless vampire in Lithuania who was drinking the town dry, giving Jasper the chance for a clean kill. We'd spent the rest of the day speaking about the corruption in the Academy—the favoritism and favor-trading—and how we might clean it up. I must have said something encouraging, because he invited me back the next day. We were getting ready to leave for another simple, routine hunt to reclaim a stolen book so that he could test my basic skills and determine whether I had the potential to become an asset. He was in his office, and I was waiting for him in his sitting room, anxious to leave and to prove myself better than the day before. I even bought a little notebook," he chuckled, patting his pocket. I had put it back before dragging him out of the delivery truck. His smile faded, as he likely considered that he'd never gotten to use it. Then he continued. "Jasper got a phone call and everything changed. His door was open a crack, and I..." he blushed faintly, "I eavesdropped a little, overhearing his side of the conversation."

I leaned back in my chair, my head propped on my palm in a dubious pose. I waved my hand vaguely for him to carry on before I got bored.

He cleared his throat, and then started speaking in a burlier, deeper tone, obviously trying to replicate Jasper Griffin, Justice Extraordinaire.

"Only three people know that cursed artifact exists! Me, the Grandmaster, and you. There is no record of it anywhere, because I fucking destroyed every record of it, and then I killed anyone who had ever heard even a whisper about it. For damned good reason. If anyone knew we had such a nefarious artifact at our disposal, absolutely no one would trust us. Ever. So, Cyrilo, how the hell was it stolen? And do I need to shorten the list of people who do know about it to me and the Grandmaster?"

Kára was leaning forward, engaged in the story. I had to admit, I was too. Because I loved dangerous toys, and to hear that the Academy had some super-secret artifact that they didn't want anyone to know about was extremely curious. It didn't sound like something they even wanted to have, referring to it as cursed. They must not have been able to destroy it, otherwise they would have.

Aiden had paused, staring down at the ground. Then he resumed his story in his usual voice. "I panicked, realizing that Jasper would add me to that death list for what I had overheard. But the floor creaked and Jasper spun, lashing out with bands of air to trap me. The way he stared at me..." Aiden whispered, shaking his head. "His eyes were wide, bloodshot, apologetic, and fully committed to what he had to do. I had to die."

Kára appeared to be holding her breath, frowning cynically but still drawn into the story.

"Realizing his position, I met his eyes and told him that I understood. *'I never would have been promoted to Justice anyway, not without selling my soul. But it was inspiring to learn from you. More fun than I've had at the Academy in years.'*

"And then I waited for him to kill me. But time stretched on, and I finally lifted my head. He was clenching his jaw, looking torn, and I realized that I might just have a second chance for some goddamned reason.

"Finally, he rounded on me, and his voice was hoarse. *'It's already stolen, so more people will know about it soon enough. Unless I...we...can get it back. Do not make me regret this, boy.'*

"I couldn't believe my luck," Aiden murmured. "I vowed I would do whatever he asked and carry the secret to my grave. Because I wasn't naive. I knew that once we got it back, I would only be a loose end. But I was going to be part of a real fucking adventure with Jasper Griffin before I died.

"He grabbed me by the shoulder, placed a finger over his lips for me to be silent, and then Shadow Walked us to a warehouse in Illinois. We saw a few dozen wizards working in teams. Hackers, welders, battle wizards, and some loading and unloading trucks. But Jasper looked annoyed, not seeing the artifact he was looking for. We must have set off an alarm, because they suddenly attacked us, overwhelming us. Jasper took out ten of them, but more kept coming from offices deeper within their warehouse. There had to be fifty of the bastards and, at some point, numbers matter. They captured us and slapped these on," he said, tapping a fingernail against his cuff.

"And then they interrogated us. Jasper would not talk. At all. They did the most sickening things to him, bringing him to the brink of death and then healing him. Repeatedly, for days. Still, he said nothing. So, they decided to try me, seeing if they could break him by roughing up his apprentice while he watched. Because he had growled instinctively when one of them hit me—the first response they'd managed to get from him, despite his own torture." He absently reached down to touch his swollen ankle, grimacing. "Thankfully, they only worked on me for a few hours before Jasper somehow managed to break free of his handcuffs and grab a gun. He shot three of them before one of the wizards blew a hole through his chest, but I thought there was a chance he might have made it because that's how notorious his reputation is. You ask why he's the most legendary Justice ever? I witnessed why. The man was made of diamond, only getting stronger beneath their pressure for him to cave.

"Then someone kicked me in the head, and that's the last thing I remember. The next thing I know, I'm waking up here with you," he admitted, "getting hit in the head again," he grumbled, rubbing at the spot where he'd banged his head on the chair after Kára had dumped him onto the floor.

CHAPTER 11

He folded his arms uneasily, waiting for our reaction. I let out a whistling sound through my teeth, not knowing what to say. I was entirely confident that he hadn't fed us lies, but some of what he'd claimed was actually provable. Kára could look into the Lithuanian vampire and see if anyone knew more about Jasper Griffin. Or Cyrilo, the man on the phone with Jasper about the artifact. Was he a wizard at the Academy?

And this secret artifact had my interest piqued. Someone had obviously known about it, despite Jasper's confidence, because it had been stolen. I'd never heard a whisper of such a thing. Hell, I might have been tempted to steal it myself, legitimately earning the ire of Jasper Griffin.

Unfortunately, I still had no idea who the assassins had been, but they were highly organized, according to Aiden's story. I glanced at Kára, and she nodded, mouthing *Niko*. The mercenary was our best bet.

Aiden surprised me by letting out an annoyed breath. "Look. I don't really give a shit if you believe me or not. I'm dead either way once the Grandmaster learns that I heard about this artifact—whatever it is—and that Jasper died. She will kill me just to keep the secret, based on how many *others* they've killed to keep it secret. So, do what you will. I'm already on borrowed time," he muttered. "Fucking Academy, man. The one damned thing that went right in my entire life at that cursed place, and it ends up being the thing that fucks me."

I frowned. "Cursed place?" I asked. "That doesn't sound like the brainwashing we all know and love."

He grunted, smirking. "Yeah. Tell me about it. Why do you think I was so unpopular? I wanted the hell out of that place, dreaming that I could one day do something like Jasper. Maybe not a famous Justice or anything, but living life on my own, away from the bureaucracy of hypocrisy."

"So, what the hell were they coming at me for?" I asked. "I've never heard about an artifact, and I have nothing to do with the Academy. I've never met either of you clowns."

Aiden held up his hands with a look that should have earned him a slap, but I found myself smirking. His personality was very similar to mine, and I found it refreshing that he wasn't some milksop apprentice.

"The thing that bothers me," he said, scratching at his jaw, "is that I have no idea if they got this artifact or if they were just a lead Jasper decided to chase. He didn't tell me before taking me to the warehouse. And I have no idea who Cyrilo is, but it sure felt like we walked into a trap."

I nodded. "My thoughts exactly," I admitted. "He's not a Justice or a member of the Academy?"

Aiden shook his head. "I've lived there my whole life and that was the first time I heard the name."

"Nickname?" I mused. "Last name?"

"Not that I've ever heard."

I still didn't understand why these assassins would come to Falco, and why they would have brought Aiden and the dead Justice in the truck. Maybe to frame me and send the Academy after me? But their plan had been to blow me up, kill me, or die trying, and get it all on video, so... maybe raise enough noise in the fight that the cops would come and find the three dead bodies? I shook my head, deciding to mull it over with Kára in private—

The door to the office swung open and Carl sauntered in, tugging the red boa back and forth across his neck, humming to himself. He did not realize we were here.

"What the fuck is *that*?" Aiden shouted, sounding panicked.

Carl froze, slowly turning to look at the strange wizard, and then me and Kára. "Hi." He turned to Aiden and showed off his scarf. "It is a boa. We have more if you want one."

Aiden sputtered incredulously, looking pale as a sheet. "E-Elder…"

"Elder Carlemagne, at your service, impotent wizard," he replied, eyeing Aiden's cuffs. Kára burst out laughing at his new name. I'd never heard it before, so it must have been given by one of Gunnar's clan. Calvin? Then he turned to me. "The Randulfs are still waiting for you. And this was with the goats," he said, handing me a dark envelope.

Kára got up and held out her hand to accept the envelope, but Carl suddenly hissed at her, and the spiked crests on his neck abruptly expanded, fanning out and rattling menacingly. Aiden yelped, tried to run, and tripped over the table, falling on his ass with a groan.

Kára placed one fist on her hip and arched an eyebrow at the Elder, not remotely taken aback by his reaction. "I told you to stop doing that, Carl. I don't want the stupid boa, just the envelope."

Aiden sat up, nursing his ankle as he stared, bug-eyed at the Elder and Valkyrie. Finally, Carl shoved the envelope into her hands and then sprinted out the door, clutching his feather scarf tightly to protect it from thieving Valkyries. I sighed, shaking my head. "Fucking Carl," I muttered.

Aiden watched me, struck speechless. I walked over to Kára as she opened the envelope and pulled out a small black card with silver writing on it. I leaned over her shoulder and we read it in silence so Aiden didn't eavesdrop on us like he did with Jasper.

Not as traditionally important as Mistletoe, but just as vital.

It was unsigned. Kára turned to look at me with a frown, and I held a finger to my lips before discreetly pointing my thumb at Aiden.

She nodded in understanding. "Mistletoe?" she breathed.

"It's a warning. The goats are protection," I whispered. "And we know someone allergic to mistletoe."

Kára scowled, giving me a single faint nod. "Baldur." She looked ready to spit nails.

I gripped her bicep and squeezed reassuringly. "We'll figure it out."

"I'm still here," Aiden said in an annoyed tone. "Just making sure you didn't forget."

Kára burst out laughing and then turned around to lean over the back of the chair and face our prisoner. "So, what are we doing with him?"

I frowned. "Well, I was going to have Carl watch him while we went to Fae to hunt down that ogre who pissed you off yesterday," I lied, deciding to fuck with Aiden's head.

Kára clucked her tongue, instantly catching on to my tactic. "I thought we were going to Olympus for Zeus' funeral. Just because you executed him doesn't mean you're not invited."

Aiden stared at the two of us, his face paling.

I let out an annoyed sigh. "I guess we could divide and conquer." We both stared at Aiden and he began to fidget. "Well, apprentice, it looks like you have a decision to make. You can play human pincushion for the scary Elder, you can play human shield while Kára heads to Olympus to disrupt Zeus' funeral, or you can play human bait in the deadly Fae realm with me."

He blinked rapidly, mouthing the choices. "That is so fucked up. Just lock me up in a prison cell or something. Christ."

I shook my head. "Nah. The prison cells are for the prisoners I know I can trust. Oh, time's up. Looks like you're coming with me, apprentice. Ever been to Fae? If not, I suggest you go potty before we leave. If you piss yourself, you'll attract every Fae monster within ten miles, like sharks to blood."

"But I'm crippled," he said, pointing at his leg.

"Well, I'm not going to hold it for you, Aiden," I said, folding my arms. "But I can walk you to the restroom, at least."

He clenched his jaw, his cheeks reddening. "No. I meant I can't help in Fae because of this," he said, pointing at his leg again.

I grunted, walking over to the side of the room where an umbrella stand was tucked against the wall. "Why do you think I want you for bait?" I asked from over my shoulder. I pulled out an old cane with a silver handle that featured the Temple Crest on it. Nothing fancy, but it had been one of my dad's favorites for sentimental reasons. I turned to Aiden and tossed it to him. "If the ogre comes for you, just bonk him over the head with that, but make sure to stand on your good foot."

Aiden caught it, pursing his lips. "Bonk," he repeated in a flat tone, somehow drawing the word out into two syllables. "The ogre's head."

I nodded, snapping my fingers. "But if you break that, I'm shoving all the splintered pieces up your ass."

He blanched. "What if I break it over the back of the ogre's head while he's trying to hurt you?"

I thought about it for a second. "I'll take the nuances into *consideration*." Then I smiled. "No promises."

He grunted, and a whisper of a smile tugged at the corner of his mouth. "Gee, thanks."

I clapped. "Talk about a stroke of good fortune, Aiden. On Team Temple, you've already been promoted to henchman, first class. Way higher than apprentice."

He smirked, shaking his head. Then he heaved himself to his feet, using the cane for support. "Well, I guess it's better than an Elder poking me or a god punching me to death, or the Grandmaster erasing me from existence for overhearing a phone call."

Kára smiled warmly. "Think of it this way. If the ogre hits you, you'll burst like a broken watermelon before you even have time to *feel* it."

I held up a finger. "But remember. Bonk. At any opportunity."

Aiden smiled crookedly and mimed bonking an imagined foe with the cane. "Like that?"

"Yep. Perfect."

He rolled his eyes. "Okay. Tell me where we're really going. I know you're just screwing with me."

I chuckled, shaking my head. "Mind watching him for a few minutes while I get changed?" I asked Kára.

She nodded. "Sure."

I briskly walked to the door but paused before leaving the room. "You really should go potty, Aiden. You'll regret it if you don't." I caught one last glimpse of his utterly confused face before I slipped out of the room, biting back my laughter.

CHAPTER 12

I shook my head, wondering what to make of Aiden Maxon. On a personality level, I liked him and definitely understood why he hadn't thrived in the Academy. He was against authority, even when it was in his best interest. I could definitely relate to that.

His story seemed completely genuine, but that didn't mean he knew the full story. He knew what Justice Jasper Griffin had told him, and I wouldn't feel completely confident until Kára hunted down a few of the verifiable tidbits Aiden had mentioned. Like the Lithuanian vampire. Maybe some information about this Jasper Griffin. If he was hundreds of years old, some of my allies had to have at least heard of him.

But I was grateful that his moral code had deemed me a good guy, despite the Academy's opinion.

And after realizing Aiden's magic level was mediocre at best, I couldn't find any good reason for him to lie. He was pretty much stuck between a rock and a hard place, and everything about our conversation supported that—his mannerisms, frustrations, and even the story itself.

My suspicion arose from something bigger than Aiden. I was wary of the Academy itself—of them possibly using Aiden in some elaborate ruse to trip me up and arrest me, without him even realizing it. The Academy would welcome me back into the fold the day strippers accepted loose change for tips, and not a day sooner.

The Temple family was a dark stain on their pristine history of wizards. Both my parents had turned their backs on the Academy and had been swiftly ex-communicated, branded as thieves and power-hungry bastards. The funny thing was...the Academy wasn't wrong.

They were simply *worse* than anything they accused us of being. And they hated that we knew it. That we didn't conform and give in to their petty declarations of authority. On that note, I'd *really* gotten under their skin, threatening to destroy them if they set foot in St. Louis without my express permission. They had exactly no jurisdiction here. Period.

But now a renowned Justice had died here. I was almost certain that Justices were going to be popping into St. Louis very, very soon, demanding to know what had happened to him, and they were going to be asking me since I'd claimed the city as mine.

So, I definitely wasn't going to release Aiden until I figured out exactly what was going on. Right now, he was my only bargaining chip. The only one who *knew* I hadn't killed Jasper Griffin.

I made my way down the hall towards the Master Suite.

I rounded the corner and skidded to a halt to find Carl with his back to me a few paces ahead, standing utterly still in the middle of the hall.

I frowned, glancing past to see Makayla standing ten feet in front of him, also motionless, blocking his way. She had his feather boa wrapped around her shoulders, and I had no fucking idea how she'd taken it from him. He'd almost challenged Kára to a literal fight for the mere suspicion she wanted to take it from him. Carl stood in a ready stance, but not necessarily an aggressive one. More like he was ready to flee if the young bully made any sudden moves.

Makayla stared at the Elder, her face blank, and her hands hanging loose at her sides. The tension in the hall was as thick as steam from a sauna and it didn't seem like either of them were breathing. They didn't acknowledge me at all.

Then Makayla abruptly lifted both of her tiny hands and splayed her fingers out like claws. Carl hopped laterally, like a spooked cat, and crashed into a side table, destroying it. Then he turned tail and ran past me as if the world was ending, completely giving up on his prized red-feather boa. I grinned and flashed Makayla a proud smile. She gave me the vaguest of smirks and shrugged, tugging at her new accessory. Then she calmly turned down a side hall and continued her leisurely exploration of Chateau Falco.

I stared after her, grinning despite the bizarre encounter between her and the Elder. Because I'd just seen her act like a kid without being prompted. She'd even smiled at me and shrugged. Nonverbal communication was a huge step forward.

It was no understatement to say that the Randulf teenwolves had been destroying the fabric of reality both at home and at Chateau Falco these last few weeks since they'd transformed into humans for the first time.

Calvin was as sharp as a tack, hyper-rational, and quickly coming to terms with his drastic growth spurt into adolescence and humanity. With each passing day, he had grown more confident and it was beginning to look like he might actually be an extrovert of sorts.

Makayla was pretty much a closed door. She did not talk. Ever.

Yet she was a physical powerhouse. She was swift and agile as hell and way stronger than her tiny frame suggested—both as a human and a wolf. Kára and I had gone hunting with the Randulfs twice in the last few weeks, and the adults had all been relieved to learn that, yes, the kids could shift into wolves at will. Not bipedal monsters like their parents, but exactly like they had looked before taking human forms, just larger now. They were about the equivalent of late-stage Great Dane puppies, with Calvin about thirty pounds bulkier than Makayla.

Despite her delays on the social side, Makayla had been the first to kill on both hunting trips—smoking her brother, who was no joke himself. She was a fucking natural at it. She took down a full-grown buck elk her very first hunt. Her bigger brother took down a smaller doe...thirty minutes later.

But in her human form, she would sit in silent observation rather than participating in group conversations with us. Same thing during movie nights or family meals. She would simply watch each person when we spoke, her face devoid of any emotional reaction yet hyper-aware of everything that was said. We could ask her to do something and she would not hesitate to go do it, so there was no issue with comprehension or understanding. But Gunnar and Ashley had begun to fear that she suffered speech issues of some sort.

Where the other adults talked behind closed doors about therapists, doctors, cures, and any other number of solutions...

I hung out with her. A lot. Every time they stopped by, I made a point to pull her aside and ask her help with some task I had on my plate. Or to simply join me on strolls through the mansion. I treated her like *my* therapist rather than acting like *hers*. I would ramble on about petty annoyances of my day and ask her rhetorical questions. When she didn't answer, I would nod along like she'd given me some pearl of wisdom. "You're probably right. I'll think on it a little more."

Comments like that.

I took her to lunch once and let my mouth run for thirty minutes about nothing in particular. I basically just opened up my subconscious mind and spoke the unvarnished thoughts that had been tumbling around in my head throughout the day.

She would stare at me intently, absorbing everything I said. But she wouldn't smile or show any outward reaction. She would just be present, waiting for some action-based activity.

I took her to the garage and had her help me clean up and organize boxes. She helped me dust and re-shelve old magical texts in the Sanctorum. I covered the Round Table in pillows and sleeping bags and invited her and Calvin to a sleepover with me and Kára. We stared up at the gemstone stars embedded in the ceiling high above as we pointed out the constellations. We read the kids stories about the Knights of the Round Table from Chrétien de Troyes. We played hide and seek in the arcane library before passing out from too much hot chocolate and marshmallows. That was the night I'd earned my first whisper of a smile from her—nothing more than a twitch at the corner of her lips.

But damn it, I'd worked my ass off to earn it, so I was rightly proud.

In short, I'd decided to treat her like I wished someone had treated me. Not as a friend, but as a trusted informant and confidant. I tried to be the Pan to her Wylde. And I'd earned a faint ghost of a smile from the sprite-like little blondie.

Worth it.

This altercation with Carl was the second maybe-smile I'd earned from her, and that was enough to turn my gloomy day entirely around.

I wasn't sure what the deal was with Carl and Makayla, but he was fucking terrified of her when she was not under the direct supervision of her parents. Every time Makayla walked by Carl, he would freeze and stare at her, his nostrils flaring. He watched her as if anticipating an immediate assault, slowly sidestepping around her while he refused to even blink. Like two wild animals on the savanna. Makayla would stare back at him, her face blank as she slowly pivoted so that she was always facing him head on. He would, as quickly as possible, find a way to carefully leave her scrutiny without having to turn his back on her.

This was the first time I'd seen Makayla actually screw with him rather than letting him escape freely.

And it was the first time I'd seen her give me a direct smirk. Maybe she was finally opening up. The strangest part of their dynamic was that neither would answer questions about it after the fact. Makayla never spoke anyway, but even Carl pretended like he didn't know what I was talking about whenever I asked. As far as I knew, I was the only one who had seen any of these silent confrontations.

It wasn't necessarily aggressive or confrontational—I wasn't scared of Carl attacking her or anything. He was definitely the scared one in their stand-offs.

"This place is so fucking weird," I laughed, making my way to the master suite so I could get changed into normal clothes for the first time today. And wash off the damned face-paint.

One didn't visit a king in one's bathrobe, looking like a clown.

CHAPTER 13

I'd washed the pretend runes off my face and changed into boots, jeans, and a sweater. I'd tossed on a light jacket just to be safe, and then slung my satchel over my shoulder before heading back to my office.

Aiden seemed to be moving well with his cane, and I was glad I didn't have to worry about a broken ankle, since the swelling also seemed to have gone down after his long story. I opened a Gateway from my office to Camelot, holding out my hand for Aiden to enter first. He swallowed nervously and gave me a faint nod. Then he hobbled his way through, looking as if he anticipated the ogre to attack at any moment.

Kára smirked at the nervous wizard's back. "Ogre bonking?" she whispered, fighting back a laugh.

I shrugged. "I need to keep him on his toes until I figure out what I'm going to do with him, and it's also the easiest way to throw a wrench in a story. Keep them distracted and elements of their story accidentally slip."

She nodded her agreement. "So, where are you really going? Asgard?"

"Yes. I want to discreetly look into the Baldur threat. I also want to see if Odin recognizes the picture we took of Jasper Griffin. If he's that old, Hugin and Munin would have likely seen him at some point. Enough to verify Aiden's story. Maybe even this Cyrilo guy," she added with a shrug.

I nodded. "Just be careful. If Baldur's a threat, he might try to find out what you're doing in Asgard."

She shot me a stern look. "Really?"

I grinned. "And you can call Niko, right? Maybe she's heard of this Cyrilo guy." I raked my fingers through my hair and let out a sigh. "Anything helps, Kára. See what you can learn, and I'll figure out what Alex's message was really about."

"I got it!" she laughed, shoving me. "Go!"

"I'll see you back here in a few hours," I said, glancing at the open Gateway. "Oh, and can you apologize to Gunnar if you see him on the way out? Let him know I'm just running an errand and that everything is fine. Relatively speaking. He's probably freaking out about this morning's...incident."

She arched an eyebrow. "You want me to lie for you. Not just about your errand, but that you have a wizard as a prisoner."

I nodded. "Because you're amazing and beautiful and—"

"Fine!" she said, shaking her head with a resigned smile. "I'll see what I can dig up and be back before dinner. Hopefully." With that, she blew me a kiss and left the office.

I hopped through the Gateway after Aiden, sweeping my gaze from left to right to search for my henchman—

I grinned to see my oldest friend, Talon the Devourer, holding the axe blade of his white polearm against Aiden's throat. Except now he was Sir Talon, a Knight of the Round Table. His gleaming white armor glistened in the sunlight, and the feline warrior looked downright noble. His fur was reddish brown, except near his lips, where it changed to a thick white beard. His long, shaggy ears sported three golden earrings, and his eyes were silver and striking. Flowers were blooming, and I heard birds chirping in the air. I feigned surprise. "Ah, there you are!" I said to Aiden. "You didn't bonk *him*, did you?" I asked, noting the cane lying on the ground.

Aiden swallowed very carefully. "I tried. On reflex."

I tsked my displeasure. "He's a Knight of the Round Table, Sir Talon the Devourer." I bowed at the waist, grinning at my old friend. "Sir Talon, this is my henchman, Aiden Maxon. It's his first day on the job, so don't break him."

Talon finally lowered his spear and took a step back, shaking his head at the wizard. "You fucking moron. You try that again and I'll rip your spine out with my bare claws and eat your liver."

Aiden's eyes bulged at the coarse language from the Knight. He shot a perplexed look my way and I shrugged. "Camelot's a little different from the stories. And yes, he would do all of that to you."

Talon used his foot to flick the cane up at Aiden. The wizard hadn't been expecting it, so it struck him in the nose with a solid *crack*. He let out a cry as his bad ankle gave out, and then he fell down on his ass. Talon grunted, casting a disgusted look my way. I shrugged, ignoring Aiden's whimpering groans as he tried to clutch at both his nose and his ankle, resulting in a rocking fetal position. "I told you not to break him, Tal," I said, grinning.

The beefy feline smirked and began purring loudly as he approached. His armor evaporated in a puff of mist and then he wrapped me up in a tight, furry hug, patting his paw against my back as his purring threatened to shake my fillings loose. "Wylde! I've missed you, brother. It's been forever since I've almost died for no good reason. I need some *adventure*."

"Oh?" a new voice asked in a stern tone. "Getting bored, Sir Knight?"

Talon pulled away, flashing me a guilty wince. "Ah, now I remember what it feels like to be around you," he chuckled. His armor puffed back into existence.

"Me?" I demanded in mock outrage. "That was you putting your paw in your mouth. I had nothing to do with it."

We turned to see Alex standing behind us. He wore white and gold armor that was even more resplendent than Talon's, and the legendary Excalibur hung at his hip. He was frowning down at Aiden. "Who made the wizard cry?"

Aiden muttered unhappily, his stuffy nose altering his voice. "I'm not cwying! Well, my eyes are weaking because he bwoke my fweaking nose, but I'm not weeping." Aiden stubbornly climbed to his feet with the aid of his cane. His nose was crooked and dripping blood, so he quickly pinched it with his free hand, trying to act tough in front of my friends.

Alex arched an eyebrow at Aiden's over explanation and turned to face me. "It's good to see you, Nate." His eyes discreetly flicked in Aiden's direction. "I had hoped for a bit of privacy."

I nodded, extending my hand. "He's...pwotecting me fwom any... woving ogas."

Talon's tail twitched as he grinned at Aiden, who was scowling at my mockery of his voice. Alex shook my hand firmly. "There are no...roving ogres here," he said, smirking. "Are you always such an asshole to new guys?"

I puffed my chest proudly. "It builds character. Aiden Maxon, meet King Alex Pendragon. It's a long story but only level two henchmen are permitted to hear it."

Alex turned to Aiden and dipped his chin in polite greeting. "Welcome to Camelot, Aiden."

Aiden bowed respectfully, still pinching his nose with one hand. "I've heawd a wittle, King Pendwagon," he said, his eyes flicking to Excalibur on Alex's hip. "It's an honna' to meet you." He turned his head and spit out a glob of mucus and blood, opening up his airways.

Alex somehow managed to keep a straight face. "Perhaps Talon could take you to the healer for your nose." Talon nodded obediently.

I cleared my throat pointedly before Talon could lead him away. "His ankle is sprained as well. Maybe the healer could take a look at it for him? But under no circumstances is he to be left unattended or have those bracelets removed. He's technically my prisoner. But he's been obedient and respectful. So far."

Alex clenched his jaw upon hearing Aiden was my prisoner, studying me for a moment. Finally, he nodded. "Have the healers see to him, Sir Talon. Do not let him out of your sight."

Talon abruptly held his spear again—since he could summon up the armor and the spear independently with a thought—keeping a wary eye on Aiden now that he knew the wizard was a prisoner. Rather than taking offense, Aiden gave Alex a warm, appreciative smile, and his speech impediment was vastly improved. "I do not need to see a healer, but I appreciate the offer."

Alex glanced at me, forwarding the question my way. I studied Aiden thoughtfully, wondering if he was simply being polite. Finally, I shook my head. "Go get yourself cleaned up, or I'll have to make fun of you all night. When a king offers you aid, the only acceptable answer is gratitude. Fae is a little different than our realm. Offers of gifts are almost as significant as the gift itself."

Aiden paled, licking his lips. "I meant no offense." He tested his bad foot on the ground and abruptly recoiled with a wince. "It would be nice to get rid of this limp."

I grunted. "That, and you'll look like a raccoon in a few hours if you don't get your schnoz checked out."

Aiden dipped his chin at Alex. "Thank you for the gift, King Alex." Then Talon was leading him away, frowning over his shoulder at me, likely wondering what the hell this was all about.

Alex turned to look at me. "What the hell is this all about? Why bring him with you?"

"My sitter cancelled on me." He arched an eyebrow in question. "Carl," I explained.

Alex grunted. "You were going to let Carl watch him for you? Do you want him to die?"

I waved a hand. "Enough about me. Why did you send me that strange letter?" I asked. "Is everything okay?" I glanced around the empty courtyard, noticing the lack of citizens. "Is it just you two here?"

Alex motioned for me to follow him and I sensed the heavy mantle of responsibility settling over his shoulders. "I have a few hundred Fae living here. Mostly the undeclared—those who prefer not to play the political games required in either the Winter or Summer courts. Some of the wild Fae are trickling in and I have a few of Tory's...more difficult students... here on a foreign exchange program of sorts."

I arched an eyebrow. I hadn't known Tory had started sending students here. It was an idea we had discussed a while ago, but I wasn't aware she'd begun the first wave. Some of her students came from very unforgiving childhoods and were more feral than civilized. Coming to Fae sometimes had the positive effect of calming inner demons. So, for out-of-control shifters, they sometimes experienced an aura of serenity upon coming here. "That's great news. Is Talon working them hard?"

Alex nodded. "And they love him for it."

"So, what's up with the—"

"Not out here," Alex interrupted in a firm tone that abruptly reminded me he was a king. The authority was natural on him, and I saw that he'd come a very long way since I'd first found him here, fleeing from the Wild Hunt. "Follow me."

One thing was becoming increasingly obvious. The Knightmare situation was not good.

CHAPTER 14

Alex guided me through the mostly bare castle and I caught my first glimpse of other inhabitants. Woodworkers, painters, builders, and other Fae craftsmen were hard at work furnishing the place and it was actually coming along quite nicely. Rich carpets lined many of the floors and the smell of freshly carved wood from the new furniture decorating the halls and rooms permeated the air.

I paused at an opening to a large room and stared in horror. "What is *that*?" I hissed.

From up ahead, Alex frowned at my tone and took a few steps back to see what had so offended me. He grinned. "That's going to be the throne room," he said calmly.

I shook my head. "No. Get *that* out of there," I said, waggling my finger again.

Alex was on the verge of laughing. "Oh, that," he said, patting his palm against the cheap plastic circular table for two that looked to have cost less than twenty dollars. It featured two cheap folding lawn chairs, one on either side. "That's our Round Table until *someone* gets off their ass and brings me the real thing. After they help me with getting the actual Knights, of course."

I narrowed my eyes at him. "People won't take you seriously if you don't treat this seriously. That is offensive," I said, kicking the leg of the table. "And I don't know *how* to bring it here." I glanced at the crumbling castle. "And this place needs real work before we put something that valuable here."

Alex smirked. "Then Betty stays."

I closed my eyes and counted to three, resigned to the fact that I couldn't win in this situation. Merlin probably never had to deal with shit like this. Plastic tables and cheap chairs. Pah!

Of course, I didn't tell him that I'd used *his* Round Table for a sleepover with Kára, Calvin, and Makayla.

Alex led me down a circling stone stairway that ended in what had to be the bedrock of the land. We walked through a dank, dark hallway illuminated by flickering torches. Pairs of elven guards stood with their backs against the walls every ten feet, making the hair on the back of my neck stand on end as we walked between them. They each saluted King Alex, and I could tell by the looks in their eyes that they genuinely adored him.

Huh. Bully for him. Maybe I needed to move back to Fae to get some of the respect I deserved.

Alex halted before a thick iron door and glanced over his shoulder at me. Rather than speaking, he let out a faint breath and unlocked the door with a key from his belt. Then he pulled the door open and led me inside. He closed it behind him and took a few steps into the large circular room.

I saw eleven sets of pristine white armor sitting in a row against the wall. I frowned uneasily. The last time I'd been here, nine of them had been black and cursed with a red, inverted rune of the legendary Knight trapped within. "Why are they empty and no longer black, Alex?" I asked in a soft tone.

Alex turned to look at me and there was no ignoring the pain in his eyes. "They are dead," he said in a hoarse voice. "The infamous Knights of the Round Table are all dead. With their link to Mordred broken, the armor eventually consumed them—slowly, at first, and then all of a sudden. They wilted away, weaker and weaker by the day. My healers could do nothing for them. They gave up the will to live. By the end, they were starving, savage animals who would bite the very hand that tried to give them bread or water. Not long after, they lost the will to live and the armor turned white," he said, crouching down in front of one set of armor.

He rapped a knuckle against it, producing a hollow tone that echoed off the walls. "These are blank slates, Nate. Anyone could strap one of these on and gain the power of a Knight...or a Knightmare."

I shook my head uneasily. "That shouldn't be possible. When we killed the other Knightmares, the suits didn't turn white and put up a For Lease sign. I had to dump a shitload of magic into them to clean them."

Alex nodded. "I know. I was there. It was when Talon joined me." He placed a palm on one of the sets and let out a resigned sigh. "Maybe it's because they died of their own accord? The armor and the man consuming each other, breaking the curse by destroying it in each other?"

I grunted. His theory actually made a lot of sense, but I was supposed to be the wizard in this relationship, so I'd have to rephrase it and claim credit. "It's never that simple," I said in a sage tone, lying my ass off.

I knelt down in front of a different set of armor, placing my fingers on it. I sent my magic into it, searching for any sign of power or life. He was right. They were humming with power just like the ones I'd healed with an insane expense of magic. I frowned. "I almost killed myself to heal those two sets for you," I said, pointing towards the end of the row, "and these nine managed to heal themselves?"

Alex shot me a disapproving frown. "Your empathy is overwhelming, dad."

I waved a hand dismissively. "In my mind, they died the night Mordred woke them up. I've already mourned their deaths. And the path to hell is paved with good intentions and overly empathetic people." I shot him a stern look. "And if you wanted empathy, you wouldn't have sent me a letter. Son."

He smirked faintly, seeing the familial plea hadn't swayed me. He waved a hand, capitulating. "I want to have a royal funeral in their honor, but I cannot announce such a thing without everyone realizing the suits are up for grabs."

I felt a cold sweat break out on my neck at the thought. "Good god. That would be like ringing a dinner bell." He nodded his agreement. "We will do something for them, but just hold off for now."

He nodded his agreement. "You probably want this back, too." He pulled out a coil of silk ribbon and handed it to me in a blasé gesture. Gleipnir, the cord designed to bind freaking Fenrir, for crying out loud.

I snatched it up with a muttered curse and shoved it into my satchel. "What the hell, man? You're just carrying this around in your pocket?"

He arched an eyebrow at me. "Safer than anywhere else," he said, resting a palm on the hilt of Excalibur at his hip. I grunted. He had a point. "Speaking of safe," he growled, "we need to get these out of here. This castle is a long way from being secure. Years, perhaps."

"Is that why you sent that bizarre letter?"

He nodded. "I need you to be my Merlin and get them the hell out of here. No one can know where you put them. When I find a worthy knight, I will contact you for a suit. Having eleven of these in the same place makes my skin crawl." He leaned close, staring into my eyes. "I haven't been able to sleep a wink since this happened. Any one of my guards—or enemies— could break into Camelot and take all of them at once."

I nodded my agreement and rose to my feet, trying to calm my racing heart. "Fuck, Alex. I don't know where I could put them either. I have plenty of good hidey-holes, but nothing is foolproof," I said. "Not even the Armory. When facing a temptation like this, some of my freaking allies might weigh the pros and cons of my continued friendship."

Alex nodded. "I know. But you have more defenses than Camelot does. And you have more places to hide them. Maybe split them up. I'm trying my best to find worthy men and women to pair with each set. Let me know if you have any suggestions, but for now, just get them out of here and somewhere safe."

I nodded, recalling that I had Aiden with me. I couldn't risk him learning about this in case he later decided to tattle on me to the Academy. I briefly imagined eleven Justices getting their hands on the suits and I shuddered involuntarily. "Okay, Alex. I'll do it, but I have to get rid of Aiden, first. Just keep this place locked up and I'll be back tomorrow to take them."

He nodded and clapped me on the shoulder. "Thank you, Dad."

"Don't ever have kids, Alex. They're nothing but trouble, I tell you. Especially the adopted ones."

He laughed, shaking his head. "I believe you."

We turned back to the door and I hesitated. "You trust every one of those guards, right?" I whispered. "Because you need to trust them with every fiber of your being."

Alex hesitated for a moment before nodding. "Yes. As much as a king can trust anyone, I imagine."

"A trusting king is a dead king," I said, my whisper echoing off the walls like a sinister specter.

Alex sighed. "I'll make sure Talon is on guard duty tonight. Or me. Or both of us."

CHAPTER 15

I sat in the office at Chateau Falco, staring into the fire as I sipped a glass of a new brand of absinthe I'd recently acquired. I drank it straight rather than making a cocktail because cocktails were for closers, and I'd yet to close anything. I'd tossed my satchel onto my desk, and I'd been staring at it for a few minutes, thinking of all the dangerous weapons and artifacts tucked inside the white, Elder hide bag. Gleipnir was in there now, and I had no idea what I wanted to do with it. I also had the new peace treaty staff I'd made in Olympus after killing Zeus, Ares, and Apollo. Odin's Devourer—taken from Gungnir—was affixed to the top, and I wasn't exactly sure how I wanted to use that either. Before all this assassin crap had spilled onto my porch, I'd been considering heading to Olympus to talk with the gods about next steps for the Omega War. Same with Asgard.

But now I had Knightmares, goats, assassins, Baldur, the Academy, and likely the Masters to deal with.

Our trip back from Fae had been quick and silent. Aiden's sprained ankle, bruised face, and broken nose had been healed and he'd actually seemed in pretty good spirits when we met back up in the courtyard.

I sure hadn't been in good spirits. I felt like I had a million pairs of eyes watching me from all angles, and I hadn't even collected the armor yet. I wasn't even sure if I'd said goodbye to Alex and Talon before ushering Aiden through my Gateway back to Chateau Falco.

Aiden sat in a chair across from me, clutching his whisky like it was a lifeline in a stormy sea. I felt him watching me, picking up on my obvious tension. But he didn't press me, knowing he wasn't privy to my trust. But it left him in a pretty confusing place.

A nicer wizard would have reassured him. But the nicer wizards were all dead.

Where the fuck was I going to hide eleven suits of fucking magical armor? What if a god got their hands on a suit? Would they become a supergod? Did I know anyone I had absolute trust in to recommend to Alex as a candidate to become a Knight? On the other hand, a very selfish and unfatherly thought crept into my mind, screaming for attention. If I did have a person I trusted that much, didn't I want to keep them in *my* circle rather than giving them away to Alex? I bashed the selfish thought over the head with an imagined family photo frame. A metal one.

This was so fucking stressful.

And what was taking Kára so long? Had she asked the wrong questions of the wrong people and been taken off the board? Should I go to Asgard and check in on her myself?

I closed my eyes and took a deep breath, mentally imagining my stress condensing into a ball. Then I hurled that ball into the empty halls of my mind, listening as it bounced and rolled into the darkness of my subconscious.

I opened my eyes and appraised Aiden. He stiffened under my abrupt and intense scrutiny since I'd been blatantly ignoring him for the past twenty minutes. His ice-cubes tinkled in his glass before he steadied his hands. He took a sip to cover his uneasiness, jerking his head to get his hair out of his strangely light green eyes. "You...um...okay?"

I stared at him, unblinking, and I gave him a very, very slow nod. "Dandy."

"G-good." He glanced around the room. "Am I sleeping here, or—"

"What's your angle, Aiden?" I asked in a soft tone, interrupting him. "Why are you working for the Academy if you hate them so much? Apparently, it's more lucrative to go rogue," I said, holding out my arms to indicate Chateau Falco. "The assassins seemed to be doing okay for themselves, too. You expect me to believe that you really want to be a Justice? A Freak hunter? I hate to break it to you, but you're not going to be the next Jasper Griffin. That's not a dig at you, by the way. He came from a different era, but the establishments squash hope like that these days. They want obedient little automatons they can control. So, I ask again. Do you really want to be a Freak hunter?"

He pondered my words in silence, staring into his glass with a pensive frown. He looked up and shook his head firmly. "A hunter? No way. I do not want to hunt anyone. I want to help people, as lame as that sounds."

I nodded. "You read my mind," I said, studying him. "Tell me more about yourself."

He sat up, taking a sip of his drink as he gathered his thoughts. "What do you want to know?"

"How did you become a member of the Academy? You tried out for Jasper's contest for fifteen years. That's a very long time to hate an establishment but to continue working with them."

He curled his lip, and I saw that he was squeezing his glass so tightly that his hand was shaking. "My sweetheart of a mother gave me to the Academy as a baby," he rasped in a furious growl. I froze, feeling like I may have pushed him a teeny bit too hard. He looked like he needed a hug. About thirty years ago.

"Damn," I breathed. "That's...really messed up. I have a friend in Kansas City who was also abandoned as a baby, but she was left on the steps of a church. She's a wizard, too." I realized I was babbling, trying to make him feel better by telling him about Callie Penrose. "I'm sorry, Aiden. I had no idea, and I'm on edge right now. I could have handled the questions better, instead of being a dick to you."

He waved a hand. "I get it. The Academy hates your family more than anyone else, so when I show up as a lifelong, card-carrying member, I can empathize with your suspicions." He met my eyes. "I would be suspicious, too."

I nodded. "So...what's the deal with your mom? Is that all you know, or is there more to the story?" I was waiting to hear him say they'd also killed his dog

He waved a hand dismissively. "She didn't have time to take care of a kid, I guess. So, staying in an establishment I hated was really the only option on the table for me. Jasper's contest was the light at the end of the tunnel." He took a sip of his drink, his eyes growing distant as he rifled through his memories. "I grew up as the resident orphan. It wasn't too bad, really. I had grand dreams that I would one day become a legendary wizard like Jasper Griffin, despite my low beginnings. But it quickly became apparent that I was average, at best. When I finally got the opportunity I'd been waiting for with Jasper, everything blew up in my face. Now he's dead, and I'm your prisoner or whatever we're calling it. All I know is that it's better than the execution waiting for me at the Academy. Everyone knows I was working with Jasper that day, so when they find out he's dead, their sights—and blame—will swing to me." He lifted his glass with a defiant chuckle. "Cheers for saving me."

I had been watching him closely searching for any hint of deceit, but I had found none. He was genuinely glum and irritated about the orphan topic, exactly the way Callie had felt about her own story.

I liked the fact that he seemed annoyed he'd even had to tell the story. Aiden had a chip on his shoulder and didn't like playing victim. He wasn't pleased about his current situation, but he hadn't given up either. And he hadn't told me the orphan story up front, which would have been a great way to manipulate our emotions. If I hadn't asked, I wouldn't have ever found out.

The door to the office opened and I glanced up, hoping to see Kára.

Instead, Carl walked in. Again. He studied us in silence, his tongue flicking at the air. Aiden cringed as if the back of his neck was itching under Carl's scrutiny.

"This is the third time today that I've had to tell you the Randulfs are waiting for you, Master Temple. I believe they are going to open all the presents if you don't come down and stop them. They have been very patient."

I smiled at the thought of the kids tearing through all that wrapping paper, and let out a sigh. "Sorry, Carl. Do you mind watching over Aiden tonight? I think he's been through enough today without me tossing him in a warded prison cell."

"If the alternative is having a sleepover with an Elder, I'd prefer the prison," Aiden said, looking up at me earnestly. "Handcuffs. Chains. What-ever. I'm game. Seriously. Do not leave me with him."

I chuckled. "Carl grows on you. You two will have a blast," I said, rising to my feet. "Just don't do anything to startle him and you probably won't die."

I turned to Carl and nodded. "Thanks, Carl. Keep an eye on him."

Carl cocked his head. "I am not Gunnar. I will keep *both* eyes on him. I do not need sleep."

"Jesus," Aiden grumbled. "The darkest, coldest prison would be better. Please."

I turned back to him. "I haven't figured out what to do with you yet, Aiden. I'm no fan of the Academy, but right now you are my only bargaining chip with them. And I might be your only bargaining chip to get out of this with your head still attached," I said, meaningfully. "You're right. As soon as they hear about Jasper Griffin's death—in St. Louis—they'll come knocking on my door. If I turn you in, I'm going to be tied to his disappearance, even though I had nothing to do with it. If I keep you away from them, I'll be seen as aiding and abetting a potential witness, which will only make you look more guilty. No matter what happens, we're both stuck in the same finger-trap, and we need to find a way out by working together."

He nodded thoughtfully. "Logical and reasonable."

"The Academy wants a culprit, and it's either you or me. Rather than accepting that choice and granting them the moral authority to make such a demand, let me offer an alternative."

Aiden cocked his head curiously. "I'm listening."

"Be a man of principle like Jasper. Don't grant them the moral authority to force you into a decision where both options are terrible. Otherwise, you're nothing more than their puppet. They only have that power if you grant them that power. That's why they hate my family. We don't accept the premise of their accusations."

He frowned. "Are you offering me a job?"

I stared at him, considering the question. "I don't know you well enough to offer you a job. Instead, I offer you the chance to be your own man. Make your own decisions. Rather than letting them set the terms of your immediate future—or me, for that matter—set your own terms. Don't accept the two choices they are giving you as the only options available. You should spend tonight thinking long and hard about what you want out of life. Right now you are very valuable—to them and me. They want you to spill secrets. After your use has expired, they will likely toss you back into the Academy machine to continue being a nameless puppet wizard of average ability. I can guarantee that they will never let you be a Justice with this stain on your record. Even if you're vindicated. The optics already killed your chances."

He grimaced. "Inspiring. What about you? How would you use me?"

I shrugged. "That's what I'll be thinking about tonight. Reconsider the options before you and we will talk tomorrow. Try to think of new solutions that benefit you—not them, and not me. I'll do the same and we'll touch base in the morning."

He nodded thoughtfully. "Thanks for not killing me."

I grunted. "There is always tomorrow, Aiden. Memento Mori," I said, jerking my chin towards a painting of my family crest on the wall. "Tomorrow we may die, so live today with purpose and fulfillment."

He studied the family crest in silence. Carl gave me a nod and then took the chair I had vacated. I saw Aiden's shoulders tighten and I smirked, shaking my head as I closed the door behind me.

"Poor guy," I murmured. "Tonight's going to be the worst night of his life."

I made my way downstairs to finally spend some time with the werewolves, hoping that Kára would return soon so I could tell her about the vulnerable suits of armor.

CHAPTER 16

Gunnar folded his arms, leaning his back against the wall as I caught him up on my day's adventures and apologized profusely for leaving him hanging. He had cursed seven times, been chastised by Ashley twelve times for cursing—even though she was in the adjacent room, she was a werewolf and a wife, granting her *double* enhanced hearing. Wife math was tricky, but apparently accurate. Gunnar had quickly resorted to drinking straight whisky as I finished telling him everything.

And people wondered why men lived shorter lives, driven to drink at early ages for 'no explicable reason'. Wife hearing, I tell you. Wife-hearing and wife math.

"Christ—"

"Gunnar Randulf!" Ashley hissed, putting up a thirteenth point on the scoreboard. "The kids hear just as well, or better, than we do!"

I smirked. "If you write a cuss word can she hear—"

"Watch it, Nate," Ashley warned from the other room. "I'm not in the mood."

I winked at Gunnar. "Everything okay?" I asked.

He nodded. "Just more runaways at Shift."

I jolted in surprise. "Wait. *More*? As in, this isn't the first runaway?" I hissed. "Was anyone going to tell me?" I demanded.

He shook his head. "We wanted to keep you out of it. Give you some time with Kára. But Tory's beginning to panic. She's been calling Ashley all day, so we sent Drake and Cowan and two dozen wolves to the school to search for where they might have gone. It's probably nothing," he reassured me. "Kids feeling alone during the holidays," he said in a lame attempt to appease my concern.

"We delivered all the Christmas presents to the school, right?" I asked, wondering if I hadn't done a good enough job in giving Tory everything she needed to run the school. Because it wasn't just a school. It was a community where the students actually lived.

Gunnar smiled, patting me on the shoulder. "Yes. Don't worry. We'll take care of it—"

Makayla abruptly stormed past us, turning to mist as she drifted *through* her father rather than stepping around him. She coalesced on the other side of him and continued storming down the hall. Ashley raced towards us with a pained look on her face, holding out a hand towards her daughter. "Makayla!" she called out in a heart-wrenching tone.

"What happened?" Gunnar asked, splitting his attention between his wife and daughter, unsure whether he was supposed to be angry with his daughter or concerned for her. Apparently, Gunnar's ability to eavesdrop was far surpassed by his wife's, because he hadn't overheard them arguing.

Ashley flung up her hands. "Calvin asked if we could go to Shift tomorrow, and I said no."

Calvin stepped up behind his mother, staring at the ground as if fearing a reprimand. "Mac wants to give the other kids presents," he said in a soft voice. "She's sad that they don't have family with them during Yulemas."

Ashley lifted a hand to her mouth and her eyes began to water as if she'd been stabbed in the heart. "I..." she croaked. "She didn't *say* any of that. How was I supposed to know? I tried asking her why she was upset, but she wouldn't talk to me," she sobbed in a truly miserable tone.

Calvin shrugged, shifting from foot to foot. "She doesn't feel like talking yet," he said, staring after his sister. "And she doesn't understand why you don't understand how she feels. She considers the other kids her family and she wants them to be happy."

Gunnar wrapped his arms around his wife and kissed her forehead. Then he discreetly shot me a desperate look. I sighed. Time to pull out the big guns.

"I'll need two juice boxes, a stack of printer paper, two pairs of scissors, and my Bluetooth speaker," I said. "It should all be in the security room and kitchen." Ashley lifted her head from her husband's shoulder and the two parents stared at me with baffled looks.

"Give it to him," Calvin said, staring at me with a strange intensity in his eyes. He no longer looked like the awkward, nervous child from a moment ago. His eyes were practically blazing with inner light, and his voice had been an absolute command. "Now."

Gunnar opened his mouth wordlessly. Ashley abruptly peeled back and shoved him away with a stern glare. "You heard him. Now!"

The alpha werewolf turned and ran towards the nearby reading room that Kára had turned into her security nexus for Chateau Falco. It was loaded with computers, printers, guns and ammo. Calvin raced towards the kitchen and swiftly returned with the juice boxes.

Gunnar returned a few moments later and shoved the requested items into my arms. Calvin stacked the juice boxes onto my collection and then ushered his parents back, herding them far away from whatever he imagined I was going to do. I made my way down the hall, searching for Makayla in silence, gathering my thoughts and focusing my mind on the sad little girl and how best to help her.

My goddaughter needed me.

She hadn't run very far. I found her in a dark sitting room sitting on the couch, staring into a cold fireplace. She didn't acknowledge my arrival. "Hey, Mac. Your dad has crappy hand-eye coordination, and I need an extra set of hands to finish these," I said by way of introduction.

She glanced up at me, her eyes bloodshot.

I spilled my collection onto the coffee table, pretending not to notice her eyes. "Snowflakes. It requires a deft touch, so I obviously didn't ask your brother." I said, pointing at the papers and scissors. "I was thinking we could make a few for Shift and hang them in the dormitory to brighten up the place. But it will take me all night by myself."

I pulled out my phone and turned on John Mayer's *Continuum* album, starting with the best song, *Slow Dancing in a Burning Room*. The soothing music began playing and I brought the wireless speaker to the mantle above the fireplace. I frowned at the logs and lit them with a small tendril of magic.

I nodded satisfactorily, glancing over my shoulder with an impish grin at cheating with my fire-starting skills. "I was chilly. Hope you don't mind."

She gave me a faint shake of her head.

I walked over to the couch and sat down. "Hey. I heard a riddle earlier, and no one else has gotten it right. Want to take a stab at it?"

She shrugged uncertainly, not meeting my eyes. She picked up a piece of paper, frowning at it.

"It is kind of hard. Maybe when you're older—"

She dropped the paper and slowly turned to look at me, frowning competitively.

I grinned. "Okay. There are 30 cows in a field and 28 chickens. How many didn't?"

She brushed her hair back behind her ear, thinking for about thirty seconds. Just when I was about to reassure her that she could let it simmer and answer later, she tapped my thigh. I looked down at her to see her holding up ten fingers.

I arched my eyebrows in genuine surprise. "Wow. Yes. It's ten. I had to look the answer up on the internet," I admitted. It was a homonym riddle. The 28 was actually *twenty ate*. I scowled down at her. "No more riddles for you, girl genius."

She smiled faintly, looking proud. Then she turned to the table, waiting for instructions.

I began separating the stack of paper. Then I started making a paper snowflake, murmuring the steps in time with my movements. She watched me like a hawk, nodding along as I folded a few times, and then started cutting small shapes out of the paper. Once I was halfway through the first cut, she grabbed one of her own papers and began folding it in on itself, biting her lower lip in deep concentration.

We worked like that for five or ten minutes, comparing the finished snowflakes and silently voting on who made the better of the two with finger pointing. I showed her different shapes to start with, cutting the pieces of paper into circles and triangles before handing them to her to begin folding and cutting. Soon, we'd cracked open the juice boxes and I caught her bobbing her head to one of the songs, not fully aware she was doing it.

CHAPTER 17

Kára walked by the entryway, saw me, and froze. I was relieved to see she'd returned, but her attention shifted to Makayla, and her faced cracked with emotion to see the little werewolf focusing so intently on her scissor work that she hadn't even noticed Kára's presence yet.

An idea came to me, and I leaned towards Makayla, speaking in a secretive whisper that only she could hear. "You know that I really like Kára, right?"

She nodded, furrowing her eyebrows as she continued cutting.

"I'm not sure if she knows exactly how *much* I care about her. Hugely. Bigly. Giantly," I whispered, jerking my chin to indicate the spy in the hall. "I don't know what to say to her, Mac. How to tell her. Any ideas?"

Makayla turned to look directly at me, pursing her lips.

I shrugged, resuming the cutting of my snowflake. "Yeah. Me neither. I just figured you were a girl, she's a girl. Maybe you'd have some good advice for me. I never know the right thing to say to people when it really matters. Anyway, we still have more to do. And then we have to get them to Shift tomorrow, but we can save some for Falco. Maybe we can get Calvin to help us hang them tomorrow."

Makayla was silent for a few moments. Then she turned to look back at

Kára again. I kept cutting my snowflake, not looking up. But I heard Kára's breath catch as Makayla hopped off the couch and trotted over to her, grabbing her by the hand and tugging her along to join us. She plopped Kára down onto the couch beside me and handed the Valkyrie her scissors. Then she began to silently teach Kára how to make a snowflake. I didn't look up from my work, knowing that this was the most direct contact Kára had ever had with Makayla.

I noticed every wet tear that splashed onto Kára's snowflake as she followed Makayla's silent demands. Then Makayla commandeered my juice box and handed it to Kára, motioning for her to take a drink as she walked over to my phone and turned the music up.

I bit back a smile.

Kára took a sip of the drink and Makayla nodded satisfactorily.

Soon, we were down to our last paper. I was halfway through folding it when Makayla snatched it from my hands and gave it to Kára. The Valkyrie hesitated before accepting it. Makayla nodded eagerly, pointing down at the paper and miming a folding motion. Kára nodded and finished folding the paper. Makayla handed her the pair of scissors, and then Kára cut out a triangular shape from the edge. Before she could make another, Makayla swooped in to pass the snowflake back to me, gesturing for me to make my own cut-out.

Then back again until we were each taking turns with the last snowflake, cut for cut, creating it together in silence. Even though Makayla didn't know it, the silence reminded me of how my first relationship with Kára—as Othello—had also started in silence. We had bloomed in silence, struggling to learn Russian together. The fact that we weren't talking now actually made this experience seem more deeply personal. Idle chatter would have taken away from this perfect, focused quiet.

Makayla took the finished product, unfolded it, and hung it between us. We smiled at it, seeing each other through the cut-outs. I stared at Kára through the shapes of our paper snowflake, mesmerized by her dual-colored eyes, feeling like I was staring at a wintery kaleidoscope.

Makayla gently shoved the back of my head so that my lips were almost touching the paper snowflake.

She did the same for Kára on the other side, guiding her towards the paper to mirror me.

Right before Kára's lips touched the paper, Makayla yanked the snowflake away so that our lips touched. We froze, totally caught off guard by Makayla's swift movement, and then Kára flung her arms around me, kissing my lips and forehead and cheeks in rapid pecking motions, grinning from ear-to-ear.

Makayla beamed with a smile that literally took my breath away, and she was clapping delightedly.

Something she had *never* done before. Not the clapping, and not the brilliantly exuberant smile.

Then she handed the snowflake to Kára and pointed at each of our chests individually before pointing back at the snowflake and clasping her hands and fingers together in a tight embrace.

Kára let out a happy sob and held her arms out wide in invitation for a hug. Makayla hesitated for only a moment, and then she hopped onto Kára's lap and wrapped her arms around the Valkyrie in a full body embrace, even resting her head on Kára's shoulder. Kára didn't even try to hide her happy tears, and I pretended not to notice the tear that rolled down Makayla's cheek.

The beautiful little girl extracted herself from the Valkyrie and studied the mass of snowflakes on the table with a proud smile. Kára got up from the couch and smiled at the two of us. "I'm going to get some sleep. You two don't stay up too late, okay?"

Makayla smirked and shrugged. Then she shot me a conspiratorial wink that made me burst out laughing. Kára rolled her eyes and left the room, shaking her head and muttering under her breath about unruly kids. It was obvious by her dramatic tone that she was teasing, so Makayla and I grinned at each other. She took Kára's place on the couch and let out a weary sigh as if the emotional display had been particularly exhausting to her.

I nudged her with my shoulder. "Thank you for helping me, Mac. I think she understands now. Did you see her keep the snowflake?" I asked, leaning back into the couch with a happy sigh. I held out my hand for a high-five.

Makayla slapped it and nodded, smiling proudly.

"I was so nervous. How did you know it would work?" I whispered, lowering my hand with a grin.

She leaned back and rested her head on my shoulder—the first direct affection she'd shown me. She waggled all the fingers of her hand in a dramatic flourish.

I chuckled. "Magic. I use that line all the time. The suckers always fall for it."

Makayla nodded sleepily, and I even heard her let out a deep yawn. I stared into the fire, watching the flames dance as Makayla's breathing grew deeper and slower. Soon she was out cold, melting into my arm like a barnacle of love. I was fairly certain she was drooling on my sleeve, but I wasn't about to wake her.

Some short while later, I felt a presence creeping towards the hallway entrance. I kept my body relaxed and still, not wanting to wake Mac. I saw Kára tug Ashley into the open doorway, holding a finger to her lips to indicate silence. Ashley stared at us in stunned disbelief and then broke down into silent tears. Gunnar loomed over her shoulder, his lone eye glistening as he saw his daughter passed out cold, nuzzled against my shoulder. He nodded at me one time, seeming to tremble with a beautiful, soul-crushing pain.

Makayla stirred and I petted her hair in soothing strokes. "It's okay, Mac. Get some sleep. I'm not going anywhere," I told her, scowling at the adults ogling us.

She nuzzled her cheek deeper into my shoulder and even draped a tiny arm across my waist in a hug. "I love you, Godfather," she murmured sleepily.

I looked up in time to see Gunnar's face crumple in happy agony, and then he slipped back into the shadows.

"I love you too, Mac," I whispered, blinking back tears of my own. I closed my eyes and let out a breath, feeling tired myself.

I felt a light rush of air and peeled open my eyes to see Kára gently draping a light blanket over Mac. The werewolf murmured contentedly but didn't wake. Kára silently walked up to me and gave me a long, warm kiss on my forehead. Before I could do anything else, she was already walking away on silent feet.

I maybe lasted another ten seconds before I was out cold.

CHAPTER 18

I woke up to the smell of coffee and let out a deep, contented groan. Bacon was the only better thing to smell upon waking up. I stretched my arms out and arched my back. I immediately hissed in pain as my back locked up on me. I collapsed to my side with a curse and opened my eyes to see that I had fallen asleep on the couch. I carefully sat up and turned to see Makayla's spot empty. She must have woken up already.

"That's what you get for not coming to bed last night."

I flinched, not having noticed I had company. Kára sat on the chair near the smoldering fireplace, smirking at me. She held a steaming mug of java in both hands and jerked her chin to draw my attention to the coffee table.

I looked down to see a second mug sitting beside a small, intricately detailed snowflake that I knew we hadn't cut last night. All the others were gone. I scooped up the coffee and the snowflake, holding it up to the light with a thoughtful frown.

"The coffee was all me, for the record," she said, territorially. "But Makayla made that for you before she left," she said, smiling adoringly at the snowflake. "You really had a breakthrough with her last night. Who knew you were so good with kids?"

The sunlight from the window struck her hair and green and blue eyes, making her face look like spun gold and gemstones. I smiled at the snowflake, shaking my head at the complexity of the heart-shaped paper.

"It's cute," I said, setting it down and trading it for the mug of caffeine. I took one sip before something else she'd said registered. "Wait. They left?" I asked, glancing out the window. "What time is it?"

Kára snorted. "Almost noon. I already had time to go out and fix the keypad at the gate. Temporarily, at least. Ashley took the kids to Shift to deliver your snowflakes," she said with a smile, "and to check in on Tory. Apparently, she's pretty concerned about the missing kids."

I cursed, recalling Gunnar mentioning the runaway students. I couldn't take care of everything, so I shrugged it off as I set my coffee back down and rose to my feet. I snatched up the snowflake and carefully folded it up before slipping it into my pocket. Then I plucked up my coffee and motioned for Kára to follow me. "We need to go to Fae," I urged, and then gave her a quick rundown of the armor situation.

Her face paled and she swallowed nervously. "Are they safe?"

"Nowhere is safe for a temptation like them. One Knightmare killed both Talon and Gunnar in Fae, remember?" Her face paled and she nodded. "That's how dangerous they are. Alex wants me to hide them until he can find people to adopt them—people who won't abuse the power." I took another sip of my coffee as we walked down the halls. "What did you learn?"

Kára grimaced. "I spoke to Odin," she began, furrowing her brow. "I got five seconds into my questions and he silenced me, looking over my shoulder as if fearing someone might have overheard. Then he rushed me to see Tyr, the god of justice, using only back hallways so as not to be seen," she said, meaningfully. I frowned at her uneasily, wondering what could make the Allfather paranoid in his own palace. "The two of them think Baldur is preparing to make a move against you or Gunnar for killing Thor. Odin sent the goats to act as a buffer in the event their suspicion is correct."

I halted, turning to face her. "He sent me Thor's goats to keep me safe from Thor's brother? Won't Freya have a really big problem with me killing Baldur?"

Kára nodded grimly. "I imagine she would. Then again, it is no secret that Baldur is emotionally unstable." She shrugged. "Who knows where a mother's love stops?"

I grunted, shaking my head. "What makes him think Baldur is acting shady?"

"Tyr was walking past Baldur's house yesterday morning when he saw a flash of sparks through the window. He saw a hooded wizard step through and speak to Baldur in a heated discussion, leaving the Gateway open behind him. Tyr crept up to the side of the house to see if he could loop around and catch a glimpse of the wizard's face through a different window."

I stared at her, confused but also alarmed. "And?"

"When Tyr was creeping along the wall, he overheard part of their conversation—which was what prompted Odin to *immediately* send Tanngrisnir and Tanngnjóstr to you and Gunnar," she murmured, using the goats' real names. She took a nervous breath, meeting my eyes. "The wizard told Baldur that he had his hands on *a dangerous magical artifact that would upend Nate Temple's world. Do your part, Baldur.*"

I felt a dark anger creeping over my shoulders like a warm, heavy cloak. Gunnar really was in danger if this artifact would upend my world—every friend of mine was in danger. But the *Do your part* was particularly ominous. It could mean anything, and none of it was good. "Who was he?" I rasped. "Did he get a look at this wizard's face?"

Kára clenched her jaw. "For a brief second, as the wizard was turning back to his Gateway, and..." she let out a soft breath, averting her eyes from my seething anger as if she felt I was mad at her. I took a breath to dial my rage back, but her next comment set me right back off again. "Right before his silver Justice mask shimmered back into place."

I stared at her with wide eyes. "A fucking *Justice* was behind the theft?" I hissed in disbelief.

Kára grimaced. "Tyr said he would recognize the lower half of the face if he saw it again, but that he couldn't reliably describe it due to the shadows from the hood, and the mask distorting his memory—since the designs on their masks form an animated face. It happened so quickly that he didn't even see hair or eye color."

I gritted my teeth, screaming on the inside. "Fuck!" I shouted out loud. Had Baldur's Justice been this Cyrilo guy who called Jasper? Or one of the bajillion other Justices? But the most significant part was that it seemed to have been an inside job—and that opened a veritable Pandora's box of new questions and suspicions.

Had this Justice gone rogue or was he on official business? If he was defecting, was he acting alone or alongside other like-minded wizards within the Academy?

Were the wizards who took Jasper and Aiden—and then tried to kill me—partners of his?

What if this was a coup? A civil war within the Academy? Or, worse, what if this was all official business, stamped and approved by the Grand-master to finally put me in my place?

Jesus.

"I showed Odin and Tyr the three pictures we took in the delivery truck," Kára continued in a soft tone, rubbing my arm in a soothing manner. "Tyr didn't recognize any as Baldur's associate, but he instantly pointed at Jasper Griffin with a big smile. Apparently, the Justice really was as legendary as Aiden claimed. He was close friends with Tyr. He even showed me a picture of him and Jasper from World War II in Germany. Looks like Justice Griffin was a Nazi hunter, and that's just scratching the surface. He said the best Justices he's ever met all spent time learning under Jasper, because the man was an astute stoic of the rule of law, and was always impartial in his judgments. Tyr couldn't say enough good things about the man, and he was devastated to hear of his murder."

Good god. A Nazi hunter? Pals with Tyr? Talk about a badass—Jasper Christ.

This Justice's death wasn't just bad, it was super fucking bad. If my name was attached to it, I would look like the worst person in the history of ever.

But Kára's other news quickly rose back to the surface. I found myself chewing over the Academy's attempt to cover up a theft of something they didn't want anyone knowing about. "So, Baldur is tied to, or at least knows about, the theft at the Academy. The one Jasper was sent to resolve," I murmured, slurping my coffee. "Right after this Cyrilo guy called Jasper to warn him about it," I added, pursing my lips. "What if Cyrilo was the Justice speaking to Baldur, and what if he set up Jasper to be killed? That would mean Baldur is behind these assassins, and it explains why they came at me," I finally said, feeling like a conspiracy theorist.

She shrugged uncertainly. "That's a lot of what if's, but it does connect the dots. Unfortunately, Odin and Tyr had never heard the name Cyrilo."

I grunted, lining up the facts in my mind and searching for any other possible connections. The Masters were all about the long game, so it was entirely possible they were finally beginning to make moves, and that Baldur had nothing to do with them. I'd personally made the god look like a fool in front of all of Asgard, so he could simply be working independently to get revenge on me.

Occam's razor or convoluted tinfoil hat logic?

Also, a very important fact to note was that Baldur was not the brightest person in the world. He was a petty, emotional, spoiled little brat. Strong and vindictive as hell, but not clever. He never had to be when he lived in a world where nothing but Mistletoe could hurt him. The world was his safe space, so he'd never needed to scheme and claw his way toward a goal. Evil genius did not describe dear Baldur.

I sighed, shaking my head. "What about Niko? Maybe hitting the problem from a different angle will shake something loose."

Kára linked her arm through mine, guiding me on through the halls. "I called her this morning. She said that after the last contract on you, the app was shut down and the mercenaries have been relatively silent. She wasn't sure if her name got leaked as your associate, but she hasn't received any jobs since. She'd never heard of anyone named Cyrilo either—not at the Academy or among her fellow mercenaries. She has heard chatter about a lot of Justice activity all over the world, but no one seems to know what they're doing or why. The Academy is searching for something, and they're using every Justice to do it," she said, sounding concerned.

"Fuck. They must be looking for Jasper and Aiden, because the theft is supposed to be a secret."

"Unless the Grandmaster was vague when she gave her Justices their orders. Maybe they were told to hunt down any bands of rogue wizards, all at once, to make a statement to the world. They would have no idea they are really looking for this secret artifact." She noticed my frustration and squeezed my arm affectionately. "Just playing devil's advocate. I did verify the Lithuanian vampire story, though. Niko thought it had been a contract closed. The vampire had been feeding on a nearby village's children," she said with a snarl. "When I told her the 'rumor' I heard about Jasper Griffin being behind the kill, she basically squee'd all over the phone. He was her hero. Her inspiration for breaking off from the Academy and choosing to become an honorable mercenary." Kára shrugged. "I didn't tell her about his death, though. If she shared that information to the wrong person, St. Louis would be inundated with Justices."

I nodded my agreement and then glanced over at her. "I'm surprised you're not angry."

She cocked her head. "I'm plenty angry. Were you not listening to me? It's a fucking circus out there. And it all leads back to you, whether they know it or not. Whether it's true or not."

I shook my head. "I was talking about Odin. He sent Thor's goats to protect me, but you're my official protector. Does he not think you're enough—"

"The goats," she said in a frosty tone, "are officially here for the Randulfs, since Gunnar technically killed Thor. They work for him. But they will also keep you safe as a second line of defense. Behind me."

I smiled, kissing her on the cheek. Her shoulders relaxed slightly and she let out a soft sigh.

"Looks like I might need to have an uncomfortable conversation with the old bag," I said.

"You mean the Grandmaster of the Academy?"

"I mean the old bag who is also the Grandmaster of the Academy. G-Ma."

"So, your solution to keeping your eyes out for Baldur, the Justices, and these rogue wizards, is to directly pick a fight with the Academy." She wrapped her arm through mine. "I missed you, Nate. I really, really missed you. You're eighty-percent offense, twenty-percent more offense."

I laughed, nodding. "Yeah." I realized that she might be the only ally who wouldn't challenge me on my plan. "Keeps things interesting."

I felt my stomach rumble with hunger and I took a big gulp of my coffee to squash the mortal weakness with excess caffeine. "I want to keep Aiden close until we figure all this out. Let's go collect him. We should probably feed and water him before we leave for Fae. We can hit up my favorite sandwich joint downtown."

"Six Inches to Heaven?" she asked, grinning. "I swear you only like that place because of the name."

I clutched at my chest, offended. I opened my mouth to stand up for the delicatessen when I caught a rich, savory smell in the air. I frowned. "Why does it smell like kababs in here?"

Kára winced. "Carl is cooking for Aiden..." Her tone was one of disgust, so I waited. "Goat leg," she said.

I felt my stomach churn as I remembered his comment from yesterday. "He's cooking our new security goats?" I hissed. And then I bolted for the kitchen.

CHAPTER 19

A few minutes later, we burst into the kitchen to find Carl ripping a bite of meat off a half-eaten leg of roasted goat. He was dressed in fighting gear today, as if he expected violence. After yesterday's attack, I didn't blame him. Leather straps crisscrossed his chest, supporting daggers in the front and two twin bone blades over either shoulder. All his weapons were made from the bones of his victims. Despite being one of the world's scariest beings, the Elder was quickly becoming an entirely too normal fixture of Chateau Falco. If he'd been wearing an apron and baking cupcakes, I probably wouldn't have taken a second glance.

Aiden sat at the table, chewing on a slice of meat that Carl must have sliced off for him. He waved at me, looking more relaxed than yesterday when he'd been so frightened of spending the night with Carl that he'd requested to spend the night in a dismal and dank prison cell instead. "Morning. You should try some of this. The Elder's surprisingly good at grilling," Aiden said, pointing his fork at his apparently new best friend.

They weren't technically doing anything wrong by eating...well, whichever of Thor's goats it was.

According to myth, Thor had killed and eaten his goats every night.

The next morning the goats would be reborn to continue their job of carrying Thor's chariot across the sky.

Still. Ick. Roast mythical goat just didn't do it for me.

"What the hell, Carl?" I demanded.

Carl smiled as if I'd meant it as an astonished compliment. "The talking goat was a noble warrior. And I wanted to honor him by making a dagger from his leg bone," he explained, tearing off a hunk with his teeth.

Aiden dropped his fork and stopped chewing, staring down at his plate. "Wait. What? A talking goat?"

I opened my mouth to reassure him he hadn't unknowingly offended an elder goat god, but a loud *crash* from the pantry stopped me cold. I spun to face the sound, lifting my hand at the ready to call up a shield. Again, no warning from Falco. What the hell was going on with her? She didn't respond to my disappointed mental query, which was concerning.

Carl drew a dagger and shoved past me, still gripping the leg of meat in his other hand. He flung open the door with a snarl but the threatening hiss abruptly cut short.

I called up my shield and backed up so that I was between Aiden and the threat. Carl slowly backed away, frowning in confusion as his eyes darted between the leg of meat in his hand and the pantry.

Two mastiff-sized goats hopped out of the small room, scraping their hooves against the floor and glaring at Carl. They both wore the *emotional support goat* vests from yesterday, but now I had time to notice the embroidered names on each lower back: *Snarler* and *Grinder*. They'd shortened the definitions of their names to make it easy on their new boss, apparently.

Tanngrisnir meant teeth-barer or snarler. AKA Snarler.

Tanngnjóstr meant teeth-grinder. AKA Grinder.

Which was helpful, because they looked practically identical except for one stark difference: Snarler's eyes were the bright blue of a summer sky, and Grinder's eyes were a viridescent green like fresh grass. They both had horizontal black bars for pupils, which had always creeped me out, but that could have been a result of one too many close encounters with shifter dragons, who had similar pupils.

The two giant, stout and burly goats had long, shaggy coats of thick, wiry, gray hair, and their tall, curled horns—although chipped and seemingly ancient—were sharp as spikes and harder than sledgehammers.

"Gobble me down, snake-boy," Snarler cheered, shuffling forward on only three legs—because his back leg was missing. My brain had a momentary hiccup, wondering how the rebirth process actually worked because I'd sent many of his body parts to a desert on the other side of the globe. Was it because Carl and Aiden were eating him?

I did not ask for clarification. Or I would never eat meat again.

"Doesn't my brother taste honey sweet?" Grinder hooted in a rasping baritone that was much deeper than his brother's. "Don't chew with your mouth open! It's bad table manners." He lifted his head to take stock of the elegant kitchen with an approving whistle. "Speaking of manors, check out this fucking spread. Score!"

Aiden choked, spitting out the meat in his mouth as he stared wide-eyed at the talking goats.

Carl slowly set the meat down on the counter, looking utterly confused. "The goats are back," he murmured absently. I must have forgotten to tell him about their abilities.

"Eat me!" Snarler taunted, scraping his front hoof—on the opposite side of his missing back leg, so as not to tip over—across the floor like he was gearing up to charge the Elder.

Kára grimaced. "That's just not right."

"No," Carl said, carefully folding his arms since he still clutched his dagger. "I'm no longer hungry."

Snarler didn't like that one bit. He lunged for the Elder, screaming and bleating. Carl sidestepped and drop-kicked the beast across the kitchen. The handicapped goat slammed into the fridge, denting the hell out of the metal. He landed on three hooves, wobbling precariously as if dazed, but he was laughing maniacally. "Oh, that felt so good. Try out the Elder, bro. He's a real riot."

Grinder barreled forward and Carl promptly slammed a toaster down on his head.

"Hey!" I snapped at the casual destruction of my toaster. "Those aren't cheap!"

Grinder stumbled a bit and then began thrashing his horns back and forth in an attempt to gore the Elder. Carl stabbed him in the ribs with his claws, but the goat merely burst out laughing. "Fancy some ribs with that haunch of leg?" he crowed.

"Yeah! Tickle his ivories, snake-boy!" Snarler cheered.

Carl flung Grinder into his taunting, hooficapped brother and then hopped up onto the counter and shot me a desperate look. "Make them stop, Master Temple, or I will kill them. Again," he added, pursing his lips.

"This is so fucked up," Aiden stammered, rising to his feet and shoving his plate away.

The goats spun towards me and abruptly gave me formal bows. "Team Temple!" they cheered, and then they began hopping about in an excited dance, gouging and scraping the hell out of my floor.

At least I finally had someone else saying my phrase. I dipped my chin at the sadomasochists. "Snarler, Grinder, welcome to Chateau Falco."

Their eyes widened and they squeed excitedly. "He read our vests!" Snarler gasped.

"He's the best co-boss ever!" Grinder added. A steady flow of blood was oozing from his ribs and onto the floor, thanks to Carl's claws. The Elder was studying his bloody claws, sniffing them curiously. Grinder noticed and chuckled. "Try me," he urged, "I'm finger-licking good." Carl wiped his claws off on a hand towel, shaking his head.

"Well, it's great to see you guys again—"

"Ah. There you are, Nate," Gunnar said, walking into the kitchen. "What the hell did you say to Mac?" he asked, grinning widely. "She was smiling and holding Ashley's hand this morning—" He cut off abruptly, noticing the goats, and skidded to a halt. "The goats are back."

"Observant for a big, one-eyed bastard," Grinder growled, chuckling.

"Hey, boss! Like our vests?" Snarler piped up in his higher-pitched, almost sing-song tone.

Gunnar seemed to notice Aiden for the first time and flinched. "Who the hell is that guy?"

"I, the hell, am Aiden Maxon," the wizard muttered, unhappily.

Gunnar grunted dismissively, already distracted by the steaming goat leg on the counter next to Carl. He was practically drooling. "You going to eat all of that? I'm starving."

The Elder shook his head. "I lost my appetite."

"I'm going to throw up," Aiden said, sounding quite literal. Kára burst out laughing.

Gunnar was making his way past me to snatch up the fresh leg of meat, so I held up a hand, stopping him. "No, Gunnar. Count his legs," I said, pointing. Gunnar frowned and turned to look. Snarler wiggled his rear, showing off the missing thigh in a grossly provocative dance. Gunnar shot me a confused, grossed-out look, and then his eye shot to the roast leg. He recoiled, snorting as if to banish the savory smell in his nose.

I turned to Carl. "Give it back to him. We're all going for a ride. I'm hungry and I just became a vegan."

"Booooo!" The goats catcalled in unison.

"Go milk an almond, plant murderer!" Grinder hooted.

"Fuck you, tofu!" Snarler began chanting over and over again. Grinder joined in.

Then Carl tossed the leg at Snarler. "Stop singing!" he begged them.

Snarler caught it in his teeth and then shoulder-bumped his brother. "Mind giving me a hoof putting this back on?" The two of them trotted out of the room and around the corner. I heard a sickening squelching sound and then a scream of joy. "Oh yeah! Good as new!"

The two goats trotted back into the kitchen as if nothing strange or disgusting had happened. Everyone stared at his new, completely healed leg in disbelief; he looked just like his brother with four normal goat legs.

Snarler bowed politely. "Thank you. But may I suggest using garlic salt and fresh-ground pepper next time? That was Thor's favorite. Before those two killed him anyway," he added, jerking his horns toward me and Gunnar with a dark, entirely unsympathetic laugh for his old boss.

I turned my back on the goats and motioned everyone to follow me. "We're leaving," I said, snaking my arm through Kára's and gripping her hand as I led everyone out of the kitchen and made my way towards the stable where I parked my vehicles. I would need one big enough for all of us, but I had that covered.

Aiden quickly rushed up beside me, wanting to be as far away as possible from the Billy Goats Snuff.

The goats galloped up behind us, flanking Gunnar. "We're your new service goats," Snarler said. "You know, since you only have the one eye. Odin gets the ravens; you get the mighty Snarler and Grinder!"

"Security goats," Grinder corrected in a low rasp. "We kill things. All the things."

Gunnar frowned down at them. "I'm a werewolf."

"They saved my ass during the wizard attack yesterday," I reminded him from over my shoulder. "Thanks for the whole bomb thing," I said, not sure which of the two goats had been responsible.

"It was delightful," Snarler said, judging by his higher-pitched voice. "Felt like I'd swallowed a ghost pepper and then BOOM! SPLAT! My guts were everywhere," he said, chuckling.

"This is not normal," Aiden muttered. "Why is everyone acting like *any* of this is normal?"

I glanced over my shoulder and smiled at Snarler. "Yeah. Your head landed on the van thirty feet away."

"So cool," he chuckled.

"I let them light me on *fire*," Grinder chimed in, as if it was a competition. "And I didn't hit you in the nuts," he added smugly.

"I. Ate. A. Bomb." Snarler sneered, and then they began cracking their heads together behind Gunnar, arguing and crashing into a side table.

I sighed, shaking my head. "No fighting in the house!" Kára laughed at my fatherly shout, shaking her head. Damn. She was right. I was becoming my father.

"I can't believe anyone is *hungry*," Aiden complained, shuddering at the thought of eating.

"You sure that taking this crew downtown is a good idea?" Kára asked. "The city is swarming with police and National Guard."

I nodded. "They can stay in the car while we order the sandwiches to go. We can get a feel for the city while we're at it." I held up a finger. "And you will be six-inches happier."

She rolled her eyes at me. "The whole city can't be crazy..." she said, sounding doubtful.

"You guys want to take our chariot?" Grinder asked.

"NO!" everyone shouted in unison.

CHAPTER 20

Luckily, the snow hadn't continued overnight and the roads were already mostly cleared. There had been enough accumulation to blanket the city, but the temperamental Missouri weather had already begun fighting back. Pretty soon, the pretty white snow would turn into icky gray slush.

The Knight XV was a literal beast of a luxury vehicle, clocking in at close to one-million-dollars. It looked like the edgy, rebellious, chip-on-the-shoulder love child of a drifter military tank dad and a flashy Mercedes G-Wagon grifter mom after the two hooked up for a one-night stand. But then daddy tank went to go buy lottery tickets at the gas station and never came back home, leaving mommy to raise the seven-ton baby all on her own.

The Knight XV had inherited the best genes from both parents.

On a structural level, it had been built from the axles up as an armored vehicle, whereas other 'armored' vehicles were simply luxury SUV's with a figurative Kevlar vest slapped on after the fact. The XV had floodlights, bulletproof everything, night vision cameras, run-flat tires, a built-in oxygen survival kit, ballistic steel and fiberglass plates and fenders, and anything else one might need to survive the end of days.

But he was pretty on the inside, too. Flat-screens, handcrafted leather seats, oak trim, LED lighting, automatic window-tinting, and intercoms—because it was twenty feet long.

Only one hundred of them had been made in the entire world, and I'd bought ten of them. I'd given one to the Randulfs, but the others were all mine.

The ride downtown consisted of the goats grossing everyone out with competing stories of their innumerable grisly demises. Thankfully, the SUV was massive, so I was able to tune them out as Kára caught Gunnar up to speed on everything, speaking to him in low tones. I kept my eye on Aiden via the rear-view mirror, wondering how his night had gone, and checking to make sure he wasn't eavesdropping on Gunnar and Kára. Of course, Carl sat right next to him and was turned so that he stared directly at the prisoner. Aiden seemed both engrossed in and horrified by the goats' stories, so I shifted my attention to my driving.

When we entered downtown, the police presence was insane, and my reflexes shifted my hands to ten-and-two rather than my usual one-handed steering. I parked the SUV on a side street near a spot that didn't have a lot of potential pedestrian traffic and fewer police vehicles. I would hate to have to explain my passengers.

I turned to address my team and lifted a finger in warning. "No shenanigans or we'll start a war with the police."

Gunnar nodded with a grim frown, understanding the severity of the situation. "How about we find a different sandwich shop," he said, sweeping his eye across the dozen or so police vehicles in the near distance.

"I want to get a general feel for the city, especially after that truck blew up yesterday. We'll only be a few minutes," I said, wanting desperately to get out of the car. I'd already envisioned eating the sandwich, so there was no deterring me. "It's just around the corner."

He relented with a look that told me he disagreed completely with my reasoning but knew there was no dissuading me. Aiden licked his lips anxiously, staring through the windshield at the police.

I climbed out of the SUV and joined Kára on the sidewalk. She grasped my hand and played doting girlfriend as we adopted a casual pace along the slushy sidewalk. We swiveled our heads back and forth in a perfectly natural observation of the perfectly unnatural number of police vehicles occupying downtown. It would have been strange *not* to gawk, so we did it openly and huddled close together as we approached the famous shop.

"This is insane," I told her. "I can't believe Prometheus crashing into the Arch drew so much attention. I mean, I get it, I guess, but I've never seen anything like this before."

She nodded. "At least no one saw him leave the scene or there would be a lot of questions."

I pursed my lips, nodding my agreement. "He came straight to Falco afterwards, so I should count myself doubly lucky."

We rounded the corner and waved at a pair of police officers standing across the street. They smiled back in a polite manner and then resumed their conversation. They looked bored—which was great. I saw the sign for *Six Inches to Heaven* about fifty yards away, and I was relieved to see no police officers lurking directly outside.

We entered the discreet sub shop—a hidden gem known only to locals —and the bell above the door tinkled in a welcoming sound. I spotted the owner, Laurie D, behind the counter as she spoke to a young delivery guy holding a transport bag over his shoulder. Three customers in my peripheral vision sat at a table, talking quietly as they munched on their sandwiches. I took two steps and I came to an abrupt halt as I felt the aura of other magical practitioners in the room. Kára bumped into me with a grunt. My eyes darted to the trio at the table and immediately narrowed.

Wizards. Fuck.

They absently turned to take note of our arrival and then froze in unison like they shared a hive mind.

"Master Temple!" Laurie D called out in a jubilant tone, bustling around the counter with a bright, welcoming smile. "It's so great to see you again! And with a *lady* friend," she cooed, swaying her hips salaciously. "Oh! Our new aprons just came in. You like them?" she asked eagerly. I managed a crooked, brittle smile and glanced over at it.

Nobody beats our meat. It wasn't an apron; it was an a-pun.

"It's great, Laurie D," I heard myself say as my eyes darted back to the wizards. They had lowered their food to their trays and were staring at us like we were freshly baked cupcakes.

"It's funny because it has a naughty connotation," Laurie D explained, giggling at her own rapier wit.

"Yep. I get it," I said in a strained voice. "Give me a minute," I told her. "I think I forgot my wallet in the car," I lied, sensing the collective animosity from the wizards. I wasn't scared of them, but this was the worst possible place to get into a fight. Cops everywhere outside and I didn't want to destroy Laurie's place.

"Let's get the hell out of here, Nate," Kára murmured in my ear, "or there's going to be a bloodbath."

"Master Temple," one of the wizards said, scooting her chair back with a chalkboard screech. "Just the man we've been looking for. I'll buy you a sandwich. Come join us," she said, her voice dripping with venom even though her face was smiling.

"Oh, how kind of you!" Laurie D chortled, clapping her hands together as she smiled at the wizards. "It's so nice to see genuine acts of kindness these days. "

I narrowed my eyes, trying to speak low enough for only them to hear, but the floors and walls were glossy tile, so it was practically *designed* to create echoes. "If you're friends with the delivery guy, you won't leave this place alive," I growled to the lead wizard.

The delivery guy at the counter gasped, clearly hearing my threat and assuming I meant him. He threw his hands up, dropping his delivery bag. "What the hell did *I* do?" he squealed, sounding panicked as he lifted his hands in surrender. "You know what, Laurie D? I quit. Immediately. I want nothing to do with whatever this is."

He stormed out the back door, shooting me furtive, apologetic glances.

Laurie D frowned, looking bewildered. She obviously hadn't heard me threaten the wizards. "But I just gave you an apron!" she complained, chasing through the back door after him as if she intended to physically wrangle it off his neck.

I pointed at the back door and eyed the wizards. "Not *that* delivery guy, in case any of you are confused."

The three of them stood up and lowered their hands to their sides. "Know anything about a coworker of ours who was in town yesterday?" the woman asked in a frigid tone. "Seems like the city was too hot for him and his apprentice."

Alarm bells began going off in my head as I realized that these particular wizards had not been friends with the assassins who attacked me at

Falco. They had been friends with the late Justice Jasper Griffin. Double-fuck.

But if I gave them any hint that I knew what they were talking about, I would incriminate myself, confirming my involvement in the clean-up and my kidnapping of Aiden. I had to play dumb about the whole situation.

On the other hand, one of these three might be the Justice Odin and Tyr saw speaking with Baldur. So, how to bring it up without incriminating myself? I chose my words very carefully. Blatantly calling them out on the Baldur thing might tip off the god, which would take away the element of surprise I currently had.

I frowned. "Wait. Apprentice? Are you guys Justices or something?"

Kára cursed under her breath. They nodded. Slowly. Hungrily.

I burst out laughing and their smiles faltered. "You fucking morons," I said, shaking my head. "St. Louis is off limits to Justices. I thought I made that perfectly clear to the Academy several months back. I gave a speech and everything. Whoever your buddy is, he must have missed the memo." I shrugged. "This town doesn't take kindly to nosy members of the Academy and your pathetic attempts to grab power from your betters. In my eyes, your Grandmaster just learned a valuable lesson." I let my gaze sweep over each of them, resting for a moment on each. "I hope she doesn't have to learn three more."

"You know," the lead woman said in a conversational tone, sidestepping to my right in an overly casual manner, "I've always wondered about your feud with the Academy. How your thieving family turned your noses up at us little people. How you so bravely came to our school and frightened all those little children."

"How big that must have made you feel, Master Temple," the second man said, casually sidestepping in the opposite direction to fan out around us. The third man was murmuring under his breath and I saw the glass windows beginning to frost up, obscuring the view from outside.

"Think long and hard about this before you make a decision you won't live to regret," Kára warned.

The woman sneered, eyeing Kára up and down. "One of your worthless gold diggers?" she scoffed. "Run along, little girl, before—"

The front door jingled and the five of us jumped in alarm. Two beat cops strolled in, bantering back and forth with each other.

CHAPTER 21

One cop was fumbling with something on his body armor while the other was shaking his head in resigned amusement at his partner's complaint.

"I always get the shitty body cam," the first officer muttered, still fumbling with his shirt.

I gritted my teeth in frustration, hoping they wouldn't recognize me as I casually guided Kára out of their way and averted my face. I was a local celebrity, so the odds weren't in my favor.

But...they were wearing body cams. We might have just stumbled upon a solution to our disagreement with the Justices before it escalated to violence. Violence that would have likely resulted in a swarm of cops storming into the place in about two seconds, judging by the police presence we had seen outside.

They seemed to finally pick up on the pregnant tension in the air and they looked over to frown at the three Justices, Kára, and then—

"Master Temple!" the first officer croaked excitedly. He didn't grab his taser or handcuffs, so I took it as a positive development.

The second officer—the one with the unreliable body cam—grimaced, recognizing the political shit show he'd just stumbled into. "Ah, shit."

"Officers," I said, trying to keep absolutely everyone in my line of sight. "Thank you for your service. I hope it hasn't been eventful out there."

Until now, I thought to myself.

The first officer shrugged, smiling warmly. "Not too bad, thankfully."

The second officer was frowning at the mess left behind by the retired delivery driver, possibly wondering why a perfectly good sandwich was splattered on the floor and why absolutely no one was moving, including Laurie D, who had returned at some point in my argument with the Justices. Her silence—and the *I just crapped my pants* look on her face—told me she had heard entirely too much of my argument with the Justices.

"Is everything alright here?" the second policeman asked in a suspicious tone, shifting his attention from the mess to the Justices and finally, to Laurie D.

She nodded adamantly. "G-great, officers! What can I get for you? It's on the house!" she all but shouted.

Instead of answering, the second cop shifted his attention to the three Justices again, and his instincts must have picked up on their offensive formation. He casually shifted his hand to rest on the grip of his gun, making it look more like an innocent lean. "And how are y'all doing?" he asked in an overly casual tone.

The lead Justice dipped her chin. "Fine, thank you for asking. Just taking a lunch break from the chaos at the courthouse," she replied, discreetly revealing a lanyard around her neck. One I hadn't previously noticed. I realized they each wore one, and I felt my heart skip a beat. Employee ID badges for the courthouse.

Motherfuckingshitballs. The Academy Justices were working with the *government*? What in the ever-loving hell was happening to my neat little world?

The cop instantly relaxed, letting out a sigh to realize that they were all working for the same organization. "Oh." He was silent for a beat and I could practically hear his brain overheating as he connected some unfortunate dots.

Three alleged employees of the Justice department who were likely looking into the alleged terrorist attack on the Arch looked to be having a Mexican Standoff with St. Louis' favorite asshole billionaire.

The odds had just gotten incredibly worse for the home team, and I couldn't shake the sudden tune of the annoying Twelve Days of Christmas jingle out of my head.

On the third day of Yulemas, my true love gave to me: three jaded Justices, two beat cops, and the Guard waiting outside for me.

And their body cams prevented me from using magic to shut down the situation before they could call for backup or whip out the handcuffs. Also, the first sign of anyone using magic would result in everyone simultaneously lashing out with *their* magic. I very carefully kept my hands where they could see them and I shot them a hapless smile. With nothing else up my sleeve, I glanced at the friendlier of the two officers. "Is Kosage still wearing...couture underwear?" I asked, knowing my old nemesis on the force was mostly hated by every low-level officer.

Kára—back when she'd been Othello—had been the one to humiliate Captain Kosage by finding embarrassing pictures of him in risqué underwear and blasting them all over police headquarters. And the internet. And I think she even had flyers plastered on walls downtown. In fact, that was back when I'd had my first altercation with the Academy Justices. That was when Othello had died...when Death had secretly made the switch, putting Othello's soul into the Valkyrie beside me now, and putting a fraud with a memory shard into the old Othello to deceive everyone.

Talk about full circle.

Kára made a soft sound, apparently sharing my thoughts and recalling the night she truly died.

The pair of cops tensed as if I'd just double-barrel nut-tapped them from ten feet away. I held my breath, hoping my grin looked genuine rather than a mirror image of Laurie D in her wildly inappropriate apron.

The friendly cop casually reached for his body cam as he spoke to his partner. "Damn. Now my camera is malfunctioning, too, Thomas," he said.

The second officer casually reached for his and gave his partner a hesitant nod. "Maybe we should reset them," he suggested in an overly casual tone.

"I didn't hear your question, Master Temple," the first officer said as he unplugged the wire hooked up to his cam. Officer Thomas did the same and I held my breath, maintaining my smile even though I felt like making a run for it.

Had they turned their mics off so they could whoop the hell out of me or was it because they didn't want any record of them trashing Kosage?

The Justices were frowning, discreetly shifting from foot-to-foot as they watched in tense silence.

The friendly officer waited until he was certain his partner had actually unhooked his gear before letting out a breath of relief and flashing me a big grin. "Kosage is the fucking *worst*, man," he said in a rush. Then a deep laugh bubbled out of his mouth, erupting from his belly. "Goddamn that feels good to say out loud."

Officer Thomas nodded with a half-hearted smirk. "Fucking asshole, for sure." He seemed to abruptly remember the three Justices were also listening, and his smile slipped. "Shouldn't you be getting back to work?" he asked in a warning tone.

The lead Justice smiled and dipped her chin apologetically. "Of course. My apologies."

Then she suddenly let loose a blast of air that sent both cops flying across the room. My eyes almost popped out of my head to see the Justice so flagrantly break her own Academy's laws to not use magic in front of Regulars, let alone to attack the fucking police directly.

They hit the wall hard and I saw their eyes flutter closed as they lost consciousness.

Well, shit. Now we had a real problem on our hands.

CHAPTER 22

I didn't have long to worry about being surprised because I was too busy throwing up a shield of air to deflect her follow up attack that was aimed straight at my face. Kára had already called up her trident and was halfway through the motion of impaling the second Justice's head.

"Don't kill them!" I hissed at Kára as I used my shield to deflect my own foe's first attack. Heeding my warning, her trident's poky bits disappeared at the last instant, transforming her weapon into a metal staff. She struck the wizard in the forehead with a resounding *crack* like she was breaking a cue ball in a game of pool. He went flying across the room and slammed his back against the wall. He must have blocked some of the force of her blow because he landed on his feet with an incredulous look on his face and a noticeable dent in the center of his forehead.

I lashed out with a tendril of magic and grabbed a table, swinging it high into the air before slamming it down on the back of the third Justice's skull so hard that he headbutted his own table for a double knock-out. He fell bonelessly to the ground as the lead Justice continued peppering me with blasts of magic, cursing under her breath.

I could tell she was itching to use deadlier magic but knew she couldn't without risking alerting all the police outside.

"You really working at the court?" I growled as I used tendrils of magic to toss chairs at her in rapid succession. I was exceedingly careful that none of them went near the external windows. If those broke, we were all fucked. Thankfully, the windows were still frosted over so I didn't have to worry about any police officers noticing our rapid restaurant renovation.

"As a matter of fact, yes!" she snapped. I blinked, dumbfounded. The Justices really were working with the government? What the fuck was going on?

My thoughts were interrupted by the universally familiar sound of a cocking shotgun. I spun instinctively, shifting my shield to prevent a twelve-gauge hole in my ass. Laurie D was aiming the gun at the lead Justice with a furious, proprietary twinkle in her eyes. "Master Temple is one of my founding Six-Inch Heroes!" she shouted.

My face flushed beet red with embarrassment. "It's a rewards program, not—"

"It is *not* a rewards program!" Laurie screamed, swinging her gun across the room to get everyone's attention and let them know that she was the craziest person in the room. "It is a lifestyle!"

If she pulled that trigger, we would have an army of cops rushing to the scene.

When Laurie's gaze slipped to Kára, the lead Justice in front of me snarled and her hand began to glow. I physically grabbed a chair and swung it at her ankle as hard as I could. I heard wood and bone crunch and she let out a shriek as she cartwheeled at the exact moment she let loose a blast of bright sparks. The attack missed Shotgun Laurie but knocked the fan hanging over her head loose. I leapt up onto the counter to try and get the shotgun away from her while using the shield to protect both of us from above and behind.

Still on the ground, the Justice let loose a blast of air that missed my shield and sliced into my hip. I felt a flash of pain as I crashed into Laurie, tackling her to the ground behind the counter. The shotgun slipped from my hands and went flying into the mayonnaise, splashing it everywhere.

Ironically, it had not suffered an accidental discharge, all visual evidence to the contrary.

"Stay down!" I shouted at Laurie as I hopped to my feet, ignoring my wounded hip, and used my sleeve to wipe the mayonnaise from my face. I spotted the broken-ankled Justice still on the ground and, without missing a beat, I flung a blast of air back at her. With the storefront windows now behind her, I couldn't risk anything too powerful, so I resorted to relentless short-ranged hammer blows that she easily swatted aside like they were Nerf bullets.

Since she was preoccupied with those, she didn't see it coming when I altered one of my blows to knock down the dangling fan over *her* head. Or the second whip of air that I used to then grab the free-falling fan and slam the fixture down on her face with a resounding *crack* that shut her up for good.

I let out a breath of relief, glancing over at Kára on the other end of the restaurant.

I watched as Kára hit the second Justice about two dozen times in two-point-three seconds with her metal staff, and then she headbutted him hard enough to make my own skull hurt. He crumpled to the ground, his eyes rolling into the back of his head. Her staff winked out of existence as she verified that he was down for good.

She turned to check on me and I threw both hands in the air. "I'm a Six-Inch Hero!" I wheezed.

"Damned right you are!" Laurie cheered loudly, climbing to her feet from behind the counter. Her hair was wild and disheveled, and I silently thanked god that she wasn't covered in mayonnaise or I would have died of shame.

Kára burst out laughing, shaking her head. I winced as I felt blood trickling down my hip. I pressed my palm over it and caught my breath as I scanned the five bodies for signs of movement. The cops were breathing easily but still unconscious, and the three Justices were battered but not dead. Kára jogged over to the policemen and swiped their handcuffs and one of those zip-tie shackles. Then she calmly walked over to the Justices and began binding them to tables. She accidentally kicked the lead Justice in the nose. "Whoops." She repositioned herself and accidentally kicked the Justice in the broken ankle, earning a sharp groan. "Whoops," Kára repeated. I grinned. Pettiness was endearing. Finally, she managed to close the handcuffs.

"Was that..." Laurie began, licking her lips as she glanced down at the lead Justice, "magic?"

I let out a tired sigh and turned to Laurie, realizing that I had a whole lot of explaining to do. "Yes. But you can't tell a soul."

"Are you kidding me? No one would believe me if I tried!" she said, shaking her head. But something about her reaction told me she was more excited than afraid. Relieved to finally hear a truth she may have long believed. It...wasn't what I'd expected. "You used magic...to save *me*. Your meat dealer."

Kára coughed lightly, turning her back on us. "Sorry. Something in my throat."

I turned back to Laurie. "This is serious. You can't tell anyone what you saw here. It would be dangerous for you. Men would come to try and silence you. Permanently. Understand?"

She nodded, smiling to herself. "I'll do anything for one of my founding Six-Inch Heroes. Tell me what you need, Master Temple."

Kára fake-coughed again. Repeatedly. She was terrible at hiding her amusement. "S-sorry, Six-Inch Hero. You were saying?" she asked, keeping her back to us.

I turned back to Laurie. "Ignore her. I'm proud of my status. Now, when we leave, you need to wake the police up and thank them, profusely, for arresting those three," I said, pointing at the Justices. "They are very dangerous and they attacked us. They also used stolen ID's to get high-level security access through their jobs at the courthouse."

Laurie frowned. "Won't the cops know that they didn't actually fight or arrest them?" she asked, frowning. Then her eyes widened. "Oh, are you going to magic them into thinking—"

I heard a two sharp *pops* behind me and I spun around in alarm, only to see that Kára had relieved the cops of their tasers and that she had shot two of the Justices in the chest. They spasmed, arching their backs for a few moments. "There. Magicked." She dropped the guns between the cops and the targets and put her hands on her hips. She frowned at the last Justice and then glanced at Laurie. "You heroically cracked him over the head with a table when he was distracted. Good job."

I turned to Laurie and shrugged. "Sounds plausible to me. If they don't remember very well, it's because they had drawn their tasers on those two for throwing tables and chairs all around the place when that third guy snuck up behind them and hit them in the head with a chair, causing their tasers to fire and hit those two. Which was when you snuck up and single-handedly saved the day with a table of your own. Then you handcuffed them," I said, grimacing at the loopholes. "But it all happened so fast and you're confused."

"And we left *before* the fighting started," Kára added. "That part is vital."

"This is like a movie," Laurie said, shaking her head.

I noticed a stack of sandwiches on the back counter—at least a dozen of them. "Who are those for?"

Laurie turned to look. "That was supposed to be Cameron's next delivery," she said with a frown. "I always thought he was too pretty for this job. I should have known better." She sighed, shaking her head. "They were going to the courthouse, so you can have them."

I reached into my pocket and grabbed my wallet. I pulled out six hundred-dollar-bills and placed them on the counter. "To pay for the sandwiches and the damages. I know it's not enough, but it's all I've got on me. I'll pay you the rest later, deal?"

"For my number one Six-Inch Hero? Of course!" She grinned and then turned around to bag up the sandwiches for us. "And I can give you some merchandise, too." She pointed at the door. "Disguises." I sighed, nodding. Less than a minute later, we were each holding two bags of sandwiches and wearing aprons and hats with the company logo proudly displayed. *Nobody beats our meat.*

We paused at the door, grinning like idiots to see how ridiculous we both looked. "Let's take the long way around the block and loop back," I told her. We waved at Laurie D one last time, and then slipped out the door to do our jobs as deliverers of six-inch surprises to the citizens of St. Louis.

Thankfully, no cops were waiting outside for us. None were in sight at all, which was a blessing. We hurried down the street, waiting until we rounded the corner before letting out nervous breaths of relief. We continued on at a steady pace. "Why the hell are Justices working at the courthouse?" I murmured, shaking my head. "That can't be good."

"Maybe they were fake badges. Or even magical illusions."

I muttered a curse. "I meant to check them for their silver masks to see if they were telling us the truth. Too late now."

Kára frowned. "You think they were lying?"

"They attacked the police when we could have easily defused the situation. Justices were willing to openly attack Regular cops. They wanted me *that* badly." I shrugged. "That could make them more of the rogue wizards or some of the Justices Niko told you about," I admitted. "Anything to find Jasper's murderer."

She nodded, looking troubled. "I took pictures of their faces. I'll text them to you for what it's worth."

I grinned at her. "You're kind of amazing."

"I'm no Six-Inch Hero," she teased.

"I've never heard you complain," I muttered.

She nudged me with her shoulder playfully. "I can take the new pictures back to Odin and Tyr and see if they recognize any of them as Baldur's Justice friend." I nodded. She let out a breath. "I'm just glad Gunnar and the others didn't come to check on us."

My eyes widened and I picked up my pace. Soon, we were all but running.

CHAPTER 23

W e had gotten back to the SUV without incident, even though a pair of cops were admiring the strange and unique vehicle from across the street, looking as if they wanted to get a closer look. There was nothing alarming in their attention, just curiosity in the strange-looking vehicle. I made sure to jump in and start it up before their curiosity got the best of them and they decided to strike up a conversation. Especially if they began to wonder why two delivery people—from the same sandwich shop—got into a million-dollar SUV. Or why they had passengers waiting for them.

I was pulling away from the curb when Kára finally turned around and lobbed the sandwich bags into the back like she was feeding a pack of lions. "Shut up or you're walking home!" she snapped, overriding the eruption of a dozen simultaneous questions.

The ride was tense and silent for a few moments before I saw Carl raise his claw in the rear-view mirror. "Yes, Carl?" I asked.

"I like your hats."

The car was silent again and then Aiden burst out laughing. "What kind of sandwiches do we have?" he asked, digging into one of the bags.

Gunnar tapped me on the shoulder. I glanced back to find him sniffing the air and scowling.

I frowned, offended, turning back to the road. "It wasn't me. You're the one sitting in a car with a bunch of guys on high-protein diets," I grumbled.

"Heh-heh-heh," the goats bleated from way in the back cargo area.

Kára grinned, shaking her head. "It's like high school all over again," she said, drumming her fingers on the dashboard.

"No," Gunnar growled. "Not that. I smell blood. Why are you bleeding?"

Everyone's ears perked up, waiting for an answer. In the rear-view mirror, I saw the goats slowly lifting their heads from the far back of the SUV. Kára muttered a curse, annoyed that I hadn't told her about my injury. Then she snatched a few napkins and physically lifted my arm out of her way so she could shove them under my waistline where the blood had seeped through my jeans.

"Don't worry. It's not serious. I actually forgot about it," I admitted, frowning. "That's weird."

Kára unbuckled my pants faster than she ever had before—and that's impressive, folks—and tugged at my waistline, making it difficult for me to keep the car in the lane. I swerved a little as she went completely still, staring into the gap between my pants and hip. "It's no longer bleeding. Looks like it's a few days' old," she murmured, sounding troubled.

"Um...good?" I asked, awkwardly. I waved off their concern and re-buckled my pants. "It wasn't that bad, trust me," I said, having no idea if that was actually true or not. I addressed everyone in the back, speaking louder so they could hear me. "We ran into a few Justices," I said, shifting my eyes to Aiden in the rearview mirror. "We took care of them and arranged for them to be arrested. They attacked two police officers."

Gunnar cursed.

Aiden stiffened in shock, lowering his sandwich as he met my eyes. "Who were they?"

I slapped the steering wheel as if I'd just realized my mistake. "That's the thing about sudden unexpected attacks. I always forget to ask their names before I take them down," I said, locking eyes with him. "Did you get their names, Kára?"

"Darn. I forgot." She pulled out her phone and tapped the screen a few times. "But I got pictures." She lifted the phone to Aiden and I could tell by the uneasy look on his face that she was staring directly into his eyes. Her gaze could be extremely unsettling when she wanted it to be. The target found themselves hesitating between which eye to focus on. They weren't even consciously aware of it, but their brains noticed the two starkly different colors and it caused the person to fidget and twitch—even *more* noticeably once the person became aware they were doing it.

Kind of like when someone had a wandering eye and you couldn't quite tell which one to focus on. Your intentions were honest—wanting to show that you were paying attention—but the result was often offensive.

Aiden squirmed under her gaze, and it took him a moment to glance down at the phone. I watched him closely, wondering if I would catch a flash of recognition or any form of deceit if he denied knowing them.

He nodded thoughtfully. "I recognize them. Joanna, Gustavo, and Erik," he said without missing a beat. He licked his lips as he lifted his gaze to Kára. "They...aren't very popular with the students, but they're respected among the other Justices. Were...they looking for me? Do they know what happened to Jasper?"

Kára turned back to the front, staring down at her phone, leaving me to answer.

I considered my answer, studying him. "They think he died by fire," I said, "So I assume they found the truck I torched. They mentioned his apprentice but I couldn't exactly let them know I knew what the hell they were talking about without incriminating myself."

Aiden nodded, looking pensive. "Why did they attack the police?"

"We were interrupted. Wrong place at the wrong time. Strangely enough, they seemed more interested in picking a fight with me for the simple fact that they might be able to claim bragging rights for it if they won. I think they were in town to investigate Jasper, but they sure forgot about him once they thought they could take me down in a three-on-one fight."

Kára chuckled, staring at her phone as she replied. "They mistook me for a Regular. Whoops."

Aiden nodded. "That sounds about right for that particular team. They are more interested in being feared and notorious than doing the job a Justice should." He let out a resigned sigh. "The Justices seem to be a... mixed bag these days. They used to be a unified band, but lately it seems like they are a collection of individuals with individual goals, all aiming for clout. They pursue their own causes, only teaming up when the Grand-master calls for a larger operation."

I nodded, deciding that I really did want to have a meeting with G-Ma to find out what the hell kind of Academy she was running if even the Justices seemed to be going rogue. Because it sure seemed like her house was tumbling down. First, Baldur's mysterious Justice buddy and now the three at the sub shop.

"Master Temple?" Carl asked in a strangely polite tone, which instantly set off alarm bells in my head. Like when, as a kid, I proactively did a bunch of chores, knowing I had a big Ask for my parents later and I really needed to butter them up, first. Kára sunk low into her seat, grinning wide and trying not to laugh.

"Yes, Carl?" I asked, ignoring her.

"Can I please get a magic tongue tattoo? Please, please, pleeasse," he begged, leaning forward.

I blinked, entirely caught off guard. "What?" I sputtered, trying to imagine how the hell anyone would even be able to tattoo his snake-like forked tongue. Then the rational question came to mind. "Where did you get that idea?" I asked, bewildered. I glanced out the window, wondering if he'd seen a billboard.

"Prisoner Aiden has one," he said. "I want one, too."

"I told you that in confidence, Carl," Aiden grumbled. "And it's not magic."

I spun my head around so fast that I swerved a little before turning back and readjusting the mirror to focus solely on Aiden. "What the hell is he talking about?" I demanded. I glanced over at Kára to see her shrug with a knowing smile. I hadn't noticed Aiden's tongue tattoo.

Aiden sighed. "Can we talk about this later?" he asked, sounding genuinely embarrassed. His ears were bright red and he looked to be sinking down into his seat.

"Aiden," I growled, "I will turn this truck around so fast, and send you straight into my warded prison cell," I warned, knowing how dangerous some runes could be. Like the Omegabet, for example. I couldn't take the risk. "Show me."

He sighed, begrudgingly. Then he stuck out his tongue. I squinted, noticing a small black rune of sorts tattooed into the center of his tongue. A wave of anxiety washed over me, wondering if it really was some kind of actual spell or magic like Carl had claimed. I committed it to memory, frowning because it didn't look finished. As if it was only part of a rune. And I sensed none of the eerie familiarity of when I saw an Omegabet symbol.

Aiden retracted his tongue and took a deep breath. "When I was thirteen, I didn't have much in the way of friends at the Academy. In fact, I had exactly none. A group of boys started talking to me, treating me like normal for once. After a week, they asked if I wanted to join their secret club. Of course, I said yes. They told me I had to prove myself and get the club's secret power rune tattooed on my tongue—so it would be hidden from the professors—like they had done. That it would make me stronger. They showed me theirs, so I easily agreed."

He'd said it wasn't magical, so I had a feeling Aiden had been taken in. I shook my head, recalling the cruelty of middle-school bullies. Looking back as an adult, they were always glaringly obvious mistakes, but in the heat of the moment as an awkward teen, just wanting to make at least one best friend, it was ridiculously easy to fall for crap like that. "You're shitting me."

"It's not even finished because a few of them began laughing halfway through and I got suspicious. Turned out that their 'tattoos' had been a permanent marker to trick me. The whole thing—the entire *week* of them buttering me up—had been a prank to pick on the penniless, resident orphan," he said, growling angrily. "The Grandmaster gave them slaps on the wrist but made me keep that tattoo as a reminder to not be so gullible in the future. *Justices cannot be fools, Aiden*," he mimed in a faux G-Ma voice that was alarmingly accurate.

"Damn, Aiden. That's messed up," I said, lamely. "I wouldn't have pressed if I'd realized..." I sighed. "I'm an asshole. I've seen some truly terrifying runes lately, and it set off my scorched earth instincts. I promise to tell you an embarrassing story about me some day," I said.

Aiden nodded absently, staring out the window with a dark shadow in his eyes at the memory. "I get it. Carl noticed it last night and asked about it. I lied to him," he said, letting out a sigh, "so I guess karma just fucked me," he said with a weak laugh. "To be honest, I forget I even have it until someone notices."

"And if Nate won't tell you an embarrassing story about himself," Gunnar chimed in, nudging Aiden with his elbow, "I'll tell you *five*."

Aiden smiled, glancing over at the werewolf with a nod. "Deal."

My phone vibrated in my pocket. I pulled it out and saw a text from... Kára? I lifted it so I could discreetly read but still focus on the road.

Not Omegabet. Carl asked about tattoo this morning. I checked internet— zero results. Didn't know bully story or I would've stopped you.

I glanced over to see Kára nodding vehemently, still ducked down in her chair. Kára had worked diligently with me to transcribe all the symbols of the Omegabet that I had come across—from my memory up on Olympus as a prisoner, to Pan's stack of journals, and to conversations with Alice. She'd put them all on a computer that had exactly zero connections to the internet or anything else that could be hacked. So, it wasn't a complete list, but it was fairly impressive. Carl must have sketched the image of Aiden's tattoo, or Kára had taken note of it herself and investigated it without telling me—that was more her style. To come to me with a solution rather than a problem or question. I was a lucky, lucky man.

Which meant I needed to listen to her now. I nodded at her, mouthing *thank you.*

I glanced back in the mirror. "Hey, Aiden." He looked up at me. "Did you get those fuckers back?"

A wolfish grin split his cheeks and he nodded. "Twice-over, but it took a few years," he admitted with a smug smirk.

"Good," I said with an approving nod. "It doesn't matter that we got hit, just that we got up and hit back twice as hard."

He scratched his chin thoughtfully. "I like that. Thanks. Just embarrassing is all." He glanced at the passengers. "Hope you enjoyed the show."

Snarler piped up. "This one time, at hammer camp—"

"No!" Grinder said sternly. "We do not talk about hammer camp."

The pair of goats slowly slunk back down out of view, whisper-arguing in unintelligible sounds.

"Hey, babe," Gunnar said, inadvertently changing the subject as he answered his phone.

"We're just—" He cut off abruptly and I frowned, glancing back at him.

I watched as he clenched his jaw and narrowed his eye, seeming to hold his breath as he listened. I felt the hair on my arms rise up. "We're on our way," he snarled, hanging up. He wrapped up his sandwich and blindly shoved it back into the bag as he shot me a dire look. "Two of the were-wolves I sent to Shift to help find the runaways were murdered. By fire," he said, meeting my eye. "The campus is going into lockdown and everyone is gathering in the auditorium. We need to get there as fast as we can," he growled, leaning forward anxiously to look through the windshield. The fear in his eye was raw, and I felt the capacity for extreme violence rippling off him like heat waves. I heard threads popping in his shirt and pants as he struggled to control his own shift. The outside of the SUV was armored, not the interior. If the werewolves were murdered by fire, that only meant on thing.

Wizards. But only one thing mattered in my mind, and it was a throat-ripping scream of profanity. My best friend needed me. My enemies had become his.

His wife and kids had gone to Shift this morning, and now they were in danger.

My godchildren were in danger.

CHAPTER 24

I glanced down at the GPS, frantically studying the streets to recalculate our route. "We're not far. Five minutes," I said, taking the next turn to get onto the highway. I floored it and the engine roared like a great beast. "Easy, brother," I reassured Gunnar. But my mind was racing, imagining Baldur laughing with glee.

Kára spun in her seat. "Murdered by *fire*? No one saw anything?"

Gunnar squeezed his armrest in frustration. "No, but they were burned to a crisp, so I'm guessing wizards."

At the verbal mention of wizards, I snarled furiously, wondering which faction they might be—Academy or mutineers, or...

Baldur and his Justice friend finally making a move. Not on me, but on Gunnar.

I swerved into the fast lane, cutting someone off. The driver looked so surprised by the bizarre design of my SUV that he simply held his hand above the horn, staring at us with his mouth open, forgetting to honk or yell. He probably mistook me for a presidential escort or a military vehicle. I used that to my advantage, swerving back and forth across lanes as I raced towards Shift.

The goats were eerily quiet and I glanced in the rearview to see them staring straight ahead with feral, bloodthirsty green and blue eyes, reminding me of Kára, the dreaded Valkyrie beside me. Their lips were peeled back, revealing frightening yellow teeth.

And that haunting visage reminded me of the meanings behind their names.

In Old Norse, Tanngrisnir meant *teeth-barer*, and Tanngnjóstr meant *teeth-grinder*.

"No one fucks with the Wulfric," they snarled, and then they crashed their heads together so hard that I felt it in the base of my freaking spine.

Gunnar turned to look at them. "Don't worry about me. I want you to protect my *family*. At all costs. If I know they are safe, I will have the focus to lay waste to those responsible," he growled.

They cracked skulls again, chuckling in a truly horrifying, bleating sound.

"First, the missing kids and now this," Gunnar growled impatiently. "It has to be related."

I saw Aiden flinch at Gunnar's comment. I narrowed my eyes suspiciously. "I hope you thought long and hard last night, Aiden. Your crucible moment is three minutes away."

He met my eyes in the mirror and gave me a firm nod, looking suddenly righteous with anger.

I watched as Aiden slowly turned to face Gunnar. "Missing kids?" Gunnar stared back at him for a few tense moments and then gave him a slow nod. "The Academy is terrified of the shifter school in St. Louis. They think it's dangerous—an army disguised as a school. I overheard Justices discussing how to get a look inside, but that was more than a month ago."

Gunnar grabbed him by the shirt, pulling him close. "And you are only just *now* telling us this?" he snarled.

Aiden nodded calmly. "It was old news to me, even back then. I didn't know it was relevant because I didn't know kids had gone missing until you *just said it*. If I would have randomly volunteered that information without any reason to do so, Nate would have assumed I was trying to misdirect him," he said in a calm tone. "It was a *month* ago," he reminded us. "And a dozen other times before that."

He was entirely correct, but I didn't tell him that. He hadn't been privy to my conversations with Gunnar about the missing kids at Shift. Hell, my knowledge of it was practically virginal as well. Gunnar thought they were runaways. But now coupled with two fire-bombed werewolves and Aiden's news about the Justices' fear of the place, it was looking to be something more sinister.

"We don't even know if it's the Academy," I said, watching Aiden. "Could be more rogue or mercenary wizards like the ones who jumped you and your boss. And me." I hadn't shared any of my theories with Aiden. Like what Kára had learned from Asgard, which had led me to fear there were great fissures in the vaunted Academy. Judging by the way the Justices at the sub shop had so brazenly attacked police for a chance to get street cred by taking me down, it was seemingly confirmed that the Academy's system was broken and they were on the verge of civil war.

Jasper Griffin had needed to be killed as the catalyst for chaos. No more of that old, stuffy ideology about laws and fairness. In with the new age Justices, who ruled by might, say-so, and oppression.

Aiden shrugged. "Maybe it is, maybe it isn't, but I thought you should know in case we find Justices *are* involved. If we go in assuming we're up against run-of-the-mill wizards—like me—it could cost us."

Kára glanced back at him with a look of respect. "That's actually a really good point that everyone here needs to realize. Justices are not a joke. Some are, but most earned their rank on the battlefields."

Aiden didn't smile like a kid given a gold star. He smiled like a soldier in a bunker finding a spare clip.

"Are you picking a team, Aiden?" I asked. "Or simply being a cooperative prisoner? Because it will take more than words for me to even consider taking off your cuffs."

He clenched his jaw and narrowed his eyes—but not at me or my threat. I saw an inner anguish in his eyes. Some old, familiar pain. "They're *kids!*" he snarled, passionately. "No one should fuck with kids. Not ever. I don't care if they are shifters or...Elders," he said, grasping at the first thing he could think of. "I'll kill anyone who threatens a child. That's *my* fucking hill," he said, panting angrily. And I suddenly remembered the story of his upbringing. That he'd been an orphan abandoned at the Academy. A kid without the protection of his mother and father. Shit. "This is exactly the kind of shit I was trying to tell you about with the Academy last night—why I wanted to work with Jasper or quit. They are *different* these days, Nate. Different like *this!*"

The car was silent for a few moments. "These Justices you overheard," I said, "were they the ones Kára just showed you pictures of?"

Aiden thought about it for a few seconds. "They had their masks on, so I can't be sure."

"Do you have any solid evidence on what they were planning to do?"

Aiden paled. "I ask that you remember I am simply repeating their words," he said warily. Gunnar narrowed his eyes and nodded. "They were joking about burning the place down in the middle of the night. They said that...every beast is scared of fire," he whispered in a hoarse tone.

Gunnar snarled, cracking his knuckles.

"Calm down, Gunnar," I warned. "Aiden is the messenger."

"Drive, Nate," he growled, turning his back on Aiden as if he feared he might kill him if he had to look at him one second longer.

I met Aiden's eyes in the mirror and gave him a grateful nod. "I hope you brought your bonker," I told him, smirking. "These are Justices, after all."

He lifted the cane I had lent him. I hadn't realized he'd brought it to the kitchen earlier.

"Remember," I warned him, "if you break that—"

"I know, I know," he said, rolling his eyes. "You'll shove the splintered pieces up my ass," he said, chuckling. "Unless I bonk someone trying to hurt you. Then you *might* reconsider."

I grinned back at him. "Bingo."

I saw the exit for Shift and hit the off-ramp at full speed. I saw a large cloud of black smoke in the distance, and my heart skipped a beat. I pressed the pedal all the way down, refusing to slow for any reason whatsoever. I would run over anything in my way if I had to. Thankfully, no one else had noticed it yet. They would see soon enough, but it would only make things worse if I said it now. If Gunnar lost his shit, he would tear out of the car and destroy it in the process, leaving us all on foot—where we couldn't help the students.

Elder Carl laughed. "We should go on car rides more often." Then a new thought hit him and he cocked his head. "You are going to let me come out and play, too, right? If the zombie goats can go, I should be allowed."

Gunnar clapped him on the back, nodding his agreement. "I *insist,*

Carlemagne. In fact, I want you to fucking cut loose, Brother. Everyone is welcome to play at Shift."

Carl's nostrils flared and he bared his teeth, rubbing his palms together greedily. "Delightful."

I was bringing an Elder to the battlefield, escalating the stakes. My thoughts drifted to the Masters and their devious machinations. Were *they* somehow breaking the Academy from within? Was Baldur a Master? Dozens of other questions zipped through my mind as I raced onward, so I took a calming breath.

Then I shot Kára a grin. "Nobody beats our meat."

She laughed, nodding. Then she turned to address the rest of the crew, grinning excitedly. "Let's go kill some fucking wizards!"

Everyone in the car cheered.

Even henchman Aiden, although not as confidently as the others since I caught him eyeing his bonker rather dubiously. I sighed, debating internally.

Did I trust him enough to take the cuffs off, or would he bolt at the first opportunity and rat me out to save his own ass? He sure seemed dedicated to protecting kids, but everything changed once the fighting started.

"Everything changes..." I murmured under my breath.

CHAPTER 25

Part of me still found it strange that the old Temple Industries property was now encircled by a twelve-foot-tall, stone wall to protect the newly-constructed, and still expanding, campus for wayward shifter kids. There was currently only one main complex, but it was massive, featuring a main hub that connected three wings: an auditorium and gym; a dormitory; and an area comprised of dozens of classrooms and lecture halls. Behind the complex was an outside obstacle course that looked more like a military training circuit, and the entire property was surrounded on the inside of the wall by tall evergreen trees to blind prying eyes. They were breaking ground on new buildings that would someday flank the main complex, but they hadn't started construction yet.

Cranes, trailers, bulldozers and other construction machinery peppered the grounds.

And almost every one of them was mangled or burned, looking like charred skeletons or the remains of abandoned pirate ships after a sea battle. Black smoke billowed into the sky and oozed across the surroundings, blocking out the sunlight and casting a sinister pall over the scene. The threat had escalated significantly since Ashley called Gunnar.

"What the fuck?" Kára whispered, rolling down the window. I counted a dozen dead werewolves—not two—and an equal number of mutilated human remains.

"Wizards," I growled, pointing out the bodies to Kára. "I hope they died horribly, without finishing the last season of *The Nanny*."

She stiffened, and then slowly turned to stare at me with an incredulous look. "You...watch *The Nanny*?"

I blushed, shaking my head. "What? No. Of course not. We need to focus," I said, pointing at the school.

"Fire," Gunnar rasped in a voice that sounded like tires over dry gravel, slowly turning to look at Aiden. "You said *fire*."

"Save it for the enemies, Gunnar," I warned, picking up on the barely restrained fury in his voice. It was as if he hadn't heard me, and he leaned closer to Aiden's face, clenching his jaw. "Your family needs you focused, Wulfric!" I shouted at him.

That last comment hit him like a slap to the face and he growled loud enough for me to feel it in my chest.

Before anyone else had the opportunity to turn on each other, I drove up onto the sidewalk and across the grass, tearing through meticulous landscaping that I had likely spent a lot of money on as I tried to get as close as possible to the school. I slammed on the brakes and the giant SUV skidded to a halt mere feet away from the entrance. Thankfully, the building itself wasn't entirely ablaze, but I did see pockets of fire here and there, making several of the upper windows look like demonic eyes. I hoped the inside wasn't as dire as the outside. Most of the smoke seemed to be coming from the burning construction equipment rather than the buildings.

Still...this had the potential to become a real fucking fire. If left unchecked, the school was done for.

Kára handed me my satchel and we hopped out, scanning the grounds, searching for immediate threats. I slung the satchel over my shoulder and swung it so that it was behind my hip and out of my way. Carl tasted the smoky air with his tongue, and his nostrils and ear holes expanded and contracted as he tapped into his enhanced senses. I felt magic in the air—a *lot* of fucking magic. Aiden licked his lips and shot me a grim look, picking up on the same sensation. Despite his cuffs, he could still sense magic—

that was the worst part about the contraptions. This wasn't the work of a few wizards; this was a goddamned invasion.

And shifters were known to be slightly...territorial. As were hormone-crazed teenagers, who comprised about eighty-percent of the student roster. It was a powder keg of chaos and I knew it was only a matter of time until a Good Samaritan noticed the cloud of black smoke and called the fire department or police.

Or both.

Furious howls erupted from within the school and my blood froze in my veins. The iron handles on the massive, wooden, double-front doors had been looped with heavy chain so no one could escape the school. Gunnar noticed the same thing and abruptly exploded into his alpha werewolf form. A colossal white monster was suddenly towering over us as bits of fabric rained down all around. Aiden's eyes bulged in disbelief to see the abnormally giant werewolf and he took an instinctive step back, lifting his cane in futile reflex.

Kára had already shifted into her golden Valkyrie armor and opened the back of the SUV to let the goats out before they decided to simply ram their way out.

I leapt in front of Aiden and flung up a shield as I saw Gunnar approaching the chained door. Kára and Carl were safely behind the armored truck, thankfully. Aiden shot me a confused look, not seeing any enemies. I pointed at Gunnar. "He'll huff, and he'll puff..."

Gunnar didn't open the doors.

He tore them off the fucking *hinges*, chains, framing, brick, and all. A staccato of chain links, shattered brick, shrapnel, and pieces of the doors slammed into my shield as the werewolf hurled the doors to the side with a coughing snarl. Aiden's eyes were as wide as I'd ever seen them. I nodded. "Who's afraid of the big bad wolf," I said, grinning as I lowered the shield.

"I am," Aiden whispered, staring at Gunnar's back.

I chuckled and then turned to my team. "Stay close to each other and keep your head on a swivel!" I shouted. "The place is huge and the shifters' blood is up. They might not know friend from foe and could mistake us for the enemy."

Aiden gave me a ghost of a hopeless smile and lifted his cane.

Gunnar took a deep breath and lifted his head to the sky. A howl tore out of his throat that made the hair on my arms stand on end, and set off every single car alarm in the parking lot. It made me fucking stutter-step and almost face-plant into the pavement.

A chorus of howls answered from within Shift and I sensed magic being thrown about inside.

I snarled. "Any wizard who lays a hand on a shifter will die this day," I vowed.

Gunnar let out a coughing snarl of agreement, and then he raced into the main hall and lifted his snout, sniffing at the air. Then he took off again, loping towards the auditorium.

The goats raced after their boss and soon overtook him, remembering their promise to watch over Gunnar's family above all else. Carl followed suit, caught up in the excitement. Seconds later, they rounded a distant corner, leaving the olfactory-impaired humans in their dust.

Kára and Aiden followed me into the main hall, pausing to observe the place. It was completely empty. If everyone was in the auditorium, like Ashley had told Gunnar, Tory could manage their wilder instincts, but if any had missed the call and were spread out all over the building, they would see anyone walking the halls as a threat.

Like us.

Shifters were territorial. The very fact that the place was being invaded was enough to set most of them off. Add in the fact that many were also adolescents with raging hormones, and Tory had her work cut out for her this afternoon.

Two massive paintings hung at the top of a giant staircase leading to the second floor. One was of me as the Founder of Shift and one was of Tory Marlin, Headmaster. We'd both opted to wear Victorian royal garb so as to make us look like we were hundreds of years old. She had opted for a crown, but I'd thought that a little much. I'd chosen a big honking golden scepter for my pose.

"My painting is on fire!" I hissed, indignantly. Queen Tory's painting was perfectly unharmed.

Aiden arched his eyebrow at me. "I am fatigued with your unorthodox display of unparalleled hubris."

Kára belted out a surprised laugh. "Wow. Couldn't have been said better, Aiden."

I scowled at the pair of them. "I am humble as all hell."

Kára leaned towards Aiden in a conspiratorial whisper. "He commissioned a twelve-foot-tall marble statue of him slaying a pair of lions." She pointed at the base of the stairs, indicating a walled circle fountain that featured an empty pedestal in the center. "It's going right there."

Aiden stared at me with a disgusted look, shaking his head in judgment.

I stormed past them. "I told you that in confidence," I grumbled at Kára. "And it's me riding Grimm, not slaying lions. That would be inconsiderate in a school of shifters—"

"Incoming!" Aiden shouted, tackling me into Kára. We collided in a tangle of bodies as a ball of fire struck the floor where I'd been standing.

Kára was first to leap to her feet and she hurled her trident towards the second floor. I heard a stunned grunt, and looked up to see a wizard flip over the upper railing and crash down to the main floor twenty feet below. I grimaced at the echoing, broken watermelon sound and then disentangled myself from Aiden. I stared down at him, panting. He'd just saved my life. I held out a hand and pulled him to his feet.

"Sorry," he apologized. "I reacted on reflex—"

I raised my hand, cutting him off. "No. Thank you."

He nodded brusquely, turning his attention back to our surroundings to drop the apparently awkward moment. I could tell that he wasn't used to hearing praise, judging by how his hand was shaking, causing the cane to wobble noticeably. He was used to the military camaraderie of trash-talking each other. It was messed up, but that was how he'd been raised. Kára shot me a meaningful look and I nodded. I hadn't expected for Aiden to be of any real use, but his quick thinking had saved me from a fireball.

"Let's go," I growled. "Gunnar said they were in the auditorium, but we don't know how many wizards are left roaming the halls. Or angry shifters. Stay close to me, Aiden. Hopefully, they'll recognize me, but they'll definitely attack you on sight."

He nodded grimly. "I figured as much already."

"We need to get the large group of kids out of here before we split up to hunt down the invaders or straggler kids."

Kára led the way, calling her trident back to her hand with a snap of her fingers. Aiden studied the Valkyrie discreetly, admiring her armor. I saw an opportunity to give him shit and pounced, hoping it would wash away any awkwardness he felt at me thanking him a moment ago. I leaned close, whispering into his ear. "Do you like your eyes? Because prisoners don't need eyes."

He grunted, immediately averting his gaze. "I wasn't checking her out, you psychopath. You think I'm ogling her metal ass because it's oh-so flattering?" he grumbled, but I saw him smirking at the familiar territory of rapier banter. Okay. I'd read him correctly.

Kára slowed and glanced over her shoulder with a pointed look. "Are you calling me fat?"

I let out a long whistle. "Now you're going to lose your tongue and your eyes. Good thing we fixed your ankle or you would have looked downright ridiculous."

He grumbled under his breath, doing his best to keep his eyes anywhere else but on his two allies. I shot Kára a grin and a thumbs up.

CHAPTER 26

We ran towards the auditorium, chasing the screams, explosions, snarls, and wet ripping sounds of Gunnar, Carl, and the murder-goats. We didn't get to them in time to help, but we saw plenty of truly grisly sights that even gave *me* pause. One wizard had been hanging from a chandelier, and just so happened to fall to the solid marble floor the moment we entered the ballroom.

Another wizard had been shoved into a fireplace upside down, hanging out from the throat above the firebox and missing an arm. Strangely enough, the two chairs before the fireplace had been completely undisturbed. Their pillows even had the little fold in the top like it was a photoshoot. Whoever had shoved the wizard up there had done so calmly and intentionally.

I sort of blurred the rest of the house of horrors from deeper scrutiny after that. Aiden had thrown up twice, and even Kára looked mildly queasy before we jogged around a bend in the last hallway before the auditorium.

I let out a sigh of relief to see Gunnar, Carl, and the goats standing before the doors to the auditorium. Gunnar was speaking to his Geri and Freki—the top two generals in his wolfpack—Drake and Cowan. They were currently in human form, probably to more easily communicate with cellphones since they were wearing earbuds. They also held military grade shotguns. The wolves had acquired quite a few gun nuts from the backwoods of the midwest. Veterans and lifelong hunters. I'd once seen the pack's military stockpile—an underground bunker as big as a warehouse —that they'd set up in case any more packs across the nation decided to come piss on a tree that was one inch too close to St. Louis.

It had happened once before. People still talked about all those wolves Gunnar and Ashley had killed.

Gunnar's white coat was liberally splashed with blood and his steadily dripping claws were forming large crimson puddles at his sides. Carl was licking blood from his daggers, humming to himself, and the goats were playing tug of war with a severed arm, bleating and laughing playfully.

"Well, we know what happened to the chimney guy, at least," I said, grimacing as I pointed at Snarler and Grinder. "Oddly, that doesn't make me feel better."

Aiden dry-heaved, having nothing left to expel in his lil' apprentice stomach.

Drake and Cowan were an enigma. They were the best of friends, even though they hadn't known each other more than a few years. In fact, they were more like adopted brothers. They weren't just different; they were different in almost every single documentable way.

Drake was a handsome but scrawny white guy of average height with a mop of unruly, light brown hair. His eyes *always* glittered with mischief, and I constantly found my hand reaching for my wallet, feeling as if he'd robbed me at some point during our conversation. That wasn't to say he was sleazy or anything. He was the exact opposite. He was the notorious confidence man they make movies about, capable of stealing everything you own while getting you to say thank you and feeling as if he'd done you a great favor.

Cowan was tall and dark with skin almost as black as charcoal and light brown eyes that bordered on caramel. He had a perfect flat-top and a thick, bushy beard that he maintained on a weekly basis at the pack's barbershop—run by a fellow shifter. His face had the emotional capabilities of a granite boulder, looking as if he took absolutely everything seriously, at all times. He was the kind of guy you wanted with you in a dark alley in the middle of the night.

To say the pair were opposites was an understatement, yet I had never seen a stronger friendship between two men. I even looked up to them as an inspiration on how to be a better friend to Gunnar. In recent years, our lives had driven us further and further apart, and most of our recent engagements were either heading to battle, in a battle, or immediately after a battle. And I knew that I took advantage of his loyalty and steadfastness. For the umpteenth time, I promised myself that I would take him on a hunt soon. A guy's trip. Maybe we could take Calvin and Talon. *Soon*, I promised. Kára had vehemently agreed, even encouraging me to make that my gift to him at our Yulemas exchange—which had probably been shot to hell, now.

I sighed, frustrated.

Cowan dipped his chin to his alpha in a respectful bow. "Your family and the students are inside, Wulfric, and all the entrances are guarded," he growled. Gunnar's shoulders visibly relaxed. Maybe an inch. The blood kept dripping from his claws.

I let out a breath of relief. "How many casualties on your side?" I asked. "We saw bodies outside."

Drake snarled. "I brought two dozen with me to investigate the runaways. I think I have four left. They took most of them out while they were on patrol. They struck fast and hard. This was coordinated."

"See any silver masks on these wizards?" I asked.

Drake turned to Cowan who shook his head. "Not that I've seen. Just the wizards and the cowardly Fae bastards sleuthing about," he snarled, baring his teeth at the situation in general, looking like he wanted nothing more than to avenge his dead wolves but knew the priority was keeping Gunnar's family and the other kids safe.

"Wait. *What*?" I demanded, only just now registering his additional comment. "What are the Fae doing here and why are they working with wizards?" I hissed, struggling to process the insanity. I'd expected Baldur's involvement, not the Fae. At least they hadn't seen any silver masks. We hadn't either so far.

But a sickening feeling started to roil in my gut. The only thing I currently had going on in Fae was protecting the sets of Round Table armor. Was it 'give Nate a panic attack week' or something?

Drake nodded. "The pointy-eared bastards run and hide in the shadows at any sign of confrontation, but the wizards attack on sight—whether Fae or shifter. It's either the fog of war or they did not come here together."

A second cold pit settled in my stomach as a chilling thought came to mind. "You had more kids disappear, right? These supposed runaways? How many are we talking?"

Drake nodded. "Six kids disappeared last night, four others over the past week. And Tory said five more were not in the gym when she did a roll call after the attack started. Why?"

I gritted my teeth. "Because Fae like to steal children. I don't think this is a runaway problem."

Kára stared at me, her eyes sparkling with rage. "I. Will. Kill. Them. All." Aiden stepped up beside her, thumping his cane as he clenched his jaw and nodded his agreement.

I held up a hand, forestalling them. Then I pointed at the door. "I need to speak to Tory. Maybe I can open a Gateway for her to get the kids out of here. Then we can scour the halls room by room and execute anyone who doesn't belong. At least Tory has been able to keep the kids in line. If we didn't have a Beast Master on site, I couldn't imagine what shit show this might have turned—"

"The Beast Master is not in the gym," Drake said in a grim tone. He stepped to the side and pointed at the doors, revealing metal bars twisted around the handles in a makeshift lock. "We're not keeping the enemy out, we're keeping the kids *in*," he said in a grim tone.

I stared at the twisted metal in silence, stunned.

Aiden cursed under his breath. "This is a fucking powder keg," he whispered, mimicking my earlier thoughts.

"Where is my family?" Gunnar snarled, taking an aggressive step forward. Cowan and Drake wilted in submission, lowering their eyes.

"Wulfra *ordered* us to guard this door with our lives—from within and without," Cowan said in an appeasing tone. "They are inside."

"Your wife and children are the *only* reason the students haven't broken through," Drake added.

Now that I was focused on the door, I could hear snarls and growls from the other side, followed by sharp yelps as shifter fought shifter.

Something slammed into the door and began clawing at the wood, but was abruptly cut short with a piercing cry and then a loud crash deeper within the auditorium.

CHAPTER 27

G unnar reared his head back and let out a howl so deep and loud that my vision momentarily wobbled. The chaos from within the gym dimmed as the shifters took note of the king of the jungle beyond the doors.

A cloud of mist drifted out from the door and everyone jumped back in alarm. Everyone but Gunnar, who fell to his knees and threw his arms wide as he let out a whine of sheer joy. Makayla shimmered into existence, sporting a few scratches on her cheeks and looking physically exhausted but mentally energized.

"Daddy!" she cheered excitedly. She ran forward and wrapped her arms around her father, and the giant werewolf whined even louder, looking as if he wanted to absorb her into his chest. Was that their first hug? She looked even tinier now that her daddy was in full on beast mode, ten times her size.

Makayla giggled and shoved him back. She caught sight of me in her peripheral vision and grinned toothily, pointing at me with a wicked gleam in her eyes. "Dark Horse," she said, clapping happily.

Everyone turned to face me with confused looks. I had no idea what that ominous nickname meant or where it came from, but I played it cool, knowing it would only diminish the victories I had gained with her communication improvements over the past few weeks. I ignored the stares and patted my pocket. "I've got my lucky snowflake," I told her. "I'm so glad you're okay."

She nodded. Then she grabbed her father's giant paw and tugged him towards the door. "Come play with us. We're having so much fun."

Aiden choked and devolved into a coughing fit.

The goats looked at each other with approving nods. "That girl is so fucking *metal*." Grinder said.

"Can we play, too?" Snarler asked Gunnar, skipping about on his hooves.

Carl stepped forward. "I can put the shifters down," he said, eyeing Makayla as if anticipating a violent attack. I shook my head, hissing at him as Drake and Cowan shot him horrified looks and adjusted their grips on their shotguns to bring the barrels closer to the Elder.

"Fuck me," Aiden murmured, grimacing at the Elder. "That's a little drastic, eh?"

Carl cocked his head, realizing he'd said something wrong but not knowing what it had been. "I can put them...to sleep," he said slowly, checking with me.

I winced, shaking my head as Aiden let out a long whistle and took a step back as if to say he was not friends with the white lizard man.

"With a *song*," Carl clarified in a frustrated hiss. "I can *sing* them to sleep you fucking imbeciles!" My eyes widened at his frustrated outburst, but I gave him a shaky thumbs up.

"Oh," Aiden said. "That's a great idea. Not the other thing. And *maybe* don't call the stressed-out guys with guns idiots." He held up his palms in a *don't shoot* gesture.

Carl frowned. "Not idiots. I called them imbeciles. Pay attention. Words matter."

"Yeah," Aiden said, eyeing the armed werewolves warily, "that's kind of my point."

Carl sniffed, dismissively. "Imbecile wizard. I thought we were friends." Aiden sighed.

Elders were no joke with their mysterious Singing powers. He'd once been able to take control of my magic like a puppeteer, effortlessly showing me things I hadn't even known were possible. If he said he could sing them to sleep, I believed him.

"Where is Tory?" I asked.

"She went searching for the five missing kids I told you about," Drake said, pointing to my left down a dark hallway. "The dormitory."

Makayla walked up to the door and frowned. Her hand abruptly shifted into a claw and she sliced entirely through the metal lock Drake and Cowan had spent so much time making. They grunted, looking startled and offended at the same time. Makayla shot her father an impatient, expectant look. His tail curled low between his legs and his ears wilted. It took him a moment to realize that the tiny death princess wanted the doors opened for her. He chuffed and approached the door, his tail slowly beginning to wag as Makayla gave him an eager nod.

Gunnar grabbed both handles and heaved.

Like he'd just opened the front door during a tornado, a vortex of screams, cries, snarls, and growls struck us like a physical force. A chimera stood facing Makayla a dozen feet away. Chimera's were a demonic combination of three different predators, and this one was as tall and stout as Gunnar's current Wulfric form—maybe larger.

Above the shoulders, it was a fiery-eyed, horned ram. On the broad chest was the head of a snarling lion. But to top it off, a hooded cobra as thick as an anaconda made up its tail, swaying back and forth as it bared its fangs at the tiny, tow-headed girl. In unison, the lion's head on its chest and the horned goat head atop its shoulders let out a coughing, bleating roar. Makayla crouched, flashing her teeth at the giant shifter in a playful grin, and then she laughed. "Tag me, Daddy!" she said, extending one hand behind her.

Gunnar blinked rapidly, and then slowly swatted her palm with his massive paw.

"I'm *IT!*" she squealed. Then she bolted forward in a blur. The chimera's cobra tail struck, but Makayla effortlessly spun at a forward angle, swatting the cobra head past her opposite shoulder like she was dodging a tackle on a football field. Aiden gasped in awe, but my goddaughter was just getting started. She juked left and right, dodging both of the giant paws that tried slashing at her, and then she shoulder-charged the chimera in the gut while shoving her fingers into the lion's nostrils and wrenching it to the side.

The lion yowled in agony as the ram's head let out an explosive grunt from the wind being knocked out of its gut, and at *least* half-a-ton of shifter went flying across the gymnasium, sailing over the heads of dozens of other battling shifters. It crashed into a basketball goal and the glass backboard exploded into a billion shards.

"*That* is why I watch her!" Carl snapped, glancing back at me as he pointed a claw at Makayla and then the broken chimera.

I nodded absently, unable to speak.

I saw Ashley in her full Wulfra form wrestling with a pair of weregorillas, but her tail was wagging back and forth. Calvin was blipping between mist and gangly teenwolf as he barreled through vast swaths of various huddles of fur, fangs, and claws in his way. He was cackling like only a kid could, having the time of his life. The overwhelming sound of laughter in that auditorium would haunt my dreams for years to come.

The goats cheered and galloped into the room rather than waiting for permission.

Gunnar turned to Drake and Cowan with a silent command to remain guarding the doors. Then he took off into the chaos, howling eagerly.

Kára shot me a questioning look but I shook my head. "I need you to be the playground referee with Carl before everyone kills each other. They will need all the help they can get, and you two are technically the only non-shifters available. If I can't find Tory..." I trailed off, meeting her eyes, "they'll need some Valkyrie-level military school instruction." Carl beamed at the responsibility and Kára gave me a firm nod. "Aiden and I will go find Tory and the five kids, and kill anyone who disagrees with us."

"I'm going to *die*," Aiden said, emphasizing the last word in a higher pitch and nodding to himself as if verbally accepting an empowerment mantra. In fact, I wasn't sure if he knew he was actually talking out loud. Drake and Cowan shot me uneasy looks, cocking their heads at the mentally-cracked wizard. "And that's *okay*, because today—as scary and nutty as it's been, Aiden—it's still better than your life at the Academy. And dying is *way* better than going to recess," he finished with a resigned smile, pointing his cane at the gym.

He nodded and then glanced over at us. He froze to see us all watching him with baffled expressions and his cheeks flushed red. He opened his mouth wordlessly.

"Yeah," I said. "That was on stereo." His mouth clicked shut and he stared down at the ground in silence.

Kára kissed me on the lips and then she and Carl entered the gym. Drake and Cowan closed the doors behind them and gave me encouraging nods. Aiden? Not so much.

I turned to Aiden and grabbed him by the shoulders. "It happens to all of us. It's actually a great coping mechanism. But it's time to focus now. No more breakdowns."

He nodded firmly. "Got it."

I let him go and straightened, glancing towards the dormitory for a moment. "The Justices at the sandwich joint weren't wearing their masks either. It's possible these wizards are using the same tactic, so we can't underestimate them."

He lifted his cane with a committed gleam in his eyes. "I'll be the bait and flush them out for you," he said. "If they are actually from the Academy, they might recognize me and think I'm on their side. That's when I go bonkers on their bitch-asses."

I met his eyes and pursed my lips, debating an inner decision back and forth in my head. I let out a breath.

"Fuck it." Before I could change my mind, I broke his cuffs with a slice of magic. He gasped in surprise, staring down at his naked wrists. I was relieved to sense that he didn't suddenly triple his power-level—an unfounded fear I'd had that his cuffs had been hiding a deeper well of magic.

I really needed to start trusting people a little bit more. Just a sliver short of paranoid would do the trick.

But not just yet. Maybe once this current insanity was all over. A New Year's resolution.

I grabbed him by the shirt and pulled him close. "If you betray me, I swear to all the gods that Prometheus himself will envy what I do to you, Aiden Maxon." Drake and Cowan watched the uncuffed wizard warily.

Aiden nodded with a sober and grateful expression, determined to impress me. "I know."

I let him go with a shove, cursing myself for nine kinds of fool. "Prove yourself to me with action, not words—hey!"

"*OW-OW-OWOOOOO!*" he howled, sprinting past me and down the dark hall leading to the dormitory. I almost cast a ball of fire at his back before I realized what he was doing. He was sticking with his original plan to flush out the wizards for me. Drake and Cowan cheered behind me, laughing.

I grinned. "Okay. Let's do this." I chased after him, keeping my head on a swivel as I maintained my distance from the howling wizard apprentice. That way I could sucker-strike any wizards who might fall for the ruse.

Dozens of questions swirled through my mind as I stalked the halls of the shifter sanctuary.

Was Tory alive? Had she found the missing kids?

Why were the wizards and Fae here at the same time? It didn't sound like they were working together.

Was Baldur involved with his mysterious Justice associate?

But the biggest question of all was one I'd pretended not to notice...

Why Makayla had called me Dark Horse, and why had it sounded symbolic?

I shuddered, focusing back on the task at hand.

CHAPTER 28

W e'd finally reached the dormitory and had yet to run into any wizards or Fae. Similarly, the remnants of magic in the air had drastically dropped. Before, the entire school had seemed full of activity, but now there was only a trail leading deeper into the dorms. We'd snuck through the entrance to this wing, sticking to the shadows as we found physical cover.

Aiden hid behind a statue at the base of a set of curving stairs that led to upper-level housing, the girls' section, if I remembered correctly. He stared at me from the shadows, silently asking me our next step. I hid behind a couch, questing out with my senses for any signs of life in the large open space ahead. It was eerily silent despite us making all sorts of noise on our way here. The invaders had to know we were close.

Had they really left? Was that why the sense of magic had faded?

What about the Fae?

Aiden had definitely risked his life on the way here. If there had been any wizards, I would have been hard-pressed to save him before they killed him—even with the regained use of his magic, he might not have been strong enough to stand up against a potential Justice. Then again, if these assholes were from the Academy, perhaps they had recognized him and let him pass without breaking their cover. Maybe we'd run past a few of them without knowing, and after spotting me chasing after their colleague, Aiden, they were now creeping up behind us to trap us in the dorms.

I craned my neck, glancing back to entertain my paranoia. I smiled at a thought. Using magic would alert any wizards of my presence, but maybe I could tap into my Fae side without alerting anyone. Fae magic worked differently from a wizard's magic and wasn't as simple to detect from one practitioner to another.

I formed a thread of air and stretched it across the entrance to the dorm, making it sticky and impossible to see. If anyone crossed that line, the thread would wrap around them like a spider silk boa constrictor, immobilizing them. I called up a few more and spaced them a few feet apart in case there was more than one sneaky wizard or Fae following us. In the back of my mind, I debated whether it was Summer or Winter behind the kidnappings that everyone had mistaken as runaways.

And I considered what I would have to do about it when I discovered the answer.

I would *have* to hold the queen accountable, but there were allegedly huge consequences to fucking with the queens. Primarily, killing one of them could send the world itself into chaos, turning nature in on itself. That would impact Earth just as significantly as Fae. Hell, it could mess with every realm out there. Olympus, Asgard, the Elder Realm. All of 'em.

I shook my head, silently chastising myself for my anxiety. I would do what needed to be done.

Aiden waved at me, suddenly looking frantic. I saw him pointing behind him towards a pool of dark shadows. I frowned, looking closely, not comprehending what he was trying to tell me. After a few moments, I turned back to him and lifted my palms in confusion. Then, out of my peripheral vision, I saw something in the shadows move. I couldn't see who it was, but they were human and looked to be lying in wait.

Aiden lifted the cane, miming bonking the attacker over the head. I frowned, shaking my head as I mimed back by waggling my fingers in a magical wiggle. But he must not have wanted to alert any nearby wizards by using his magic. Before I could stop him, he had already slipped from cover and was creeping up behind his target, stepping into the shadows as he hoisted the cane over his head. I held my breath, prepared to grab onto my magic if this went horribly wrong or he whiffed his ninja Whack-a-Mole attack.

Aiden darted forward, disappearing into the shadows as he brought the cane down hard. I heard a sharp *ping* as the metal handle struck something solid, scoring a direct hit. I leaned forward, frowning at the pregnant silence. I couldn't see shit.

Then I heard a choking sound and saw Aiden levitating in midair as a hand held him by the throat so that his feet kicked wildly in the air a few feet off the ground. He started battering his unseen attacker in the head and shoulders with his cane until his opponent smacked it out of his hand. The angle made it impossible for me to see or strike his attacker without hitting my ally. Aiden finally made the brilliant decision to call on his magic, and his hands began to glow. His enemy stepped fully out of the shadows in a rapid motion and fucking *threw* Aiden across the room at an upward trajectory before ducking back out of sight. Aiden's hands were still glowing, so he looked like a firework as he sailed past my head and over the bannister, landing on the second-floor walkway. He struck the wall with a loud grunt and then dropped out of view with a crashing sound of broken furniture.

I stared in disbelief, wondering if he'd survived the throw. Or landing.

Then, like a dud Roman candle, I saw the world's saddest fireball lob over the railing—barely clearing it—before falling down to splash onto the couch that I was hiding behind. The flame washed over it and I muttered a curse as I rolled to safety and called up my magic, spinning to face the threat who had bested Aiden.

I heard an astonished grunt. "Nate?" Tory Marlin hissed, stepping out of the shadows with a baffled look on her face. Her eyes glowed with green fire as she tapped into her Beast Master powers, but that wasn't her only trick. She was also freakishly strong, as displayed by the paper Aiden-plane she'd just thrown forty-feet across the room. "Are you okay?" she asked, patting my arms in a concerned gesture.

I smiled sadly. "My painting caught fire," I said, sadly, grateful that someone *finally* cared to ask how *I* felt.

She blinked. "My heart bleeds for your terrible loss," she said in a flat, unimpressed tone. "I just took out a chump wizard," she said urgently, heartlessly dismissing my feelings as she pointed up at the landing. "But he's not alone, and we have Fae to deal with. I think I sense the last few kids around the corner," she said, pointing deeper into the dorms. "I was scoping out the area when he hit me in the head with a stick."

"Bonked!" Aiden chimed in, his echoing voice sounding dazed and slightly loopy.

Tory tensed, shooting a quick glance my way to nonverbally coordinate our attack against the resilient wizard on the second-floor.

Instead, she saw me grinning and shaking my head. "Um. He's with me," I explained, trying not to laugh.

"Wait!" Aiden wheezed, and I turned to see him using the railing to weakly pull himself to his feet. "You *know* her? Why the hell didn't you *say* anything?" he demanded, swaying back and forth as he held onto the railing for support.

I opened my mouth to answer when I felt the hair on the back of my neck stand on end. I shoved Tory behind me and called up a shield of air just in time to catch a ball of fire screaming through the air from the entrance to the dorm. I had been right! It splashed over my shield and splattered onto the tile with sizzling hisses. I blindly hurled spears of air back at them and shuffled away from the center of the room, ushering Tory to keep her behind the shield. When we got close enough, she ducked behind a pillar and I crouched down behind another couch, hoping that this one would be safer than the last.

I heard a mournful howl further into the dormitory, but it was very close. Right around the corner. Before I could react, I heard Aiden stumbling down the stairs as he gracelessly ran towards the crying shifter. I gritted my teeth and hurled more blasts of air to cover his escape. Tory made as if to run towards the attacking wizard but I hissed at her to stop, reminded of the traps I'd set. She frowned at me, obviously unable to read my mind. I heard Aiden trip and eat it at the base of the stairs, striking the ground with a grunt and then a horrific squealing sound that instantly reminded me of the knee and elbow burns earned in my formative years by sliding across a polished wooden floor during gym class.

Goddamn Aiden. He was worthless.

And he was an easy target sprawled out on the floor like that. I closed my eyes and strained to call up a cloud of fog as quickly as possible, feeling beads of sweat pop up on my brow at the effort of producing it so rapidly and without any outside precipitation to draw from. It wasn't as thick as I would have liked, but it did the trick and saved Aiden from a quick death while also concealing the movements of Tory and me.

"Tripwires across the entrance. Stay five feet back," I whispered to her as I heard Aiden scurry off, deeper into the dorm.

She nodded, and then crept through the fog, cautiously approaching the door but heeding my advice.

Upon me calling the fog, the inbound fireballs had ceased and I heard two people muttering to each other as they cautiously approached, likely holding up shields of their own while moving from cover to cover. I held my breath, keeping an eye on Tory who was angled to flank them from the side once they entered the dorm.

Two men went through the entrance, spaced a few feet apart as they swept their gazes back and forth, wary of the obvious trap I'd set with the fog. One of them took another step and immediately let out a curse as the sticky tripwire lashed around him like a boa constrictor. The other sprinted into the fog at an angle, not wanting to get caught in whatever trap his partner had just triggered.

He only made it three steps before he struck the second sticky tripwire I'd left and crashed to the ground with his hands stuck to his sides. Tory calmly walked up to him and pointed a pistol down into the fog. She pulled the trigger before I even had time to open my mouth. The shot echoed off the walls, loud as hell. She did the same to the other wizard, executing him at point-blank range like he was vermin.

"Waste of good lead," she murmured. Wow. Great line. And a deeper look into why she hadn't been too concerned about my painting.

She wasn't wrong, so I kept my mouth shut. This was her school. These were her kids. There were consequences to pushing a mother too far.

I heard another howl and then felt a rapid flurry of magic coming from farther into the dorm. Where Aiden had fled to get to the kids. We turned and sprinted towards the sounds of battle, knowing that even a few seconds delay might cost a child his or her life.

Oh. And Aiden.

CHAPTER 29

I followed the back-and-forth pulse of magic in the air, but I could have just as easily used my ears to follow the explosions and destruction from the room at the end of the hall. Tory made as if to rip the door open but I slapped her wrist and shook my head, holding a finger to my lips. Perhaps we could sneak in and surprise them under the cloak of all the noise.

She clenched her jaw and nodded, only willing to entertain me for a few more seconds before she took care of things her way. I grasped the handle and quietly twisted it. The door swung open and I saw a wizard with his back to us hurling magic at Aiden, who was crouched down on the floor with a shield, protecting a fallen kid who looked injured, judging by the blood on the floor.

Aiden saw us but his face showed no reaction.

Tory walked past me and tapped the wizard on his left shoulder with the barrel of her pistol. She then immediately stepped to his right, as he spun to his left, and she set the barrel at the base of his skull and pulled the trigger, splattering his brains all over the side wall. She didn't even look at him as she executed him, her glowing green eyes fixated on Aiden and the shifter he was protecting. I stared at the dead wizard, realizing that she hadn't wanted to execute him from the front and risk the bullet hitting an ally, or one of her children.

Aiden dropped his shield, and then collapsed sideways, panting heavily, clutching at his side. His fingers were coated with blood. He rolled over onto his back with a groan and then he surprised the hell out of me by lifting his cane in the air with a weak cheer. "Bonk lives!"

I grinned and gave him a slow clap, impressed that he'd managed to grab the cane in the fog before heading this way. The little girl was scared and anxious, but Tory's mere presence had an immediate calming effect, and she began blinking tiredly as Tory calmed her with her Beast Master powers.

She glanced down at Aiden and gave him a grateful, although grim, nod. "Where are the others?"

Aiden lowered his cane and met her eyes with a look of dread on his face. "Fae took them. I managed to pull this one from the group before they leapt through a Gateway. A very cold, blustery Gateway," he added, meaningfully. He glanced up at me and twisted so I could see his wound. He peeled his fingers away and I saw that his side wasn't only bleeding, but that it was partially frozen from the icicle wedged into his side. "I'm not a gambling man," he said with a wince, "but I'd wager a nickel it was the Summer Court," he said, his sarcasm so dry that it was dusty.

Tory studied him in silence, not looking even the least bit amused. Not because it hadn't been hilarious, but because all she could think about were the four shifters who had been taken.

"I'll get them back, Tory. I swear. Even if I have to burn half of Fae down to do it."

She nodded determinedly, her eyes practically crackling with green fire. I crouched down to get a closer look at Aiden's wound. It definitely looked like Winter, and I could smell the Fae magic on the icicle, otherwise I would have entertained the possibility that a wizard had been throwing icicles at him.

"S-saved me," the little girl murmured, looking on the verge of passing out as she reached out a grateful hand to Aiden. Then she let out an exhausted breath and rolled over onto her side, dead asleep.

Tory turned to me, arching an eyebrow. I saw her eyes abruptly flash a much brighter green and she whipped her head around to stare over her shoulder towards the open door and the hallway beyond. She was perfectly motionless.

Aiden cleared his throat. "I'm bleeding—"

"Shh!" I said, blindly reaching back to palm his face as I watched Tory with wary apprehension. My thumb accidentally slipped into his mouth and I yanked it back with a frown as Aiden began spitting furiously. I ignored him as I wiped it off on my shirt, wondering if Tory had sensed danger, because I sensed no magic anywhere near us, leading me to believe we had taken out the last of the wizards.

Tory turned back to us with a hungry grin. "Gunnar is on his way with Ashley. They'll take care of Ella," she said, smiling down at the sleeping child. She glanced at Aiden. "You're lucky she didn't shift. Jaguars are wicked dangerous when they're frightened. She would have eaten you alive. Girl's got an appetite like I've never seen," she said, fondly brushing a strand of hair out of the innocent-looking child's eyes.

Aiden's eyes widened as he flicked his gaze to Ella. Tory chuckled and pulled him to his feet, completely ignoring his grunts of pain. "What's your name? Punching bag?" she asked, in a much cheerier mood now that she knew help was on the way.

He stifled his whimpering and shot me a wry look. "Well, first it was Apprentice. Then Prisoner. Then Bonk. Then Henchman. But my name is actually Aiden. Aiden Maxon." He winced again. "Damn that hurts!"

I rose to my feet, brushing my hands together to wipe off some debris from the floor. I winced at a sudden flash of pain in my pinky. I lifted it up to get a closer look and saw a splinter I'd picked up at some point in the exchange. I tried plucking it out with my fingernail and hissed as I drove it deeper by accident. "Ow! Do either of you have tweezers?" I asked, waving my pinky at them. "Splinter!"

Aiden looked at my hand, then down at the icicle piercing his side, and then back at me. "You're such an asshole," he muttered, shaking his head. But he was smirking at the familiar banter he now viewed as affection.

I tried using my teeth and pulled it out on my first try. "Oh! Got it! *Now* we can leave for Fae."

"I take it that I'm not allowed to stay here and recover from the six-inch icicle dagger wedged into my ribs?" Aiden asked me, hopelessly.

"No, Bonk," I said absently. "And nobody likes a whiner."

Tory watched the two of us, highly amused but not interfering. She'd dealt with a few messed up youths, so probably suspected what I was up to. Aiden rolled his eyes with a resigned sigh, leaning on his cane to alleviate some of the pressure from his little scratch.

In truth, I was highly concerned about it, but something wasn't sitting right about this whole thing, and I knew the quickest way to heal him from a Winter Fae's blade would be to get a Winter Fae to heal it.

I tapped into my Fae side and noticed a very faint residue in the air. A trace of the kidnappers' Gateway. I latched onto that essence, pulling it into my own gathering magic, and then I ripped open a Gateway.

It surprised the hell out of me to see a tall-backed, blue crystal throne not twenty paces away from me on the other side. A beautiful, deadly, conniving Winter Queen reclined in said throne, and she had her legs crossed. She flashed me a beatific smile and then called upon her inner Sharon Stone a la *Basic Instinct* to slowly uncross her legs, pause for a very notable second that made Aiden murmur appreciatively, and then recross them in the opposite direction.

"Oh, look. We caught her by surprise," I said, drily, stepping through. Tory and Aiden followed in my wake like two angry little ducklings.

CHAPTER 30

W e stepped into the throne room of the Winter Court and it was hard not to take a moment to stare at the icy beauty surrounding us. I casually adjusted my satchel, absently debating which weapon I wanted to try out when I killed the Winter Queen. I felt Mac's snowflake crinkle in my pocket, and the totem centered me, calming my bloodlust so I could focus.

Dark Horse, her words trotted across my cerebral cortex, but I silenced the thought.

The queen wore a simple, shimmering blue dress with no frills or layers that hugged her frame in a flattering manner, leaving her delicate shoulders bare and enough of her thigh exposed that her legs would have passed the height requirements to ride most rollercoasters without supervision. The negligee was obviously designer and part of the *Elsa's Toy Box* catalog of evening wear—the *Let her ho!* collection.

I elbowed Aiden for gawking, and he hissed in agony as it destabilized his wound.

Massive spires of crystal climbed thirty feet overhead, supporting blue banners with a darker blue snowflake on proud display. The ceiling was a thick, fluffy cloud, and heavy snow drifted down through the air but seemed to evaporate moments before hitting the ground, leaving the blue-tiled floor dry.

Guards lined the walls, clad in extravagant armor seemingly made of solid blue ice that was so vibrant it seemed to glow from within. They held spears of white metal at their sides and stared straight ahead, reminding me of England's fabled Beefeaters. Frosteaters?

Clouds of vapor formed in front of my face with each breath and I felt my Fae roots taking charge of my muscles, warming them from within to fight against the chill, so that I soon felt rather toasty.

All-in-all, the throne room was downright beautiful, although rather nipply.

Not only for the brisk temperature, but also for the wonderful attendants working so hard to keep their queen happy. None of them—male nor female—wore shirts. Some of them sported fur capes or fox pelt scarves but nothing to keep the nipples warm and cozy. The attendants were all mesmerizingly pretty, and I knew they were all mercilessly murderous.

What I hadn't expected was to immediately see four Shift students sitting at a long table while topless fairies served them hot wine, steaming pastries, and platters of fresh meats and cheeses. Tory snarled and took a step forward upon seeing them, but then hesitated, realizing they all appeared perfectly happy and hale. Were they the four just taken today? By my count, we needed to rope up fourteen runaways in total, but four was a good start. The students turned in unison, saw their Headmistress, and grinned at her.

"Ms. Marlin! Isn't this wonderful?" one small young boy asked between stuffing his face with jellied pastries. An attending fairy smiled warmly and dabbed the excess jelly off his cheek with a steaming towel before stepping back and curtsying. "She said we are honored guests for being so brave," he added, but not before winking at his curvaceous fairy servant, of course.

Tory stared back at him with a hollow smile, looking like a startled deer. "That's...great to hear, Desmond."

Desmond had used the word *guest*, which carried great weight here in Fae. The Queen sat in her throne, smiling warmly at us but not saying a word. She had not corrected Desmond, and I began to feel very twitchy, wondering what the fuck was going on here with these apparently benevolent kidnappers.

"*Still* bleeding to death," Aiden reminded me, whispering out the side of his mouth.

I ignored him as I stared at the icy queen, unable to shake the scene from that children's book, *The Lion, the Witch and the Wardrobe*. How the icy queen was oh-so-nice to the young boy, Edmund Pevensie, stuffing him full of treats, but only so she could later turn him against his three siblings.

"Um. Stop this. Whatever *this* is," I told the Winter Queen, scratching at my head. "Or I'll have to kill you. I mean it."

Aiden shot me a look that silently said he was embarrassed to be standing by my side after such a weak threat. He winced as the movement must have pulled a muscle in his side, and his hand darted to his wound with a groan. Served him right.

The Winter Queen laughed, waving a hand at me in a playful manner. "Ah, Wylde," she said in a warm, familiar tone. "Your presence is an unexpected, and entirely beneficial, development. I should have anticipated your concern, dear cousin. But where are my manners?" She cleared her throat and everyone grew as silent as a midnight forest under a thick blanket of fresh snow. "Wylde Fae! Nate Temple! Catalyst! Horseman of Hope and leader of the Dread Four! The Winter Court is honored by your presence and welcomes you as a distant cousin and guest."

The servants clapped politely and the guards hammered fists to breastplates with a resounding *thud*.

She shifted her attention to Tory and dipped her chin. "Tory Marlin! Beast Master! Headmistress of Shift! The Winter Court is honored by your presence and welcomes you as a distant cousin and guest."

Another round of polite claps and another icy *thud* from the guards, but tack on a round of cheers from her four students. I scowled at them for making me look bad in front of the queen.

The queen turned to Aiden and hesitated. "The Winter Court welcomes Nate Temple's henchman as a guest." There was only a hesitant smattering of claps but at least he received a *thud* from the guards.

Aiden grumbled unhappily but he wasn't stupid enough to say anything out loud. I grinned at him.

The Winter Queen clapped her hands, signifying an end to the formalities, and the servants resumed tending to the kids, drawing their attention away from us.

Why had the queen been so quick to offer us guest right? And why had she feigned surprise to see me?

The queen turned to face Tory and flashed her a bright smile. "I've heard so much about you, Tory Marlin. You've been kissed by Fae, haven't you? I can practically *taste* it on you."

Tory nodded. "I have," she said in a careful tone. The queen was referring to how she had acquired her Beast Master powers in the first place. During our first major encounter with the Brothers Grimm at Chateau Falco, Tory had lost her left arm at the elbow. A green sprite had sacrificed her life to heal Tory and regrow her arm.

"My sincerest apologies on my actions over the past several days," the queen continued, dipping her chin in an entirely sincere manner. "I must admit, I was shocked to hear that you hired wizards for security after the first ten children went missing. My people—those who survived—were caught entirely off guard this afternoon. Bravo."

I risked a discreet glance at Tory but her face was a cool mask. Did the queen really think the wizards had been working for Tory, or was she fishing for confirmation? I kept my face blank. When ignorance strikes, mask it with confidence and silence.

"Where are the rest of my students?" Tory demanded, her green eyes crackling with fire hot enough to melt the queen's throne.

CHAPTER 31

T he Winter Queen smiled compassionately. "All ten of them are either resting in their rooms or bathing in the hot springs," she assured her. "They each have their own coterie of servants and have been treated like royalty. On this, I swear," the queen said, lifting a hand in a symbolic gesture.

"What is the meaning of all this subterfuge? Speak plainly," Tory growled, clenching her fists at her sides.

The queen didn't seem remotely offended by her anger. In fact, she looked downright empathetic and compassionate. "I wanted to get your *attention*, Ms. Marlin, without drawing the attention of my associates. My men were supposed to leave rather obvious clues behind that would lead you to me, but it seems they either failed or the clues were overlooked. My apologies for the misdirection," she said, indicating the children, "but as you can see, they are perfectly fine. They feast under no obligation whatsoever, but rather as a reward for what they endured at my request. They were never in danger from my people, although I'm told that your new security wizards killed a few of them this afternoon. Several of my soldiers died nobly to keep them safe so that the rest of my team could abscond with these precious little monsters," she said, smiling fondly at the table of students.

Tory turned to look at me, not knowing how to react to the queen's words. I could tell that she was on the verge of losing her shit but the queen's words were compelling.

I studied her warily, trying to convince myself that she was lying. But the harder I looked, the more certain I felt that she had not been working with the wizards who attacked Shift. Which meant someone else had, bringing me back to my earlier suspicions. Baldur and his mysterious Justice pal? Or maybe the Justices from the sandwich shop had made bail and decided to retaliate against me for humiliating them.

Or maybe the delivery wizards I'd killed outside Falco had friends who wanted a little payback.

That was neither here nor there. What mattered now was making sure all of Tory's students were okay, and finding out why the queen was so eager to catch Tory's *attention*, as she put it.

The Winter Queen had been trying to get Tory's attention for some time now. The wizards had only begun pestering me yesterday.

I realized my earlier thought of the queen mimicking Sharon Stone's infamous *Basic Instinct* scene was more appropriate than I had intended it to be. Was she trying to pull a Catherine Tramell on me?

I racked my brain. *Motive*, I thought to myself. *What are her possible motives?*

"Alliance," I murmured, squinting at her. "You want an alliance with Tory, and you thought the best way to do that was to kidnap her students."

The queen nodded shamelessly, but she addressed her answer to Tory rather than me. "To show you how vulnerable you are in St. Louis, surrounded by enemies and solely responsible for protecting and guiding hundreds of unstable shifter teenagers. An alliance works both ways." Her words were soft but impactful and I licked my lips anxiously, realizing that the queen...had a very solid point. And after the wizards' attack, it was even more poignant. She continued, speaking directly to Tory. "Your power is part of Fae. There are those who would attempt to take advantage of your gift. You should be among people who have the capacity to watch your back. How long until your ruse about a school for wayward children draws the ire of the Regular authorities?" she asked in a conversational tone that made the hair on the back of my neck stand straight up.

The queen leaned forward, her pale as milk skin seeming to sparkle with inner frost. She drummed her long, icy fingernails on her armrest. "A Beast Master could climb great heights in Fae," she said in a meaningful tone. "And, as you can see, our realm has a calming effect on one's inner monster. Your students claim they have never felt more serene."

Tory studied her students, nodding thoughtfully rather than outright rejecting the tempting offer. Her current school was on fire, so she was primed to negotiate. Had the queen set this whole thing up, possibly hiring the wizards to attack—for the precise purpose of motivating Tory to move to Fae?

But the queen had been at this for a week, and the wizards had only attacked today.

"What about their Wild Sides?" Tory asked.

The queen laughed. "You mean their *true selves*?" She smiled, drumming her fingers over the armrest again. "I am easing their transition, but their Wild Sides are something to be embraced and loved, not feared and reviled. I would argue that addressing their Wild Sides directly would only expedite the cure for any control issues they may have. They would not have to hide in Fae. They could be truly free, no longer seen as monsters. Here they could even become nobles, worthy of status and respect."

Tory cocked her head thoughtfully, processing the queen's words.

The queen waved a hand again. "All I ask is that you consider it. Not just for yourself but for your students. Sleep on it."

With that, she turned to Aiden, eyeing him up and down with a thoughtful look. "And what is your name, wizard? One of the security members who killed my soldiers?" she asked. She grinned at the nervous look on his face. "I knew the risks when I sent them. You need not fear my reprisal. It was just business. Some juice is worth the squeeze."

He licked his lips, neither confirming nor denying her supposition. He glanced at me, silently asking my permission to respond. I nodded for him to answer. "Aiden Maxon," he said. "Former Academy."

I managed to mask my surprise at his last comment. Not the Academy affiliation, but the *former* he'd tacked on in front of it. Had he come to that conclusion before the Shift attack? During his night of thinking?

The queen nodded pensively, studying him for a few more moments—likely wondering why he hadn't claimed credit as one of the security wizards. Especially with the Fae icicle-dagger in his ribs.

"Okay!" I said, clapping my hands. "Let's circle this conversation back to the center of attention," I said, pointing my thumbs at my chest. "I'm feeling ignored. And I know you're hiding something. If it sounds too good to be true…"

The queen smirked. "Yes, *let's*," she said, licking her lips in an eerily hungry manner. "Perhaps in my private chambers." It didn't sound like a request, and the brief intensity of her gaze told me that something very significant was on the horizon and that she didn't want anyone else hearing it.

She snapped her fingers and a stream of servants filed into the throne room with long fur coats and steaming goblets. They swarmed Tory and Aiden, draping them in the fur coats and ushering them over to a private table already laden with food.

I looked up at the throne to find it already empty and the queen walking towards a set of massive arched double doors at the back of the room. They looked to be made of solid ice. She moved in a swaying, eye-captivating stroll, coming to a halt before a half-dozen guards who bowed and then worked in unison to pull open the giant doors. Once her path forward was clear, the soldiers saluted her and then returned to their stations against the wall, three of them on either side of the entrance. The queen resumed her stroll forward, lifting her hand over her shoulder and curling her finger in a slow, come hither motion intended for me.

I glanced back to see Aiden grinning as a shockingly beautiful fairy sat on his lap, feeding him grapes. Another fairy was kneeling at his side, tending to his injury, but Aiden sure didn't look like he remembered he was wounded.

Tory had a pair of big burly men waiting on her hand and foot. A third was even massaging her shoulders! A violinist struck up a soothing tune on a small stage off to the side, and dancers clad in silk ribbons and streamers skipped into the room. I decided that my life was unfair, and turned my back on the revelry.

"Traitors," I muttered as I fully committed to plunging myself into the icy private parts of the Winter Queen's impregnable castle. Badump-bump.

I gave a stink-eye to the three guards on either side of the tall doors. They didn't make eye contact or acknowledge me in any way whatsoever.

This place sucked.

CHAPTER 32

The doors closed behind me with a solid *thud* and I spotted the Winter Queen seated on the edge of a huge bed that was laden with furs and pillows. Braziers burned on either side of the headboard, looking like hellish nightstands. The room was large, dimly lit, and cozy compared to the one I'd just left. To put it mildly, it wasn't what I'd expected. Which was usually a warning sign.

I folded my arms. "What's really going on here? I know it wasn't just about schmoozing Tory. You *knew* I would come."

She studied me intensely, and I could tell that she wasn't entirely committed to telling me whatever was on her mind. We'd had our differences in the past—trying to kill each other a time or two—yet she'd still made moves to get me here, to a place where we could speak in private. I remembered I was in Fae, and then I took a breath, reconsidering the known facts from Wylde's point of view.

"You know a *secret*," I abruptly mused in a whisper, narrowing my eyes. "You want to tell me something but you don't want anyone to know," I continued, pointing a thumb over my shoulder. "You're either snitching, scheming, or both."

She scowled and I knew I'd scored a point. "You are closer to your Fae side than you care to admit, cousin," she said in a begrudging tone. "It would serve me well to remember that," she commented, and I saw her shoulders relax as she finally came to an internal decision. "The answer is both. But I fear my palace has ears so I needed a pretense to get you both here. When the first abductions went unnoticed, I doubled down this afternoon. Time is of the essence."

I frowned. "You did so well with the first abductions that Tory thought they were runaways. I didn't even hear about it until yesterday. But when I got wind of the all-out-assault today, I decided to get involved."

She cocked her head, reading between the lines. "The wizards were not yours?" she whispered, sounding deeply troubled.

I took a gamble and slowly shook my head. "Nope."

I saw a flash of very real fear flicker in her eyes, but she quickly regained control and took a calming breath. She locked gazes with me and the intensity in her eyes was compelling, imploring me to believe her next words. "I have been deceptive, but only out of necessity."

"Says the trickster spinning tapestries of lies and calling them exotic to pad the sales price," I growled.

"Not a trick," the queen assured me in a troubled whisper. "An absolutely *vital* false flag operation." I stared at her, trying to ignore the imagined sound of knives sharpening in the shadows. "I believe my sister was working with Mordred in the plot to acquire the Knights and abduct Fenrir. Worse, I suspect they had a third associate in Asgard, Baldur."

My eyes widened. "What?" I demanded, stunned. I thought about the completely unharmed kids outside. How the damage at Shift had been caused by the mysterious wizards, not her people. How the Academy and rogue wizards really, really seemed to want me six-feet-under. And underscoring it all was Odin and Tyr's warning about Baldur having a part to finish in the upending of my world. But to sprinkle the Summer Queen onto this shit storm as well? And for her *own sister* to turn on her? "Why would I believe you? What evidence do you have to support this claim? And why the hell would you bring this to me rather than extorting her directly?"

She licked her lips, her eyes flicking past me to the tall doors leading out to the main throne room. And now I realized why the violinist had started playing—to conceal our words from potential spies. She tapped her ear with one fingernail. "When snakes are in the grass, one needs a scythe," she said, pointing at me with a smirk. "You are my lawnmower, or I fear she may turn on me next."

I folded my arms. "What do you mean *next*?" I asked, frowning.

She licked her lips nervously. "My sister marches on Camelot as we speak." My heart skipped a beat, thinking of the legendary suits of armor locked in Alex's dungeons. I waited, keeping my face blank so as not to give anything away. She took a deep breath, as if gathering up her courage. "I believe she intends to collect the suits, and possibly Excalibur, in light of Mordred's failure. That's what I would do in her stead. To capitalize on the death of her business partner. Bargains must be honored. Even in death. And to lay waste to any and all conflicting stories and evidence of my wrongdoings."

The sisterly love was overwhelming. "I find it very convenient that you are pointing me at her when it could just as easily be you."

She rose from the bed and approached me in a slow, determined walk. I stiffened, lifting my hands in warning. Rather than stopping, she knelt before me and bowed her head. "If you believe that, take my head."

I stared down at the back of her head in stunned silence, opening my mouth wordlessly. Her delicate neck was *right there!* It would be so easy to do it. One swift move. Why? Why would she put herself at my mercy like this unless she spoke the truth? This was an act of desperation. Commitment. I let out a shaky breath. "No," I breathed.

She let out a soft gasp as if she'd fully expected me to actually kill her. "If you do believe me, however," she continued in an entirely different tone as her fingers lightly danced up my inner thighs, "Take my head—"

The doors behind us shattered in an explosion of icy shards. The queen gripped my thighs firmly, limiting my movements to a swift glance over my shoulder. I saw Kára standing in the center of the destruction, gripping her trident at her side. The guards outside were writhing and groaning on the ground. Kára looked from me to the Winter Queen kneeling before me in a very incriminating position. Combined with the strained and startled look on my face, I knew I had just earned a free vacation to Chateau Falco's doghouse.

"This is most *definitely* what it looks like," the queen murmured to Kára. "He looked tense and hungry—"

"Okay," I interrupted. "Meeting adjourned," I said, forcefully pulling away from the Winter Queen.

"That's a tactic I use to keep him in line," Kára replied smoothly. "Like fishing. Cast him out and then reel the worm back when it catches a big fish for me to skin, debone, and then fry," she said, her voice light and sweet but looming with deadly shadows.

The queen rose to her feet, slowly and confidently, smiling warmly at Kára. "It is a pleasure to meet you, Lady Valkyrie. I think we would get along quite well. I am also a hunter at heart."

"You two finished?" I muttered, drily.

They both turned to shoot me cool, withering looks and I felt my shoulders wilt.

"Happy hunting," the women said to each other at exactly the same time. Then they smiled brightly, flashing teeth at each other.

"Yup. Let's go," I said, striding away from the nuclear fallout as fast as possible. Kára didn't look at me as I very meekly tip-toed past her.

Kára's glare, however, did burn into my back and I felt like I was in one of those nightmares where the monster was chasing you but you could never run fast enough. Where you were sprinting and it was walking, but it was still gaining on you.

I motioned for Aiden to join us with a harsh, jerking gesture. "Thanks a lot," I muttered.

He arched an eyebrow, speaking out the side of his mouth. "You can't honestly have expected me to get in her way. She already docked me a point for suggesting she was fat. No way, man."

Tory was beaming, way too amused at my walk of shame. "Nate, you look pale as a sheet," she said innocently. "What *happened*?" she asked with feigned concern, biting back a laugh.

"Let's get the hell out of here," I growled. "We're going to Camelot. Now."

Tory frowned at my tone. Then she swiftly rounded up her students. I realized that the remaining ten had joined her at the table, bringing the total to fourteen abducted shifters. All accounted for. She glanced back at me and gave a nod that she was ready. "Could you take us to Shift afterwards? I want to make sure everyone is alright."

Kára placed a hand on my shoulder and I jumped like a startled rabbit.

"They are all healthy and resting. Carl calmed them all down and Gunnar's entire pack arrived to search every nook and cranny."

Tory let out a breath of relief. "Thank you," she said. Then she turned to her students. "Now be on your best behavior. Nate is taking us to Camelot."

Their eyes widened excitedly and they grinned toothily. I idly wondered what kind of shifters they were. They ranged from twelve to eighteen, both boys and girls, and none of them looked particularly threatening. But beneath each gangly kid was a monster. And beneath that monster was a Wild Side.

Maybe the Winter Queen had a fair point about bringing them here.

I ripped open a Gateway to Camelot and we stepped through. With every fiber of my being, I hoped the Winter Queen was wrong about her sister. Invading Camelot would take her all of ten minutes with Alex's limited forces. I found my eyes settling on Tory and her shifters and I realized that the Winter Queen had been more successful than I'd thought, because I was already considering the possibility of turning them into soldiers, too.

The queen had wanted powerful allies all right, but not for future gain.

So that she might withstand her sister's dark ambitions *now*.

Anyone else order our famous civil war special to-go? I imagined a cute and cheerful server asking me as she blew a huge pink bubble.

And I imagined three customers raising their hands with eager grins—Baldur, the Summer Queen, and a Justice. The server then turned to me and handed me the bill as her giant bubble popped like a gunshot.

CHAPTER 33

We stepped from one court to another, and the sudden spike in temperature was enough to make it feel like opening the door to a sauna. I let out a breath, glancing left and right to make sure we weren't attacked on sight. The courtyard was bustling with so much activity that it seemed like no one even noticed our arrival. I realized that I would need to establish a safe and secure Gateway spot or I might rip an innocent passerby in half next time I came here. I'd ask Alex later.

I saw men and women in armor gathering weapons from an armory and then rushing up a set of stairs to reach the top of the walls that overlooked the front gates. I turned, looking up, and saw dozens of archers lining the exterior wall. They stared out into Fae, seeing something that truly terrified them.

"Nate!" a familiar voice shouted. I turned to see Alex and Talon on the upper rampart, both wearing their armor and looking grim. Rather than yelling back at him, I turned and quickly ascended the stairs, feeling my crew following close behind. I skidded to a halt near the outer ledge and clasped forearms with Alex. His eyes were strained and tired, but also full of a fury that was obviously fueling him. He slowly pointed towards the horizon beyond Camelot's walls.

I leaned on the wall, gripping the stone in my hands as I clenched my jaw. A black swarm plagued the distant hills, slowly descending the slopes like oozing molasses. It was too far away to clearly distinguish what it represented, but I knew.

The Winter Queen had just warned me about this.

The largest army I had ever seen was marching towards Camelot.

"Summer is coming," I growled, shaking my head.

Alex didn't miss a beat. "You know nothing, John Snow." Without looking, we bumped fists.

Kára surveyed the approaching army with a critical eye. "We have a day or more until they arrive," she said absently. "Twenty-thousand of them versus..." She turned and swept her gaze over Alex's pitiful forces. "Less than twenty-thousand," she said in a flat tone.

Tory stared outward, her green eyes ablaze. Her arms were shaking and she was gripping the stone wall with her hands as if it was the only thing holding her up. She squeezed and the rock crumbled to gravel. Her gang of students instantly huddled around her, giving her affectionate touches and even hugs. She let out an embarrassed breath and smiled back at them, shaking her head as she apologized and casually lectured them on the insidious nature of unchecked anger. "It can be a poison or a fuel, and we must all learn to use it appropriately or we are nothing more than savages..."

I turned away, feeling pretty poisonous inside. Alex gave me a meaningful look and jerked his chin to indicate his desire to step away and speak in private. Aiden moved as if to shadow me but Talon slammed his spear into the stone at his feet, barring his way with a warning shake of his head.

Kára placed a hand on Aiden's shoulder and smiled at Talon. "We are all friends here, Sir Knight. He meant no offense."

Talon dipped his chin. "Then he can *mean no offense* about ten feet away from this spot, Lady Valkyrie."

I sighed. Aiden had been my prisoner yesterday, so Talon's suspicions were warranted. "Take it easy, Tal," I said. "She'd give you a run for your money. And I wouldn't have brought him here, or taken his cuffs off, if he wasn't mildly useful to have around." I gave Kára a warm smile, discreetly flicking my gaze to Aiden, silently asking her to keep an eye on the wizard. She smiled back.

Aiden smirked at my comment, having not broken his stare-off with Talon. "Mildly useful. I'll take that as a compliment."

Kára chuckled and then dipped her chin at Talon. "Hugin and Munin have told me much about you, Sir Talon. Much..." Talon curled his lip in embarrassment, but Kára was already guiding Aiden towards the wall and Tory's clan. I grinned, shaking my head. The ravens' feud against Talon would never end.

Rather than halting a safe distance from eavesdroppers, Alex continued on, walking the walls with his hands clasped behind his back. Excalibur hung in the sheath at his side but he moved as if he'd been born with the legendary blade. I caught up to him and matched his pace. We strode on in silence for a time and I found myself reminiscing about the first time we had met—when I'd saved him from the changeling operation and the Wild Hunt.

And now he was back in Fae as a king, which brought my thoughts to Tory. She'd had a brush with Fae twice in her life, and now she was back, being offered free real estate to move her school here. This place was intoxicating and addictive.

"I told my people that our enemies want Excalibur," Alex said, glancing at me sidelong, "but I think we both know what they truly want." I nodded. "You need to move them. Now. In case we fall."

I wanted to argue with him. To tell him that he wouldn't fall. But...the odds sure weren't looking good.

"I just spoke to the Winter Queen," I said in a soft voice. "She warned me of this. I immediately came here to see for myself."

Alex furrowed his brow, turning to look at me. "How did she know?"

I came to a halt and leaned my elbows on the wall, staring out at the beautiful landscape in the distance. Purple trees and forests of red grass swayed back and forth in the gentle breeze. The air was sharp and crisp like new spring and I tried to breathe it all in, knowing that the air would soon be full of smoke and the sharp tang of fresh blood.

I felt Alex watching me intently. "She thinks Summer helped Mordred. With the Knights and Fenrir. Worse still, that Baldur was also part of the plot and, with Mordred now dead, everyone's looking to cash out and clean up loose ends."

Alex stiffened, resting his hand on his hilt. "I'm the loose end preventing her from acquiring the suits she thinks she is owed," he growled.

I shrugged. "That's what Winter thinks, and she was pretty damned paranoid that she has spies in her own court. She wouldn't tell me anything until she convinced me to come inside her private chambers."

Alex choked, quickly lifting a fist to his mouth.

I rolled my eyes and shoved him with my shoulder. "So childish," I said in a condescending tone.

He chuckled. "That's rich, coming from you." He let out a tired sigh, shaking his head. "Well, whether she's right or wrong, it seems like the safest bet."

I nodded. "I'll need you to distract everyone. No one can know what I'm doing. What I'm moving."

"I will gather the men for an announcement," he said, scratching at his chin. "I'm not sure how to inspire them against such a massive opposition. The only chance I can think of is abandoning Camelot and using guerrilla tactics," he said, sounding disgusted for even mentioning it.

"Tory! Wait!" Talon shouted.

We spun to see Tory storming towards us, her green eyes crackling with light. Her students and a small crowd of nervous soldiers trailed in her wake but I had eyes only for the furious Beast Master striding our way. Alex rested his hand on his hilt and shot me a wary look. I held out my hand and stepped in front of him, shaking my head for him to stand down. "What's going on, Tory?" I asked. "Did Aiden do something stupid, because you can totally throw him over the wall if he did."

Aiden popped his head out from the crowd. "What the hell, man? It's almost like you *want* your friends to kill me—" Kára's golden gauntlet flashed out from the crowd to grab him by the lapel, cutting his words short, and then she tugged him back out of sight like he was a barking dog on a retractable leash. Talon had hopped up onto the wall and was sprinting towards us in an effort to bypass the crowd rather than slicing his way through a dozen allies.

Tory halted a few steps away and stared at Alex, clenching her fists. He met her gaze levelly, waiting.

"It has come to my attention that St. Louis may no longer be the optimal location for my students and their needs. My school was assaulted and is now in great disrepair." Alex watched her, knowing she wasn't finished. "They need an environment where they can open up and be themselves. A place where they will not be feared but respected. A place where they can be free to live their own lives on their own terms."

"Have you considered Montana?" he asked, not bothering to hide his smirk.

Her anger fluttered at his unexpected quip and a small smile split her cheeks. "Not Montana, jerk." She lifted her hands and spun in a slow circle. "I see a lot of potential here in Fae."

I leaned towards Alex and spoke out the side of my mouth. "In case that wasn't clear, she was not suggesting she wanted to take *over* Camelot." I straightened and gave Tory a faint nod. "I got you, girl."

She rolled her eyes, turning back to Alex. The two studied each other in silence and I felt like I was watching history being born. That something very significant would result from this moment and ripple through the pages of time. And I needed to be a part of that immortal story.

"Are you willing to fight for your new home?" he asked in a sobering tone.

Tory nodded and the kids behind her growled their agreement, their eyes flickering with the monsters just beneath the surface. Thankfully, they didn't shift or it might have knocked a few of them off the wall. "My children have been waiting for me to cut them loose. Most of them were raised in an arena of violence as gladiator slaves. Civilization is harder for them. And beasts are rather territorial, so I don't think you could ask for a more resilient, determined ally. None of mine will run away from a fight. Ever."

I took note of her using the word ally rather than subject. I wasn't sure if Alex caught it, but I wasn't going to point it out. Girl power was a force of nature. Ignore it at your peril.

Alex nodded, extending a hand. "It would be my honor to have you fight beside Camelot. Whether that is as subjects or neighbors is your choice."

So, he *had* caught it. I'd raised him well. My chest puffed up with pride and I tried to look official, as if this had all been my idea. I embraced my inner Merlin and nodded sagely. This was it. The historical moment. I casually shifted my satchel so that it was in better view for the gathered crowd and I took a stoic pose.

Tory extended her hand and they shook forearms. A bolt of lightning cracked across the clear blue sky and slammed into the ground just beyond our wall, followed by a wave of rolling thunder. Everyone murmured in awe, whispering back and forth as they stared at Alex and Tory, who were still clasping forearms and staring at me with startled looks on their faces.

I slowly looked up at the sky and gave a slow nod. "It is done," I said in a loud, somber, wizardly baritone.

Silence.

"Nate totally called that lightning!" Aiden shouted, shattering my moment of glory. Jealous asshole. "I felt him use his magic—gah!" he abruptly cut off again as Kára wrestled him into a headlock and shot me an apologetic look.

Everyone turned to stare at me. I managed to maintain my sagely visage and repeated my historical line. "It is done," I lied, lifting my arms to the air in a dramatic gesture that I hoped would convince everyone.

CHAPTER 34

Tory burst out laughing. "I can't *believe* you, Nate," she hooted, shaking her head as she wiped at her eyes. "Just when I think your ego can't get any bigger, you have to fabricate a bolt of lightning and a catchphrase to steal back some of the spotlight." Her laughter slowly bubbled down and she shook her head. "Come on, kids," she said, turning away to usher them back to the courtyard. "We will have a lot of work to do when we get the others to join us..."

I turned to find Alex staring at me. "Did you really just—"

"Don't be ridiculous," I snapped. "It was an omen."

He narrowed his eyes dubiously. "Uh-huh..." Then his face split into a grin and he burst out laughing. "It was pretty fucking cool. I'm sorry he called you out."

My chest deflated and I let out an annoyed sigh. "Aiden is *definitely* going on the front lines for that," I said, speaking loud enough for him to hear me despite Kára still holding him in a headlock at her side. "Well, it looks like I need to make them a Gateway to get the rest of the kids here. A Tiny Ball wouldn't stay open long enough, and I imagine the students will need to pack food and supplies for an extended stay. Oh, and I need you to specify a specific spot for my Gateways so I don't hurt anyone by accident when I return. Somewhere close to the courtyard would be ideal."

Alex nodded. "Of course. I want to gather everyone around and tell them the good news about Tory and her students," he said, meaningfully, letting me know that now was my window to move the suits. "You could begin transportation after the speech."

I nodded, biting back my instinctual comment that I was the one who had come up with the idea for Shift and then paid for the damned thing. It sure seemed like everyone had forgotten that part.

I assessed Aiden pensively, debating what to do with him. Talon was crouching on his heels, balanced on the wall, and he was curling his lips at Aiden just to fuck with him. Kára still held him in a firm headlock, frowning at me because she could read the cryptic undertones of my conversation with Alex.

"Perhaps Talon could take us on a tour while you give your speech," I suggested. "I want to get a feel for the place in case the fighting breaks through the gates and we find ourselves battling within these very walls."

Alex nodded at Talon and the feline warrior obediently hopped down off the wall. "Come out when you're finished and I will make sure I have people ready to assist our new neighbors," Alex said, turning away.

I motioned for Kára to let Aiden go and then followed Talon. He obviously knew where I really wanted to go because he went straight for the dungeons, not even pretending to give us a tour.

After a few minutes of walking, Aiden piped up behind us. "Do you think Tory will bring Nate's statue here to Fae? It would be a damned shame for that work of art to not see the light of day."

"Asshole," I muttered, unable to hide my smile. He chuckled proudly. I didn't want Aiden to see the Knights, but I also couldn't afford to leave them here a moment longer. I would just have to make sure that I kept my eyes on him until I had time to move the suits elsewhere.

We finally made it to the stone staircase that led down to the dungeon and I gathered my thoughts, formulating a plan. I tapped Talon on the shoulder before he could descend. He glanced back at me, his ears twitching anxiously. "Tell them I'm setting up a protective ward and must not be disturbed until I'm finished."

He nodded, took a deep breath, and then descended.

"I get the feeling," Aiden began, "that we're doing something we shouldn't be doing—"

I heard a sharp grunt as Kára elbowed him in the gut. "Oh, Aiden. Whoops. I didn't mean to do that."

He wheezed, struggling to catch his breath and I shot Kára a grin from over my shoulder. We stepped out into the hallway leading to the dungeon and I eyed the dozen guards lining the walls with a faint shudder. Talon came to a halt in front of the first guard and clapped his paw to his heart. "King Alex wishes for Master Temple to place a protective ward around the cell. I will wait here with you and keep an eye on them until he is finished."

The guard eyed the three of us, taking stock of Kára's elegant armor with an impressed grunt. He dismissed Aiden, which made me deliriously happy, and finally settled his eyes on me. He smiled, recognizing me from the last time I'd been down here with Alex yesterday.

"Of course, Sir Talon. Master Temple. Valkyrie..." he assessed Aiden with a pensive look, not knowing how to address him.

Aiden sighed and called up a tiny ball of flame in his palm, looking annoyed.

The guard involuntarily flinched at the unexpected magic, but immediately realized it was not a danger of any kind. "Wizard," he finally decided, dipping his chin.

Then he motioned for us to proceed, and Talon led us to the door. He opened it with a key and ushered us inside. He met my eyes, speaking loud enough for the guards to clearly hear him. "Knock four times when you are finished, Master Temple. I will lock the door until then."

I nodded, and he closed the door on us. Kára and Aiden both let out sharp gasps to see the eleven suits of armor on the ground. I grabbed them both by the shoulders and gave them a rough shake to get their attention. "Do not say a word," I whispered, using my serious voice.

I waited for them to nod before I let go. I glanced over my shoulder to see Talon's shadow standing directly in front of the door so that no one could risk a gander through the sliding peephole.

Without waiting to explain, I ripped open a Gateway to Chateau Falco's Sanctorum, angling it so that it would conceal the Round Table from Aiden's view. I made the Gateway wider than normal so we could each carry the suits through simultaneously rather than taking turns—and taking three times as long. I lifted a finger to my lips to remind them, and then I pointed at the armor. Then I moved my finger to the Gateway.

Aiden swallowed audibly, but Kára set right to work. It was hard work moving all that armor while trying not to make any noticeable noise. Clanking heavy metal is very difficult to move without sounding like banging pots and pans together. After ten minutes of hard work, all eleven sets of white armor rested on the floor of the Sanctorum. I let out a deep breath and used my sleeves to wipe the sweat off my forehead. The gurgling waterfall in the Sanctorum was a cruel temptation but I managed to ignore it.

We hopped back through the Gateway and I let it close. They turned to look at me, noticing the obvious problem before us. If any guards looked into the cell, they would find it empty and freak out.

I drew deep on my Fae side and closed my eyes, imagining the pile of suits as they had been. I reached out to the stone element of the floor and asked its help in keeping my upcoming illusion spell powered up even after I left. I told it how we would soon be fighting for Camelot itself and that this was the best way it could help us. It agreed, seeming to rise up from the depths of the earth as if it had been slumbering. It had been long years since it had spoken to anyone and was glad to be of assistance.

"Thank you," I whispered, earning a sharp grunt of surprise from Aiden and Kára.

I ignored them and called upon my wizard's magic to fuel the illusion spell. I felt it whip out of me in a rush, taking my breath away. I opened my eyes to see a hazy image of the suits slowly clarifying until it finally settled. I felt the stone beneath my feet vibrate warmly as it latched onto my spell and fed the power of the earth into it. Firm. Bedrock support.

I stumbled as a wave of dizziness washed over me. Aiden was first to catch me, staring into my eyes with a nervous look. "You okay?" he breathed with an anxious look in his eyes. "What was that last part you did? Where did that huge fucking wave of power come from?" he asked, staring down at the floor with a decidedly nauseated look on his face as if he feared it might swallow him up. "Do you have some kind of amplification artifact?" he asked suspiciously.

I smiled back and straightened, feeling the strength of the earth reaching out to empower me as well. I smiled in gratitude. "Real men don't need toys." Kára coughed, biting her lip to swallow a laugh. I turned back to Aiden. "It was just an old, old friend," I told him in a cryptic, offhanded tone. "Now, play it cool until we're out of Fae. The only thing anyone needs to know is that Talon took us on a tour. I'll tell you the truth later."

I knocked on the door four times and Talon swiftly unlocked it and opened it for us. He glanced over my shoulder, saw the illusion, and then a wicked smile split his cheeks. "Is the ward in place?" he asked, loudly enough for the other guards to hear. I nodded. "Good. King Alex will be pleased."

CHAPTER 35

I sat down on the couch in the office at Chateau Falco and let out a long, weary sigh. The mansion was eerily quiet. Then again, maybe it was normal and the day had been so loud and chaotic that it sounded strange now to not have dozens of kids screaming and arguing back and forth. It reminded me of when I once attended a loud concert for a few hours. After leaving, the sudden lack of noise had been so absolute that the silence felt like a profound physical presence—resulting in a persistent yet faint ringing in my ears.

I reached out to Falco, recalling her temperamental assistance over the last few days. *Miss me, old girl?*

The mansion's sentient Beast remained silent, although I could still sense her. I frowned pensively.

Kára reclined on the armrest beside me, leaning on one elbow as she toyed with my hair. Aiden stretched his hands high overhead and let out a loud yawn before collapsing onto a chair and leaning his head back as if to fall asleep right there on the spot.

Transporting the students at Shift had taken longer than even I had anticipated. Close to five hundred students had been on the roster—a number far higher than I had realized—and Tory had even hired more faculty to boot. Served me right for not looking into the budget I received every month. Well, someone received it. Likely Ashley Randulf or Othello 2.0. Once a week, I was lobbied with sweet words, vague assurances, and a glass of fifty-year Macallan that never seemed to empty as one of the vixens encouraged me to sign *here*, *here*, and *here* until I couldn't see straight and fell asleep at the desk.

So, I'd learned a lot about Shift in the past few hours since we'd left Camelot. Tory had hired two or more shifter adults of almost every persuasion she could find—gorilla, panther, lion, wolf, coyote, and even a rhino couple. Those teachers had organized the students into Families—kind of like classes—to both receive their general education as well as the particulars of their flavor of shifter.

That chaos in the gymnasium during the attack had been under the *supervision* of these teachers, so it was rather obvious that Tory needed even *more* help. To that effect, Gunnar and Ashley had already been sending a dozen or so werewolves on rotation to the school to act as substitute teachers, chaperones, and hall monitors.

Long story short, the place had already been a powder keg waiting to explode without the inciting event of the Winter Fae abductions and the wizards' attacks. Moving them to Fae was actually a godsend, because from what I'd heard, the school was now a total loss. Especially with Tory preferring Fae.

I was still suspicious of the Winter Queen and the family drama she was involving me and Tory in, but the solutions were solid and made the most sense, given all other variables. The kids needed a place to stretch their legs without getting into altercations with Regular police—like accidental homicide if someone cut them in line at a gas station or shorted them a quarter when they got their change back at a restaurant.

Aiden had held open the Gateway while Gunnar walked me through the updates on the attack. The kids had suffered mild injuries from their shifter mosh pit in the gym, but with their rapid healing abilities, most of them were already completely healed. Drake and Cowan had led two teams of a dozen werewolves to scour every square inch of the property, but they had found no other wizards or Winter Fae. That had really gotten under everyone's skin because I could tell they had really hoped to find a target for their pent-up frustrations over the attack. In total, twenty wolves had been killed, which I supposed was good news because that meant no more had died after our arrival.

Gunnar's security teams had gathered the dead bodies of the attackers —fifteen in total, including the three Tory had personally executed—and searched their pockets for any signs of identification, magical artifacts, or any other evidence that might indicate who they were or who they had been working for.

An *I Heart Baldur* tattoo would have been swell, but no dice.

He had found no silver Justice masks, and I hadn't yet decided if that was good or bad news.

He'd forwarded me a barrage of photos of the dead wizards so that Kára could work her magic and hopefully identify them with internet sleuthing when we got a minute to catch our breaths. Unfortunately, the Academy didn't have a website that displayed professional photos and bios of each of their hitmen—I mean, Justices. Aiden hadn't recognized any of them either.

It was looking more and more like I needed to have a direct meeting with G-Ma, but that would require me to set foot onto her turf, and if her Academy was disintegrating before her eyes, that could very well be my death sentence. Even if she was in full control, walking into that place with my Team Temple jersey on full display could be grounds for my immediate execution as an enemy of the wizarding world.

After Gunnar's security analysis, we'd spent an hour over a bottle of wine in Camelot, discussing the amazing developments of his daughter in the last day. He spent at least ten minutes telling me about his first hug and how big his heart had swelled when she cried out Daddy at the gymnasium. He hadn't taken offense to me being the one to finally crack through her defenses and earn the first *I love you*.

"That's exactly what a godfather is *for*," he'd grumbled, seeming surprised that I'd been concerned over his feelings. Which meant that I was habitually terrible about ignoring his feelings if he was surprised to see my empathetic side. So, we'd sipped our wine and watched Calvin and Makayla kick a makeshift soccer ball back and forth in Camelot's courtyard. It...had been surprisingly refreshing to hang out with my old friend. I soon caught him up to speed on all the insanity behind the scenes, explaining why he'd had to hang out at my house for hours and hours after the delivery assault, and why Shift may have been attacked.

He'd taken the goats much more seriously after that. In fact, they'd been sleeping at his feet the entire time and he hadn't known. After a time, I'd made my goodbyes, telling him not to worry about me but to get Camelot in order so I could work on the players pulling the strings. I also told him a few sneaky attack suggestions for the war that he found particularly appalling. And worthwhile.

"I wouldn't have called you out for the lightning thing," he'd said by way of farewell. "Aiden's an asshole."

I'd grunted, grinning back at him. "It would have been on your bad side, cyclops!" I'd shouted, tapping my eye and cackling as he threw the empty wine bottle at me, laughing.

I'd taken a walk with Kára, telling her about Aiden's upbringing as an orphan and the rest of our conversation from the night before, hoping she might notice a few details that would lead us to a culprit on the Baldur angle. She'd looked stunned to hear about his rough upbringing, but then nodded proudly. "Those childhoods either break you or shatter you. Like Callie," she'd said, elbowing me gently. "They are victors, not victims, and I can get behind people like that." I'd then told her about Aiden in Shift, and him getting his ass kicked repeatedly but not giving up. She'd burst out laughing. "Yep. Definitely *behind* a person like that—far, *far* behind. So, they took out the uncoordinated passionate guy first." But I could tell she was touched by him protecting little jaguar shifter Ella.

In fact, we caught him talking to little Ella beside the Gateway when I went to relieve him of his duties and give him a break. He'd walked away holding a flower bracelet she had made for him, and he'd slipped it on proudly.

As I'd watched streams of Shift students and faculty lugging suitcases, potted plants, trolleys of food, and trains of make-up crates, I'd been surprised to find groups of werewolves slipping through the Gateway. They carried bug-out bags and gun bags. One of them even backed a box truck up to the Gateway and a dozen men began unloading crates of ammunition, shotguns, and rifles into Camelot.

Ashley had then told me of their decision to get involved in the fight.

Five-hundred experienced werewolves were moving to Fae—at least temporarily—to fight for Camelot.

And every single one of the crazy bastards had been grinning like idiots. I counted twenty different werewolves using the term *Alamo* as they shuffled past me through the Gateway.

I'd spent a few minutes trying to come up with a clever way to combine *Camelot* and *Alamo* in order to give the werewolves a better rallying cry, but the best I managed was *Remember the Cameltoe*, which just didn't work for so many reasons.

With nothing else to do but play human battery to my expanded Gateway—which had been much larger than Aiden's, thank you very much—I'd felt my hopes rising for the fight ahead. We were still vastly outnumbered, but Camelot would have two Horsemen, a Valkyrie, two murder-goats, two mistwolves, and an Elder on their side. That had to count for something.

I had considered calling on Grimm, but there really wasn't much for him to do until the big battle, and if I warned him about the upcoming danger, he would freak out and immediately rush to join me, which would only get in the way of some of the things I had to do to prepare.

Part of me was surprised that he hadn't checked in on me of his own accord. Maybe he was trying to give me some privacy with Kára, because *that* was going so well for me the past two days. I was so tired that she could have flashed me right here and now and I probably would have had to work very hard to convince my body to raise my hand for a quick obligatory feel.

Okay, that was a lie. Us menfolk had the instant ability to perk up— heh—at the sign of a naked woman, no matter if we were halfway dead or dead asleep.

I heard a tinkling sound and my mouth instantly salivated via Pavlovian reflex. I snapped out of my reverie and looked up to see Kára twirling a glass of aromatic absinthe by my ear. I hadn't even noticed her getting up to make it. I smiled and accepted the glass. She'd even used the French Method—placing a sugar cube on a slotted spoon over the glass and then slowly dribbling chilled, distilled water over it so that the sugary drops mixed with the absinthe below, permitting the flavors of the drink to blossom as the emerald green absinthe transformed into the final cloudy, opalescent louche that signified the cocktail was complete.

To my surprise, Kára had even made one for Aiden. He looked just as startled as me to be treated as a fellow human for the first time in the last few days. "Don't get used to it," she said with a warm smile.

He grinned back, accepting the glass. He still wore Ella's little flower bracelet. In fact, I was pretty sure that was why Kára deigned to serve him a drink. "What's the next tier above henchman?" he asked me, smiling. "And does it include health benefits?"

I grunted. "Some of us will start using your actual name. And no, to your second question."

He smirked. "Just when Bonk was starting to grow on me," he mused, sadly.

Kára lifted her glass to the both of us. "Skal." We echoed her and took deep drinks.

I felt myself melting into the chair and knew I needed to get up before I gave up. "You did well today...Aiden," I said, grimacing at the name as if it tasted particularly nasty.

He shrugged. "Wasn't for you. I did it for the kids."

"What about you ogling that fairy waitress? I asked, smirking. "The one with the big—" I flicked my eyes towards Kára to find her arching an eyebrow at me, "personality," I amended.

Aiden chuckled. "That was *also* for the kids. I'm a relatively healthy male with a pulse. Sue me."

Kára grunted. "Be wary of frostbite. I've heard one too many stories in Asgard of men who fell for a Frost Giant only to find their junk turned into a popsicle." She snorted. "A cocksicle."

I arched an eyebrow, wondering if she was lying. She was an excellent liar, so I couldn't quite tell.

Aiden stared at her, looking like a child who had just been told Santa wasn't real. On Christmas Eve. Right before bed. I smiled. "Don't worry. You'll see your waitress again soon. We're going back to Fae tomorrow afternoon."

He looked less optimistic about his hopeful dalliance. So, like a hero, he swallowed his pain and chased it with a big gulp of absinthe. He stared down at the glass, smiling. "Never had absinthe quite like this. What brand is it?"

"Same one you had last night when we returned from Camelot," I replied absently.

Aiden shook his head, frowning. "You had bright green absinthe, not this cloudy stuff. And you gave *me* whisky. I specifically remember because you acted like you wanted to murder me and gave me the cheap stuff rather than the fancy Macallan," he said, pointing at the bar.

I frowned, sitting in silence. "Huh." Something was picking at my brain, but I couldn't quite place it.

Aiden was staring at me strangely in my peripheral vision. Kára piped in to crush the awkward silence. "I was going to buy you some more but the label is just a sticker that says *Pimp Juice*. In crayon."

I chuckled. "Alice brewed it for me after researching it online," I said. Kára choked on her drink. "It's the real deal, as opposed to the over-the-counter stuff with no wormwood. This is au-natural. I put the sticker on there." That nagging sensation came back with a vengeance and my hand tensed as my eyes darted to my glass. I swiftly locked down my face so as not to give away my sudden suspicion.

When the Justice had sliced my hip at the sandwich shop earlier today, I had self-healed remarkably fast...after a night of drinking Alice's absinthe.

Aiden had been stabbed in the side with an icicle earlier today, and he had not self-healed at all—which was totally normal, of course. And he had not been drinking Alice's absinthe.

Had...the little girl made me a fucking healing liquor without telling me?

Kára placed one hand on her hip in a scolding pose that all girls naturally acquired during puberty. "Alice is a child, Nate."

"She was under adult supervision," I argued lamely, snapping back into the conversation to hide my theory. "It was more like a science project."

"Boot-leg absinthe brewed by a minor is not a science project. And the adult supervision argument is debatable," she added, teasingly. I waved a hand dismissively.

Aiden studied his drink a little more suspiciously. "So, we literally have no idea what's in this?"

"Welcome to Team Temple," I said, raising my glass. "We drink anything and fight anyone." I rose to my feet, fighting against my protesting muscles and heavy eyelids. "Let's take a walk before we turn in. And let's see if we can get Alice to make more of this," I said, raising my glass and licking my lips. "It *is* rather delicious…"

CHAPTER 36

I knew they were both anxious for me to tell them about the magic armor—especially Aiden, who quite literally had no idea what they were. But he was a wizard. The act of merely touching them had likely let him know that they were very, very fucking dangerous. But, like a true team player, he'd helped me in what pretty much looked like Grand Theft Armor and he hadn't cracked under the pressure.

That was both admirably loyal and potentially a warning sign of a darker inner psyche.

But that was the name of the game with wizards. Principled wizards died young. I lived in a glass house.

Kára brewed another round of the questionably dangerous—and apparently restorative—drinks, coming to the conclusion that it was better to make a bad decision twice rather than only once. Then we left the office, and I decided to take us on a tour. As tired as I was, I had enough stress on my shoulders that walking was a great way to burn off some energy. Otherwise, I might wake up in the middle of the night with restless legs as anxiety gave me a malevolent little poke, followed by a litany of bizarre questions and statements intended to send my thoughts into overdrive. I had a mental list of the damned things.

Do all dogs bark the same language?

If I die in my sleep, will I know?
Why isn't the word lisp spelled lithp?
Many animals probably need glasses, but nobody knows.
What is the speed of darkness?

I took a sip of my drink, realizing I was already doing it. I led them up to the third floor to walk through areas of the house I didn't typically explore on a regular basis—which is easy to do in a mansion the size of Falco. In fact, I was entirely sure that even I hadn't seen all of Falco. There were hidden tunnels and rooms all over the place, and it would take X-ray vision and a team of ghost hunters to map the place out with any degree of certainty. As we walked, I came to the conclusion that Aiden's subconscious curiosity about the story behind the armor could wind up being more dangerous than telling him the truth.

I had *not* learned that lesson from my parents, obviously. Maybe I'd learned it in *spite* of my parents. Another question to keep me up late at night.

I cleared my throat and began telling them the highlights. Nothing about Mordred or the numerous conspiracy theories behind the Masters and gods working together to pull off the suspected armor heist, but I shared the facts that were relevant to the next few days—especially the upcoming war. Namely, that Summer likely wanted Excalibur or the armor sets, and that they were ridiculously powerful because anyone could put them on and be bonded to the suit for life.

Aiden had turned pale upon hearing the story. "All the original Knights of the Round Table are dead?" he asked, sounding deeply heartbroken. I'd completely neglected to consider his hero and idolization coping mechanism. "I thought they might have been reborn or something—like how Alex now carries Excalibur."

I nodded, empathizing with his reaction. When legends died, honorable men and women cried. I'd heard him speaking to Tory earlier today, asking about Alex. It seemed that the Academy was not that up-to-date on current events, which was concerning. Aiden had been working with a Justice in the field and he hardly seemed to know anything relevant to the world these days.

"So, Talon is bound to his suit for life?" he asked, looking up at me with a concerned frown.

"Part of the job. Great power has a cost. Alex wants to remind the world that power doesn't have to be scary. That, in fact, power wielded by men of principle got humanity through its darkest hours." I grunted. "That would also be reason enough for Summer to want him dead. For many to want him dead." I arched an eyebrow at him. "Especially the Academy."

Kára had been relatively quiet up until now, so I glanced over at her to make sure she was all right. She looked exhausted and was halfway through stifling a yawn. She blushed at my attention, stammering an excuse. "I wasn't yawning at your story. It just felt like the last straw on the camel's back," she said, cryptically, and I knew she was thinking of Baldur, likely trying to determine if any of the murderous threads over the last few days directly connected him to the armor.

Almost anyone who *wanted* a suit disqualified themselves by that simple admission. I briefly entertained the horrifying thought of the Academy getting their hands on them, turning the Justices into nigh-impregnable sheriffs. With how self-righteous and sanctimonious they'd become, the potential for abuse was terrifying. Especially given the fact that Baldur had already proven that at least one of them was corruptible.

I knew the Masters had to be playing in this game, but I simply saw too many cracks for them to sneak into for me to determine where they might be focusing. Every single player could be making moves under their guidance—or the players making the moves *were* the fucking Masters: Summer, Baldur, Cyrilo, Nameless Justice.

Moving up from the nightmare that Justices could become new Knights, the potential for chaos and tyranny only grew by an order of magnitude.

What if the gods got hold of them? Or the Masters? Or the Fae Queens?

The more I thought about it, I was actually surprised more people hadn't rallied to Summer's cause, all fighting to get their hands on the prizes supposedly buried beneath Camelot's upcoming smoldering ruins.

Perhaps they were simply laying in wait, hoping to sneak in for the prize while Summer kept us busy.

I sighed, shaking my head. Kára stepped up behind me and began massaging my shoulders, sensing my anxiety. I slowed my walk, stifling a groan. When it came to massages, Kára had learned an exceptional amount in her brief tenure as a Valkyrie. She'd once told me that it was basically a requirement for them to learn. Not too long ago, I'd questioned her on who she'd learned it from if the Einherjar she saved for Valhalla were already dead and didn't have much need for loose muscles when they spent their afterlife drinking and fighting, preparing to be called back for Ragnarok.

With a devilish smile, she'd teased me that the Valkyries practiced on *each other*. Before bed. After attending the bath house together and washing each other's backs. Since I was an eternal adolescent, my mind had instantly gone down the rabbit hole of fantasies involving gorgeous babes having pillow fights in lingerie.

But the way she had smiled after accurately accusing me of my unspoken thoughts let me know that I probably wasn't far off, and that I was probably giving it more of a Disney spin than it had warranted. After all, they were savage Vikings with hot berserker blood. She never confirmed nor denied her own involvement in such sordid affairs, but she told me a few doozies about some of her sisters that ended up cutting our gossip short and postponing our night's sleep for a few hours as she tried to reenact the story in person.

Those hours had turned into days. Blissful days of sex, reconnecting, sex, cuddling, sex, and playing Shamans and Sheriffs, as well as dozens of other silly games—board games, card games, any kind of game. In short, we'd been wild at heart for a few weeks, popping out only to spend occasional time with the Randulfs, and I hadn't cared if the world was burning beyond the walls of Chateau Falco.

Until I'd stepped out the door yesterday to accept a package from a delivery man and the reality of current events had hit me like a bomb in a Christmas box.

Kára surprised me by suddenly placing a finger over my lips and pointing ahead with her other hand. "Look," she breathed, and I could taste the healing absinthe on her breath as I looked where she was pointing.

CHAPTER 37

Aiden had continued on, not slowing with us. His glass hung limply in his hand and he was staring at each picture of past Temple ancestors. Some of them were family portraits, some were pictures of children playing, and some were simply pictures of husband and wife doting on each other. I saw a tear roll down his cheek as he turned to look at the next picture, completely oblivious to our observation. I felt a fist squeeze my heart.

Kára made a breathy aww sound in my ear, but Aiden must have heard her because he abruptly jolted, glancing back at us with an embarrassed look. "Sorry. I..." He trailed off, unable to finish his sentence. Or maybe he saw no need in finishing his sentence. We each gave him genuine smiles, waving off his anxiety. "What was it like growing up here?" he asked, turning his attention to a particularly strange cabinet of curiosities that featured a pipe, an old rusty dagger, and a—

I glared, pointing for Kára's sake. "A real Native American headdress!" I complained. "We had one the whole fucking *time*?" I growled, recalling the feather boa I'd used as a substitute yesterday morning.

Kára pinched me, reminding me of Aiden's question.

I shrugged, turning back to Aiden. "Pretty normal, I guess. I didn't know anything different at the time," I admitted. "It's not until later that you learn the truth. That even your mother and father, who claim to love you unconditionally, can turn out to be a pair of liars."

Aiden was quiet for a time, staring at a picture of mother and son. "I would have taken a lying mother over no mother," he said in a soft tone, as if to himself. There was no malice in his statement, but...

I winced, not having foreseen how my harsh personal comment would obviously cross over and apply to his own orphaned childhood, making me seem callous. In case I'd missed the point, Kára gave me a very sharp, reproachful pinch to the lower back. I yelped, hopping forward to escape her judgmental claws, even though she had been right. "I'm sorry, Aiden. I didn't mean—"

He waved a hand. "No. I wasn't being passive aggressive, moron," he grumbled, shaking his head. "It's just..." he trailed off again, the smile slowly returning to his face as he stared back at the painting. He let out a wistful sigh. "Would have been nice, I guess." He shrugged. "To have all of *this*...even if it came with a life of lies, seems worth it," he said.

What really drove the point home for me was that he wasn't staring at anything of monetary value when he'd said *all of this*. Not the expensive paintings or priceless artifacts or expensive furniture. Instead, he was staring intently at a family portrait of a mother kissing a young boy on the forehead as he cried over a scraped knee. I didn't even know which ancestor it was, but it looked to be a few hundred years old.

"We all have our chipped shoulders," I admitted.

I accepted the fact that I was unintentionally coming across as being pretty ungrateful for my high-society upbringing, even tossing in a hissy-fit, victimhood mentality to boot.

Aiden had been an orphan, where I'd had loving parents and a long, illustrious family history of ancestors who'd passed on the same principles.

Despite keeping him at a safe distance for the past two days, I realized that he really was kind of growing on me. He had the same kind of snark that I had, wasn't afraid or offended by casual banter—even when he'd been the brunt of most of it—and he had no problem calling me out on my shit. Like the lightning bolt ruse I'd tried in Camelot. I was actually proud of the prick for doing that one, even though it was at my expense.

In many ways, he was exactly like me. In most others, we were exactly the opposite.

He'd come from nothing, and I'd come from many somethings. Yet we were pretty goddamned similar. Kindred spirits, perhaps. Aiden had never had a real family. And the holidays were creeping up. Something he may have never experienced at the Academy. To never have a Christmas was the worst type of crime.

Kára gave me a light shove, and I stepped up to Aiden. With a guilty sigh, I wrapped my arm around his shoulders and began pointing things out to him as I guided him down the halls of Chateau Falco. I indicated ancestors I did know and the things they had achieved in their time. I pointed out areas of the house where Gunnar and I had played as children, sharing a story or two about priceless vases we'd broken in our childhood ramblings. Some of them we'd gotten away with, some we definitely had not. We stopped at more cabinets brimming with strange items and inspected them together, wondering aloud why they might have been saved and cherished enough to put on display.

After what seemed like no time at all, I realized that Kára had masterfully guided us back to the Master's Suite. I checked my phone and realized that Aiden and I must have been chatting back and forth for over an hour. And Kára had let us do it without a single complaint or hint that it was time to turn in for the night.

I turned to her with a guilty smile, ready to acknowledge her selfless act of compassion—

"It's time to wash my back, wizard," she demanded in a stern, no-nonsense tone, snapping her fingers and pointing at the door to our rooms. She followed suit by pushing open the door and entering the darkening room, stripping off her shirt and flinging it on the bed without an ounce of regard for Aiden's presence.

I grinned, shaking my head. Not so selfless, apparently.

Aiden burst out laughing.

I sighed, shaking my head. "The things I endure," I said in a despairing tone. I turned him around by the shoulders and continued walking down the hall. "I'll show you to your room," I said. I hesitated at the door to the room butting up against mine, thought of Kára's declaration of back washing, and continued on. *Better to put a sound buffer between us for the night*, I thought to myself.

I opted for three bedrooms of buffering before finally opening the door to the fourth room. I walked up to the nightstand and flicked on the lamp, motioning for Aiden to make himself at home with a vague gesture. I walked up to the wardrobe and was relieved to find it well-stocked from Odin's tenure. I collected a folded towel from the shelf and turned around, shoving it into Aiden's arms. Then I pointed at the adjoining bathroom. "Shower up, man. Things are going to get hectic soon. You should have everything you need. My old butler made sure all the bathrooms were stocked with unopened necessities, so you should have a toothbrush, razor, soaps, and all of that."

I didn't really think about how any of that might have come across to a man who'd been raised as an orphan until the words were already out.

He opened his mouth to say something and then let it click shut.

"What is it?" I asked.

He raked his fingers through his hair and let out a sharp sigh. "Thank you," he finally said, unable to meet my eyes. "This might seem small to you, but I've never been treated like this before. I was always a nuisance or, at best, an inconvenient piece of furniture. Military living, I guess you might say. The only kid who stayed at the Academy during the holidays when everyone else went home to their families."

I smiled, playfully elbowing him in the chest. "Worked out pretty well for Harry Potter," I said, hoping to cheer him up.

He glanced up, smiling. "Yeah. I guess it did, didn't it?" He hefted the towel. "Thanks again."

I rolled my eyes. "Stop getting sappy. You might die in twelve hours," I said, cheerily.

His fragile smile fractured and then shattered on the hard floor of my barren wasteland of empathy. "Wow. You really know how to kill a moment."

I laughed. "Called brotherly love, man. Go," I said sternly, pointing to the bathroom. "You stink."

He chuckled and nodded. "Truth," he admitted, and then he walked into the bathroom. He closed the bathroom door behind him as I left the room. I closed the door and began walking down the hall to stoically serve out my sentence as back washer to a Valkyrie. A few steps later, I paused, glancing back over my shoulder

My smile slipped away as if it had never existed. "Keep an eye on him, Falco," I murmured. "I can't afford the price of trust. Not with the armor here."

The house rumbled softly, sadly, compassionately, finally responding to me, even though she seemed groggy. What the hell? Was she pregnant again? But I smiled at her empathy for my trust issues.

"Oh, hush. I've got *you*, old girl—"

"Goddamn it, Nate!" Kára shouted from behind me. I jumped and spun, gawking to find her standing in the hall outside our door. She was dripping wet and holding up an entirely too small towel. "Quit talking to yourself like a crazy person and get in the fucking shower before I change my mind on picking up where we left off when we were interrupted yesterday—"

I flicked out a tendril of magic, ripping away her towel. She squawked indignantly, spun on a heel, and giggled as she fled the great, all-powerful, dark wizard now racing after her.

In my haste, and because Kára hadn't turned on any lights, I banged my shin on a side table. I cursed up a storm as I kicked the door closed and began tearing off my clothes. Hopefully, Alice's absinthe washed that injury away by the morning. It would be a good way to test my theory, actually.

But I forgot all about it as I entered the steamy bathroom and the ten-by-ten-foot, walk-in shower.

Through the steam, my Valkyrie slowly stalked forward like she was emerging from a foggy battlefield. Her blue and green eyes sparkled hungrily. "Memento Mori," she whispered, extending a hand.

I grinned and pulled her close, forgetting all about orphan Aiden, rogue wizards, lying Fae queens, magical suits of armor, and the war to come tomorrow.

I kissed her lips, drowning in the sweet taste of alchemical absinthe and Valkyrie lust.

CHAPTER 38

I stepped out of the shower, humming to myself as I grabbed a fresh towel. The first thing I had done upon waking was to check in with Falco to see what Aiden had been up to since I'd last seen him. To my great relief, she had replied again rather than giving me the cold shoulder. But she'd seemed just as lethargic as yesterday, reminding me of when she'd been pregnant with Ruin. I needed to talk to her about protection.

Aiden had remained in his room the entire night, not even leaving it to explore, let alone do anything shifty.

I had slept fitfully, but not entirely restlessly. I'd simply had a lot of bad dreams, causing me to wake up several times. Kára had done her best to exhaust me after our shower last night, but it hadn't been enough to exhaust my anxious mind. Her hard work did, however, require us to both rinse off again in the morning—separately, just to be safe. Accidents happen in the shower.

Throughout the night, the topic of the wizards had plagued me. Mainly because I'd dozed off after making the mistake of tallying up the dead bodies in my mind. Then during the delivery attack at Chateau Falco. Jasper Griffin in the truck. Fifteen at the Shift attack.

Twenty-six dead wizards, and only one of them verified to have been a Justice—the most notorious, non-establishment Justice in apparent history. And, unfortunately, he had been coincidentally removed from the playing field after being sent to find a deadly magical artifact that no one seemed to know anything about except him, Mr. Cyrilo, and the Grandmaster—

Oh, and Baldur's turncoat mystery Justice, who claimed to *have* the artifact, and that he intended to upend my life with it. The convenient coincidences were all in the Academy's favor and undeniable.

Hell, had this freaking whatsit that Jasper guarded ever really been stolen? What if the whole thing had been an act—a carefully crafted lie masterminded by the Grandmaster, or her Academy colleagues, to split the Academy down the middle. Even Baldur's buddy's act strengthened the theory. He had told the god about it in order to get him to *do his part*.

That...actually made a lot of sense.

How *else* would Jasper's alleged assassins know they could pin him down at a specific place at a specific time? They wouldn't, because the legendary Justice did not follow the Academy's typical dictates and commands.

He was a wild card in the way of their plan. A catalyst for upheaval.

That would have been the only way to take him out, and then they needed a patsy. Insert Aiden Maxon, poor little orphan wizard with authority issues. Then give some no-named wizards a bullshit mission to drive a delivery truck with the bodies to Nate Temple's house, knowing he would kill them all and then sit on or destroy the evidence to protect his own ass. *Then* the Academy gets to swoop in and look like the good guys— when they were really investigating their own. Fucking. Crime.

I blinked. "I need to stop watching the Discovery Channel," I murmured.

The problem was that I had no way to concretely prove anything, and a dozen ways to justify a dozen different theories. I needed hard fucking evidence. I sighed, returning to the figurative drawing board.

Had the other twenty-five bodies been Justices as well? How many fucking Justices were on the Academy roster these days, anyway? Had they beefed up their numbers after my threat a few years back? I felt a nagging sensation in my mind, but I couldn't quite grasp it.

On *top* of the dead wizards, I'd also run afoul of three more alleged Justices at the sandwich shop. Luckily for them, they'd survived. But the same question remained. Had they *really* been Justices or part of my insanely logical conspiracy theory? They'd claimed to be searching for Jasper, but they'd also claimed to be working at the courthouse. Had both claims been true? Neither? Fifty-fifty?

The best person to interrogate was Cyrilo. He'd made the call to Jasper that had started this whole thing. Begging that, I could ask G-Ma, although I wasn't confident I could trust a word out of her mouth, and she was ridiculously well protected. Especially from Nate Temple, the one man who was not permitted to walk into the Academy for any reason whatsoever.

I was the perfect scapegoat.

I shook my head, wondering if we had time for Kára to go to Asgard and show Odin and Tyr the rest of the pictures we'd collected. I needed to find out who Baldur was working with, because for all of Odin's concern, the wizards attacking Shift had been the only event to justify him sending Gunnar the two sadomasochist goats. Unless all these wizard attacks were tied to Baldur.

Which brought me to the Winter Queen's equally rational theory—that Summer and Baldur had been partners and were now trying to play a race of *to the victor go the spoils.*

For the hundredth time, I considered simply going to the Academy to personally ask G-Ma what the hell was going on. But if there really was a coup in play, I'd be strolling into a house where both sides wanted me dead —just for different reasons: my lineage or my knowledge.

My stained lineage as a Temple warranted execution from the establishment Academy.

My knowledge of the crimes in play warranted execution from...the wizard revolt.

I would be assassinated or arrested on sight.

Even if they didn't, G-Ma wouldn't trust *me* enough to confide in me, even if I was right—because this magical artifact wasn't supposed to exist, and G-Ma's hands were dirty. Even though our interests might currently align, there was simply no way we could openly resolve the situation.

I realized I had mostly air-dried while thinking, so I made my way into the bedroom, aiming for the closet to get a fresh set of clothes. What did one wear to a war with fairies? Denim or plaid?

I'd neglected to put my dirty robe and pants from the day before into the hamper, tossing them on the chair instead. I grunted to see the sleeve of the stolen delivery guy's jacket peeking over the top of the chair, hanging on for dear life as if refusing to be banished to no-man's land behind the furniture. "Memento," I chuckled, shaking my head as I continued on towards the closet.

I took two steps and froze as that nagging sensation from earlier suddenly screamed at me. The Justice's mask! I'd shoved it into Jeff Stevens' jacket pocket before I torched the delivery truck. I'd completely forgotten about it, more concerned about Aiden's interrogation that night, fearing he was an assassin or something.

And then Alex had bombarded me with the armor drama. And then... well, *life*. Mac's snowflake cutting—which was neatly propped up on my nightstand as my first proud godfather art piece, thank you very much— the goats, the sub shop, the attack at Shift.

I frowned. But what was the jacket doing in here? I remembered taking it off in my office and throwing it on the chair. Kára must have brought it here for me to keep as a memento, knowing I would laugh about it. And she'd been right.

I hastily turned around and snatched it up, shoving my hand into the pocket. I cackled as my fingers touched the cool, silken metal, and a pair of perfectly smooth balls. I fondled them, frowning. Then my eyes widened again, recalling the unmarked Tiny Balls the Justice had been carrying. I pulled the collection back out and tossed the coat on the ground. I studied the Tiny Balls, wondering where they might lead. I lifted the silver silk up to my face for a closer inspection. I stared at it for a few seconds, my smile fading as I realized that finding the mask and Tiny Balls did very little to actually progress me from this level of the game.

In fact, the items only served to incriminate me, which was another reason why I had completely forgotten about them.

"Kinky, but I'm not into men's lingerie," Kára said, startling the hell out of me. I looked up to see her leaning against the doorframe, grinning at me. I realized I was still naked and that I was holding a shiny slip of fabric not much larger than a washcloth.

I shrugged nonchalantly, lowering the cloth. "Your loss." I tossed it onto the bed and walked into the closet to finally get dressed, rolling the marbles in my palm. "Feast your eyes, woman," I said, pointing my thumb at my ass from over my shoulder.

She laughed and I heard the door close, followed by the sound of her sitting down on the bed.

I pulled on some underwear and jeans as I scanned my shirts, debating my options. I finally decided on a white t-shirt with a wide neck and a leather jacket. I plucked up a pair of boots and walked back into the room, sitting down beside Kára. She was studying the mask with a pensive frown, obviously recognizing it for what it was.

She dropped it to the bed with a tired sigh. "Got your war undies on?"

"Always," I said in an epic growl, reaching out a hand to pat the silver Justice's mask.

She arched her eyebrow and folded her arms. "Prove it."

I will neither confirm nor deny that I put the mask of the most legendary Justice ever on my private bits.

Never.

But Kára knows the truth...

CHAPTER 39

After I finished getting dressed, Kára pulled out a sheaf of papers and a small tablet I hadn't noticed her carrying. Apparently, based on what I could see on her tablet, she really had spent some time researching Aiden's tongue tattoo. Carl had first asked her about it, bringing her a sketch of it and asking if she could tattoo him herself. That answer had been an emphatic *no*, of course, which was why he'd swiftly asked me. The old *Mom says no, go ask Dad* strategy.

Kára had already noticed the tattoo but hadn't been able to get a complete look at it until Carl showed her his sketch, which Aiden had uncomfortably posed for during his sleepover with the Elder—probably terrified out of his mind what would happen if he declined to comply.

With the sketch in hand, Kára scoured the dark web, our Omegabet database, a catalog of runes from almost every recorded pantheon, and then an entirely proprietary catalog she'd begun building out from all the magical texts in the Sanctorum. A full analysis of all those millions of books would take decades or more, but I'd helped her single out the top three-hundred books that I considered likely to have the most dangerous symbols, runes, or sigils.

This morning, while I'd slept in like a slob, she'd basically worked the job of fifty military spies to decode Aiden's rune, and...

"Nothing," she said, shaking her head. "I tried reverse-image searches with symbols that looked even remotely similar to his tattoo and widened the limiting parameters to get broader hits, but I found nothing. It's literally a garbage, bullshit doodle. It doesn't even resemble a general theme related to any lexicon of symbols," she said, holding up a page of Old Norse runes, waving it in my face as if that would help me read it easier. "You know how you can see one of these and instantly know it's Norse, or Greek, or Kanji, or Enochian?" I nodded. "His doesn't follow any of the characteristics of any of these. And you can see where it cuts off abruptly so that it looks incomplete," she said, pointing at Carl's sketch.

I had to admit that it didn't look like any symbol I'd seen before. If I had seen it drawn in crayon, I would have nodded at the toddler artist and said, *That's a beautiful giraffe*, before patting their head and carrying on with my day.

"And my last piece of evidence," she said, eyeing me with a warning glare, "I sent it to Odin, since he's famous for searching out runes and hidden magics." She waited, eyeing me expectantly.

"I...don't need to hear Odin's evidence after seeing all of yours?" I asked, crossing my fingers.

She kissed me on the cheek. "Exactly. But he said it's garbage, too. So, it's a bully's doodle," she said with a shrug. "Case closed."

I sighed. "Well, I've been around him without his cuffs on and I've sensed absolutely no power coming from his mouth other than his snark. He's a moderately powered wizard with limited field experience, judging from what I've seen in action, which makes sense. He was sheltered in the Academy as an eternal student until less than a week ago." I assessed her work and bent low to kiss her on the forehead. "Thank you for looking out for me, Kára. Really." I kissed her on the forehead again and bumped my shin lightly against the base of the bed. I grinned, realizing I didn't sense any pain from where I'd bumped my shin the night before.

"What are you grinning at?" Kára asked, coyly.

"You know how my wound healed so quickly yesterday?" She nodded, her smile fading at the abrupt change in conversation, probably assuming it had been about to take a more romantic turn after my kiss and abrupt grin. "I think it's from Alice's absinthe," I whispered excitedly. And then I explained my theory about Aiden and me having different drinks the night before. And my bruised shin being healed this morning.

"Wow," she murmured, torn between concern and excitement, since we didn't know what other properties the little alchemist had cooked up without telling us. "Why would she keep that a secret?"

I shrugged. "No idea. But that's the only thing I can think of. How else did it heal so quickly? It's not as good as a shifter's ability, but it's better than anything I've seen."

"I guess it's a good thing we drank some yesterday, but let's hold off on drinking more until we have a long talk with Alice about secretly drugging our booze."

I nodded my agreement. Another question came to mind as my eyes drifted to her stacks of papers. "Hey, when you spoke to Odin, did you happen to ask him whether he knew about this supposed artifact that Jasper was so concerned about?"

She nodded. "Tyr had never heard of it, despite their friendship. If Jasper never told him, he probably never told anyone. Just like Aiden overheard on the phone call with Cyrilo," she said with a sigh.

I nodded. "What about the new dead wizard pictures? Did Tyr recognize any of them as Baldur's pal?"

She lifted her hand and made a goose egg with her thumb and fingers. "Zilch."

"Damn. I guess the only way we're going to learn anything about that artifact is to get our hands on Baldur or the Summer Queen since we still have no leads on Cyrilo or Baldur's Justice pal."

She nodded grimly. "What about paying a visit to the Grandmaster?"

I scoffed, sharing my litany of reasons why setting foot in the Academy would cause nothing but trouble for everyone, with limited or no gains achieved. "Even if I wasn't arrested or killed, I couldn't trust anything she would tell me anyway. If I admit I know anything about Jasper, I'm instantly incriminated." I shook my head, frustrated. "I'm pretty sure every student at the Academy knows my face on sight anyway. I'm like their Lord Voldemort. I wouldn't be surprised if they take classes on how evil the Temple dynasty was—and still is. They probably know more about my family history than I do," I added, shaking my head. "I couldn't sneak in if I tried."

Kára scooped up the mask from the bed. "Just wear this and walk through the front door," she teased. "On your face, just to clarify," she added with a grin.

I was halfway through tying my shoelaces when I froze.

"I was kidding, Nate," Kára said, suddenly concerned. "That's the dumbest idea ever."

"It just might work. Those masks cover up the whole face," I said, feeling my spirits lifting. "I still have no reason to go because I can't trust G-Ma's answers—which is the only reason worth going. But it's always good to have an Ace up my sleeve," I said, shoving the silky mask into my satchel. I shoved the two Tiny Balls in there as well, wondering if Aiden might know where they went. Probably not, since they had belonged to Jasper, but it was worth a shot.

"We don't have long before we need to go to Fae. Thankfully, the time distortion has been relatively nonexistent for us so far," Kára said, glancing down at her watch. "I estimate their attack starting no earlier than this evening, Camelot time zone."

I frowned, cocking my head at the good news. "I thought you said the afternoon?"

She flashed me a dimpled smile. "I did a flyover while you were showering. Summer will be within striking distance tonight, at the earliest. Unless they have Gateways," she added, "but she couldn't make a Gateway large enough for an entire army to march through. Regardless, I gave Alex and Talon a totem so they can alert me the moment anything changes, and we can be there within moments of the first assault."

I grinned, nodding. "Great job." After axing the Academy field trip idea, and knowing I couldn't set foot in Asgard without alerting Baldur and a flock of his goons, it was looking more and more like going to war was the only option ahead of me.

That's when you know you're on the right path.

The warpath.

"Why don't you take a break while I finish putting my face on," I said, flipping my hair back like I was prepping for a commercial shoot.

She snorted, grinning as she scooped up her paperwork. I turned and headed into the bathroom, closing the door behind me. As I went through the basics of putting on deodorant, brushing my teeth, flossing, and mouthwash, my mind wandered. I envisioned Aiden's tattoo and then sketched it on the mirror with my wet fingertip. It really was kind of ridiculous. I'd seen plenty of strange Omegabet symbols, and I'd always experienced a euphoric visual of them glowing, or rising up off the ground, or flickering and shimmering. I'd also felt a kind of resonance or whisper in my mind, taunting me to recognize it or remember it from...

I knew not where.

I got none of that from Aiden's symbol.

I sighed, shaking my head as I stared in the mirror. "Sometimes bullies are just bullies," I murmured.

CHAPTER 40

I exited the bathroom and paused to see Kára still seated on the edge of the bed. She'd packed up her work and neatly arranged it on the dresser, but she had obviously sat back down and now looked lost in her own thoughts.

I smiled and walked over, sitting down beside her. "You okay?" I asked, concerned.

She smiled weakly and nodded. "Just some things on my mind."

Alarm bells went off in my head, but Gunnar had trained me for this moment—this trap. Ashley used it often on him, and the only chance to avoid it was to flee, because you were most definitely the source of the 'things' on her mind, and none of those 'things' were healthy for you to hear. "Well, I'll just leave you to your thoughts—"

She grabbed my wrist as I stood up in an attempt to escape, and then tugged me back to the bed. I landed on my ass with a grunt and she shot me a cool look. "Nice try, Mister. We're going to have ourselves a talk."

"It's *Master*," I corrected her, rubbing at my sore wrist.

"Not today. Shut up and listen for a few minutes. This is important," she said, her amusement fading to a look of dead seriousness.

Gunnar had tried to warn me, but I hadn't acted swiftly enough. I nodded, resigned to survive this battle and live on to fight another day. "Okay…"

She took a deep breath as if mustering her courage, and then grasped my hand, meeting my eyes. "The way you're treating Aiden is enough to give anyone whiplash. Either you decide to trust him or you don't. You can't do both." She leaned forward to stare into my eyes. "You've been doing both."

I frowned, realizing I should have expected this talk sooner. Like the moment Aiden was out of earshot. "Can you blame me?" I asked. "He showed up in a delivery truck with a dead Justice and a dead Regular."

She nodded. "So you distrust him?" she asked.

I hesitated. "Well, not necessarily," I said. Then I let out a sigh, realizing I was only proving her initial point. "Okay. What are you trying to tell me?" I asked, warily.

"How about we put Aiden to the side for a minute. This first part is more of a general address on the topic I want to discuss."

"Christ. This has *parts*?" I wheezed, realizing why Gunnar had been so adamant in his warning.

But I took a breath and reconsidered the situation. I realized that I actually felt more curious than argumentative. I loved this woman for a reason, after all. To take offense when she wanted to help me right my figurative ship would be as foolish as an airplane pilot taking a hammer to his control panel in midair.

I valued her opinions when it came to assessing others, so I couldn't outright dismiss her opinions when she directed her intelligent insight on me. Especially if it made me uncomfortable. That only signified that I definitely needed to hear it.

I sighed, facing the green and blue firing squad with aplomb. "Okay. I'm listening."

She smiled as if she'd read my mind. "You need to learn how to trust again," she said. "We both know how dangerous it is, so don't bother listing off a bunch of justifications or excuses. Consider your general arguments and bullet points noted, and that I already agree with you on their principles." I nodded, dizzied by the whiplash she created with her sudden full-throated attack and prediction of my own legal arguments. "Trust has both risks and returns; that's why it's always a choice worth thinking about. To trust or not to trust." She met my eyes and I gave her a hesitant nod. "And yet I'm *still* urging you to learn how to trust again, otherwise you are opting to live a life of distrust, and that spreads to all areas of your life. You cannot trust everyone, right?"

I nodded. "Of course not," I said gently but firmly.

"So, shouldn't the same be said about *distrusting* everyone?" she asked.

I folded my arms stubbornly, and I gave her a begrudging nod. She was obviously talking about Aiden, so we must have moved to part two of her lawsuit.

"I watched you two last night, walking through Falco together," she said, smiling wistfully as she squeezed my hand. "I've never seen you that animated and engaged in something non-violent...or non-Kára," she added with a wink. "Perhaps that is what truly bothers you. You only know battle-trust."

"All the other kinds dicked me over good and hard a few times," I said, shrugging. "Exhibit one, Peter."

She pursed her lips at the name, but it swiftly faded into an excited nod, as if I'd just proven a wonderful point. "And that is *life*—experiencing and surviving pain. That is being a victor. An existence of *avoiding* pain is not a life. That is being a victim. Walling yourself in a suit of impenetrable armor is a subtle form of cowardice."

I shifted on the bed uncomfortably. This was getting deep. And personal. "Wow. Irony *and* philosophy?" I teased. She stared at me, neither angry or amused but extremely focused and determined. She was testing my listening skills. I sighed, knowing what she was trying to hint at. "Yesterday in Fae, when we were talking about victims versus victors in regards to Aiden's actions during the fight at Shift, you weren't just speaking about Aiden. You were talking about me as well," I said.

She smiled brightly, nodding. "Yes. A life of avoiding all trust is actually a life of devout distrust—by its very definition. A rot of poisonous cynicism that will spread to all areas of your heart. It is the life of a victim running away from their fear of someone betraying their trust because it hurts. It is the fear of pain. The virtue of the victim."

I considered her words rather than fighting against them. Because I'd frequently given advice to others over the past few years that were bits and pieces of this little summation, yet I'd apparently been breaking my own advice, thinking strength meant refusing to budge, when it really meant rolling with the punches and learning from your mistakes. Not hiding from any and every possible future mistake.

"Did you see Aiden's face last night? As in, really see it?" Kára asked, softly, breaking the silence. I frowned, shaking my head. "His smile...it's broken," she said in a sympathetic tone.

I furrowed my eyebrows. "How can a smile be broken?"

"By the smiling muscles atrophying from lack of use," she said. "From a life of very, very few genuine smiles. On a man that handsome, it is a shame—"

"Hey!" I snapped. "Objection! You're losing ground, now."

She laughed, leaning forward to kiss me on the lips. A long and very good kiss that made me feel slightly dizzy when she pulled away, leaving my tongue tingling. I forgot my objection.

Kára nodded matter-of-factly. "Now, where was I?" she mused, tapping her lips with a thoughtful expression. "Oh, yes." She grabbed my hand and pulled me to the headboard of the bed, encouraging me to lean back beside her. I complied and then waited for my punishment like a good little boy. "When you were exploring with Aiden and showing him your old hiding spots, he was trying to smile along with you. Really, really trying. I swear you two looked like a couple of six-year-olds, ducking and playing in the house. It was transfixing," she whispered, a distant smile on her face—and her smile was radiant, definitely not broken. "I am willing to bet my very soul on this next statement," she said in a serious tone. I glanced over at her, waiting. "That was the happiest hour he has ever experienced in his entire *life*."

My breath caught in my chest and I turned away to stare at the wall... feeling...*things*.

Things deep, deep down within me. It was dark and scary down there. But I didn't run away.

I nodded stiffly. "I agree," I admitted, "but that doesn't earn *trust*. It means he is worthy of compassion. Trust is a much higher bar, Kára."

She nodded. "It's supposed to be. The greater the risk, the greater the reward." She lifted up her other hand and began ticking off fingers. "Alucard was your enemy. Carl was Carl," she said with a smirk, "Alex was a risk, although a child, still a risk. Yahn was a dancer. The Reds were the daughters of Misha, a dragon who was initially your enemy. Tory was a stranger, and you later trusted her enough to *adopt* the Reds. Raego was a hot mess, yet you gave him a chance. Callie didn't even live near you and you ended up working with her on a case for the Vatican." She waved her hand in a roundabout motion. "The list goes on with many more. You brought these misfits together and made them a family. There is always the possibility that the risk wins and you are betrayed, like with Peter," she growled. "But you get up and learn from it—you don't run away from the decision."

I nodded woodenly, unable to speak.

"All I'm saying is that you have to face Aiden squarely, weigh the pros and cons, and decide. No more back and forth. If you can let Carl in, you might be able to let Aiden in."

"Not fair," I growled.

"All's fair in love," she said, kissing me on the forehead, "and Fairy wars," she added. "You need allies, and I've tried my goddamned hardest to rip apart Aiden's story. Trust me. There's nothing. Period. And now you're justifying bullying on an orphan."

I narrowed my eyes. "That's hyperbolic. You know how I feel about bullies."

She shrugged. "And? That makes it doubly true. You had Falco spy on him last night, didn't you?"

"Jesus Christ. Are you the Spanish Inquisition?" I wheezed, clutching at my back as if she'd planted a dagger in my kidney. "Is she hooked up to the WiFi or something?" I asked, suddenly paranoid.

She smirked, shaking her head. "I'm good at investigating. I was a hacker. If there was dirt to find, I would have found it. On the other hand, we have so much corroborating evidence pointing at the obvious bad guys. Freaking Tyr—the god of justice—even gave you evidence and indirectly backed up Aiden's story."

I let out a frustrated breath. "I don't know, Kára. I want to, I really do. But I've been burned badly way too many times. I don't care about the personal pain of failure so much as the fact that people *die* when I trust the wrong person. My people trust me to take *their* concerns into account. Me trusting the wrong person opens them up to danger," I said, exasperated. "I'm not hiding from trust for my own sake. I swear."

She nodded, grasping my hand in hers. "I know, Nate. And that's why I love you and wanted to push you around on the subject. Because I think *that* concern for your people is your Achilles' heel. As much as you pretend to not care and work diligently to show everyone your arrogant side, I think you might be more compassionate than anyone I know...and that scares the living hell out of you. When you choose to back someone, you back them on a nuclear level. So your trust comes with those nuclear launch codes attached, and it's difficult to safeguard that weapon while lowering your defenses to trust a new person."

I nodded, unable to speak. Again.

"How do you feel when the members of the Academy stubbornly hold onto a belief that you are the devil reincarnate? I know you can personally shrug it off, but how many times have you heard it from the lips of strangers? And how did that make you feel? To know that no one believed you despite your actions to the contrary—actions you took that resulted in a direct benefit to the very people decrying your name? Every time you saved them, they distrusted or hated you just a little bit more."

I grumbled affirmatively. "Are...you arguing for *my* side now?" I asked, frowning.

She smirked, shaking her head. "In a milder manner, you're doing to Aiden what the Academy does to you." I felt a chill run down my spine at the words. "He doesn't get referred to as the devil, he's presumed to be a worthless gutter rat instead. But you know who saw good in him?" she asked, leaning forward. "The greatest Justice in the history of ever, Jasper Griffin. Tyr's good friend, the Nazi hunter. That Justice—who opposes everyone in the establishment and who was likely murdered *by* that establishment—saw something worthwhile in Aiden Maxon." She squeezed my hand. "Maybe we should, too."

I let out a long breath, leaning my head back to bump against the headboard as I let her words run through my mind, battling with any and all suspicions, theories, and fears I held. As I watched that battle unfold, I began to see a whole lot of my little stick figures dying, and the Valkyrie's stick figures surviving. Winning by a significant margin, actually.

"Okay, Kára. I'll try."

"Don't try. Do," she said, horrifying me with an absolutely horrendous Yoda impersonation.

I burst out laughing, shaking my head. She collapsed onto the bed and rested her head on my stomach, looking up at the ceiling.

"It could fail," I said.

She squeezed my hand firmly. "Then let it fail spectacularly. I'll still be here."

I felt a big, goofy grin split my cheeks and I squeezed back. "Okay."

CHAPTER 41

After talking with Kára about my trust issues, I felt as if a massive weight had been lifted off my shoulders. It wasn't so much that she had wanted me to trust Aiden—although she believed in him fully—it was that my hot and cold treatment regarding him had been indicative of a deeper crack in my moral foundation, and Kára was concerned about *that*.

Because she kicked ass.

And, in all honesty, I had been judging Aiden with an extremely jaded eye. I'd been at war with myself because of my recent failings with Peter after Zeus brought him back. That old failure in trust had come back and almost gotten Kára killed. So, yeah.

I had fucking trust issues.

But Aiden wasn't Peter. Hell, he'd been willing to run around like a lunatic with nothing but a cane to bonk my enemies over the head with... all so that he could get a chance to do what wizards were *supposed* to do.

I was asking him to go to war with me, for crying out loud.

And he'd risked his life to save Ella, taking an icicle Fae dagger to the ribs for it. Actions speak louder than words, and his actions had spoken very loudly. So, I was kind of anxious to give him a real chance. I would still push him and hold him accountable because that was what apprentices needed. And if I was going to be a replacement mentor, it wasn't a very good example to show him that I was a suspicious, grouchy, distrustful asshole. He needed to be taught, shaped, and molded.

But a few days of knowing him wasn't enough to get the BFF tattoo either. All I could do was give him an even shake and see where the dice landed. To be...a blind arbiter of fairness and truth.

What a fucking Justice was *supposed* to be. I was no Jasper Griffin, but I had plenty of things to teach a rookie wizard, so I would start teaching and leading by example.

I had spent the last hour gathering supplies and tools from the Armory and my own personal stash. I returned to my office once finished, and I found Kára and Aiden waiting for me. I patted my satchel and gave them a nod, letting them know it was time to leave. It was loaded up for war, making me feel both conspicuous and slightly insane. We'd agreed that if we were going to wait until nightfall, we might as well wait in Fae and coordinate with Alex's gathered forces on strategy. That way we didn't have to worry about any time-slippage between realms.

I frowned, remembering something. I reached into my satchel and pulled out one of Jasper's Tiny Balls. "Any idea where this takes you?" I asked Aiden. "I found it in Jasper's pocket, but it's unmarked."

Aiden gawked at it, backing away and shaking his head. "Get rid of that," he whispered. "I think that goes straight to the Academy headquarters. The Hall of Justice," he breathed, looking like he was about to vomit.

I glanced at Kára, thoughtfully. Then I shrugged and put it back in my satchel. "No thank you," I agreed.

Aiden was studying my satchel with a frown. "Did I see you put a spear in there earlier?" he asked, frowning as he visually assessed the impossibility of the question. "I could have sworn I did."

I frowned. "Let me check," I said. I reached into my bag and pulled out a spear. "This one?"

Aiden's eyes bulged and he sputtered in disbelief. "B-b-but...that's impossible!"

My phone rang and I glanced down to see that it was Yahn—the glass dragon shifter who managed the research and development arm of Grimm Tech. He was also dating both of Tory's adopted daughters, the Reds, so he was probably calling to get an update on what their crazy mother was doing fighting a war in Camelot. I tucked the spear back into my satchel and answered it on speaker, already imagining him gathering some shifter dragons to join in on the fight. "Hey, Yahn!" I said as Aiden was downing a glass of water and staring at my satchel as if it might attack him.

"You're still in love with that Valkyrie, right?" he asked by way of greeting.

Aiden choked, spitting out a mouthful of water and almost dropping his glass. Kára glanced up from her phone with a cool look on her face, baselessly indicting me as an accomplice to Yahn's crime. "Hello, Yahn. This is *that Valkyrie*."

"You have me on *speakerphone*?" Yahn squeaked. "That's rule number one!"

"*Still* on speakerphone," Kára clarified, drily. "Yahn, dear, we should really do brunch soon. Just you and me," she suggested in a calmly homicidal voice.

"Did you have a point, Yahn, or am I about to suffer *that Valkyrie's* wrath for no apparent reason?" I growled.

"Two guys dressed up in cosplay are trying to break into Grimm Tech. They have axes and everything."

Aiden grunted. "In the middle of the fucking day?" he muttered incredulously.

I scowled at my phone. "Did you just use the word *two*? Call our security guards, moron. They're armed and ex-military. They'll make short work of these clowns."

"Oh, I did," Yahn said. "One is now wedged halfway through the engine block of his patrol car and the other is being used as a very ineffective human battering ram against the front door," he said in a clipped tone. "Why the hell do you think I'm calling *you*?!"

I stiffened in disgusted shock. "What the hell?"

"Has he tried killing them?" Aiden asked with a thoughtful frown.

Yahn growled. "Whoever the smartass is can eat a dick. And to answer his question—five times."

I shifted my satchel to my side and prepared to open a Gateway on the spot, but Kára grabbed my arm, holding up a finger. "What kind of cosplay are they wearing, Yahn?" I frowned, not understanding why that mattered, or why she suddenly looked so concerned.

"Viking. That's why I asked if you two were still in love," Yahn grumbled. "Figured if Nate pissed you off, you'd probably send zombie Vikings like this to his front door."

Kára beamed, batting her eyelashes at me. "I forgive you for your earlier offense, Yahn. You are very wise for one so young," she said, turning to stare straight at me. I rolled my eyes, grinning at her joke. She did not smile. Mine slowly withered and died of despair.

Yahn grunted. "They're kind of stupid but they don't give up. I locked the door on them, hence their idea to use the security guard as a literal battering ram."

Kára checked her nails and answered him in a conversational tone. "You won't be able to kill them, Yahn. They sound like Einherjar—dead heroes from Valhalla. And if you killed them five times already, then they must be berserkers, who have to be killed *nine* times," she said, sounding as if she was reading off a grocery list. "Oh, and be sure they are not holding a weapon in their hands on the ninth death. Then they must be beheaded."

The other line was so silent that I heard a wet, meaty slamming sound on the other end and I almost threw up, now knowing what it was. Aiden gagged.

"Did you need to write it down?" I asked impatiently.

"Can you guys just come help with this?" Yahn complained. "With the dead guards, now I have to worry about wiping our security feeds and getting rid of the evidence. In broad daylight. Like the guard's brains that are now firmly embedded into the door," he said, sounding like he was about to throw up as well.

I nodded, agreeing with his answer. Because any slip-ups on his part would only incriminate me as the owner of Grimm Tech. "We're on our way. Which door?" I asked.

"Main entrance—in full view of everything. I'm just glad it's Sunday and no one else is here."

I hung up and shared a long look with Kára. We both had the same question. Was Baldur finally *doing his part*, like Tyr had overheard the mystery Justice say at Baldur's home? I didn't see how Grimm Tech was going to help him, other than to keep me busy—which Justices had been doing a whole lot of lately.

"Is this an ex-boyfriend situation?" Aiden asked, interrupting our silence. "Einherjar are the dead warriors you Valkyries carry off to Valhalla, right?" He kept risking glances at my satchel, shaking his head in confusion. As his new mentor, I decided that it was good for him to harbor unanswered questions.

Kára snorted. "This is not an ex-boyfriend situation, Aiden. And yes, Einherjar are very, very competent warriors. Berserkers even more so."

The lack of further elaboration only served to increase Aiden's visual discomfort. "Can I sit this one out?" he asked. "Zombies. Yuck."

I thought about the suits of armor in the Sanctorum. Even with my reconsideration of trust, I wouldn't have left anyone but Kára and my Horsemen here alone with them. Way too much temptation and risk for danger. Also, they weren't mine to neglect. I'd promised Alex I would keep them safe. I shook my head at Aiden. "The house doesn't permit guests if I'm not present," I lied. "Come on. It'll be fun. Who doesn't like zombie Viking bonking time?"

CHAPTER 42

We hopped through the Gateway and into the parking lot at Grimm Tech. Two large, bearded Vikings—who did not look remotely like zombies, thankfully—were shouting and cheering as they heaved their fleshy battering ram into the large, wooden front door to Grimm Tech. I frowned at the oddly surreal scene, taking note of the bright sunshine and the strobing lights of the totaled security car behind them.

"No witnesses, at least," Aiden said, glancing behind us nervously.

"When we get closer, I can throw up an illusion shield to conceal the clean-up," I murmured, shifting my satchel further back on my hip so it wouldn't get in the way. "A really big one."

He grimaced at the two Einherjar and pursed his lips. "Yeah. I'll work that angle while you take them out," he said, obviously not wanting to get involved with the undead heroes.

The unspoken question was loud and I had no answer. What the hell were they trying to accomplish? Only two of them, and why here? Baldur couldn't be stupid enough to attack a building I hadn't visited in weeks.

One of them happened to glance back and notice us. He stopped heaving and dropped his half of the mutilated security guard, throwing his partner off balance and almost knocking him down in the process. He opened his mouth to demand an explanation of his buddy, only to find him pointing in our direction.

Kára stormed forward, her armor whispering into place, along with her trident.

They saw the furious Valkyrie and cheered like maniacs, drawing their axes. Then they rushed towards her in a hopeless attempt for a fair fight.

Kára lunged forward and impaled the first one in the stomach before flipping him into the air and overhead like a catapult. "Alley-oop, Bonk!" she cackled, already blocking the second warrior.

Aiden let loose a blast of fire, lighting him up before he even hit the ground. He screamed as the flames engulfed his precious beard, and then he grunted as he hit the pavement face-first with a sharp *crack* that signified a broken neck. His head lolled to the side and his body grew still. Aiden let out a breath and shot me a nervous smile. "Should we assume that's number six?" he asked as the sounds of metal on metal continued from Kára and the other Viking.

I walked up to the smoldering Viking, prepared to wait for him to rise back to life so I could kill him again. Three more times. He was still gripping his axe, so I kicked it out of his hand, remembering Kára's advice. I'd already known that little superstition—that to go to Valhalla upon death, one must be holding a weapon at time of death. My peripheral vision caught movement and I instinctively grabbed Aiden's arm and Shadow Walked us twenty feet away.

Aiden grunted to see a much larger third Viking slamming a two-handed axe into the ground where he'd just been standing. I'd barely gotten him clear. I gritted my teeth. So, that was Baldur's angle. The first two had been bait for the trap. Duh.

"Your friend sucks at counting," Aiden growled, glaring at the third Viking. He only thought so because we hadn't told him about Baldur. Another appeared out of thin air, but this one was accompanied by a wizard, explaining how the first three had arrived.

I grinned wolfishly to see that this wizard—unlike all the rest I had encountered—was actually wearing the familiar silver mask of a Justice. "Bingo," I snarled, hurling a spear of air at the wizard. He Shadow Walked away, leaving the Viking to take the spear in the throat. I let out a curse and began spinning in a slow circle. Aiden instinctively backed up against me so we could get a full circle view.

"That Justice is Shadow Walking them in," I snarled. "Which means he's been watching this entire time. Waiting for us to arrive. No illusion wall for you. I need my Bonker."

Aiden swore, casting out dual fireballs. Judging by the immediate screams, he had good aim. "Two more of them?" he complained from over his shoulder. "That's four."

I called up my whips of fire and ice, wanting to be ready to strike in an instant. Baldur's apparent plan wasn't half bad, to be honest. Especially if he happened to be recording this.

But it was too late to worry about that danger. The only way to avoid it was to let them kill me or flee—and fleeing would ultimately result in police coming to the scene and finding dead cops at the front door to my company. I wouldn't be immediately guilty, but the press would slaughter me and the attorneys' lawsuits would be the equivalent of death by...filing squad.

I kept my eyes unfocused, counting on the instincts of my peripheral vision. "We have to take out the Justice or he's going to keep sending reinforcements," I muttered.

Aiden grunted. "Take out the Justice. Just like that. One of the Academy's most powerful wizards," he griped, launching more attacks. I saw Kára flicker into view, decapitating the newest Viking who had almost killed Aiden, but I paid her no mind. If that Justice didn't die, we would be here all day, and any moment a police car might drive by on a casual patrol. Luckily, I heard no sirens, so no one had called in a disturbance.

"I'll take the Justice," I said in a calm tone. "You're the zombie bonker. Just keep them back."

"The one Kára just killed didn't get back up," he said, thoughtfully. "I'm switching to decapitation."

"It's probably because she's a Valkyrie, so she doesn't need to kill them nine times, but pick your poison and keep them back. Three left," I added, wanting to keep up a verbal count.

I let out a breath and waited. I heard a Viking get alarmingly close before Aiden sliced him in half with a blade of air. Blood sprayed across my face and a one-handed axe skittered across the ground, before the haft slammed into my shinbone. I cursed at the flash of pain and kicked the axe away. "Do *better!*" I growled at Aiden. "I'm trying to focus over here."

He responded in an apologetic grunt.

Kára swooped back into view, her metallic wings catching the sun's reflection like a flare. It almost caused me to miss the flicker of movement to my right, but my reflexes were just sharp enough and I instantly lashed out with both whips, fueling them with as much power as I could. They wrapped around the Justice's throat a millisecond after he reappeared with a new double shipment of Vikings, bringing the living total to five. Before he could counter, nullify my magic, or escape, I heaved my arms wide open and ripped his head from his shoulders. The force of my motion also caused my screaming whips to slice through both Vikings he had transported.

"Got him!" I crowed for Aiden's benefit. "That's a threefer!"

He stumbled into my back with a grunt, blocking something before returning fire. "Stop distracting me," he growled.

Kára raced down from the sky and buried her trident into the chest of one of the newest arrivals. Then she plucked the hatchet from his dead fingers and buried it in his throat, decapitating him. She swiftly disarmed the other Viking and used his own weapon to hack his head off as well. Then she rose to her feet and kicked the heads away for good measure. She turned to face me and my heart momentarily skipped a beat to see the dreaded Valkyrie holding an axe in each hand, her armor and face dripping with blood that seemed to sparkle in the sunlight shining down upon her. She smiled at me with her teeth and winked.

From computer hacker to Valkyrie hacker, I thought to myself, sweeping my focus across the parking lot to check how many we had left. Aiden hurled a rapid series of fireballs and then let out a deep breath. "That's the last one," he wheezed. "Have Kára do her Mortal Kombat Fatality thing."

I chuckled, lowering my hands as Kára hopped to it of her own accord. Her trident was no longer buried in the Viking's chest, so she must have used her power to call it back—or however that bit of recall worked. I opened my mouth to congratulate Aiden, but I was interrupted by a wet squelching sound, and then a metallic clang. I frowned, spinning to face him. Hadn't he just said he got the last one a few seconds ago?

He crashed to his knees, clutching his stomach. I mimicked him, crashing to my knees to try and help him staunch the blood flow. My eyes widened to see a fatal amount of blood pulsing out from behind his hand and liberally dripping down his fingers and wrist.

It looked like he was holding his insides...*inside.*

CHAPTER 43

Alice's absinthe wasn't going to fix this one. "I thought you got the last one?" I growled, furiously.

He nodded, grimacing in pain. "Not before he threw an axe into my gut," he whispered, indicating the bloody axe next to us. I remembered him stumbling into my back with a grunt and my blood ran cold.

He'd kept fighting after being impaled by an axe? Kára rushed over, and I saw Yahn and the Reds sprinting across the parking lot from the now open door to Grimm Tech.

I stared down at his wound and pursed my lips. "I need to get him to a healer. Now," I told Kára. She nodded with a nod that wasn't even remotely optimistic, but I ignored her pessimism. Without Aiden, that last Viking would have had a clear shot at my back. I had to at least try.

"We will clean this up," she said, just as the dragons skidded to a halt.

I clenched my jaw, having forgotten all about clean-up. There was no way they could get rid of all these bodies, the blood, and the security car without magic. What if a pedestrian's curiosity convinced them to discover the source of the strobing red and blue lights?

Aiden collapsed to his side with a groan. "Do your best and as fast as you can," I growled, scooping Aiden up into my arms in a cradle grip and rising to my feet. "I'll be back as soon as I can." I ripped open a Gateway to

Fae, remembering the healers Talon had taken Aiden to yesterday. I ignored the gurgling, whimpering, panting gasps coming from Aiden's throat the same way I ignored the alarming amount of blood dripping down my hands as I leapt through the Gateway and stepped into the clear spot Alex had designated for me near Camelot's courtyard.

"HEALER! NOW!" I screamed at a gang of startled shifters less than ten feet away. They took one look at Aiden and then burst into action, shouting as they raced towards a man in beige robes who was carrying a stack of blankets towards a tent on the other side of the courtyard. He had already turned to look upon hearing my hoarse scream. He blindly shoved the blankets into the first shifter's hands and sprinted towards me. His hands began to glow before he was even halfway to me, and then dozens of streamers of golden light lashed out of his fingers and slammed into Aiden like harpoons. I stumbled as my apprentice cried out, arching his back in agony, and then he went limp in my arms right as the healer reached me.

I stared down at Aiden with wide, guilty, fearful eyes. *No, no, no, no, no!* I screamed at myself. *He was your responsibility and you failed him! He trusted you, but you didn't trust him. Some mentor you are...*

I ground my teeth together, silencing the self-sabotaging taunts as I felt a tear roll down my cheek. Had the healer been too late to save him? "Come on, Aiden! I can't go to war without Bonk!" I snarled, holding him tight to my chest in an effort to slow any blood loss, or at least comfort him.

Aiden took a shallow breath and my knees buckled in relief. The healer took him from my arms as if Aiden weighed nothing and turned away from me, already taking swift strides towards the tent. I saw a trio of women inside preparing a cot and motioning for the man to hurry. I jogged after him, ignoring the blood literally soaking my clothes as I kept my eyes on Aiden. As I stared down at him, I cringed at how fucking *big* the axe wound was. It had almost sliced halfway through his waist. My eyes flicked to the healer with an idle frown, recalling his strange power. I hadn't sensed magic or anything from my Fae side. Yet it had seemed familiar.

"What was that?" I asked, keeping pace at his side. "Your magic wasn't from Fae and you're not a wizard."

He wouldn't meet my eyes. "A gift."

I studied Aiden's shallow breathing, recalling the golden tendrils of power. I sucked in a breath, suddenly remembering where I'd seen something similar. It hit me like a punch to the gut. "*Pan* healed like that," I whispered.

The man closed his eyes and clenched his jaw. "Yes. He *did*." He opened his eyes again and turned his head to glare at me. "Unless you want him to die, I implore you to fuck off."

I skidded to a halt, stunned at his crass words to me—a complete stranger. He continued on, shouting out demands to the three women under the tent. I saw him set Aiden down and then the four of them began fussing over him, cutting off his clothes with shears. The man saw me watching, glared, and aggressively tugged a rope that released a curtain, cutting off my view.

Gunnar and Talon skidded to a halt beside me. "What happened? We heard you arrived covered in blood and screaming for a healer," he said, checking me over with a critical eye. Seeing that the blood soaking me was obviously not mine, he followed my gaze to look inside the tent.

Talon sucked in a breath. "The Valkyrie?" he spat furiously, his pupils narrowing to slits as his ears tucked straight back and began to quiver.

I shook my head, feeling numb. "Aiden. Took an axe to the stomach to save my life," I said, woodenly.

Gunnar placed an arm around my shoulder. "You look like you need to sit down, Brother. Let's grab a drink while we wait to see what the healer says. He's rough with his tongue, but great with his hands and his magic. We have hours until Summer arrives with her army—"

I shrugged off his arm and shook my head. "I can't, Brother. I need to go. Tell Tory that Yahn and the Reds will be here soon," I said in a hoarse, hollow voice.

I didn't wait for a response as I Shadow Walked back to Grimm Tech.

I hit the parking lot and stumbled, feeling hollowed out and numb. I beat it down, knowing this was not the time to lose my shit.

A hose was stretched out across the parking lot and I saw Kára spraying a jet of water at the bloodstains, directing them towards a storm drain. She was soaked as well, apparently having washed off the blood that had covered her armor and face from earlier. Aria was already rolling up a second hose, and I saw the results of her work on the water-soaked, paved walkway leading to the main entrance. I couldn't see a drop of blood anywhere. I sent up a silent prayer to the climate gods of Missouri, thanking them for the fifty-something-degree weather.

Kára spotted me and froze with a nervous smile on her face. I shrugged to let her know I had no answer on Aiden. Then I hurried over to the patrol car to do my part of the clean-up. I gagged as my eyes processed the fact that they had piled the bodies and severed heads onto the seats, turning it into a macabre clown car. And, of course, the two security officers were on top—the only two victims that I actually felt empathy for. I didn't even know their names.

I turned away and took several deep breaths, making sure I wasn't going to vomit. Then I reenacted my double Gateway trick from Chateau Falco and sent a waterfall to punch the nightmarish scene into a desert on the opposite side of the world. I let them close and shook my head at an idle thought. Whoever someday stumbled onto that patch of earth was going to be forever confused and broken inside.

Yahn was furiously scrubbing the door with two wire brushes and Sonya was steadily walking backwards with a big plastic gas canister in her arms, pouring a trail of the flammable liquid over the bushes in her wake. Why not add arson to our list of crimes? Aria joined her with a second canister, covering the grass and mulching around the pavement—where any blood would have been sprayed. Yahn got out of Sonya's way and she liberally soaked the door with the accelerant before pouring the rest on the bushes on the opposite side of the door. She flung the container behind her and I saw that both girls were wearing gloves to prevent fingerprints. Aria finished up the other side of the walkway and tossed her empty canister into the parking lot as well. I was both creeped out and proud of how calm and efficient their criminal operation was.

Yahn spotted me and jogged over. Behind him, Aria and Sonya stripped down to their skins and abruptly shifted into red dragons. Without missing a beat, they unleashed a wild torrent of flame that covered the whole front wall and the entirety of the landscaping. The gas went up in a *whoompf,* spreading the flames for them as they focused their attention on the most problematic areas for evidence collection. Especially the thick wooden door, which likely had flesh and bone embedded in its axe-marred surface.

Yahn slowed as he drew closer, glancing back at his girlfriends with an approving nod.

I frowned at the charred, still-burning, hacked door. "Clever, but not inconspicuous," I said, not wanting to invite an opening for him to ask about Aiden.

Yahn grunted. "I'll call it in as someone who hates you fire-bombing the place. Our security guards took off after them and we haven't seen them since. They ran that way," he said, pointing a finger in a randomly chosen direction. Yahn turned to me with a smug grin. "I'll take care of their families," he said sadly. "That's all we can do."

I forced myself to smile and shook my head. "Good job." I didn't mention my fear that Baldur may have been recording the whole thing anyway. It wasn't worth mentioning because if it were true, he would have already caught us using magic on camera. What was a little crime scene clean-up on top of that?

But in the back of my mind, I couldn't figure out what he'd actually accomplished. Other than possibly killing Aiden, maybe. But why would that matter? They'd been trying to kill all of us. And I now had my own proof that Justices were working with Baldur. Had I just killed the half-face Justice Tyr had seen?

Yahn took note of my distraction and made a shooing motion with his hand. "I need to call the police, and you need to leave. I still have to spray the fire extinguishers everywhere to further contaminate any evidence the fire might have missed. If I make it look dramatic enough, they won't have any reason to look for evidence."

Kára had finished and was rolling the hose back up to the wall on the side of the building. The Reds had shifted back and were hurriedly tugging their clothes back on.

Yahn glanced over at me, sensing that my nerves were raw. "Tory informed us of her relocation decision. Raego is already gathering his forces and intends to join in on the fight," he said, casually.

I closed my eyes and nodded. "Thank you," I whispered. That could make all the difference in the war. Or none at all. Twenty-thousand was a big number to take on.

"We will head that way once we finish up with the police," he added.

I frowned at a new thought. "Why were you even here?"

He turned to face me. "I wanted to make sure the Vault was securely locked up before we left town." I frowned, not following. "It just felt too empty in St. Louis. Too quiet. Gave me the willies, so I wanted to double-check."

I stared through him, processing his words in stunned silence. How had I not seen that? St. Louis...had been gutted. Emptied. Was that Baldur's part of the plan? Why?

Yahn pulled his phone out and cleared his throat. "No one likes a micromanager, Nate," he said, teasingly.

It took me a moment to catch the obvious hint. I managed a weak laugh "Right. I'm a little distracted."

Kára joined us and grabbed my hand with a weary smile. "I got a picture of the Justice," she assured me. "You ready?" she asked, her hair dripping wet.

I squeezed her hand, turning to Yahn. "We'll see you in Fae." I waved at the Reds. "Thank you."

And then I Shadow Walked us back to Chateau Falco, not wanting anyone to see my destination. A Gateway would have given me away.

CHAPTER 44

Kára froze upon realizing we were back in my office at Chateau Falco. She slowly turned to look at me, cocking her head. I walked over to the bar and poured myself a glass of Alice's absinthe, not caring about the potential risks and not patient enough for a cocktail. I slammed it down and drank in the fiery burn. Then I placed my hands on the counter and hung my head, taking a deep breath.

"How did Baldur convince Einherjar to do his bidding? Don't they work for Odin? Or the Valkyries and Freya?" I asked, my throat hoarse.

I heard Kára sit down on the armrest of the chair, which seemed to be a favorite spot of hers, like a cat to a laptop. "Before today, I would have said he couldn't. But *this* seems to confirm it."

I glanced over my shoulder, frowning at her emphasis on *this*. She held a bearded axe in one hand and was pointing at the haft with a finger. I approached, leaning forward to see that she was indicating a message carved into the handle. "From Asgard with love," she said, holding it out for me.

I waved a hand and then leaned back against the desk, folding my arms. "That's too easy. Anyone could have written that. I'm not very popular in Asgard."

She nodded her agreement. "We could take it to Fenrir and see if he recognizes the scent. Or Loki might know something. Loki usually learns the important gossip before anyone else."

I grimaced, annoyed that we hadn't considered it sooner. "That's a great idea," I said, but I knew it came across sounding angry. I couldn't help it. I felt rage burning deep inside of me, and I didn't know why.

The room was silent for a few moments, and I could tell Kára didn't know what to do to make me feel better. The only thing I wanted to do was hurt someone. Wylde's instincts were scratching at my skin, struggling to break free and cut loose, but I didn't know where to direct him. It wasn't any one thing, it was all the little things. The tiny questions like hundreds of little needles, *poking, poking, poking!*

I heard the sound of shattering wood and I glanced down to see that my hands were now gripping the desk and that I had squeezed entirely through it. Hadn't my arms just been folded? I saw Kára rise, her face a mask of raw anguish and a desperate desire to comfort me. I let out a shaky breath and closed my eyes as I let go of the splinters in my fist and held up my palm to tell Kára to remain where she was.

I felt like I was holding a feral beast on a leash, and that beast was *me*. I realized I was grinding my teeth but I couldn't figure out how to stop doing it.

I definitely didn't trust myself with Kára's affections while struggling to hold myself together.

"I'm...okay," I rasped, lying as I struggled to withstand the tornado of questions screaming within my mind. The healer using Pan's magic. Aiden possibly dead. Baldur and his Justice. Einherjar. Cyrilo. Rogue wizards. The Masters. The Academy. The Queens.

I needed a totem. Something to latch onto and ignore the questions plaguing my mind. "We need to move the armor," I croaked, rising from the desk. "Come."

And I walked out of the office, desperately needing to move. I felt my veins glowing beneath my skin as I began to lose the perilous grip that kept my Godkiller powers under wraps. Golden light abruptly bathed my surroundings and I realized I was panting, snarling.

Something tackled me to the ground, jarring me out of my panic. I hit the ground on my chest and bounced. I spun in the air, flipping onto my back to face my attacker. Kára pinned me to the ground, wearing her full set of golden armor. Her dual-colored eyes blazed and she was crying even as she gritted her teeth.

She punched me in the jaw, rocking my head to the side. I bared my teeth and grabbed her hips, pulling her close as I straightened my neck to glare at her. She punched me again, even harder than before, rocking my head to the other side.

"FIGHT IT!" she roared, making my ears pop. She lifted both fists above her head and brought them down, aiming for my chest. "FIGHT IT!"

I bucked her up with my hips and flipped our positions, slamming her down to the carpet beneath me. I loomed over her, panting. "STOP!" I shouted in a beastly roar.

She punched me in my side and I grunted in surprise, curling in to protect that side from another strike—which was when she pounded me on the other, now exposed, side. I bent my elbows, trying to cover both, and she hit me with an uppercut to the chin, sending me flying off of her and into a side table. A vase on the top wobbled and then tipped, soaking me with cool, earthy water.

I gasped, choking at the plant-based waterboarding, shaking my head and sputtering until it was finished. I rolled over onto all fours, shaking my head. I lifted my gaze to glare at Kára, rubbing my chin with my fingers. Surprisingly, it didn't hurt. At all.

She was sitting cross-legged a few feet away, cleaning her fingernails with a dagger. She glanced up at me and I saw a flicker of a smile tug at her lips. "There you are. Your eyes are no longer glowing. That's good, because I was about to resort to this," she said, lifting her dagger for my inspection.

I stared at her, feeling as if a dark cloud was drifting away and a ray of sunlight was finally breaking through to hit my face and bathe me in warmth. I spit out a leaf. "What the hell was that?" I rasped.

She sheathed her dagger and rested her chin in her palms while planting her elbows on her knees. "I have no idea. But to make this whole situation even weirder, I need to be honest with you..." I waited, furrowing my brow. "It scared the living *hell* out of me...and turned me the fuck *on*," she admitted with a blush. "If that's not masochistic, I don't know what is," she added, sounding troubled.

I plopped down on my ass and wiped the water from my face. "You've been spending too much time with the goats?" I suggested with a faint smile. "Kink is contagious?"

She grinned. "It wasn't the violence. It was something out of my control. I think it was the raw *power* oozing off of you. I knew it was dangerous but it was also intoxicating. Whatever was happening to you was starting to mess with my head, too. It was making me feel reckless, and the rational part of me feared what would happen if I didn't stop you, even though another part of me didn't want to stop you at all. That's why I tackled you. Before I could talk myself into letting you break free."

"Break free?" I asked, warily. "What made you say it that way?"

"You kept repeating it over and over again." She studied me with a calm look on her face, but I could tell she was concerned and only acting calm for my sake. "The energy seemed to spike when your eyes and veins started glowing. Your Godkiller powers, right?" I nodded. "Did you sense a god nearby or something?"

I shook my head without hesitation. "No. This...was different." I licked my lips, forgetting all about the dirty plant water until it was too late. I scooped up the vase and then spit the earthy taste into it. I set it down and put some of the flowers back inside as I tried to process what had just come over me and how.

I had only felt that out of control one other time, and it was burned into my memory with a firebrand.

"There," I said, straightening the flowers in an attempt to mask my concern. "All better."

Kára snorted. "You really do need a butler. Carl was right."

I shot her a scowl for good measure but it didn't wipe away her grin. Despite her playing along with my idle banter, I knew I hadn't succeeded in distracting her. Those green and blue eyes knew my tricks, so I wasn't surprised when she figuratively pounced like a panther—from calm and relaxed to sudden lethality.

"At first, I thought it was the axe," she said softly. "But I sensed it in the parking lot at Grimm Tech when you returned. Nothing like in the office back there, though, and the office didn't hold a candle to the hallway."

I nodded, averting my eyes guiltily. "No. Not the axe, but now I'm starting to feel angry again," I said with a light grunt. "But this was different," I whispered, not sure how to voice my theory.

"Tell me what it felt like, Nate. Why was this different? And don't pull any of that bullshit about not knowing how to share your feelings. You now have a girlfriend who can take it as hard as you dish it, and dish it *back* twice as hard," she said in a stern tone. "So...talk to me, Nate."

I realized I was smiling. "Pretty sure you cracked some ribs."

She snorted. "You were all juiced up. I could have hit you with a truck and you would have shrugged it off," she admitted. "Unless Alice's *Pimp Juice* really is some super soldier serum and not just a magical Neosporin," she teased.

I rolled my eyes. "Blaming a child? Really?" I asked, shaking my head. Then I let out a breath, focusing on her real question. "I was holding the anger back ever since I left Fae," I admitted. "Like I was holding my breath underwater and I finally had to come up for air once we got here."

She watched me, nodding along to show that she was entirely focused on me and not here to judge. On that note, she didn't immediately answer but rather gave it some serious thought. After a few moments of watching me, her armor winked away and she scooted up to me so that our knees kissed and she grasped each of my hands with a determined squeeze. I smiled down at them, idly wondering how such tiny fists could punch so hard.

"I can't help hold the door closed if I don't know what's on the other side," she said, drawing my attention back to her face. "We are all explosions of stardust, fighting to hold ourselves together. Hell, I died and chose to get zapped into a new model," she grumbled, her eyes growing misty. "You think that doesn't fuck with my head most nights? When I pass by a mirror and see a stranger?" I winced, suddenly feeling guilty. "But you *help*, Nate. When I feel like exploding, you are the core of gravity that somehow pulls me back to center. It's okay that you are made of unstable molten rock. That's exactly what *I* need." She squeezed my hands tight enough to hurt. "So, let me be the armor that keeps you safe. I can handle a few volcanic eruptions every now and then." A smile slipped through her tears. "After all, I *did* just kick your ass," she said with a giggle sniffle. "My Wild Side is fiercer than yours."

I chuckled, staring at her plump lips and sweeping my eyes over every contour of her face like my gaze was a fingertip caress. She shuddered, picking up on its intensity. "You just made geology and space sound sexy."

She perked up. "I'm an ass-trophysicist. Or a geosexual. Aannddd I've exhausted this scheme. The point is, I'm not going anywhere, and I won't let you go anywhere. I worked way too damned hard to get you back, Nate. I watched you for *years* after I switched bodies, trying to find a way to break out of my promise with Death and Odin. And I succeeded. I beat Death and the Allfather to get back to you. I am *not* going to give up over a few childish temper tantrums!" she vowed, panting.

I started laughing. The juxtaposition of her delicate, curvy frame compared to the seemingly outlandish claims she'd just made were just too extreme. It was so easy to forget that she was a Valkyrie when she wasn't wearing her armor. She was barely over a hundred pounds. I interlaced my fingers through hers to let her know I wasn't laughing at her but with her. Kind of.

It seemed to please her, which was really my main goal in life from here on out.

"What was it about Fae that set you off?" she asked. Silence stretched for a few more seconds. "Aiden?"

I shook my head, letting out a deep breath. "The last time I felt anything like that was when Pan and I fought each other," I admitted. "When he used his powers to make me panic and succumb to my unbridled rage. When he used me to commit suicide, per my parents' orders."

She poked her lip out sadly and squeezed my hands tightly. "I'm sorry, Nate," she whispered, her voice cracking.

She knew that story very well. Because...

"I was *there*," she reminded me in a croaking whisper, and I hung my head, nodding my chin against my chest. She'd been watching me from up in the sky, breaking Odin's rules by getting too close to me. Back then, her job was to guard me from afar, not to get involved and not to risk detection. "That was the day I decided I couldn't wait any longer to get you back," she whispered, releasing my hand to cup the side of my face and run her fingers through my hair, no longer bothering to hide her sobs. "When I saw how much *pain* you were in after he fell..." she whispered. "You were lying there on that cliff, screaming for help, and I fucking lost it with you, Nate. I vowed to find my way back to you no matter what it cost me. To at least let you know, once and for all, how I felt about you. Even if it was with my last breath. I never dreamed we'd get a second chance, but I'm sure as hell not going to waste it," she snarled, and then she was straddling me, kissing me with an animalistic passion as she drove me back to the ground.

We pulled apart after a few minutes and she hovered over me, pressing her forehead against mine. "I love you, Kára."

"I know," she whispered, pompously. I pinched her ass and she yelped, laughing. "Okay! I love you, too!" She rose up with a regretful sigh. "We don't have time to conclude this the way I would like."

"Thank you for reminding me," I growled.

She laughed and climbed off of me. "So...what was it about Fae that incited your panic if not Aiden?" she asked as I climbed to my feet.

My smile slowly faded. "The healer taking care of Aiden used magic like Pan's. I called him out on it and he confirmed it." I shrugged. "That hit me like a slap in the face. Coupled with my fear for Aiden, I think it hit me too fast. Like free radicals in my blood stream being reactivated. Or PTSD. Pan Traumatic Stress Disorder."

She frowned thoughtfully. "That's strange. Maybe Pan trained him," she said, glancing back down the hall. I saw my satchel leaning against the railing and I frowned. She walked over, picked it up and then brought it back to me. "You threw it off when you were talking crazy about breaking free." I nodded uneasily, putting the satchel over my shoulder and across my chest. "You seemed adamant about the armor. I assume that's still important?"

"Yes."

"Great. Let's walk and talk. There's a war on the horizon." And she tugged me down the hallway, leading me towards the Sanctorum.

CHAPTER 45

We entered the Sanctorum, and I was grateful that she hadn't peppered me with dozens of questions on the way down. Walking in silence had given me the time to recenter myself and get my head back on track. I was still concerned about the panic attack and I had a lot of questions for the healer, but I needed to secure the armor sets first. He had been upset with me—probably for killing his mentor.

Understandable, but he didn't have all the facts, and probably wouldn't believe me if I told him.

No, Pan asked me to kill him!

Riiiight...

The armor was exactly where we had left it. Kára bent down to touch it and yanked her finger back. She rose to her feet and nodded. "Okay. It's the same armor, and it's safe. So why do you want to move it out of the safest place in town?" she asked.

I shook my head. "Chateau Falco is empty. The mansion's only protection is the Beast, and she is not invincible. She's actually been acting kind of strange lately. Not sure what that's all about, but she's done it before, so I'm not freaking out about it. But even without that, she's standing against a coordinated team of supervillains who are willing to work together to either take me out or get their hands on the armor. At worst, the Academy, the Summer Queen, Baldur, and the Masters are all in cahoots. At best, they are fighting over the same thing. The old *enemy of my enemy is my friend* shtick. And that's just the people we can kind of confirm. Do you fully trust the Winter Queen's sudden desire to help warn me when we have never been friends? And why hasn't Oberon and his Wild Hunt picked a side? The Academy is either gunning for me or they really are in the middle of a coup and the two factions are vying for power."

She pursed her lips, nodding. "Okay. But you weren't concerned about those things when we first moved them here. What changed?"

"Because Yahn made a good point. Even though he didn't fully realize it, his subconscious mind did. St. Louis is empty—our fortress unprotected —because everyone's heading to Fae to fight Summer. And I don't know why Baldur attacked Grimm Tech. It makes no sense, but it does make me suspicious."

She pondered my words, pinching her chin between her thumb and finger.

I continued. "If I wanted to get to Nate Temple, the first thing I would want to do is peel away the layers of the onion—get all of his allies out of the way—while keeping him busy with bee-sting attacks. St. Louis is empty and we've seen a whole lot of unexplainable bee-stings," I repeated.

"But there is nowhere safer than Chateau Falco, even with her limitations."

I sighed. "You're not wrong, but it's also the most obvious place. When you feel overwhelmed, you go home. You keep your most coveted treasures at home. What if they're purposely encouraging me to empty St. Louis to get me alone?"

She held up a finger. "If they want *you*. But if they want the *armor*, they don't even know you have it."

I met her eyes. "What if they want both? The easiest way to get to the armor would be to make sure I'm dead. Take me out and my allies start to fall apart. Without me, Alex and Talon would likely be squaring off against Summer with almost no support. They could then *walk* in and get the armor. No matter how it plays out, they have a better chance at collecting the treasure."

"A shell game," she mused, nodding thoughtfully. "It's insane, but it kind of makes sense." She stared down at the armor. "So, where would they be safe? The Armory?"

I shook my head. "It's insanely secure, but it's also the obvious choice. Too many people have access. Possibly Hephaestus and Aphrodite. Odin, Freya," I waved a hand, implying that the list was even longer. "And technically, I lease the space from Callie. I don't know her people well enough to put this kind of temptation in front of them."

She pursed her lips. "Grimm Tech is now off limits, too, right?"

I frowned, glancing at the personalized hatchet from Grimm Tech that she'd strapped to her waist. "No way. Which was probably Baldur's aim—to ensure that if I was going to hide the armor, I would see my other safe houses were all compromised. Subliminally encouraging me to hide them at Falco, who has been acting strange and occasionally unresponsive all of a sudden," I reminded her. "Like the goats popping in and Alex sending the fairy with the letter—both arriving without warnings from Falco."

She pursed her lips, nodding. "Where is the last place they would look?" she asked, sounding flustered.

I needed a place no one would think of but that still had security measures in place. A middle of the road location that would be dismissed out of hand rather than a Fort Knox type place. I snapped my fingers at a sudden thought. "The Mausoleum!" I hissed.

Kára considered my suggestion, knowing all about the ridiculous security upgrades my parents had built into the place. It was secure, but not so secure that it drew too much attention. My parents had used it to hide important artifacts for me.

Kára crouched down. "Okay. Let's get this over with. We have a lot to do before the war," she said, tapping Baldur's hatchet at her belt to remind me of her idea to speak with Loki.

With the use of Gateways and magic to carry the heavy armor, it took no time at all to move everything into the Temple Mausoleum. I chose to spread them out throughout the building, hiding them behind particularly large tombs and statues, betting on the assumption that no one would think I'd be dumb enough to hide them in such an open space.

They were wrong. I was so brilliant that I *was* that dumb, but only because I was so exceptionally intelligent! I tried not to think about the poisoned wine scene from the Princess Bride, but that was simply...inconceivable.

Once finished, we decided to take the hatchet to Loki and Fenrir to see if either of them recognized it or could confirm that it did or did not belong to Baldur and, if not, whom did it belong to? Since I had no idea where the semi-fugitive gods were, I let Kára drive.

She grabbed my hand and...

Valkyrie-Walked? Valked? Rainbow-Skipped?

Whatever she called it, I was not a fan. I felt like I was in an elevator when the cable snapped, sending me crashing to the ground faster than my own bodyweight would have accounted for. Rainbow light blazed across the cosmos of my mind and I couldn't seem to catch my breath—because I'd left my lungs about five miles above me back in the Mausoleum.

This continued for the length of a particularly long infomercial rather than a snap of the fingers. It was absolutely the *worst*.

Then we simply stopped and I crumpled to the cold ground as if my bones had been replaced with the ephemeral light of rainbow power. Then, because I wasn't miserable enough, I fell *through* that ground. My breath fogged before my face and I shivered involuntarily, feeling the heat literally being sucked from my body. My underground prison was blindingly white and I momentarily panicked, fearing that the infomercial-lengthed overexposure of pretty lights had caused a black-out in the color-processing section of my brain.

I looked up and saw a circular hole that led to a black sky marred by a smear of neon-green. I could still see color! Kára's head appeared in said hole, and a cascade of icy snow slapped me in the face and then slithered down my collar. I gritted my teeth, realizing I'd simply fallen into a snowdrift—answering the question of why everything was white and I was freezing. Kára stared down at me with her beautiful green and blue eyes, grinning. "Whoops!" Then she extended her arm to grasp mine and pulled me out.

I shook off the snow, kicking my boots and cursing loudly. "Where the hell are we?" I demanded, rounding on her. "The North Pole?"

Kára rolled her eyes. "Norway, I think." We assessed our surroundings and the stunning beauty of it all nearly took my breath away, instantly freezing my anger into a neat little cube. The night sky seemed impossibly huge, full of brilliantly white stars, and the beautiful green smears of the Northern Lights made me think of Kai, my old Beast. The air was thin, and I realized we were near the very top of a ridiculously high mountain and surrounded by more barren mountains in every direction.

I continued spinning in a circle and abruptly jolted to find Loki only a few yards away.

The god of mischief was naked, lying on his back, and gripping his heels in his hands to assist in spreading his legs as high and wide as possible. Thankfully, my viewing angle prevented me from seeing wank or stank.

Barely.

Kára, on the other hand, had a bird's eye view of his cannon.

"Oh, god!" Kára cursed, dropping the hatchet as she shielded her eyes with her elbow.

"Yes, child?" Loki replied in a sage voice, taking her words as an homage to his glorious splendor rather than a curse of abject horror. Because he was an asshole. Just like how he hadn't acknowledged our arrival until we saw his show.

"What the hell are you *doing*?" I asked, bewildered. I was unable to peel my eyes away.

"Winking at the Allfather," he said while wiggling his ass in the snow and laughing. "With my brown eye!" he hooted.

I looked up into the night sky to see two huge ravens circling the mountain, cawing in outrage.

CHAPTER 46

I felt a huge presence behind me and I immediately locked down my thoughts to prevent any accidental mind-reading between me and my fellow Godkiller. I slowly turned to see Fenrir padding towards us. He paused a good distance away so we didn't have to break our necks looking up at him. "It's his new thing," the giant wolf explained in a resigned growl. "It's called Perineum Sunning. He claims that thirty seconds of sunlight...down *there*," he said, awkwardly, "gives your soul more energy than a full day in the sun."

I slowly lifted a finger to point up at the night sky. "No sun tonight, strangely enough," I said drily.

Fenrir lowered himself down to the snow and started panting. "He says the Northern Lights have an even greater effect on his...what did you call it again, Dad?" he asked, glancing over.

"Ass-solar Charge," Loki chimed in, proudly. "Get it? We're basically human solar batteries, but only recently discovered where our charging panels were. You guys want to try?" Loki called out. "It's quite liberating. I feel empowered."

"I can see that. We're good, thanks," I said, shaking my head as I turned back to Fenrir.

"He read about it online somewhere," the giant wolf explained as I walked towards him. "Figured it was safer to let him do it up here. I'm pretty sure he's just trying to annoy Odin, which is fine by me."

"He locked me up for hundreds. Of. Years!" Loki fired back in a clipped, petulant tone.

Between one step and the next, Fenrir's friendly demeanor abruptly changed and he let out a low growl, his hackles rising up from his back. I froze, lifting up my arms to show him I meant no harm. I realized he was staring at my shirt and sniffing at the air warily. "Your blood?"

I looked down to see Aiden's blood was still all over my shirt. I waved a hand, letting out a breath of relief to learn that he hadn't been threatening me. He'd been *concerned* about me. "Not mine," I reassured him. I scooped up the hatchet Kára had dropped and extended it to him. "Some Einherjar attacked us. The one who threw this hit a friend of mine. Another wizard. I carried him to a healer," I explained. "I was hoping you two might know who owns it."

Fenrir sniffed at the axe and abruptly let out a sharp sneeze that blasted snow twenty feet—thankfully not in my direction. He turned back to me, shaking his head with a surprised look on his face. "Your friend's blood is almost overpowering it, but I recognize one thing." he said, licking his lips with his giant tongue. "I didn't know you came bearing *gifts*," he said, and his tail began to wag, forming massive snow drifts.

We stared at him, waiting. "*Any* minute now," Kára said, folding her arms as she came to a halt at my side.

Fenrir curled his lip at her, amused. "That axe belonged to one of the men who took me and trapped me in Colorado," he growled.

My eyes widened in disbelief. "You're fucking kidding me," I breathed, staring at the hatchet. For some reason, it took me until this moment to come to the understanding that I could not tell him my suspicions about Baldur. If I did, he would confront the god and prevent me from discovering the identity of his Justice pal. Worse, he could possibly kick off another war—one that I would be required to participate in as a brand-new member of Asgard's War Council. Yet *another* civil war potential.

And that would alert any of his allies that something had changed. I needed this Fae war to happen so I would have the chance to get my hands on the perpetrators myself and find out if they really had been working together at the behest of the Masters. Fenrir would just *eat* everyone, but I needed *answers*.

I presumed that Fenrir would recognize Baldur's scent, but he hadn't said the god's name. He'd merely recognized it as one of the men involved in his abduction. Only Kára and I knew—or highly suspected—that it had come from a man working for Baldur.

Which meant that Fenrir might have just unknowingly confirmed two things: that the god really had been involved in Fenrir's abduction, and that the Winter Queen's accusation of her sister working with Baldur and Mordred was spot on.

And that was further corroborated by the Summer Queen's approaching attack on Camelot.

The Masters really were involved!

But I kept all of this sudden understanding from my face, because there were plenty more mysteries to solve. Unfortunately, this whole conclusion was based on the initial assumption I'd made about the axe...

That the Einherjar at Grimm Tech had been working for Baldur.

Not someone *else* in Asgard.

Because the Einherjar didn't work for Baldur. They worked for Odin... the man who had been so incredibly helpful in feeding me answers and information to rely on. I clenched my jaw, truly hoping that all my investigating skills weren't going to lead me to my old butler being the bad guy. That Odin was a Master in disguise, and that he was merely throwing Baldur in my path to keep me off his own trail.

Jesus. Where was the line between insanity and objective rationality?

So, without incontrovertible proof that this axe really belonged to Baldur, I was still working on theories.

"Let me see that hatchet," Loki said from directly behind me. I jumped in surprise, my heart practically exploding from my chest. Then I very carefully glanced over my shoulder to make sure he was decent. He wore a robe and his face was a cold, lifeless mask. I extended the hatchet to him. I wanted the answer, but I also had to ensure that they didn't take matters into their own hands if Loki confirmed it did belong to Baldur.

There were simply way too many questions still on the table, and allowing Fenrir's unchecked vengeance would utterly destroy any chances at me discovering the truths, allowing other culprits to get away scot-free.

Other Masters.

Loki looked at it, frowning thoughtfully. He read the message carved into the haft and grunted. After about a minute, he handed it back to me. "I've never seen that in my life. You said an Einherjar threw it?" I nodded. He turned to Fenrir. "And you're certain this belonged to one of your abductors?"

"The scent, not the axe," Fenrir clarified. "But I almost missed it beneath all that putrid wizard's blood," he growled unhappily.

Loki nodded pensively. "Perhaps it's faint because the Einherjar involved in your abduction did not carry this for very long," he mused. "It is a rather fine axe. More of a gift. And it carries a message." He turned to me. "Whichever Asgardian sent those Einherjar at you accidentally—or intentionally—delivered you one of the men involved in my son's abduction. They were not only taking a chance at killing you, but simultaneously cutting ties that might lead back to *them*."

Well, Loki was coming to the same conclusions as me. But he was crazy. So...did that make me crazy?

I cleared my throat. "I have a request."

Loki regarded me in silence for a few moments, and then gave me a begrudging nod. "I guess you've earned it," he said, sounding annoyed. Apparently he hadn't received a strong enough butt-charge to maintain his cheery attitude from minutes ago.

"I'm working on something of my own that has impacts on the Omega War," I said in a sobering tone, "and I don't want anyone alerting my target until my trap is set. Subtlety is vital. The plot likely involves an Asgardian, possibly several, and I—we—*desperately* need the secrets they hold. If we happen to be targeting the same person," I said, pointing at his chest and then mine, "I ask that you stand down and let me act first. If I fail in the attempt, I will fail very loudly, so you will have no question who Fenrir needs to go after. He could then chase him up and down Yggdrasil for all I care since I will already be dead. But my window of opportunity is limited, and the Omega War rides on my outcome."

Loki opened his mouth to respond, but Fenrir cleared his throat, interrupting his father. Loki flashed him an annoyed look, but reluctantly acquiesced. "It is my vengeance, and you are the one who freed me from my imprisonment, Nate Temple. I will honor your request. For a time. But my patience is not limitless."

I nodded gratefully. "Thank you. No one can know—or even suspect—what I just told you."

Loki sighed. "We will go to Asgard and see what we can learn. Discreetly. They have probably missed me dearly," he said with a slow-forming mischievous grin that reminded me of the Grinch.

Kára stepped forward. "I will go with you."

Loki grunted, his grin withering away. "Don't trust me, Valkyrie?"

She flashed him a wicked grin of her own. "I trust Nate and myself. But I wish to speak with Freya about...girl stuff," she said, blindly picking a topic out of a hat of lies.

Loki clutched at his heart, reading right through her bullshit. "You wound me, Valkyrie."

"That is actually part of my job description," she said with a smile.

Fenrir rolled his eyes, turning to me. "After you get your answers, make them suffer. Or deliver them to me so I can mete out my own justice. I will consider it a gift, but I am content to let you manage it how you see fit and will not hold a grudge if you are the one holding the executioner's axe at the end of the day."

I nodded, surprised at his willingness to give up his revenge. To gift it to me. "I will try."

Kára wrapped me up in a tight hug, pressing her lips into my ear. "Stay out of danger until I'm back. I'll show *him* the pictures of all the dead wizards and see if he recognizes any of them as our man," she said, referring to Odin and Baldur's inside Justice, respectively.

"I'll be fine for a few hours without your protection. I am a Horseman, you know."

"You're a petty, territorial, emotionally unstable wizard," she said, pulling away to touch her nose against mine. "And I love it."

I smiled. "Guilty."

She shot me a serious look. "If it comes down to it, don't be afraid to let the monster out. Be a savage, Nate. Something feels different about all this. Like we're being led by a bit and bridle. Like something is about to boil over. What if you and Fenrir are aiming at the same target, and both of you are wrong? That you're being misled?" I wondered if her thoughts had drifted to Odin as well, but I obviously couldn't ask her.

"We will figure it out when we come to it," I told her. "I'll meet you back in Fae."

I waved at the three of them and then Shadow Walked to Camelot.

CHAPTER 47

I left the designated traveling area and walked into the courtyard. I spotted the tent where I'd left Aiden and saw the same grouchy healer and his three assistants, except it looked like they were raising more tents in anticipation of the upcoming battle. The whole wall was lined with them, almost making it look like a pop-up street fair.

Of death.

I jogged towards him, wanting to check in on Aiden before I met with Alex and his influx of new allies to discuss battle plans. I was halfway across the courtyard when the two goats, Snarler and Grinder, skidded to a halt in front of me, physically barring my path. I didn't see Gunnar or the kids anywhere, so I felt a flicker of panic in my stomach.

"Your boy, Bonk, is one tough bastard," Snarler said. "I can't believe he's still kicking."

Grinder shot him a grim look, shaking his head in disapproval at his lack of proper bedside manner. Which meant his brother had crossed a line. Huh. Good to know they had boundaries.

But I did let out a huge sigh of relief to hear that he was alive. The healer had truly performed a miracle. Somehow, I needed to mend the tension between us and thank him. "I was just going to check in on him before meeting with Gunnar and the others. Speaking of, shouldn't you be guarding them, seeing as how you're his emotional support goats?" I asked sternly.

They shared a long look with each other, having some kind of silent conversation.

Finally, Grinder turned to me. "He doesn't quite need us right now, but we had an idea we wanted to run by you, seeing as how you are oh, so powerful."

"And we're all on the same team, right? One family. One direction!" Snarler added.

I narrowed my eyes suspiciously. "Is this a *mommy said no, so let me try asking dad* situation?" I asked, wondering how many people were going to try using this on me.

"What?" Snarler hooted, glancing over his shoulder. "That's crazy!"

Grinder chimed in. "We would *never*—"

I held up a hand, cutting him off. "What is it? Just spit it out." Their little tails started wagging excitedly and they stared up at me with their chilling green and blue goat eyes.

Snarler puffed up his chest proudly. "We want to sneak behind enemy lines and gather intel on the Sumbitches." I bit the inside of my cheek at his term for the enemy, wishing I'd come up with it. "We can hide in the grass and slip into their ranks when they pass us. Then slip out when we're done."

"Slip in, slip out! Slip in, slip out!" Grinder began cheering, chanting louder with each repetition. I shot an embarrassed smile over my shoulder at the various shifters and Fae milling about the courtyard, who were all giving us strange looks.

Then Snarler joined in and they started competing to see who was loudest. "Slip in, slip out! SLIP IN—"

I shushed them both with a frantic *stop* gesture. Then I placed my hands on my hips. "You're not even Fae. They will instantly know you're not supposed to be there."

Snarler bumped me with his horns, narrowing his eyes. "We're talking fucking goats," he argued.

"And sadomasochists," Grinder added. "We're basically second cousins by default."

That was so wrong that I didn't even know how to respond. They sensed my hesitation and doubled down.

"What do we have to lose?" Snarler pressed. "Oh no! We might be horribly murdered," he said, laughing dismissively.

"I love it when you talk dirty," Grinder bleated, hopping up and down excitedly.

I held up a hand again, quieting them. "I understand your slip-in strategy, but how exactly do you plan to slip-out, and then somehow beat their army back here? If you make a run for it, they'll just shoot you down."

Snarler grinned, baring his teeth proudly. "Oh! That part was *my* idea. Check *this* out." He craned his neck back and stuck his mouth into a little pocket on the side of his support vest. He picked up something small with his teeth and then trotted about ten feet away. He turned back around to face us and I frowned uneasily. "THTAND BACK!" he bleated at the bystanders in a lisping shout.

"What does he have in his mouth?" I asked Grinder, frowning as the crowd swiftly obeyed Snarler's request and gave him room or found someplace else they needed to be. The healer had stopped working and was frowning at me and then the goat with a suspicious look on his face.

Grinder shrugged, watching his brother. "Something about a magic marble," he said excitedly.

"THWEE..." Snarler lisp-shouted like he was trying out for a Monty Python skit.

My eyes bulged in sudden realization. "A Tiny Ball?" I hissed, waving my hands to get Snarler's attention, but he was too enamored with being the center of attention for all his curious fans.

"TWOO..." Snarler continued, drawing it out.

"Everybody get back!" I shouted at the crowd. "FAR BACK!"

"WON!" he hooted.

And Snarler chomped down on the Tiny Ball between his teeth.

The Gateway ripped open and Snarler exploded into goat shrapnel. Organs and bones and legs of meat went arcing up into the air before raining down on the cobblestones with sickening *splats*. The crowd screamed in alarm and ran away in horror.

Grinder abruptly hopped into the air as if he'd been electrocuted, his entire body going completely rigid as he suffered a catatonic seizure upon seeing his brother's grand plan turn into an unexpected suicide mission. It was *exactly* like those videos on the internet of fainting goats. He toppled to his side, as stiff as a board, and came to a rocking halt like a shaggy piñata fallen from a tree.

I ran my hands through my hair and let out a long breath, realizing everyone was staring at me as if it had been my fault. I flashed hollow, reassuring smiles at the people peeking out from behind tents, carts, and doorways. "It's okay. Crisis over! Snarler will be back tomorrow. Feel free to cook a piece of him up if you're hungry," I added with a nervous laugh. "Grinder will walk it off in a minute," I added, nudging the catatonic goat with my foot. "Get up," I whispered down at the goat out the side of my mouth.

Grinder let out a long, soft, high-pitched whine like a slowly deflating balloon.

"Who the hell made you think it was a good idea to bite down on a Tiny Ball?" I hissed, crouching low in front of him. "There's a reason we throw them in *front* of us!"

He didn't even blink to acknowledge me. He just kept letting out that sad little whine, frozen stiff.

"NATE!" a voice bellowed from the castle wall. I looked up to see Gunnar glaring down at me. His eye shifted from me, to the catatonic goat, and then to the circular blood stain and random goat pieces decorating the courtyard. "Did you just kill my goats?"

Everyone turned to look at me. I decided it was too long a story to shout back at him from across the courtyard, so I flung up my hands. "Kind of?"

He shook his head and stormed off. I pointed my finger down at Grinder. "That's the *last* time I listen to one of your crackpot suggestions!" I scolded in a low hiss.

He continued the deflating balloon sound.

I turned away to resume my trek to the healer's tent to check on Aiden. I made it three steps before the healer saw me coming, shot me a glare that said goat-bombers were not welcome in a tent of healing, and then he dropped the curtain again—before I even had the chance to catch a glimpse of Aiden.

I growled under my breath, spun on a heel, and made my way towards where I had last seen Gunnar.

I kicked Snarler's detached spleen into the wall on my way by, ignoring the sickened gasps, and jogged up the stairs to go over battle plans.

We sat at a long wooden table in the throne room and I was pleased to notice that Betty—Alex's make-shift, plastic Round Table—had been relegated to the corner. The space would be grand someday, but right now it just looked like depressing castle ruins with new furniture.

Our war party consisted of Alex and Talon, obviously. Tory had brought along the Family heads of her school—one representative for almost every kind of shifter on their rolls. Gunnar and Ashley had brought Drake and Cowan. Calvin and Makayla had chosen to come hang out with me, probably feeling sorry for me since Kára and Aiden were both absent. Carl had thought about sitting beside me until Makayla made a move. Then he swiftly got up and silently backed away from her as if waiting for her to attack.

That had raised almost every eyebrow in the room, but everyone now knew better than to ask Carl questions, so they left it alone. Yahn and the Reds had wrapped up their crime scene drama and had arrived moments after me. Raego was still gathering forces, and it sounded like he was going to be a late show.

In total, we had close to two-thousand bodies, counting all the Fae from the surrounding area who had flocked to Camelot to either escape the battlefield or stand up and fight for Alex. After spending only a short time in the courtyard, even the meekest of refugees had changed their minds, asking how they could help.

The first thirty minutes of our discussion, upon me walking through the door, had been dubbed *Two Goats One Marble*. I'd had to tell the story twice because they kept laughing too hard the first time through, and had missed key elements of the tragic tale. The second time through, even I was laughing hard enough that I had to wipe tears from my eyes, forgetting all about my anger for a few minutes.

We'd been here for about two hours, going over plans and suggestions on how we might pick apart the Summer army in such a fierce, startling manner that they were forced to retreat, even if only to regroup their scattered forces. We were still vastly outnumbered, but I had a feeling we could beat Summer back with shock and awe. Individually, we'd all experienced different forms of warfare and brought different tactics to the table that would help stem the tide. But to be blunt, there were a lot of long, poignant stares directed at the dudes with magic, magical armor, or magical weapons.

I suggested a few ideas I considered truly evil, and I was almost disappointed when they were so quickly agreed upon by everyone. Yahn had brought a trove of helpful goodies from Grimm Tech, and my satchel was always locked and loaded with party favors. Pretty soon, everyone was breaking off to prepare their teams and go over the strategies with their people. I made a few short trips to Chateau Falco with a team of shifters and was back twenty minutes later with nothing left to do.

Which left me all alone. With Carl. I caught him up to speed on my own adventures, and even shared my conspiracies about Summer, Baldur, the Academy, and Mordred. Things only Kára knew.

He grew very troubled upon hearing me speak, and vowed to stick by my side for the rest of the day. Since I knew I didn't really have a say in the matter, I thanked him. I wasn't sure when Kára was going to return, but the war was only getting closer, and the longer she was away in Asgard, the more I feared she might have asked the wrong person the wrong questions and gotten herself in trouble, and caught by Baldur.

Or...

What if my darkest fear about a second, unknown Asgardian working behind the scenes was true? That Odin was a Master? What if Odin had grown leery of her line of questioning, fearing that she was onto him? Had she discovered something directly tied to my old butler and been permanently silenced?

I shuddered, knowing my emotions were baseless and that I simply missed her. I was being paranoid. I had exactly zero evidence of Odin's involvement. Still, my gut...

Be careful, Kára. Very, very careful.

I had to trust Kára to take care of herself because I couldn't abandon all these people. If I left, a large chunk of their plan would fall apart. Especially if any of my crazy theories about the big parties were even partially correct. If they had been working together in any form or fashion, this fight wasn't just about Camelot or the suits of armor or Excalibur.

It was about exterminating me, the Catalyst. In the opinions of those in the upper echelons of power, I was getting too big for my britches and needed to be put down. Some of them meant well, and some of them meant not well. Because some of these big hitters were Masters, hiding in plain sight, hiding their moves behind altruistic-sounding causes when all they really wanted was power. Absolute power.

So, I couldn't leave until I exposed them, which meant a whole lot of people were going to die.

The louder and flashier I made it, the lower the butcher's bill at the end of the day.

I had to become a savage like Kára had urged me. I would have to be so bloodthirsty and righteous with my enemies that it would sow terror upon their followers, shattering their resolve and breaking the advantage of their numbers.

I needed to murder their hope. It wasn't difficult for me to step into that mode when in Fae. It was hard *not* to tap into that primal, Wild Side of mine. Memories of me and Talon as kids, braving the wilds of Fae, flickered and danced through my mind, and I realized I was smiling.

Not only that, but the simple possibility that the Summer Queen might have been working with Mordred and Baldur was enough to set me off. My primary goal today was personally squaring off with the queen and getting some straight answers, once and for all.

CHAPTER 48

I snapped out of my daze and realized we had made it to the courtyard. Students from Shift were huddled in small groups up on the ramparts, chatting back and forth, looking excited for the battle to come. It was almost easy to forget that they'd been raised in an arena of bloodshed, and that most of them actually enjoyed the chaos of battle. They had all been gladiator prisoners, for the most part. This was like a field trip to them.

To most of them. Some were obviously more concerned, pacing back and forth across the walls and speaking in low, anxious tones to each other. Gunnar's wolves patrolled the grounds, some in wolf form, some as men and women, but most had subconsciously agreed to leave the courtyard open to traffic rather than milling about and forming a social atmosphere that would be difficult to break up once the fighting started. Also, it was where the healers would be situated for the many triage locations.

And where all the bodies would be moved once death came a'calling.

"Let's go see if we can sneak past the healer and check on Aiden," I told Carl, targeting one of the ten healing tents now erected along the wall, confident it was the one I had sent Aiden to earlier. The courtyard was still rather crowded as last-minute preparations were made for the upcoming battle, and people ran back and forth, using the courtyard as a nexus to get to different areas of Camelot.

I spotted a pair of young, pretty women glaring directly at me with fiery looks. They were holding mops and buckets of crimson water, cleaning up the last remains of Snarler's Goatsplosion. I winced apologetically and their eyes narrowed further, as if they sensed weakness and were preparing to pounce. I shuffled on, glancing over my shoulder to make sure they didn't take chase. I saw no signs of Grinder, the depressed whoopee cushion, so I presumed he'd recovered.

If not, I'd be graced with his presence tomorrow, of course, but I would have preferred both goats around to keep an eye on the Randulfs during the upcoming war.

Shift students roved in packs of two or three, running errands for their families, and soldiers in armor hurried to the walls with bundles of arrows and spare bows tucked under their arms. Ten paces ahead of us, a short, brown-haired boy walked with his mother towards the healer's tent, both of them carrying baskets of what looked like fresh cloths or bandages. The boy was skipping happily, ignoring his mother's scolding every few steps to stop frolicking about before he tripped and scraped his knee.

They were simple folk, not warriors. Just refugees trying to do their small part to help their new home.

Calvin and Makayla stood on the opposite side of the Courtyard, kicking a ball back and forth again. I smiled to see them continuing to act more like normal kids. Especially now, on the eve of battle. Carl eyed Makayla as if he expected her to zip across the crowd and attack him. He sniffed at the air, cocking his head as he listened to god knows what, but his eyes remained fixed on the scary mist wolf blondie.

"Why are you so nervous around her?" I asked, absently.

Carl flinched as if I'd pinched him. "I am respectfully aware of her capacity for lethality."

I rolled my eyes. "Isn't that a *virtue* to the Elders? You should be worshipping her, if that was the case. And why do you not treat Calvin the same? You act skittish around Mac, but not him."

Carl continued staring at Makayla, pensively. "She is the more dangerous of the two. I am not fearful, I am respectful. A healthy, wary respect. She must be protected," he said out the side of his mouth. I dropped it, relieved to simply confirm that he wasn't harboring aggressive tendencies after all. But it was interesting that he had singled Mac out as the alpha of the twins. Through a gap in the crowd, I saw that the target tent's curtain was still closed, blocking any potential view of Aiden. That grouchy healer really had it out for me, and my thoughts once again drifted to the idea that he'd probably taken great personal offense to learn that he was healing his idol's murderer's friend. I couldn't be upset with him about that, and it still felt shameless to consider convincing him that Pan had *wanted* me to kill him.

I changed course, spotting an opening on the side of Aiden's tent that might give me an unobstructed view within, possibly letting me check on Aiden without encountering the protective, bitter healer. Carl continued on, completely unaware of my detour in his obsession with Makayla, and there were already people between us, so I decided to let him wander. I would find him after I checked on Aiden or he would realize he'd lost me in the crowd of rushing people.

I saw a pair of boots at the foot of a cot and assumed they belonged to Aiden since the other cots looked empty, but my angle was still wrong. I craned my neck, trying to verify that it was him—

I felt the thrum of magic immediately followed by the sharp, cracking sounds of wizards Shadow Walking into the very courtyard. Screams erupted and everyone started running for their lives. I cursed, calling up my magic as I tried to pinpoint the invaders through the chaos. People ran in every direction, screaming and shouting. Three people were trampled, but I helped one of them back up while keeping my eyes out for the invaders. As my eyes took in the scene, I noticed four figures standing completely still, unaffected by the turbulent crowd of panicked residents. And it became immediately apparent why.

Four Justices with shining silver masks of maniacal laughing faces and hooded black robes had come to Camelot. And they were fucking powerful. These weren't sandwich shop rookies. These were seasoned men.

And three of them held hostages with opaque blades of condensed air pressed against their throats.

Children. They'd snatched up fucking *children*.

"Attack and they die," the fourth Justice called out with his arms spread wide as he spun in a slow circle, right in the center of the courtyard. He was obviously in charge and did not hold a child as a shield, but there was no way to attack him without sentencing all the other children to instant death.

Carl stood ten paces away from him, crouched warily, but he was staring at one of the other three Justices.

The one holding Makayla hostage. Her face was calm and serene, blank as a winter pond at dawn.

Calvin was also hostage, but his face was a rictus of rage. I knew they could mist out of danger, but I also knew they wouldn't do any such thing, because they were both staring at the third hostage—the little brown-haired boy I'd seen carrying the basket with his mother. His eyes were wide and terrified as his captor stood with his back up against one of the other tents, holding the boy in front of him with a fistful of his hair and a blade of air to his tiny, delicate throat.

Not a shifter. Just a normal kid who liked to skip and who had been helping his mom carry bandages.

If Calvin and Mac shifted, the other Justice would slice the boy's throat without hesitation or remorse.

I saw seasoned werewolves and soldiers gathering on the walls, some of them drawing bows or rifles to aim down at the wizards in the courtyard, others pacing the walls with raised hackles and vicious snarls. Gunnar stepped into view on the inner rim of the castle wall overlooking the court-yard, seeming larger than life. He silently lifted a hand and the wolves *instantly* ceased howling and snarling to glance over at their alpha, even though he was in human form. His long blonde hair hung loose and almost touched his shoulders, shifting slightly in the breeze and making me think of a WWE legend in his prime entering the stadium to claim the title belt.

Rather than wearing his concealing white eyepatch like he did among Regulars and easily frightened folk, he was flaunting the black quartz eyepatch that was fused to his eye-socket. It blazed, reflecting the light of the declining sun, and his thick beard seemed made of spun gold. His arms hung loose at his sides and his fingers were splayed in a relaxed but threat-ening posture. He was at least twice as large as the helmetless, grizzled, hard-faced soldiers standing on either side of him, and they were wearing bulky armor.

Gunnar wore a tight tank-top with the word WULFRIC stretched across his massive chest, and mid-thigh athletic shorts that barely contained his bulging thighs. If he'd had a whistle around his neck and long, double-striped socks, he would have been the god of P.E. teachers everywhere.

He looked down upon the Justices like he'd just finished listening to Rammstein at full-volume on his way to Gold's Gym, only to step through the doors of his sanctuary of pain and protein to stumble into four scrawny vegans drinking coconut water as they ragged on the worthlessness of squats.

And it was fucking leg day, ladies.

The fourth Justice turned to look up at Gunnar, but it was impossible to tell his facial reaction with his stupid laughing mask on. But he did visibly hesitate, almost taking a step back from the Wulfric's intense glare before he managed to stop himself. "We have no care for this crumbling castle," the Justice began in a deep, authoritative tone. "We are here to arrest two fugitives of the prestigious Academy."

Alex stepped up beside Gunnar, wearing his royal white and gold armor and resting a hand on the hilt of Excalibur. His chivalrous aura was one of silent, righteous power, and he seemed to occupy the same amount of space as Gunnar despite his physical size difference. On the other hand, I swore I could see a golden silhouette—like the spirit of King Arthur's relatively unknown dark side—looming over him, and the menacing specter had a teardrop tattoo under one eye for doing hard time in a black-site supermax prison. He wanted to go back to prison, and the Justices were his ride home.

I'd once seen him personally kick the shit out of a Knightmare while wearing work-out garb, suplexing him on my unicorn's horn with ease. And that had been *before* he got armor and Excalibur.

"You have broken into my home," Alex said in a calm, clarion call. "Leave. Now. Before you ruin your lives and dishonor your family names for all eternity. Stay, and I vow to make you legends—for history will forever remember the cautionary tale of four cowardly clowns who briefly considered themselves righteous, only to realize they were merely smudged reflections of Icarus, who flew too close to the sun. I will write this story in the pages of history with my sword as the pen," he said, resting his palm on Excalibur's hilt, "and your blood as the ink."

I felt an icy shiver roll down my spine as Alex stared down the Justices, his eyes blazing.

The Justices did not immediately respond, looking shaken by the power of Alex's threat.

In my peripheral vision, I saw the man on the healer's cot slowly sitting up. With the curtain closed, no one could see him, especially not the Justice on the other side—the one holding the small brown-haired boy. I licked my lips nervously and kept my eyes averted, not wanting to draw attention to him. He finally sat up straight enough for me to get a glimpse of his profile, and I let out a discreet breath to see Aiden, looking ghastly and pale and clammy. But he was alive! The first visual proof I'd received.

The lead wizard let out a derisive laugh. "The Academy operates wherever shadows lurk, tiny king. We—"

"The Academy has no jurisdiction in Camelot," Alex interrupted, "because we monsters don't need dusty old books, or dusty old wizards. And we certainly don't need dusty old Justices. We have him, the Horseman of Justice," he said, pointing a thumb at Gunnar. "Rider of the Dread Four."

Gunnar didn't blink or move in any way. He just stood there, his blue eye glittering with his inner wolf.

Aiden slowly turned his head and noticed me. His eyes widened in surprise and he lifted up a pistol in a trembling hand, aiming it at the curtain where the Justice stood on just the other side. I felt a cold sweat break out on the back of my neck, realizing what he intended even though I had no idea how he'd gotten his hands on a gun.

A flicker of hope in an impossible situation. If he killed the Justice holding the boy, everyone else could act.

That boy was the linchpin, and Aiden had the means to tip the odds.

CHAPTER 49

The lead wizard snarled up at Alex, taking an aggressive step forward. "The Academy wizards are the most powerful wizards in the world, and are not to be taken lightly," he hissed. "We are the arm of Justice in a world gone mad—"

"All I see are petty, tiny tyrants hiding behind children," Alex interrupted. "I'd wager my best Knight could beat you senseless without drawing a blade."

Aiden glanced at me with wide, anxious eyes, jerking his chin towards his gun and shrugging his shoulders. It took me a second to realize he was asking for me to help him freaking aim at the unsuspecting Justice's back. My eyes darted back and forth between the target and the gun barrel. The only aid I could offer his targeting was vertical. The horizontal, left-to-right question was impossible for me to discern from my current angle, which would make a headshot harder than a chest shot. I waggled my fingers discreetly at my side, telling Aiden to lower the gun. He went too low, so I curled my finger in a slower, upwards motion. Aiden slowly lifted the gun until I made a sharp stop signal.

"There you are, Temple," the lead Justice growled and I jumped as if goosed, turning to face him. My heart was racing, but Aiden's gun was properly zeroed in on the wizard's chest. Thankfully, his hostage was short enough that there was no chance he would be in danger from the gun.

I slowly lifted my arms and held them out. "Here I am, Mr. Tiny Petty Tyrant," I said, taking slow steps forward. "This is wizard business, King Alex. Let me handle it," I said, glancing up at him.

He pursed his lips and gave a begrudging nod.

I casually swept my gaze across the courtyard, locking eyes with Calvin and Makayla for a brief moment, silently telling them to stand down. "Children hostages," I mused, getting a closer look at the boy and the Justice behind him. I took note of his relative position to where I estimated Aiden's gun had been aiming. I licked my lips and turned to the lead Justice. "Do you have no dignity *left*? Even just a *little*?" I asked, hoping Aiden picked up on my hint to shift his aim a little to the left. Then I hoped that my directions were accurate.

The lead wizard grunted. "You are under arrest for the murder of a Justice."

I cocked my head, steadying my breathing. I needed him angry and distracted. "Just one? Do I have time to go for double or nothing? I want to be respected when I get to wizard prison. I mean, one Justice? Them's rookie numbers. Any little bitch of a wizard could do that," I said, smirking.

He called upon his magic. "You put up a fight, and children die," he warned. "That goes for everyone! Especially you, Elder," he said in a menacing growl looking at Carl.

I nodded, clearing my throat and speaking loudly enough for everyone to hear. "Understood. No shifty business! One arrow or gunshot, and this place will turn into a bloodbath!" I said, glancing up at Gunnar and shaking my head. "We have to think of the kids."

He stared back at me, narrowing his eye a fraction. Then he gave me a brief nod. I turned back to the lead Justice and nodded.

"Where is the other wizard?" he demanded, scanning the walls. "Your co-conspirator."

So, the Academy was intending to frame me, and it was now officially on the record, spoken in front of witnesses. But which theory of mine was correct? A coup attempt or an establishment-sanctioned operation? I frowned at the Justice. "Oh, Bonk?" I asked. "That numbskull died.

Gunshot," I said. "Apparently, he wasn't trained very well." He pursed his lips at my dig. "Look, they're getting ready to go to war with the Summer Queen, so we should probably leave. *Now.*"

He scanned the courtyard, not buying my story, and my shoulders grew tense, waiting for the gunshot.

Damn it, Aiden! I thought to myself. *How many hints do you need?*

"Like, imminently," I pressed, louder. Still nothing from Aiden. I gritted my teeth, mentally sacrificing my own ego to the cause. "Look, man. I'm gonna' be straight with you. I have to pinch one off, and it *really* can't wait. I need to go right. *Now!*"

The Justice cursed beneath his mask, clenching his fist at his side. "Fine. He's worthless anyway—"

BANG!

I kicked the lead justice in the nuts hard enough to stub my toe on his tailbone as I heard a splintering crash behind me, followed by the boy's scream. The lead Justice with the chipped tailbone screamed so loudly that it was as high-pitched and silent as a dog whistle. He crumpled to the ground as I shouted, "MIST WOLVES!" and called up my magic, spinning around to grab the kid Aiden had just saved.

I heard the other two wizards curse as Calvin and Makayla evaporated out of their grasp, but they were battle-trained Justices, so they didn't stand around waiting for an explanation. They almost immediately Shadow Walked, judging by the sharp cracks in the air. Gunnar and a chorus of wolves howled and snarled as they exploded into their werewolf forms and then leapt down into the courtyard—Camelot's first mosh pit.

Fireballs began flying to and fro as the Justices Shadow Walked back and forth across the courtyard, sending the flames into werewolves and soldiers up on the walls with horrifying effect, but Alex's men were already pulling out shields and returning fire with crossbows and guns—which was alarmingly dangerous since we were in a stone fishbowl where those projectiles could hit anyone, and the Justices kept zipping around to strike from everywhere.

Unfortunately, Aiden's Justice wasn't down for the count. The bullet had hit his shoulder and spun him around, although it looked like it had shattered his collarbone based on how his left arm hung uselessly at his side. He was hurling blasts of magic into the tent, ripping through canvas and tables and glass jars full of salves and ointments we would later need for the wounded. He destroyed anything between him and his shooter. Except Aiden had been knocked off his cot and was sitting on the ground with his back against a table as he held out a shield to block the Justice's onslaught. He'd lost the gun and was barely strong enough to simply stave off his attacker, let alone cast back a wimpy counter.

"MOMMY!" the little boy squealed and sobbed, loud enough to strain his tiny vocal cords as he desperately tried to crawl away from the violent exchange, but his leg looked to have been broken in the aftermath of Aiden's gunshot. I struck Aiden's wizard in the spine with a blast of air and he crashed into the tent with a curse, knocking the whole thing down on top of them both. Whoops.

"Get the kid!" Aiden shouted from beneath the canvas, right as I'd been preparing to dive in and help him out of the tent. I gritted my teeth, forced to choose between Aiden, who was in immediate danger, and the kid, who was—

A magic band wrapped around my ankles and yanked me off my feet. I struck the stone with my elbow and hissed, feeling the pain shoot down to my fingers, numbing them. I sliced through the bonds with a bit of magic and looked up to see that the Justice I'd neutered was back in the game. Although hobbling and weak-kneed, his eyes were murderous. I tried summoning up my inner psycho from my earlier moment with Kára, but nothing happened.

Good old-fashioned wizard fight, here we come.

I called up my elemental whips and lashed out at him. His hands suddenly started to glow with green light as he lifted them in a futile attempt to block me. The moment my whips struck that green energy, they recoiled like I'd tried to force the wrong ends of two magnets together. I cursed, but it gave me a second to climb to my feet. I absently wondered how the same green light had repelled both fire and ice, but academia was for feckless twats, not professional duelists—wizards like me who had statues to honor their greatness.

Wylde's primal persona settled over my shoulders like a thick, warm fur, and the chaos around me abruptly changed, becoming beautiful and terrible, and I saw a song, written on the wind of battle before me.

Snarls and barks and gnashing fangs.

Flash of fur as arrows clang.
Ebb and flow of smoke and fire,
The dance of death is sung by liars.

"MOMMMMYYYYY!" the boy screamed, dimming the song, and pulling me back—a bit—from Wylde's almost intoxicating fervor for bloodlust. A child needed help, but I couldn't reach him.

"MY BABY!" the boy's mother screamed, hysterical with anguish we all heard in her injured son's cry.

"Get the kid!" I roared to anyone who was listening, unable to shake off my own foe as he disappeared and reappeared behind me with blindingly fast attacks, almost giving me whiplash as I jerked my head back and forth, trying to catch him before he blipped again.

I wanted his fucking *heart*!

I lashed out with a blast of air, but he Shadow Walked out of sight, causing my blast to barrel through a trio of wolves for the benefit of the Justice they'd been attacking. The man's arm was a gaping wound of raw meat and smaller, long, sinuous gashes where a wolf had bitten and then tugged, ripping trails through flesh. But he looked as if he couldn't feel it. I cursed, sending three more shots at him, but he also Shadow Walked out of harm's way.

I heard a sharp tearing sound and saw Aiden cartwheel through the air to land on the nearby cobblestones with a hard grunt. He used one arm to prop himself up and the other to hurl attacks back at the Justice who was tearing his way out of the ruined tent to finish what he'd started.

"Get up!" I shouted at Aiden, hurling spears of air through the smoke at his attacker to buy him time.

"I can't *walk*," Aiden snarled, scanning the scene in a frantic manner, searching for something through the smoke and fire. "The Viking's axe severed something in my spine, and they couldn't heal—

"MOMMY!" the boy wailed, maybe twenty feet away from me, but only ten from Aiden. "SAVE ME!"

Aiden's eyes latched onto him with a manic gleam. He began dragging himself towards the child as fast as possible, gritting his teeth in pain as he hurled what looked like spinning daggers of fire as fast as he could at the tent. It went up with a *whoompf* and the Justice screamed before Shadow Walking clear of the maelstrom.

I felt like I'd been stabbed in the gut. Aiden's legs were permanently severed? Oh my god. Then what in the ever-loving hell was he doing out here like a...a goddamned murder slug?

But...I *knew* why. A boy was crying out for his mommy...

And Aiden's mommy hadn't answered that cry when Aiden had been the little boy left all alone.

He wasn't going to let that happen today. Over his dead, crippled body.

And I felt a passionate fire bloom up inside my soul like an erupting volcano. A wizard needed support, and my wizard's magic was hungry to respond. And Wylde's heart was eager to feed fuel to that fire, singing his song in the back of my mind like a haunting dirge.

CHAPTER 50

The child sat on the ground, bawling as he tried to scoot back rather than crawl. "MOMMY!" he screamed, terrified, as werewolves zipped back and forth behind him, some leaping over him and gnashing their teeth as they hunted for their elusive prey. I took a step towards the boy, only to be intercepted by a Justice with an icy sword in his hands. I batted it to the side and hastily formed a blade of my own, choosing air. I swung it at his throat, but he fucking Shadow Walked out of the way at the last second. Something sliced across my ribs and I grunted at the icy pain, realizing he'd reappeared beside me. I swung my blade of air wildly in a circle and managed to score a direct hit of my own. Not fatal, but blood sprayed the cobblestones before he Shadow Walked away again.

I snarled, spinning in a slow circle to prevent anymore surprise attacks. They were fucking *good* at disappearing and reappearing somewhere else with a counter-strike, making them look like freaking speed ninjas as they blipped in and out across the courtyard.

Carl grabbed one by the face, squeezing his skull with a sickening crunch just as he Shadow Walked, sending the Elder to god knows where. Through the insanity of pissed off werewolves racing back and forth in fruitless pursuit of their prey, the courtyard of Camelot was pure madness.

I saw Calvin and Makayla snarling in outrage as they failed to catch one of the slippery Justices and ended up slamming into each other.

Through the chaos, I finally caught a glimpse of Aiden. He was on his side but still crawling towards the kid, even as a Justice wielded a massive, double-bladed, battle axe of condensed air, hacking down on Aiden's shield with a malevolent grin on his face as Aiden grew weaker and weaker.

I aimed a blast of air at Aiden's attacker, knowing that fire was the worst element to use when odds were more likely for me to hit an ally than one of the enemy. A new Justice appeared to my right, causing me to spin and send my shot wild, missing Aiden's attacker by less than a foot as I flung up a shield to protect myself from my new assailant. It was the charred, still smoking Justice from the tent. The burnt Justice hit hard enough for my shield to send up sparks, and I saw Aiden in my peripheral vision, reaching out a hand towards the child at his own attacker raised his giant axe for a second blow.

"NO!" Aiden screamed as a Justice appeared directly above the wounded boy, already swinging a giant hammer of air down at him. But Aiden wasn't close enough to reach him. Makayla was airborne, aiming directly for the boy's attacker, but she wouldn't be quick enough to stop him.

I grunted as I fended off another blow from my attacker but he winked out of view before I could hit back.

There were too many allies between me and the kid or me and Aiden, but through the chaos of battle, I could see three things very clearly as time suddenly slowed.

The axe falling down over Aiden as he reached out for the boy with one hand and held up a shield for himself with the other.

The defenseless boy staring up at the hammer racing towards his face, frozen stiff with terror.

Makayla *almost* close enough to decapitate the boy's attacker.

Those three things stood still, looking like a snapshot against the backdrop of werewolves snarling at the third burnt Justice who was now flinging fireballs in almost every direction to stave them off.

And then time resumed normal speed.

Aiden's own shield winked out, and a new, astonishingly bright one appeared above the boy. Aiden had a serene, resigned smile on his face. "NO!" I roared, racing up behind his attacker as I realized what Aiden had just done.

But I was too late.

The Justice's axe slammed into Aiden's back hard enough to hit cobblestone with a clinking sound as it tore entirely through him.

The other Justice's hammer rebounded off the boy's overpowered shield just in time for Makayla to strike the wizard's neck and rip out his throat with her fangs. A second mist wolf grabbed the boy by the back of the collar and began tugging him backwards. The shield hovered over him, following him as it slowly dimmed.

I skidded to a halt behind Aiden's attacker and shoved two swords of white fire directly into his kidneys. The Justice screamed as he burned from the inside out, in too much agony to even consider Shadow Walking.

I shoved him away and hurled a blast of fire at his body as I knelt down beside Aiden. I heard the wolves finally swarm the last Justice, and I saw a very confused Carl running into the courtyard from a random hallway—wherever his victim had tried to Shadow Walk while simultaneously having his skull crushed by the Elder's claw.

I carefully rolled Aiden over onto his back and sucked in a breath to find him still breathing. Barely. His chest was a huge, gaping slash that looked to have severed his spine a second time, along with almost every single internal organ except for...

His *heart*.

Yeah. He fucking had the heart all right, I thought to myself, proudly, feeling a tear roll down my cheek.

He blinked up at me with dazed, wild eyes. "The boy!" he croaked. "Did I save him?"

I placed a hand on his shoulder and squeezed reassuringly as I smiled, blinking through more tears. "Yeah, Aiden," I whispered. "You definitely saved him. You saved *all* of us. Without your gun, they had us dead to rights."

He let out a sigh of relief, and then began coughing violently, causing his wound to gush blood out of his chest like squeezing a full sponge. I didn't move my hand from his shoulder. Instead, I squeezed again, letting him know he wasn't alone.

I sensed a presence behind me and looked up to see the healer staring at Aiden's wound from a few feet away. He met my eyes and shook his head sadly. I blinked, gritted my teeth, and then silently ushered him away to tend to the other injuries. Those who had a chance.

Not Aiden Maxon.

Everyone gave us a wide berth, chased back by the healer. I heard Gunnar calling out orders along with Alex, setting up triage points and reassuring them that the danger was over.

I turned back to Aiden as he finished coughing. "What did they want?" he whispered.

"Us," I told him. "Revenge, probably, but they seemed pretty determined," I mused, frowning. "To pick a fight in Camelot was ballsy." How had they even known I was here? Had they been spying on me this whole time? What else had they seen in their spying?

Aiden frowned pensively, as if considering the same questions, even now. Then his eyes bulged in fear and he looked up at me. "The armor! If they knew you were here, they'll know Falco is undefended!" he panted, coughing up blood in his excitement. "They'll send more for revenge! You have to move—"

I squeezed his shoulder gently, shaking my head as I verified that no one was close enough to overhear. "Already moved to my family crypt," I breathed, reassuring him.

He relaxed in relief, letting out a sigh, and I could see the life fading from his eyes. "Thank you," he whispered.

"For what?" I rasped, knowing I had brought him into my mess in the first place. I could have left him locked up at Falco where he would have been safe. But then...Ella would have died—another child he'd saved. Goddamnit.

He squeezed my forearm weakly, startling me as he smiled up at me. "For...treating me like family," he breathed. "It was...nice to finally...feel..." His neck slowly loosened, and his body went slack as he died.

Wylde howled a lamenting song within my breast, rattling his fist at the sky.

I felt like he'd punched me in the throat. I hadn't made him feel like family. I sat back on my ass with a thud, staring down at him, feeling numb. A woman walked up, shifting from foot-to-foot. I slowly lifted my eyes, blinking through misty vision. She held the young boy Aiden had just saved on her hip. He had a bandage around his leg, and I saw the healer behind them, nodding at me as if to say the boy was fine. Both their cheeks were tear stained as they stared down at Aiden, unable to speak.

"My name's David," the boy whispered, staring at Aiden with haunted but grateful eyes. "Thank you...Mr. Wizard," he said, his lip trembling as he spoke to Aiden's lifeless body. Mr. Wizard...the hopeless bastard couldn't even get his name remembered in death. I would have to rectify that.

The mom's face broke and the boy finally lost his resolve, burying his head into her shoulder and sobbing. "I wanted to thank him...before..." She couldn't finish her sentence.

"He knows. And his name was Aiden Maxon," I said, hoarsely. "Family was very important to him, David." I met her eyes. "Honor that," I told her, jerking my chin towards her son.

She clutched him tight and nodded with a determined look on her face. "We will," she whispered. And then they left, sensing I wasn't in the mood to talk.

Makayla startled me by sitting down by my side and resting her head on my shoulder. She didn't say anything, but she loved on me, and that was all that mattered. I wasn't sure how long I sat there, but it was long enough for me to think over some things. As if she'd read my thoughts, Makayla climbed to her feet and held out her hand. I accepted it with a smile and rose to my feet. She assessed me from head to toe, brushed off my sleeve, and then gave me a nod of approval. "There. All better." She grinned and then turned away, walking up to her brother, who had been leaning against the wall, patiently waiting for her.

He bowed his head to me, holding it there for a few seconds.

Then the two of them spoke in low tones and I saw Carl watching me from across the courtyard, maintaining a safe distance from the deadly she-wolf. I rolled my eyes and walked up to him because he was holding my satchel. I must have dropped it at the beginning of the fight. I heard a light commotion behind me as a pair of men began lifting Aiden onto a gurney to carry him away. They were Gunnar's wolves, so I had no fear of a shallow, unmarked grave.

Aiden had sacrificed himself for the pack. That was how they would see it.

I accepted the satchel from Carl and slung it over my shoulder. I reached inside and took out a pen and a piece of paper. I scribbled down a quick message. *Courtesy of Nate Temple.* I folded it and scanned the courtyard, tucking the pen away as I found what I was looking for. The four Justices had been laid out side-by-side, and I made my way over to them.

Carl walked beside me, eyeing me sidelong with curiosity.

War horns erupted in the near distance, but we kept walking. Everyone around us froze, staring up at the walls. There, the soldiers were rushing back and forth, carrying orders and preparing.

I came to a halt in front of the Justices and studied them as everyone else began to panic. I crouched down to inspect their pockets, but found nothing of value. I sighed, mildly perturbed as Camelot went nuts in preparations for Summer's army—which was here sooner than we'd planned.

I turned to Carl with a smile. "Mail time," I told him.

I flicked Jasper Griffin's Tiny Ball at the ground and then lifted all four bodies with tendrils of magic as a Gateway to the Academy erupted. The area looked familiar, but I didn't see anybody around at the moment. I hurled the bodies through and then tossed my handwritten note on top.

I brushed my hands off as the Gateway winked shut. Then I turned back to the walls of Camelot, nodding. "You ready for war, Carl?"

He hissed, flicking his tongue out. "Oh, yes, Master Temple. Oh, yessss."

I smiled. "Good."

CHAPTER 51

I stood in front of the closed gates to Camelot, all by myself, facing the army of the Summer Queen. I had been in a hazy fog, alarmingly calm, ever since the Justices' attack an hour ago. But I was *beyond* ready for this moment. This war. The Academy would pay. Until then, they had a *thank you* card to put on their fridge.

Anyone who had a hand in this coup, or whatever flavor of corporate restructuring they were actually going through, was going to pay with their lives. I was going to clean the Academy from top-to-bottom. Not because I wanted to lead them—absolutely not, thank you very much. But it was long past time for them to *be better*. To do better. No more corruption and political machinations that ended up costing innocent lives. No more gambling for power. Not with the Omega War fast approaching. We would need every fighter we could get our hands on, and the Masters fed upon the greed of corruptible people, so it was time to get rid of them.

To starve the Masters out.

Hell, I might just change the name of the place to get rid of all traces of what they had ultimately become. And I was going to build a big, goddamned statue of Aiden Maxon in the entrance hall to the new home for wizards. Of him sacrificing his life to save a child.

Because that was what wizards were supposed to fucking *do*.

To keep the monsters back, not become them.

Their actions had earned retribution, and it would be devastating.

Birds chirped in the air and a gentle breeze blew across my cheeks, a cheery mockery of my inner turmoil. I was still covered in Aiden's blood from this morning, not caring enough to change. In fact, it was a statement piece, now. My battle armor.

I could see Summer's vast army arrayed before Camelot in the near distance. They had halted and set up battle lines *exactly* where Ashley thought they would. A vast, sprawling, only mildly rolling field that was free of trees. It was the obvious choice, of course, but I could tell that Ashley had picked the exact distance where they had placed their front lines.

She was good. Her time in Fae had opened up her Wild Side, too, and it had revealed the mind of a truly cunning strategist. Wulfra. She had been the one to reorganize Gunnar's entire pack into elite, agile units, so they could better coordinate in battle.

These micro decisions had helped maintain the necessities of pack life werewolves craved, yet it also permitted Gunnar's absolutely huge pack of over one-thousand werewolves to still be nimble and responsive during the chaos of battle.

And they were all waiting within Camelot's walls, eager to reap the seeds of chaos I was about to sow. Their blood was also up after the Justices' attack and Aiden's heroic sacrifice. The hordes of Shift students also waited with bated breath, eager to unleash their inner monsters against the twenty-thousand strong army at their door. It was a play date, in their eyes.

I eyed the army, sweeping my gaze from left-to-right, hoping they got a real good look at the wizard brave enough to stand all by himself outside the castle walls. We had sent the Summer Queen a messenger with an invitation to parley here before the war. It was pretty standard, even when both sides had no intention of backing down. So, here I was, attending a meeting to plan our next meeting.

But I was actually trying to buy Alex time to finish a few of the last-minute preparations, so I needed to drag my talk with the Summer Queen out as long as possible, even though I wanted to personally rip her throat out for working with Mordred and Baldur and likely the Masters.

I saw tiny goblins and hulking trolls, ogres and beautiful centaurs, thousands upon thousands of human-looking Fae who could have been royalty or epic legends, like Robin Goodfellow, who shared some kind of bond with Pan and King Oberon of the Wild Hunt. I saw creatures I didn't recognize and did not want to ever recognize. Glittering swarms of pixies and other, larger flying creatures zipped about their camp, and I took a calming breath, not spotting as many airborne warriors as I'd feared. Only time would tell, but I hadn't ever seen this many people gathered in one spot before. It was...chilling in scope.

After Aiden's death, I'd decided to quit pulling my punches and trying to 'figure out' the plots against me. I was going to get right up in everyone's face and start slapping them around until they lost all their teeth or spilled their guts out—literally or figuratively.

I wasn't getting answers.

I was *taking* them. War was already here, so I had nothing to lose except people, and I'd already lost one too many today. Kára was going to be devastated to hear about Aiden. I hoped she made it back soon or she was going to miss all the fun. I made sure my satchel was behind my back and the strap was nice and tight, concealing it from view.

The real prize was yet to come...

As if on cue, a bright yellow palanquin approached, carried by four burly trolls all clocking in at twelve-feet-tall. Rather than the usual hardened, leathery, rhino-like skin I'd seen on other trolls, these giants seemed to be neatly feathered like birds—except with tree leaves instead of feathers. As in, so many leaves that they would need to be plucked to see the skin underneath. That was their only resemblance to birds, because they were huge, ugly, thick-limbed brutes, and they had no wings.

The royal palanquin came to a halt ten paces away, and one of the trolls carefully pulled back the curtain so that the Summer Queen could see me. She gave me a condescending sneer, as if smelling me from this far away and not approving of the scum I represented. She was a swell lady. Truly.

She held out the letter I had sent her, waving it angrily. "Who dared send me this?" she snarled. "If Alex thinks he can treat the Queens of Fae with such blatant disrespect, I will break every single bone in his—"

"It was supposed to be an invitation to parley at a certain time," I said, frowning in confusion. "Now."

Her face darkened and her arm shook as she held the paper out for me to see. "It says *Time to Par-tay!*" she seethed, eyeing me from head-to-toe with a suspicious glare. "And other vile insinuations. Who. Wrote. This?"

I scratched my head. "It was one of the new guys. I can't see it from here. Can you have one of your big beautiful blokes bring it over to show me?" I asked, smirking as the feathered ogres beamed with pride. She made no move to answer me, so I took a step towards her. "Or I guess I could come over—"

"Stop!" she snarled. She then handed it to one of the giant ogres and motioned for him to approach me with the offensive invitation.

He stomped over to me, easily twice my size, and came to a halt within a few feet. "It's a pleasure to meet you, good sir," I said in a cheerful tone, dipping my chin politely. He opened his mouth as if to say *awww*, looking delighted that I wasn't treating him like dirt. "Don't make this weird, but can I touch your feathers?"

"You may NOT touch his feathers!" the queen snapped. "Give me that man's name, or my army marches right NOW!"

The ogre very discreetly slid his foot closer to me so that his knee was within my reach and gave me a faint wink out of her line of sight. I reached out and touched his feathers. They were silky smooth, and soft as can be. *Thanks!* I mouthed.

Then I cleared my throat as he slowly brought his foot back to where it had been and gave me another wink. The queen apparently missed it, which was just awesome. Insubordination was my favorite trait in evil henchmen. "Can I see that?" I asked loudly, holding out my hand. He extended the paper, pinching it between two thigh-sized fingers and I took it, glancing down at it.

It said *It's time to Partay!* at the top of the page.

Then it had a drawing of two stick figures. A man with a satchel and a woman with long hair and a crown. The man was smiling as he stabbed the frowning queen and her eyes had been X'd out.

The bottom of the page said *Come say HI! (Before Sunset)*.

I lowered the page, scratching my chin pensively. Then I winced, looking up at her. "You know what? This is kind of embarrassing. I think *I* drew this one," I admitted with a guilty shrug, using my free hand to slide my satchel into her view for her to clearly see—which was why she'd been initially scrutinizing me. "But it was just a draft copy. The messenger was supposed to redraw it with colored pencils. It's really shitty quality, and I apologize for that. There was supposed to be red blood and everything." I glanced up at the ogre and whispered, "You should probably get back now. And snarl at me for good measure."

He studied me for a moment, his eyes widening in alarm at his suddenly risky job security. Then he leaned forward savagely and roared at me, blowing my hair back and slathering me with ogre drool. Then he stomped away, growling furiously.

I wiped at my face, spitting and hacking. When I was finished, I finally looked up to see the queen's face, and that made it all worth it. She was so furious that she could no longer blush. She just kind of trembled.

I shrugged. "At least the time was right," I said, pointing at the paper with a grin. "So, let's move this right along. You tell me why you're here, and then I'll interrupt you."

The queen was staring through me, not seeming to have heard me. "Bring Alex out to discuss terms, at this instant, or I will—"

"How long have you worked with Baldur?" I asked, interrupting her. "Did you know him before or after Mordred? Do you also have a secret Justice pen pal like he does, or is that just for the Masters' favorites?" I asked, fishing for apples across my vast spectrum of theories. I folded my arms. "I'll wait."

Because she looked as if I had struck her between the eyes. All the blood had drained from her face, and she looked torn between terror, panic, and outrage at the specificity of my interrogation. "I do not know where you heard such filth, but this war has nothing to do with you, Wylde," she said in a very cold, empty tone. I couldn't quite get a read on whether she was offended at a lie or terrified I'd discovered the truth.

"Yeah," I said, nodding thoughtfully. "Okay. We'll work out our personal grievances later. Deal?"

She nodded stiffly. "That would be more appropriate."

I nodded, still unable to get a solid read on her reaction. It was puzzling. "Oh. Where are my manners?" I said, slapping my palm on my forehead. "I need to tell King Alex the nature of your visit. He's probably going to ask why you're here with an army, if I had to hazard a guess. He thinks you're here because of me."

The queen stared up at the gate to Camelot, again looking distant and distracted. Neither offended nor guilty. It was the fucking strangest thing. Maybe it was my lackadaisical commentary messing with her head.

I pointed at a significant crack in the wall. "That's where I speared Mordred with Gungnir," I explained. Then I pointed behind her. "From *way* back there. Probably my best shot. Boy, did *he* look surprised."

She slowly turned to look back at me with that alien, foreign gaze. It made the freaking hair stand up on the backs of my arms. I almost thought she had been possessed by something, but then I watched her lower her eyes and take a deep, calming breath. Three times. Finally, she glanced back up at me and most of the color had returned to her cheeks.

"My apologies," she told me. "I felt a little sick to my stomach for a moment, but it has passed."

I nodded slowly, wondering what in the hell had just happened.

CHAPTER 52

"Now," she began, "we have our differences, Wylde. I know we are not friends and that we have deep distrust of one another. But I am not here for *you*." She pointed a finger at Camelot's gates. "You took that boy from the Wild Hunt, and then he came back to Fae, thinking he could put on a crown and become a king."

And there it was. She had a problem with one of her old changelings becoming a king of Fae and getting his hands on toys she wanted for herself. She saw Alex as a thing, not a king.

I frowned. "The crown doesn't make the king. And Arthur Pendragon's sword chose *him*, not the other way around. He didn't come here looking for power. He came here to right your pal Mordred's wrongs."

She shrugged, giving me a strange look. "Arthur Pendragon had a *right* to Camelot and its treasures, even though I did not like it. Mordred Pendragon also had a *right* to Camelot and its treasures, even though I did not like it. Alex Arete has *no right* to Camelot or its treasures, and I do not like him. That is the difference. It's a matter of rights. I am here to banish the usurper who claims Pendragon blood yet has none."

I folded my arms and eyed her with a suspecting grin. "You're just here for the treasures, aren't you? Come on, you can tell me. I already agreed not to address our personal grievances with you until later."

She regarded me thoughtfully for a few tense moments. Finally, she nodded, rather stiffly and meekly. "All my points stand true," she said, even as a slow smile stretched across her face, "but yes, I am just here for the treasures. To protect all of Fae from Manlings," she added, her smile flickering away like a doused flame.

I waggled a naughty finger at her, deciding I was finished stalling after she'd chosen to throw that little nasty personal comment. "Then let's not mince words, Summer." She bristled at my familiarity but looked relieved to cease what she saw as my endless prattling. If she had been wiser, she would have seen my stalling tactics for what they were, but she was so eager to get her treasures, she wasn't being objective.

"The treasures are already forfeit," she said in a commanding tone. "Period. My army will take the castle by force before dawn, and many of his people will die," she said confidently. "But...if Alex surrenders and swears an oath to serve me as his queen, I will consider letting him live. But I must hear it from his lips."

I scratched my chin, considering her question. "I'm confused on the treasure thing and the question of property rights." She nodded impatiently, urging me to go on with a flick of her fingertips. "Do you want the sword or the armor? Because Alex no longer has the armor. I bought them from him—as in, they are mine by right. So, if you just want the real estate, that might be up for discussion. If you want Excalibur, that's up to Alex. If you want the armor..." I pointed a thumb at my chest. "Let's haggle."

She stared at me and I could tell that she had been knocked back in surprise halfway through my statement, but she was now thinking furiously, weighing all the schemes that might ultimately lead her to all the treasures.

Or, of course, wondering if I was bluffing.

"I swear on my power that I own all the Knigh—" I cut off abruptly and looked up at the sky, beseeching the all-seeing, promise-keeping god who supposedly took powers away from anyone who broke this stupid oath complex we all feared. Was he even real? "Pause, promise-keeping deity. Let me take that back from the top." I reached out for my magic to make sure it was still there and let out a breath of relief, wiping at my brow. "Phew. That could have been embarrassing," I told the queen. Then I cleared my throat and tried again. "I swear on my power that I own ten of the armored Knights."

She had been staring at me in silence the whole time, looking baffled at my skyward conversation. Then she leaned forward hungrily. "Ten?" she mused, practically salivating. In fact, I saw a desperate hope in her eyes that made me twitchy. "I am not leaving without that armor. If you give me the ten Knights, my army will leave Camelot," she said.

I studied her warily, sensing the truth to her claim. She *really* wanted that armor. She hadn't once mentioned Excalibur.

"So be it." I glanced over her shoulder at the gathered army, assessing the distance. I pointed at a boulder near the edge of the field between her front lines and Camelot. "There's no way I can carry them by hand, so I will open a Gateway right there. Stand back until they are all through."

She glanced back to where I had pointed and gave a faint nod. "That is reasonable. Unless, of course, you intend trickery."

I snorted, clasping my hands behind my back. "You got me. I was going to send all two-thousand of our warriors through that Gateway right in front of your army for a surprise attack," I said, drily. I shook my head. "If I wanted to kill you, I would do it right here and now." I ripped open a Gateway behind my back and stretched my finger through to tap her on the shoulder before she could even sense me using magic.

She jumped with a shriek, banging her head on the roof of her palanquin, but I had already retracted my finger and closed the Gateway. She rounded on me with a hiss. "How *dare* you finger a queen?!"

I sighed, wishing it weren't so easy. I unclasped my hands so she could see them. "Calm down. I would never finger a queen. I tapped you on the shoulder to prove a point. It could have just as easily been fire. "

She paled. "Why do you keep antagonizing me? This is between Camelot and Summer!"

I shrugged. "I like standing up for the little guy. Like I did when I took him from your changeling operation and shut you and your sister down." I took a casual step closer, staring into her eyes. "If I wanted you dead, you would be dead," I repeated.

Her ogres narrowed their eyes and clenched their giant fists in warning —except for my buddy. He winked at me before shaking a pathetic fist to fit in. The queen lifted a hand and they relaxed their shoulders. "You cannot kill a force of nature, Wylde," she said in a neutral, lecturing tone. "The world would be sent into chaos without someone wearing the summer crown. Not just Fae, but every realm would suffer, and we all know how you care about the little people who would all die as a result." She almost sounded sympathetic for my ignorance.

I nodded slowly. "They said the same thing about Zeus. Up until a few weeks ago anyway." I looked up at the sky and nodded. "Beautiful weather we have here in Camelot, eh?" I asked with a shit-eating grin.

She grimaced distastefully. "Zeus is...*was* a god of *one* element. I am more than a god. My mantle controls an entire season that takes every element into account, much like my sister controls Winter. I do not say that to brag, I say that for you to comprehend the scope of what I represent."

I nodded thoughtfully. "You know, I keep hearing that, but then my crazy brain starts wondering what happened to the Spring and Autumn Courts. Maybe they had queens once, too." I took very close note of the absolutely nauseated look on her face and the sudden intake of breath that made her throat jump. I pretended not to notice, though, and shrugged instead. "Food for thought."

I pointed at the distant boulder again. "Be ready."

She pursed her lips. "But we haven't shaken hands on the deal."

I laughed. "Lady," I said, lifting my gaze to stare at her. I lessened my restraint on my Godkiller powers and my eyes and veins began to glow with golden light. "If I get close enough to shake hands with you right now, I'm liable to kill you just to see what *happens*. After all, it is now *later*," I said, emphasizing the last word to remind her that I said I wouldn't deal with our personal grievances until *later*. Her face paled in recognition and she leaned back a few inches. "I've had a very trying day and I'm all out of fucks to give. A little inter-realm chaos sounds like the perfect nightcap."

She gave me a stiff nod. "We can dispense with the handshake," she said, sounding shaken.

I shoved down my Godkiller powers and smiled cordially. "Twenty minutes enough time for you to get back to your army, or do you need longer?"

"Twenty minutes will suffice."

I was about to turn around, but I paused. "How about we compromise and agree on one hour?"

She pursed her lips and shook her head, not falling for my trick. "Twenty. Minutes."

I shrugged. "Worth a shot. Twenty minutes. You get the Knights. Then you leave. Right?"

She nodded. "Y—"

I Shadow Walked back to Camelot without waiting for her to finish speaking, because I was petty.

Alex, Gunnar, and Tory were waiting for me in the throne room, seated around Betty, the shitty, plastic, round table he'd adopted for Camelot. I scowled, refusing to sit down. Tory smiled at my blatant hatred, having heard all about my distaste earlier today. "How did the 'stall for as long as possible and then pick a fight rather than negotiate parley' strategy work?" she asked, smirking.

I smirked back. "Like a charm. She *loved* my drawing."

Alex grunted, folding his arms. "So? How long do we have?"

"Twenty minutes, so I hope your people have been working hard while I was stalling her. We're out of time. You guys know what to do."

They nodded their readiness, but Tory lifted a finger and cleared her throat. "Why wouldn't she just attack us herself? Use her powers as the Summer Queen to assault Camelot and lay waste to us all?" she asked, indicating the crumbling brick. "Couldn't be that hard for her."

I nodded, surprised the question hadn't come up sooner. "I think the powers the queens choose to wield is limited in Fae, believe it or not. Think about Fae as one country and the two queens are co-equal rulers. They are two sides of the same coin, so they cancel each other out. They send their armies at each other, but they never go head-to-head, queen-to-queen. In fact, they often spend a lot of time together. Like sisters. So, a queen directly attacking a resident of Fae would probably set a precedent that could never be taken back. I believe that's what happened to Spring and Autumn, and these two have learned from that mistake. Spring and Autumn got too big for their panties and had to be shut down. Summer and Winter then stepped in to assume their mantles, making them even stronger and more turbulent than before. Or, as my mind envisions it, they evolved from bombs to nuclear bombs. Acting recklessly now would throw the entire world off and put all the power in one or the other's hands. Two queens deterring each other is safer than one with all the guns. So, when it comes to domestic stuff, they send their armies to ruffle each other's feathers and let off some aggression, but it rarely amounts to anything because neither wants to cross that ultimate nuclear line."

Tory nodded. "That actually makes a *lot* of sense. How long have you known that?" she asked, impressed.

I stared at her for a few moments. "I literally just made all that up. Did it actually sound persuasive?"

Alex choked and Gunnar snorted, howling with laughter. Tory grinned, shaking her head. "You're *impossible!* I take back my compliment, jerk."

I grinned and waved a hand to let her know I was only teasing. "I've been piecing it together for some time now. It really is just my working hypothesis, but when I just asked Summer about the Spring and Autumn Queens, she shit her palanquin, so I'm betting I'm kind of close."

"She shit her *what*?" Gunnar roared, now crying with laughter as he fell out of his chair, wheezing.

Alex and Tory stared down at Gunnar with startled looks. "It wasn't that funny," Tory said, shaking her head at Gunnar.

He reached up to grab the table, still giggling. "What the hell is a *palanquin*?" he wheezed. "I've never heard such a ridiculous word."

At that, Tory burst out laughing as well, realizing why Gunnar was so amused.

"But I am neither of those," Alex said, ignoring the wolf and changing the subject. "Camelot has nothing to do with the seasons."

"Ah, but you are a Pendragon. He has a claim here in Fae, for whatever reason. Summer refuses to accept that because she sees you as nothing more than a changeling—a gutter rat or slave, at best. Despite what you and I both know about that golden ichor you drank." He nodded, pursing his lips to hear her personal opinions on him. "I've heard a half-dozen versions of how Arthur got citizenship here, but they're mostly conflicting, so I don't know how you really fit into this. But if you weren't a true citizen of Fae, they would have destroyed you by now. Just like they haven't directly attacked me—because I'm a citizen. I was born here. They send their monsters and try to bully me, but at the end of the day..." I shrugged. "The other citizens would start getting mighty twitchy if their leaders started randomly assassinating their fellow citizens."

Alex grunted. "Makes more sense than anything I've come up with."

"So, we go to war," Gunnar said, wiping tears from his eye, "and hope she really did shit her...palanquin," he wheezed, fighting back another fit of giggles. "Because that would mean your hypothesis is correct. Otherwise, we will piss off the Summer Queen enough for her to show us her true powers."

I nodded, appreciating how hard I'd made him laugh. A happy consequence for once, after a day of very dark happenings. That was enough to lift my spirits for the hours to come. I'd made a friend laugh.

That's what life was all about.

"If Summer gets uppity, that's where I'll come in to shut her down. Leave the queen to me. That's the real reason I'm here." I turned to Alex. "Not to say that I don't want to be here, but there comes a time when a man needs to make his own legend. You don't want others to win this war for you. Not if you want to be a true king, beloved and adored by your people."

He smiled, rolling his eyes. "You just son'd me. Wow."

"Respect your elders," I growled, grinning back at him. Then I turned to the others. "Okay. Make sure everything is set just like we planned. When that Gateway opens, we give them the Knights and hope for the best. All hell is going to break loose."

CHAPTER 53

We stood in a grassy field far back from the walls of Camelot. Alex had surmised that it used to be a royal garden or a farm, given that there was no rubble from old collapsed structures. I closed my eyes and steadied my breathing. I'd really hoped for Aiden to be here with me. I was about to use a lot of magic and it would have been a huge benefit to have another wizard by my side rather than depleting myself too early.

But Aiden had been murdered by the very people he used to work for.

No matter what the real story was behind the Academy, one thing was obvious: they were irrevocably broken. They needed a clean-up crew. I knew there were good people in the Academy, but it was hard to have an open discussion with them when they had been brainwashed to hate every root, leaf, and branch of my family tree.

They refused to believe that each season birthed new offshoots. New leaves. New growth. New potential.

I was about as far from perfect as one could be, and my ancestors had apparently earned every ounce of hatred cast their way. Hell, one of my ancestors had apparently *started* the elusive Masters.

So, yeah. I understood their trepidation in trusting me.

But Kára had woken me up to the whole trust thing. Whether you misplaced your trust or not, at least you were riding the shit out of this vehicle called life. Why buy a brand-new luxury car and then never drive it? There was no such thing as a perfect world without risk. Just one without joy—from never trusting anyone enough to open yourself to the possibilities of experiencing joy. If you got burned, you learned. Next time, try it a little differently and keep trucking on.

I let out a breath, shaking my head from my reverie. I would try to honor Aiden's sacrifice today.

I glanced over at Gunnar and gave him a reassuring smile, even though I didn't necessarily feel like smiling. He knew me well enough to see through it, but he didn't say anything.

The Horsemen had to put on brave faces for all the men and women watching us.

We were their Hope.

And their Justice.

I cleared my throat and scanned the gathered army with a small measure of pride. Most had remained in their human skins and I spotted numerous banners throughout the crowd. I saw a bunch of the werewolves holding *Memento Mori* banners or fixing them to their guns and blades. They'd made them months ago per Gunnar and Ashley's command, honoring the Temple family crest since Gunnar was an adopted part of my family, making the entire pack an extension of my family. I smiled, honored.

I hadn't known how they planned to use them until a few moments ago. I hadn't known about any of the *other* banners either.

Tory's students at Shift had been very hard at work, particularly the Arts and Crafts Club—both at the school over the past few months and then here, lugging their manual sewing equipment over to Camelot after the attack. Dozens upon dozens of banners, rivaling Gunnar's pack. Theirs said *Non Serviam*. Because they had started out in life as slaves to a cruel Beast Master before Tory and I had saved them, showing them a different life. The motto held significant meaning for them—both personally and as a nod to my help in opening Shift.

It wasn't a painting.

It was better.

Tory's Arts and Crafts club had even assisted Alex over the past day in making a bunch of banners for him with his last name—*Arete*, which also meant to become the best possible form of a thing. The thing part was up to the individual, but the essence was to pursue your best self.

Like Alex had done since his own messed up childhood.

And yet...

Alex's banner was another nod to my family crest. For the hundredth time, I found myself wondering why so many coincidences circled my crest. Why it had been emblazoned across Zeus' mountain, how I'd saved a young boy from Fae who just so happened to have the last name Arete, and how I'd managed to get my hands on a hammer that just so happened to be Excalibur in disguise...

Which would later become Alex's. The circular flow was more than dizzying. But to see it all before me now, in Camelot, with a few thousand shifters and Fae willing to lay down their lives for a chunk of dirt and a chance at a new life, while sporting banners from my family's crest, that was truly awe-inspiring.

Well, it was a light at the end of a dark tunnel. I'd learned entirely too many dark aspects about my ancestors and, despite a few of my own mistakes, I was rewarded with finally seeing others associate my family name with something right and good.

And that meant the world to me after my grim afternoon, holding a new brother's dying body together—twice. *Give me some luck, Aiden Maxon, and I'll find the man responsible. I swear.*

I cleared my throat and addressed the crowd. "We all know our orders, but I want to take a minute to talk about why we're here in the first place. Some of you are here for a new home. A fresh start. A new life," I said, turning to Tory and the Shift students. They grinned eagerly, nodding. "But to be worthy of that new home, one must work hard to acquire it. You don't walk up to an empty field and simply wish for crops to grow, or walk into a forest and wish for animals to drop dead before you so you can eat that night. You have to earn it. Work for it. Bleed for it. Sweat for it. Toil for it. Nothing in this world is free. Your new home has a price," I said, pointing in the direction of the distant army. "It's expensive, but your freedom is worth every penny."

They cheered excitedly, pumping their fists in the air. Tory let it go on for a few moments before her green eyes flashed and they immediately quieted.

I turned to Gunnar and Ashley, dipping my chin. "Some of you are here because you understand the value of family and unity. Strong alliances take work, but they are reciprocal. You help them in their time of need and they answer your call when you're in trouble. Loyalty. Friendship. Family. Pack. I expect to see your Ghosts haunt the field today." A Ghost was a pack of twenty wolves that worked as a unit during battle. She probably had larger teams, but that had been the only unit name I could remember. The thousand plus werewolves cheered and hooted in a deafening cacophony, raising fists in the air.

Ashley and Gunnar smiled, nodding. Calvin and Makayla watched me, both of them smiling. Mac winked, the cute little shithead. I tried to wink back and ended up just blinking at her. She grinned even bigger.

I turned to Alex and Talon. His rag-tag crew of soldiers consisted of many of the forgotten Fae—those dismissed and neglected by either of the two queens. Most of them were humanoid, but I saw a few goblins, a thick swarm of pixies, a cockatrice, one adolescent troll and a dozen short, burly, bearded gnomes.

"And some of you are here to defend what's yours," I told them. "You've been forgotten by the Queens of Fae and you've found a new home in Camelot. You wish to build it back up, and someone has come to keep you down. You fight for the old blood. You fight for the honor of what once was, and you are stubborn, reckless, violent bastards," I said, grinning wolfishly. "My kind of people."

The Fae shrieked and screamed, lifting spears and axes into the air. Alex shrugged, nodding.

"And I am here for *chaos*," I told them, lifting the Scythe of Cronus, a sickle made of seemingly dark gray stone that positively hummed with power. Zeus had used it to kill his father, and I thought scythes looked wicked so I'd chosen it for this figurative photo-op, even though I probably wouldn't be running around the field swinging a blade. "I am here to stand against the chaos beyond these walls and even the scales. This is not *my* fight. It's *yours*, and it's time to see who is most committed to their cause. The tyrants who abandoned you once before," I said, pointing towards

Summer's distant army beyond the wall, "or the man who wants to give you a home and is willing to fight for it," I said, pointing my scythe at Alex. "Two questions must be answered by each of you, in your heart of hearts..." I said, trailing off to make sure they were all listening. "Are you worthy of your dreams? Are you victims or victors?" I leaned forward, grinning. "Because it's time to show *them* the answers!" I growled, pointing my scythe back towards our enemies.

They erupted with screams and roars, many of them shifting into their animal forms or raising their weapons and cheering. Then they were rushing to their positions. I glanced down at my phone and nodded. Perfect timing.

"You guys ready to give them the Knights?" I roared.

They screamed.

And I obliged.

I called up my magic, infusing it with the elemental power of Fae, braiding them together like two streams forming a river. Then I ripped open a Gateway to the spot I had pointed out for the Summer Queen.

Except it wasn't the right size for me to toss ten Knightly sets of armor through.

It was fifty yards too wide.

The front lines of Summer's army squinted, trying to look into the Gateway and likely wondering why it was so massive. Surely, their foes weren't stupid enough to actually attack a force of twenty-thousand with two-thousand ragtag foot soldiers, even though our entire force was screaming at the tops of their lungs.

They were right, of course.

Because why send foot soldiers when Camelot now had a fucking *cavalry*.

Ten armored luxury SUV's—my Knight XV's from St. Louis—roared to life as the drivers hit the ignitions. Their halogen headlights kicked on and they tore through the Gateway, decorated with more banners than a political rally, and loaded with bloodthirsty shifters and other precious cargo.

I'd promised to send the Summer Queen ten armored knights. She should have read the contract closer. After all, I was part Fae, and we were devious with our promises, burying truths in lies.

The Knights had come to Fae, and they were roaring, honking, blinding, wretched, armored beasts.

Rules had been broken, and stories would be sung.

Because sometimes you had to cheat like a bastard to win like a king.

·

CHAPTER 54

I slipped the scythe back into my satchel and grinned as the Knights rushed past me in an orderly fashion, honking their horns as werewolves and other shifters hung out the open windows howling and snarling at the stupefied Summer army. The armored SUV's began fanning out just like we'd planned, careful to keep their distance from each other as iron war-horses screamed across the Land of Fae for the very first time, hungry to commit as many vehicular knighticides as possible.

Guns began blasting like strings of firecrackers from every vehicle as Alex's army hung out the windows, hurling lead at the panicked Summer forces. Explosions rocked the land as some occupants of the SUV's began hurling grenades and tossing the explosive charges from Gunnar's armory. I'd promised to pay them back for their inventory if they promised to make a lot of noise. I'd also promised every person fighting for Camelot a bonus of one dollar per dead Summer warrior—each. So, if we destroyed the entire army, they would each get in the neighborhood of twenty-thousand-dollars.

Talk about motivation.

The horde of shifter foot soldiers raced through the Gateway in a stampede of monstrous beasts thirsty for blood. Werewolves, jaguars, rhinos, chimeras, coyotes, gorillas, and many, many more. Some of them had already taken on their Wild Sides—carefully transitioned with their Beast Master Headmistress' bond—producing even more terrifying shifters than most of the world had probably ever seen. Their advance was mostly concealed by the massive trucks, the gunfire, and the explosions.

The last SUV waited for me, revving its engine, eager to join in on the fighting. I rushed up to it and hopped in the front passenger seat. I glanced over at the driver and gasped to see the mother of the young boy Aiden had saved. She grinned, shrugged, and then floored it.

"What the hell are *you* doing here?" I demanded.

"You need a driver. And your driver's name is Yowza," she said, smiling at me.

"Yowza?" I wheezed, realizing that she was being entirely serious and that my understanding of the phrase was entirely different than hers. "What a pretty name," I said, smiling crookedly.

She eyed me sidelong with a suspicious glance at my strange tone, but I kept that smile plastered in place. "As a healer, I'm used to working under pressure, so this does not bother me," she said, gesturing through the windshield at the panorama of explosions, gunfire, screaming mutilated monsters, and stampeding centaurs ahead of us. "Driving is simple enough, and we wanted to help fight for our home, just like you said." She lifted a Tiny Ball, showing it to me. "I know the plan. All I have to do is drive from here to there," she said with a smile, "through to the other side of the army. Then I throw this down ahead of my truck and drive through back to Camelot. Simple." She smiled at me.

Instead of arguing with her, I gave Yowza a nod of approval. She wanted to fight for her home. I couldn't begrudge her that. I stared out my window, marveling at how effective the first waves of the Knights of Camelot were at scattering Summer's camp. They simply didn't know how to fight this bizarre cavalry that was faster than any of them and had super extra hard tough hides. The centaurs were skittish or panicked, running around in circles or scattering in confusion to see how inferior they were to these new Knights from Camelot.

I looked at the side mirror and saw that all the ground forces were through, so I closed the massive Gateway behind me with a sigh of relief. A new thought hit me and I spun to look at Yowza. "Where's your son, David? Is he safe?"

"Right here, Mr. Wizard," David chimed in from the back seat.

"Yowza!" I scolded instinctively as I flinched and spun to stare at him. Yowza laughed as if I'd complimented her.

David lifted up two grenades wrapped in iron nails and paper masking tape, and I almost had a heart attack. "You need someone to throw things, and I'm super good at that," he assured me. "To make Aiden Maxon proud."

For a moment, my mind went back to the story of David and Goliath, how the young man with the sling had defeated the deadly giant by... throwing rocks. Nah. He was too young, surely.

"That's great, David," I said, smiling, knowing I could not show him anger or I would risk destroying his self-confidence. And...he was doing this for Aiden. This might very well be a defining moment that built the foundation of his character for the rest of his life—the moment he learned values that most other children never learned. Hell, most adults.

Drake and Cowan were very meekly sitting in the back-backseat, holding assault rifles across their chests, looking like two school children shooting spitballs in class when the teacher abruptly spun around and caught them red-handed. I glared at Gunnar's commanders. "We should have a private conversation later, boys. Something I forgot to tell you before we left." I said in a cool tone, realizing we were already upon Summer's now mostly destroyed front line.

In response, they hurriedly lowered their windows, aimed their guns outside, and then began shooting in sharp bursts, tearing through Summer's army.

To my further horror, *Calvin and Makayla* decided to rise up from *their* hiding places in the rear cargo area of the twenty-foot-long vehicle. And they *also* held assault rifles. I sputtered frantically, feeling my pulse skyrocket so high that it seemed to stop beating at all for a few seconds. "Do your *parents* know you're here? Where's your chaperone goat?" I demanded. "Grinder!" I called out, fully expecting him to pop out from under a seat.

They grinned. "Our parents told us we could join you if you said it was okay," Calvin said, grinning triumphantly, knowing it was far too late for their Godfather to send them to their rooms.

"I did not say it was okay!" I snapped.

Calvin shrugged, grinning even more roguishly. "Oh, I could have sworn you did."

A body slammed into the side of the vehicle and then we ran over it with a squishy bump.

"Go Yowza!" Drake cheered, laughing as he hung his head out the window, panting.

"We couldn't find Grinder," Mac told me, shrugging. "And we wanted to keep you safe," she said, racking the slide on her rifle like she was a spec-ops sleeper agent.

"Do you two even know how to use those?" I demanded. They'd only been human for three weeks!

"Yes, Godfather," they said in perfect unison, sounding as if it was the fourth time I'd asked if they'd brushed their teeth before bed.

I had a mild conniption as one of them hit a button and the back hatch opened on hydraulic lifts. I saw Summer's army running around like crazy directly behind us, having no idea what to do against the Knights of Camelot. Two of the leaf-ogres were on fire, and a third was missing a leg from one of the grenades. I sent up a silent prayer for the winking, palan-quin carrying, leaf-ogre I'd befriended, wishing I'd caught his name. Calvin and Makayla calmly began popping off shots in short, targeted bursts in a *hey girl, hey* kind of strategy rather than going coked-up Tony Montana.

Say hello to my little friend!

CHAPTER 55

I spun back to the front and opened the sunroof, muttering under my breath. Too late to change anything now. I climbed out of my seat and braced my feet on the console, lifting my torso out of the car.

I got my first clear three-sixty view of the battlefield and immediately felt like I was in Jurassic Park.

It was sheer bedlam. I saw one of the SUV's barrel through a gathered mass of gnomes, absolutely *obliterating* them. Someone in the car tossed out a few grenades for good measure, and the vehicle was twenty feet further on before the iron-nail-taped bomb exploded.

Fae screamed and burst into flames as iron shrapnel pulverized them, doing double damage.

David, my own grenade launcher, took that as his sign to begin slinging his explosives, and he took particular note of a massive herd of centaurs racing towards his window. Drake and Cowan began unloading on the centaurs, mowing down the front lines, but the rest leapt over their fallen comrades, launching spears or shooting bows and arrows at us. They struck the armored sides of the SUV to no effect, skittering off harmlessly, but one almost ricocheted into my arm, of course, since I was hanging out the top of the vehicle. I started throwing balls of fire at them, realizing that I was cackling madly.

David's grenades exploded in the middle of the herd, destroying many but scattering the rest as they circled around, trying to discern who had just attacked them from behind—because they didn't know how grenades worked. They'd likely thought them to be rocks or something.

Yowza continued racing across the flatlands, laughing maniacally. Another of David's grenades landed near a rallying point of hundreds of Summer Fae, but they didn't notice it in the chaos of trying to reorganize their ranks and establish a new strategy for this shit show. They also didn't notice the loping packs of werewolves as hundreds of them split off to either worry at the edges of the army or slice through pockets of resistance all across the battlefield. They'd started late, but werewolves were equally as fast as the SUVs, so they were fucking everywhere in our wake, staying out of reach of our grenades and gunfire.

I glanced up at the darkening sky and saw dozens of Raego's shifter dragons flying towards us from their staging point atop the nearby mountain. Their signal to move had been the arrival of the SUV's and their halogen lights—which could be seen from their distant mountaintop. I let out a breath of relief, thankful they had made it in time. Yahn had assured Alex they would be ready to move, but I hadn't heard directly from Raego, so I hadn't been entirely sure. I wondered what colors of dragon Yahn had collected, because each color represented a different type of projectile— fire, lightning, wind, rain, ice, metal, stone or even Raego's obsidian smoke that turned everything in its radius to...well, obsidian statues. If turned into statues, they didn't actually die. They just lived inside their new turtle shell for as long as Raego wanted them to.

We still had a few minutes until they arrived to rain down hell on Summer's army, though, so I kept hurling magic at any who came particularly close to us. I saw the cockatrice—a rooster-headed dragon, believe it or not—begin crowing an alarm, spotting the swarm of dragons heading their way. I blasted it with a blade of air, ripping through its neck-sack. Wasn't that how they made their hellish screams?

It began crowing even louder—proving me wrong—flapping its wings as it tried to escape, and it was soon too far away for me to stop its alarm. Fortunately, there was simply too much chaos for that to matter, what with all the explosions, honking, screaming, and gunfire.

The other SUV's were beginning to circle inward, herding the Summer army in on itself and preventing their escape. At least, that was what we wanted them to think—that we intended to make another pass through them. We had to have taken out a third of their army so far, which was way better than I would have hoped. All because they'd been so confident that they could simply swallow up our smaller force if we tried any tricks.

Like the great Mr. Rogers always said on his neighborhood show, *attack from where they least expect it, when they least expect it, and how they least expect it.*

And this wizard had tricky attack strategies for days, and I was exceedingly malicious when it came to someone trying to attack Alex's first home —the boy I saw as my own foster son.

Pissed off dads don't play fair.

I saw Gunnar crouched on the top of one of the Knights, holding on with one claw as it barreled across the field. Alex and Carl each did the same, riding on top of their own vehicles like the three of them were playing vehicular polo. I wanted to join in, but this next part was all theirs. I had to keep an eye out for queenie dearest in case she finally reared her head to make some noise.

So, I continued hurling great balls of fire at the flanks of Summer's army, doing my best to get them closer together. This was the tricky part —because we were vastly outnumbered. If we got overconfident, they could easily shut us down or trap our vehicles. We needed momentum to keep going. Because I counted at least a hundred limping trolls, double that in ogres, and another herd of centaurs amassing in the distance.

Gunnar must have determined the same thing—that it was better now than never. He pounded a fist into the roof of the car to signal the driver. The SUV changed course and barreled straight towards the largest group he could find, which just so happened to be the ogres and trolls. Alex's car veered right to circle around and flank the same group of giants Gunnar was targeting, but from the opposite side, which would take a bit longer to reach.

But the giants were watching and waiting, already brandishing massive clubs and tree trunks to squash the annoying, honking, bright-lighted fastie-go-gos laying waste to their countrymen.

Carl was doing some strange hand thing, leaving behind a trail of semitranslucent purple mist, and anyone who crossed it instantly dropped to the ground, either dead or unconscious. I shuddered, not wanting to know.

I kept flinging fireballs, trying to cause as much chaos and distraction as possible as I swept the field with an impatient frown, wondering why the queen hadn't made a move to at least assist her soldiers somehow if not outright attack us. Was her hiding proof of my theory about the queens not going to battle for fear of a nuclear fallout when Winter reciprocated? But Winter wasn't here, and Alex couldn't reciprocate like a queen—a force of nature, as Summer had so humbly referred to herself.

Unless...was she hiding out in the center of the trolls and ogres? That would explain why they were waiting in place rather than fleeing or attacking. On that note, Gunnar's SUV slammed on the brakes when he was about twenty feet from colliding into the forest of crouching, pissed-off ogres.

Gunnar leapt into the air, using the momentum of the skidding vehicle to launch himself high into the sky. He held Mjölnir high overhead and lightning cracked down from the darkening horizon at the apex of his leap to connect with the legendary hammer, illuminating it with stored, crackling blue electricity.

Also, at the height of his aerial assault, he shifted into his huge Wulfric form in an explosion of shredded fabric confetti—since he'd been intentionally wearing layers upon layers of extra clothing for this *exact purpose* —so it looked like the lightning exploded *him* into billions of tiny pieces, confusing the hell out of the club-wielding ogres staring upwards in wait.

Only for a moment, but that moment was all he had needed—to deter them from swatting him out of the air before he could pull off his boss move to maximum effect.

Through that cloud of fabrifetti, Justice rained down from the darkening heavens.

A massive werewolf foot kicked an ogre in the jaw so hard that it broke the damned thing's neck, clearing a path for him to plummet down to the ground in the center of the towering giants. I held my breath as it seemed like they simply swallowed him into their huddle like a pebble in a pond.

Lightning flashed out in every direction and a shockwave of sizzling electricity sent trolls and ogres cartwheeling through the air, flipping end-over-end like rag dolls. In the center of the destruction, Gunnar knelt on the ground, a giant white werewolf with a hammer of living lightning. He arched his head back and howled, the sound tearing across the battlefield like a siren. And it was answered by a thousand wolves, making all of Fae quake in fear. Then Gunnar began blasting stunned ogres left and right. The survivors rounded on him; wielding clubs as big as our trucks.

Which was when *Alex's* SUV finally finished circling around the opposite side of their group and mimicked Gunnar's move, but this time with Excalibur. Since he was on the opposite side, I simply saw a whole bunch of yellow lightning zipping from one giant to another as if they were all the perfect conductors in Fae's first utility company, the Ogre-grid.

It was equally devastating, if not more.

Gunnar let out another bone-chilling howl, and one hundred wolves rose up from the tall grass behind the ogres. They silently tore forward like one-hundred arrows from the bow of Gunnar's howl, and they tore through the ogres, slashing legs with tooth and claw, snarling hungrily as they mowed down the giant enemies for their alpha, the Horseman of Justice.

And we were just getting started.

CHAPTER 56

I spotted a goat racing through the yellow and blue electric disco party, dodging and headbutting trolls and ogres alike as he sprinted up to his werewolf boss, who was dangerously close to being surrounded by his much larger opponents. Grinder hit Gunnar from behind, flipping the giant werewolf up into the air.

What the hell? Was he going to try carrying the seven-foot-tall werewolf? That was impossible. Grinder was the size of a big Mastiff, but that was still *way* too small.

The lightning from Mjölnir abruptly lashed out of the hammer of its own accord, and slammed into Grinder's horns. I winced, knowing the goat was a goner, and now Gunnar was going to crash to the—

Grinder grew so fast that he appeared to explode out of *himself*, expanding into a goat the size of a monster fucking Clydesdale, and the lightning danced across his horns, stretching them out, making them longer and gnarlier until they looked more like murderous antlers. *Grinder the Green-Eyed Goat-deer, nobody laughed or called him names*, I sang in my head. His green eyes crackled with arcs of blue electricity and he bellowed out a bleat that was more like a chorus of lions, and actually bowled over a few ogres.

Gunnar landed on Grinder's back with a stunned look on his cute, little

Wulfric face, staring down at Mjölnir and then Grinder in utter bewilderment. Then he grabbed onto a fistful of hairy goat neck and twisted his torso to start launching blasts of lightning at any ambitious giants who thought to pursue them. Grinder spotted me hanging out the sunroof and altered course to race towards me. We were in a relatively clear spot, so I pounded on the roof to tell Yowza to stop. She did, and I ducked back inside. I reached out to squeeze her shoulder and smiled. "You've done great, Yowza. And you saved our butts back there, David," I said, grinning at him over my shoulder, "but you two need to get out of here, now. Deal?"

She nodded, beaming from ear-to-ear at my praise. "We will keep our distance but will get rid of the rest of the grenades before we use the Tiny Ball." She smiled and reached back to ruffle her son's hair. "He really is an excellent shot."

"He sure is. Maybe get him a sling," I said in a conversational tone. She didn't bat an eye, nodding thoughtfully. "Aiden would be proud," I said, risking another glance back at David and shrugging off my suspicion from earlier. He sucked in his lower lip and nodded, fighting back tears of pride. I grinned, turning around to my door.

I let out a manly shriek to see a massive electric goat eyeball the size of a dinner plate glaring at me from inches away on the other side of the window—like that scene in *Jurassic Park* with the T-Rex. I took a deep breath as Grinder hopped back, giving me room to open the door. He'd ditched Gunnar somewhere because the werewolf was no longer on his back.

I climbed out and glared at him, slamming the door closed behind me. "Where the hell have you been?" I hissed, spotting Gunnar twenty feet away, talking to a mixed group of shifters—both Tory's and his.

"The queen is not here!" Grinder hissed before I could berate him about not keeping an eye on Calvin and Makayla. "I snuck into their camp. She left the moment you drove the trucks through the Gateway!"

I stared at him, stunned. "She ran away, but left her army behind?" I asked, incredulously. My thoughts instinctively feared for the armor in the Mausoleum, but no one other than Kára knew about that...

Right? I squashed the ominous thought.

He nodded. "No one seemed to know she left until her tent was trampled, but I saw her make a Gateway and leave with some of her guards. She even took a dozen or so of her ogre guards. The big twelve-footers with feathers covering their bodies," he said.

I frowned, scratching at my chin. Maybe she'd run home. Or to get reinforcements?

"Maybe we just won," I said, shrugging. The dragons had finally reached the battle and were blasting their elemental fire down upon the Summer army, preventing them from reorganizing, or ever seeing another sunrise.

Talon stared off into the distance where I had last seen Alex with the forest of ogres and trolls—who were now running away, tossing their clubs and lifting their hands over their heads. Talon chuckled and turned to smile at a woman who was calmly walking across the field, all by herself. He folded his arms, nodding to himself. I frowned, wondering what was going on.

I took a step forward to get a look past Grinder, since he was blocking my view. I grinned, realizing it was Ashley. She was walking towards a straggler troll who was swinging a club the size of a sedan at the two small packs of werewolves nipping at him from both sides before darting back out of reach. He was probably twenty feet tall and had absolutely massive shoulders. He was fat-strong, where he didn't have the sharp, chiseled muscles, and he had a bulging gut, but his arms couldn't hang straight down at his sides because of his broad back and shoulders, so he constantly looked like he was ready to start a tickle fight. His chest was hairy and matted, he wore a stained kilt, and his army green skin looked fuzzy, reminding me of moss. No, it probably *was* moss, because this was Fae and crap got weird fast here.

The lone woman let out a long, loud whistle and the wolves scattered with sharp whines and yelps; their tails tucked between their legs.

The furious troll slowly turned to glare at the unarmed human woman, cocking his head to the side and reaching across his broad, hairy chest to scratch at his armpit. He absently lifted his three-fingered hand to his nose and sniffed. Then he ate whatever treasure he had unearthed, sucking on his fingers one-by-one, and I gagged. He hadn't broken eye contact with Ashley the entire time, not even to glance at his homemade snack.

I blindly reached out to swat Grinder with the back of my hand to get his attention, only to accidentally flick him in the nostril and earn an instinctive head swing with his antlers that knocked me back into the side of the Knight XV. I struck the armored vehicle with an explosive grunt and banged the back of my head against the glass hard enough to send stars spinning across my vision and cause the world to tilt and roll as I collapsed to the ground with a wheeze.

"Odin's funky toenail. That looked like it hurt," Grinder bleated. And then he was looming over me, offering his antler like an extended hand. I grabbed it and pulled myself up, shaking my head as the stars swiftly winked out and I regained my bearings. I reached back to touch my head and felt no bump. I frowned thoughtfully, wondering if that was my Godkiller powers or related to Alice's Absinthe. I was thankful for it either way as I turned back to Ashley. She was coming close to striking distance, and the troll did not look happy about sharing his personal bubble with the woman.

She didn't hold a weapon or have on a stitch of protection.

I cupped my hands around my mouth, turning to face Gunnar. "Hey, Gunnar!" The giant wolf turned to look my way, sniffing at the air on reflex before his good eye spotted me. "Ashley's about to get the shit kicked out of her by a giant troll. He's probably going to squish her!"

He glanced over his shoulder at her and then turned back to me with a shrug. "Love is a fickle beast. It was good while it lasted, but there are other fish in the sea!" he called back in a rumbling growl.

Werewolves glanced back and forth at us, more arriving by the second until we had a few hundred.

"What about the kids?" I asked, still cupping my hands.

Gunnar waved a claw, dismissively. "Why do you think I made you their Godfather? You can *have* them!"

Grinder bleated in horror. "That is so fucked up! She loves him! And those poor *kids*!" he said, looking distraught and possibly about to have another fainting goat episode repeat, judging by his flaring nostrils.

I smiled, patting him on the neck reassuringly so he wouldn't have another—bigger—fainting episode and crush me, and then pointed towards Gunnar. He turned to look and saw Gunnar wagging his tail as he folded his arms and watched his wife square off against the troll, panting eagerly. "This is going to be a train wreck, Grinder. Watch."

He looked very anxious, shifting from hoof-to-hoof nervously. "Her werewolf form is not strong enough to survive a hit from that club," he bleated nervously.

"She's fast," I assured him. "Watch."

The troll had to be twenty times her size, if not more. Ashley picked up a rock and threw it at his face, hitting him right in the eye. He roared in outrage and clutched at his eye with his filthy, armpit fingers, raising the massive club with the other. She scooped up another small rock and hurled it at him, striking his forehead before it bounced away, and he decided that was the last offense he was going to suffer from the rude woman.

He lifted his club high overhead, using both hands, and then brought it down alarmingly fast. She did not move, and the club slammed into the ground so hard it cracked loud enough to hear it across the field, and tree-sized splinters shattered off of it, whipping into the air, along with a dusty cloud of dirt clods and grass.

"That wasn't fucking fast at all!" Grinder bleated, scraping his hoof on the ground in preparation to charge.

CHAPTER 57

I held out a hand, calming him. "Easy," I said. "Wait for it..."

The troll waved a hand at the cloud, frowning to see if there was any salvaging his club.

And through the smoke rose a shimmering—brand spanking new—Knight in bright white armor with a long, armored tail and even protection for her tall, pointed ears, despite her not even being in wolf form. The legendary armor took the individual into account, considering all sorts of facets of their nature, so you never quite knew what you were going to get. Rather than a great big sword, this Knight held two bearded axes, one in each hand.

"May I introduce Camelot's newest Knight," I said, holding out a hand in introduction. "Alex offered it to her right after the Summer Queen arrived with her army, but he wanted it to be a surprise. Until now." Of course, that had required me to make a trip to the Mausoleum to collect one of the suits, but to see her now...

Worth it. Especially so soon after Aiden had died. Replacing that memory with something noble and beautiful had been...therapeutic for me.

Grinder gasped in awe, nodding his head up and down and bleating happily. "Well, boil my kidneys and tell me you love me. I don't even know what I'm doing here anymore."

I grinned, patting him on the side appeasingly.

Ashley crouched and then leapt up into the air, spinning like a tornado with her axes out. She was a blur, but the sudden fountain of blood spraying from the troll's throat was not. She landed on the ground, facing us. The green troll frantically clawed at his throat and let out a gurgling cry. Then he slowly teetered before crashing to the side with a thunderous *boom*.

I let out a slow clap, and the audience of previously silent werewolves let out howls, cheering on their general and Alpha's wife. I saw Tory seated on the hood of an idling Knight XV, surrounded by blood-covered, giant shifters who had obviously tapped into their Wild Sides. Two were-rhinos with jagged, colossal horns and armor-thick skin, and the other four were chimeras, all fanned out like they were her Secret Service detail—Secret Furvice. She let out a sharp whistle and began clapping delightedly. Her shifters did the same, roaring and lifting their fists. I hadn't even seen her pull up, so things must have been going well, because our area was completely Summer free.

The Knight's helmet winked out and there was Ashley, grinning at us as she took three great big leaps, covering thirty feet like she was playing hop-scotch. "This is so fucking cool!" she shouted at us. "Sorry," she said, glancing about for Alex, realizing she hadn't sounded very knightly in front of her new boss. But he hadn't returned yet, so she shrugged dismissively.

Her eyes locked onto me and she cleared her throat. "It is done," she said in a sagely tone, lifting her axes to the sky. "Is that right, Nate? Is that how you did it?" she asked in a sickly-sweet tone, mocking my attempt to steal attention during Tory's agreement to team up with Alex in exchange for her own piece of Fae.

Everyone turned to look at me, snickering behind their paws or fists.

I scowled at her, shaking my head. "Kind of, but you need to sound more foreboding on the last word. It's missing something." I waved at her to try again.

She cleared her throat, and this time her voice was on track. "It is done—"

CRACK!

A bolt of wizard's lightning struck the dead troll behind her and thunder rolled across the land. She stared at me wide-eyed, and I grinned, shrugging. "Nailed it that time, smart-ass. *Told* you it was missing something."

Gunnar grinned, wagging his tail. Ashley spent a few moments trying and failing to look angry before giving in and flashing me a resigned smile.

I watched as the newest Knight of Camelot locked eyes with her husband and made her way over to him, flipping the white axes in her hands and catching them over and over again. She was grinning wolfishly, of course. Gunnar ran forward and scooped her up into his giant claws, burying her face in his chest fur for a loving hug.

"Aww," the giant goat beside me said, relieved. "He *does* love her!"

Gunnar then had the bright idea to toss his wife into the air in celebration.

"Oh, no," Grinder said, shaking his head.

"You are very easily swayed, you know that, Grinder?" I asked absently.

Gunnar only tossed the newest Knight of Camelot a single time.

When he caught her from her brief vertical flight, she swiftly lifted one of her hatchets and bopped him on the head with the haft, causing him to drop her back down to the ground and grasp at his head with a startled look. She brandished the hatchet at him aggressively, chastising him for thinking he could hurl her around like a dad with his toddler after mom left to run errands. Instead of taking offense, Gunnar merely panted, wagging his tail excitedly.

She sheathed her hatchets and flung her hands up as if to say *you're impossible! You never listen! I'm a Knight, now. You can't just go around tossing me in the air whenever you feel like it! Stop your wagging, I'm serious!*

He kept right on wagging and panting, not regretting a thing. She finally smiled, shaking her head. He wouldn't get mad at her, and she couldn't stay mad at him. They were happy even when they were arguing.

Then she spread her arms wide and did a cute little spin, showing off her fancy new white armor. I chuckled, grinning at the pair and shaking my head. That was true love—

Gunnar abruptly crouched with his arms and claws spread wide, and then he tackled her to the ground when she wasn't looking. The two of them hit the grass ten feet away and tumbled end over end, wrestling, snarling and laughing the whole time. Ashley eventually landed on her back with the giant werewolf looming over her, drooling all over her face as he panted victoriously.

She held her arms up defensively, laughing loudly as she tried to fend off the shower of husband drool. Then she kicked him in the chest and he flew twenty feet. He slammed into the ground and rolled, hopping back to his feet, still wagging his tail as he kept one claw on the ground like he was on the starting line of a track meet, and stared at her, ready to go again. She climbed to her feet and brushed off her armor. Then she shook her head, laughing. She motioned for him to follow as she turned around and started marching towards me, looking left and right as if searching for someone.

Or two someones. Calvin and Makayla.

I did the same, my amused smile at their loving wrestling slowly fading as I realized something truly unfortunate. Yowza's truck had left during the Ashley show, because I spotted Drake and Cowan shooting me anxious looks and shaking their heads before their panicked eyes flicked to Gunnar and Ashley approaching in the distance. I closed my eyes and clenched my jaw. Where the hell had they gone? Were they misting about somewhere or had they lunged into the fight at some point on our way here? Maybe they'd fallen out of the back of the truck and were injured!

I forced myself to take a calming breath and turned back to Grinder. I motioned for him to bend down low. "I need you to find Gunnar's kids. They're out here somewhere," I whispered. "Don't say a *word*!" I warned.

He backed away, shifting from hoof-to-hoof with a sickened expression. Then he turned around and ran back towards the distant battle where Alex and Gunnar had knocked down all the giants earlier.

The forces of Summer seemed to have mostly scattered, because the dragons circling the air roasted them en masse every time they tried regrouping. But there were still dozens upon dozens of major battles going on across the field with shifters, Fae, and Gunnar's wolves going head-to-head with Summer.

The dragons could do nothing about those without roasting their own allies.

Grinder bleated at the top of his lungs as if hoping Calvin and Makayla would hear his call over the sounds of war. I let out a nervous breath, shaking my head. *They were fine*, I told myself. *They can always mist away from any danger. They could mist all the way over to us.*

CHAPTER 58

I frowned, wondering where Carl was. I hadn't seen the Elder since he was doing that sleepy fog thing while hanging off the top of the SUV. He was probably claws deep into the battle, scaring the hell out of everyone, and having the time of his life. He didn't get to play very often, so he was probably making up for lost time.

I saw a lone centaur racing our way, but he had his hands up in a gesture of surrender and he looked terrified. I frowned, lifting my hand so I could hurl a blast of fire at him if this was some kind of trick—like Ashley had done to that ogre.

The centaur somehow had abs, because this was a fantasy adventure, and why wouldn't he? I'd yet to see a pot-bellied centaur. Ever. It wasn't like they could do sit ups. It was fucking magic. That was the only scientific explanation for it. "Unless it's what they eat," I mused, thinking out loud. "But everyone knows eating too many fruits and vegetables is bad for you."

Something small hit me in the back of the head and I spun to see Tory waggling her fingers at me. "Shhh. I'm trying to enjoy the free show, and you're ruining it with your anti-vegan fear mongering," she said, grinning. Then she went back to watching the fake-abbed horse-man approach. Although Tory was more amorously-inclined to favor women, she was an equal opportunity gawker. A lecher, really. She hadn't been in a romantic relationship since Misha, the Reds' mother. She hadn't had much of a personal life at all, actually, focusing more on her new role as Headmistress of Shift. So, I let her gawk...even though the abs were *obviously* fake.

The centaur slowed to a trot and I realized that he had a sword to his throat, and it was crackling with yellow lightning. Alex leaned out from behind him and gave us a casual nod. He withdrew his sword and patted the centaur on the shoulder—the man-shoulder, not the horse-shoulder.

"Thank you," Alex said. "If you want a better life, you're more than welcome to come to Camelot and discuss your future, but there will be a penalty for your actions today. A fair price, but still a price."

The centaur nodded stiffly, looking utterly bewildered as Alex hopped off his back and then swatted him on the ass. "See you at noon in Camelot one week from today, good sir."

The centaur reared up at the slap, looking more startled than scandalized. He studied us for a few seconds, baffled as he registered the appointment Alex had just set for him. He nodded and then bowed, looked surprised that he had done any such thing, and then he was galloping away, clutching at his throat to verify that he hadn't imagined the ass-slap, his appointment, or the exceedingly polite hijacker.

I saw Grinder racing our way, bleating happily to announce his passengers. Carl, Calvin, and Makayla were grinning broadly, waving at our party. Gunnar and Ashley let out twin sighs of relief.

Hell, I let out a bigger sigh of relief than both combined because it had been my ass on the line.

I stared out at the field of death and smoke and blood. Banners from discarded spears whipped in the evening breeze, and not all of the Knights XV had returned to Camelot with their Tiny Balls like we'd originally planned, making me wonder if we hadn't been way more successful than we'd ever imagined. The SUV's were dirty as hell and I saw scuffs and scrapes, even a few dents from a giant's club or two, but overall, they'd held up exceedingly well.

I'd have to let the company know that the vehicles withstood Fairies just as well as bazookas. Maybe they'd make me some more, because I had a feeling we were going to need them in the future. I had just changed the rules of engagement for war. If I hadn't, someone else would have.

Everything was going to change soon. The Omega War was coming. I didn't know when, but looking at the aftermath of our battle, it suddenly felt a whole lot closer.

I saw a flash of golden metal glimmering in the darkening sky, racing our way. I grinned. "Kára!"

Ashley was suddenly standing beside me, nudging me with her armored shoulder. Gunnar stood behind her, still in his Wulfric form. "You've got it bad," Ashley teased, glancing up at Kára with a big grin.

I shrugged. "She's all right, I guess—"

She shoved me harder, cutting me off with a louder laugh. "Sucka!" she teased. But the way she glanced back at Gunnar told me she had *it* just as bad.

Kára spread her wings wide in order to slow her descent and then land in a run, rather than the superhero pose—which was extremely hard on the knee. For healthy, long-lasting joints, always alternate, or stop doing the aerial knee dives.

I realized I was feeling almost giddy with excitement to finally see her again after worrying about her, and also worrying about the war. But both had come and gone, and everyone was healthy and happy and—

My smile slipped as I realized her golden armor was covered in blood and that she was running to me.

"We need to go. *Now*," she urged, grabbing me by the hand and pulling me close. "None of *this* matters," she hissed, staring into my eyes as she blindly waved her hand at the war zone surrounding us. "They are trying to break into the *Mausoleum*," she whispered, emphasizing the last word.

I felt an icy chill roll down my spine as I stared back at her, seeing the raw truth in her eyes and the proof of battle covering her armor. "Okay, Kára." She squeezed my hand as if she'd expected me to argue with her. "Who are *they*, and what do we need to stop them?"

"Everyone, Nate: Baldur. Summer. G-Ma. And their forces. The answer to both questions is *everyone*," she said, emphasizing the last word. "But they haven't broken in yet," she said, sounding only mildly relieved. "I was spying on Baldur's house and another Justice arrived barely an hour ago. He didn't take off his mask, but I heard him tell Baldur *Mausoleum. It's time to collect your suit, if you can manage it.* He didn't sound friendly, almost like it was a challenge. Then he left. Baldur left with a band of Einherjar within twenty minutes, so I travelled to your mausoleum to make sure I wasn't crazy. And there he was, trying to break in. I deterred his efforts, but then others began popping up. The Summer Queen. The Justices and their Grandmaster. It's a fucking party," she snarled, "but they're all fighting each other harder than they're trying to get in."

"What do you need?" Alex asked, startling the hell out of us. I hadn't heard him approach.

In fact, we were surrounded by concerned, supportive, friendly faces. Even the strangers were friendly faces. *Everyone* was right *here*. They had heard everything Kára just said, and they were not backing down.

Carl stood between Calvin and Makayla with one protective claw over each of their shoulders.

Tory winked at me and her gang of Secret Furvice nodded.

Talon and Ashley stood on either side of Alex, and Gunnar had stepped up beside me and Kára, letting out a soft whine to let us know he was here for us.

And beyond them, hundreds of shifters watched us with grim determination and not a flicker of fear.

I knew I wasn't the only one thinking of my return to the Mausoleum to collect Ashley's new armor—because that was the only explanation I could think of for how they discovered my hiding spot.

But one person took more offense to the breach than anyone else.

Ashley stepped up beside me, snarling. "I will not permit them to sully my armor's day of celebration with tragedy. This will be a day of *victory*. A christening by blood."

"Where is Aiden?" Kára asked, frowning. "Another wizard would be useful."

I hung my head, feeling like she'd just stabbed me in the chest.

"Justices attacked Camelot," Alex told her in a somber tone. "Aiden sacrificed himself to save a young boy."

Kára was dead silent and I could tell she was staring at me with an anguished look. "Well..." she began, "There are a lot of Justices to kill where we're going. Let's make them pay for taking Aiden—"

Talon abruptly hissed, interrupting her as he slammed his spear into the ground and spun to stare off into the distance. Ashley and Alex did the same, staring in the exact same direction. "A suit of armor was just adopted, but it is not tied to Camelot. It's there but not there at the same time," he snarled.

Without missing a beat, I ripped open a Gateway to the inside of the Temple Mausoleum, making it stretch wider and taller than normal to accommodate the larger shifters. I tied it off so it would remain open.

I slapped on my Horseman's Mask and everyone gasped as my transformation took place, coating me in inky quartz armor from head-to-toe. "Come with me to a land of darkness and death," I snarled. "Come with me to the halls of my ancestors. Come with me to lay waste to the enemies of Camelot."

Kára stepped up beside me, grinning like a demon. "So. Hot."

I grinned back at her. "Date night, Lady Valkyrie."

And then we leapt into the house of bones and death, leaving the giant Gateway open for whoever the fuck wanted to play with us, because it was time to pull out the big guns.

CHAPTER 59

My Gateway had apparently torn through some pilfering Justices, and they'd left behind a humble offering of severed arms and legs to appease the vengeful, unforgiving Temple Clan in hopes of purchasing their own salvation. Two of the Justices lay on the ground, alive, but bleeding out and unable to heal themselves. They took one look at the Horseman of Hope stepping through the Gateway inside the supposedly empty Mausoleum and screamed in absolute horror, knowing there would be no hope granted today. With an absent thought, the stone spines of my Horseman wings erupted out of my back and pierced their hearts, ending their pitiful yammering.

A third Justice was holding his silver mask in his hand and had died staring down at his stomach with a startled look on his face, unable to process why his lower half was no longer attached but propped against a wall a couple feet away.

Heh. Couple feet.

But the sounds of violence and chaos did not cease with their deaths. I turned to look down the hall, past all the statues and tombs of my ancestors lining the walls, and saw that the door leading outside was now a gaping, smoking wound in the side of the building. The door and part of the wall itself had been completely torn away. Outside, heavy snow fell from a pregnant, cloudy sky. I saw what had to be hundreds of men and monsters fighting each other in an orchestra of madness as blade struck blade and magic battled magic. I saw Einherjar, Justices, and Summer Fae of many types in the chaos, stretching as far as the eye could see, deeper into the graveyard. Too many factions and too many bodies in the same small spaces, tripping over tombstones and each other more often than not.

The somewhat muted orchestra of war sang to me, and I felt my heart racing with excitement to join the fray, but my primary purpose was to save the sets of armor. From where I stood within the Mausoleum, my view was limited to the hole in the wall, but I could see *heaps* of dead Einherjar— dozens of bodies—spread out around the smoldering opening, and I surmised that my enemies had likely overwhelmed the wards and door with sheer force, using the reanimating Vikings to keep hammering at the defenses until they gave up.

The Bellefontaine Cemetery drank in all the fresh death with a contented sigh of pleasure as wind whistled through the hole in the wall. My Gateway stood in the center of the wide hall, halfway between the Mausoleum entrance and the fountain with the Temple Family Tree, so it was eerily calm compared to the insanity outside. Now that we were inside the Mausoleum with the armor, and everyone outside was too busy fighting each other to remember the whole point of them coming here—to get the armor—I turned to Kára. "We need to collect the armor—"

I spotted movement to my left in my peripheral vision, and I flung out a blast of black fire on instinct. A tall, broad shouldered man in black armor —a new Knightmare—batted away my attack with a jubilant laugh before blindly hurling fireballs to cover his escape as he ran down the stairs within the fountain and into the catacombs below.

Into the Elder's Realm.

"Another three suits gone," Talon snarled, leaping through the Gateway behind me and pointing his white poleaxe in the direction of the Knightmare I had just failed to kill. He saw where he was pointing and snarled as his ears twitched and swiveled, taking stock of our surroundings and listening for any signs of movement.

Kára tightened her grip on her trident and shot me a stubborn look as if preparing to argue about leaving my side.

"No, Kára. I need you to collect the rest of the armor and guard them with your lives. We've already lost *four!* In less than *five minutes.* If they get their hands on all ten, they could start the Omega War this very night."

Gunnar had joined us, but he'd put on his lucky underwear without telling anyone. The Horseman of Justice was a towering white wolf, easily eight-feet-tall even though he was slightly hunched forward. His golden mask had reformed to fit his canine face, kind of reminding me of those Renaissance plague doctor masks. His paws sported long, black diamond claws, and he was a veritable powerhouse, making his Wulfric form seem puny.

But a Knightmare had already killed Gunnar once—luckily, I'd been able to make a deal to bring him back—so it looked like he wasn't taking any chances. Or...he just really, really wanted to hurt them.

He stepped up beside Kára and gave her a reassuring nod. "I will join you," he growled.

She hesitated only a moment before nodding. She was the only person who knew where I had hidden them throughout the Mausoleum. Kára took off, and Gunnar followed in her wake, keeping his head on a swivel.

Carl stepped through the Gateway beside Talon just as two silver-masked Justices leapt out from behind statues and threw blasts of lightning at us as they raced to an adjacent statue and tomb of a different Temple ancestor. Talon lunged with his spear, stabbing one in the throat as the other's lightning struck his armor and careened off harmlessly. Carl rolled beneath Talon's weapon and rose with one of his bone blades to stab the distracted Justice through the heart.

He rose to his feet and ripped his sword out of the Justice's chest, and then turned to stare at the fountain. "They go to my *home*," he hissed, furiously.

I stared at the entrance to the Elder's Realm and growled. "The new Knightmares are going to wreak havoc on the Elders. Break them up before they can rally. One is a wizard, but I have not seen the other three."

Carl opened his mouth to instinctively shrug off the danger, but he hesitated, remembering that we weren't talking about mere wizards or men or Fae or monsters. We were talking a new breed of Knightmares. "My people will not know the danger the Knightmares represent," he finally admitted. "They will underestimate the threat and not send enough reinforcements to stave off the attacks."

"That is their intent. To catch them by surprise and obliterate as many Elders as possible," I growled. "We have to stop them—"

"The first stolen suit is just outside," Talon interrupted, eyeing the hole in the building. "No other suits out there," he said, sounding suspicious. "I think the three who left for the Elder's realm are tied to that one much like I am tied to Alex," he mused, cocking his head in confusion. "All four wield magic, but that one..." he trailed off, sounding afraid as he stared through the opening at the battle outside. "He is...something else."

"Are you certain?" I asked. Talon nodded firmly. "Then I am going for him," I said.

"I found a set of armor," Carl said, pointing behind a statue. "It either wasn't hidden very well or it was disturbed. I think they were racing to get to it," he said, glancing at the two Justices he and Talon had just killed. I pretended I hadn't heard the unintended slight against my hiding skills, Because I had a sudden idea.

I walked up to Carl and stopped within two feet of him. He cringed slightly at my Horseman's Mask, afraid of me on an instinctive level rather than a personal one—I hoped. "Kneel," I growled.

He did so without hesitation, even though his face was a storm of questions, as if he thought he'd done something wrong to anger me. But...I was Master Temple, so he did not question it. There would be time to answer those questions later, because I knew his obedience had less to do with me and more to do with my family's history, although both were important. I called up my Horseman's spear-whip, made from my old Devourer I'd used to kill Mordred at the Dueling Grounds. The black blade and feathers hung from a white ethereal chain of crackling magic and I smiled. Since a chain wouldn't work for this next bit, I gripped the base of the blade, treating it like a hilt. Although that part of the blade was just as sharp, my armored skin protected me from getting cut.

"I dub thee Sir Carlemagne the Loyal," I said, touching each of his shoulders with the black blade. Talon started purring loudly, surprising me. I would have anticipated a warning as he faced a test in loyalty—me versus Alex. They weren't my suits, after all. But they were disappearing like free candy, so we needed to start putting bodies in them. "Put the suit on, Sir Carlemagne," I said. "You've earned it on your own merit, but you will also need it once we're done here," I said, pointing towards the Elder's realm, "so you can help us stop them."

"I second that," Talon declared firmly, purring even louder. "Your people will need you. We need you. And that has always been the purpose of the Knights. To help those in need."

Carl rose with a shocked, anxious, and humbled look on his face. "Thank you," he whispered, shedding a tear and blinking rapidly. "I will make you proud, Master Temple."

I knew we couldn't go to the Elder Realm with the door to the Mausoleum blown open and a battle raging outside with Baldur, the Summer Queen, and G-Ma and her Justices. And whoever the fuck this boss Knightmare was. I pointed my blade at the Elder Realm and stared into Carl's eyes. "You need to go warn your people before they are slaughtered. Then find out what these Knightmares are doing. Why they went there. Take Talon. He's the best tracker I know. We will join you shortly."

He nodded determinedly. "How will you find us?"

"I have a flying unicorn," I said with a dry smirk, "and a Valkyrie."

Carl squatted down and hesitantly touched his new suit of armor. It winked out of existence and he sighed as if someone had just massaged the exact right spot on his shoulders. He stood up and an epic suit of white armor suddenly rolled over him, looking like scales on a snake rather than large, bulky plates like Talon's. He resembled a robot dinosaur with his long, armored tail. I grinned, opening my mouth to compliment him—

"Nate!" Ashley called from closer to the Mausoleum's entrance. She was taking cover at the edge of the jagged opening, scoping out the battle. "You need to get over here. Now!" I hadn't seen her slip through the Gateway, but she had probably come with Gunnar. Regardless, I was grateful to have an actual Knight to protect the Mausoleum since I was sending away Talon and Carl. Especially since I wouldn't be inside to help; I was going to have a short, pointed chat with this boss Knightmare.

I patted Carl on the shoulder. "I believe in you, Sir Carl," I told him. "You too, Sir Talon."

They both dipped their chins, and then the two of them took off for the Elder's Realm.

I jogged over to Ashley to find that Tory had also slipped through the

Gateway to help. She had a Chimera and a were-rhino at her back, both shifters were waiting obediently and panting anxiously.

We stared out at a scene from the depths of Hell. An arcing line of dead Einherjar and Justices formed a barrier around the entrance—casualties of when the wall had exploded. Beyond that, a line of Justices seemed to be walling off the battle, preventing any from coming close to the Mausoleum —essentially, helping us without realizing it. I thought back on the five Justices we had killed inside and grimaced. These Justices had been buying *them* time—and the four who had actually succeeded in grabbing armor.

Beyond the magic-slingers defensive line, berserker Einherjar fought other Justices, but some Justices fought beside the Einherjar, and some Justices fought other Justices, slaughtering each other with a frenzy that set *my* heart racing. I saw the Summer Queen and a squad of Fae soldiers, including a half-dozen of the feathered ogres, fighting their asses off to try to clear a path to the Mausoleum for the queen, but Einherjar and Justices were easily keeping them back. At the same time, I saw Baldur a hundred feet away, trying to do the same with a group of Einherjar for security, but he was facing similar obstacles preventing him from reaching the Mausoleum.

So, Baldur's men had opened the Mausoleum and then the wall exploded, killing them all. Then four of the Justices had either been quick or sneaky, nabbing four suits for their team. Had the Justices sabotaged Baldur's men—using them to break in and then slaughtering them from behind so they could take the prizes instead? Then, rather than staying to help their wizard colleagues, they'd immediately abandoned them for the Elder's Realm.

Why? As I swept my gaze across the battle, I froze to suddenly see an area that was decidedly different. I don't know how I had missed it, other than the fact that it was eerily tranquil. That area had been what Ashley wanted me to see, and from the pale look on her face, it had truly shaken her.

She was staring at the back of a tall, hooded man in a black robe twenty paces away from the Mausoleum, and I could feel the power radiating off of him, even from here.

The Boss wizard Knightmare. I grimaced, wondering how to get to him without anyone seeing me.

Tory's eyes had immediately locked onto Summer with a hungry gleam, and she was licking her lips.

There were simply too many warriors involved, and everyone was fighting each other, creating a bottleneck. Still, Ashley and Tory wouldn't be able to stop them—definitely not both Baldur and Summer together—by themselves, even as a Knight and Beast Master.

"Anyone willing to enter that storm and cover me while I murder that asshole will be in the running for a suit of armor if we have any extra when all is said and done. But don't tell them that armor bit or Alex will kill me. On the same note, any who think to try taking a suit without permission will suffer. Better not to even tell them they're here. Call your reinforcements, Ladies."

They chuckled, nodding as they stared out at the chaos. "We already did," they said, almost in unison.

And that's when I heard the sound of many claws behind me. I glanced back to see dozens upon dozens of shifters loping towards us. Werewolves and the students of Shift. They paused at my back, eyeing me with fear and awe.

I pointed at the Black Knight off to the side, who seemed to be under a pale purple dome of power that no one dared cross. In fact, I saw the charred bodies of several who had tried and failed just beyond the purple haze. That was why his area looked so tranquil. It was certain death to anyone trying to enter.

"Lady Knight, guard the Mausoleum door. Gunnar and Kára are inside gathering the suits for protection." I turned to Tory and pointed at the wizard Knight. "He's mine. Give me a perimeter, Beast Master. But you can kill anyone else who is out there right now."

Her eyes flashed green and her team of shifters snarled in response. She glanced over her shoulder at them. "Let's go on a field trip, class," she said with a murderous grin.

I stormed outside, my wing spines pounding into the ground behind me like the beating of a war drum.

And dozens of monsters roared in my wake, entering the Battle of Bellefontaine Cemetery with one hell of an entrance. They ripped the wall of unaware Justices to shreds, gobbling them down to form one of their own. Then dozens more raced into the center of the insanity, howling and snarling with glee.

I had no idea how the police hadn't been called yet, but at least I wasn't the only idiot using magic out here tonight. Any curious policemen would take one look at the hundreds of monsters and trolls and then calmly carry on, pretending they hadn't seen a thing while they considered making an appointment with a therapist first thing in the morning.

CHAPTER 60

I walked up to the dome of power and reached out with my armored hand to touch it. My Horseman skin passed through harmlessly, and I wondered if it actually had anything to do with me being a Horseman...

Or if this Knightmare had been waiting for me to arrive. He *had* been the first one to steal a suit, setting up Summer and Baldur and G-Ma to arrive in hopes of claiming their own suits. That was my theory based on the chaos in the cemetery.

Kára had overheard a Justice telling Baldur that it was time to collect his suit. I could only imagine that Summer had heard much the same, likely from the same Justice. That was why she had fled the war in Fae.

Because Summer had randomly spaced out during my parley with her, almost as if she was hearing a voice in her head, receiving orders. Had this asshole Justice puppeteer somehow spoken to her, telling her to come for the suits?

The only thing that had snapped her out of her vacant stare had been me saying I had all ten suits and I would give them to her. That had gotten her attention very quickly. And Grinder had told me that she fled the moment she realized my Gateway would not give her the prized armor. So, I had accidentally delayed her from coming here. Phew.

So, this asshole Justice was obviously connected and probably a Master. And yet he was just standing there with his back to the Mausoleum, doing a whole lot of nothing. Snow still fell outside the dome of power, but none within, making it look like the opposite of a snow globe.

I took a deep breath and stepped through the purple light. The sounds of battle instantly dimmed. He didn't move or acknowledge my entrance, but I knew he'd sensed it. I stood there, assessing him.

Talon had said the other Knightmares who left for the Elder's Realm were linked to this black-hooded guy, just like Talon was linked to Alex.

So...after telling Summer and Baldur to come get a suit, this Justice had made sure to grab the first suit for *himself*, making it so that anyone who followed after him would be bonded to *him* rather than becoming rogue Knights. Then he'd given three suits to his wizard pals. Not Baldur and Summer. Mordred had achieved something very similar, but he'd used his Pendragon bloodline to do it, and it had affected all twelve suits of armor.

This man's bond had not done that. Carl's armor had been perfectly fine and evil-overlord-free.

This man had used their greed against them, promising them a suit of power but neglecting to tell them that their prize would only bond them more tightly to him. For eternity. He would have the Summer Queen and Baldur as his freaking *minions*—if they managed to get their hands on a suit, of course.

He *had* to be a Master, but his powers of manipulation made the past Masters I had encountered look like foolish children in comparison. I took a few steps closer, flexing my black diamond claws hungrily.

I took a wild guess. "Heard you've been waiting for me, Cyrilo," I growled at his back.

He didn't flinch and he didn't turn. He didn't even grab his magic. He was utterly unafraid of me. There was a silence, and then he let out a low, amused chuckle. Snow continued to fall down around us outside the dome like the ashes of a burning sky—a portent of the world he envisioned. I heard a sharp pained, high-pitched grunt, followed by a spray of blood painting the snow at his feet. I stiffened, crouching warily.

And then an old woman dropped to her knees on the other side of him, gasping as she leaned back against a tombstone. G-Ma stared up at the man with a horrified, confused expression, clutching her stomach with one hand and holding a piece of old, dirty leather in the other. What the fuck? He'd just stabbed the Grandmaster and she wasn't going to even *try* to do anything about it? She had caused this mess herself, judging by all the Justices fighting Justices. She had allowed this storm to happen by not taking care of her students and Justices.

They had revolted against her, and this man had risen to the top. Whether he'd instigated it all or not, she had failed to fulfill her duties, and she had definitely failed to do anything for me. Or for Aiden Maxon.

"I hope you liked my note," I told her in a cold tone. "You did this to yourself. I warned you to clean up the Academy or something terrible would happen. You taught your students poison, forgetting that one day they would grow *up*. That poison festered and bloomed, creating *this*," I said, holding out a clawed hand to the crazed battle in the distance. "Be proud of your creation and die in silence so I can focus on fixing your mistakes." I glanced at the hooded man—who *still* had his fucking back to me. "Starting with this piece of trash."

Cyrilo laughed harshly and began to slow clap. "Preach."

G-Ma stared at me, her eyes pleading. I stared back and slowly shook my head, making the internal decision to abandon her to her own fate. To permit her to take full credit for failing an entire nation of wizards.

Then I turned away from her, focusing on Cyrilo, who was really starting to annoy me. It was imperative that this Knightmare fall. He already controlled the three Knightmares in the Elder's Realm, but if Baldur and Summer got their hands on a suit and turned themselves into Super Knightmares...

This guy would control all of them, making him a Super-duper Knightmare.

"I'm talking to you, Cyrilo," I growled, wondering why he was so calm and not even remotely threatened by me. I mean, he was a Knightmare, but I was a Horseman and I'd killed quite a few gods. He was treating me like I was quite literally beneath him. Not even worth noticing, like dust under his boots.

"Then you should get my name right," the man said, calmly, in a bold, confident tone, "and stop calling me by my sniveling henchman's name."

His voice was distorted yet sounded *vaguely* familiar. Someone I had met at the Academy years ago? And Cyrilo *worked* for him?

"Enlighten me. I'd like to know the name of the all-powerful old-lady-stabber," I said, drily.

He chuckled again. "Oh, I suppose waiting thirty years is long enough," he said as he slowly, finally turned around to face me. He still wore a hood, but his face was clouded with shifting, living shadows that almost looked like a fireplace of black flames. His armor was black but trimmed in rich silver as well, reminding me of Alex's white and gold armor. "Love the suit," he commented, gesturing at my armored skin. "I always wanted to see it, but there was never any time. Things were just so...*busy*, you know?" he asked, sounding amused as all hell.

"Where do I know you from?" I demanded, mentally flying through any acquaintances I'd had at the Academy over the span of the last thirty years. A friend of my father's?

"Oh, come on!" he said in a cheery tone. "Don't be a stranger, Nate. It's *me*. Bonk."

My breath caught as he reached up and flipped his hood back. The black flames disappeared from within his hood, and I stared into a devilish, smirking face.

Aiden Maxon.

"I'm baaaaack," he said, grinning toothily, his light green eyes twinkling with vibrant life.

CHAPTER 61

I stared at Aiden Maxon, unable to comprehend what was happening.

He was no longer the same man. Physically, he was. But this man radiated power and control and an aura that seemed twice as big as his body. The Aiden who had died to save the young boy in Camelot had been a troubled, angsty, self-conscious wreck of a wizard, but he'd had a noble, steadfast heart. This man…had eyes like a shark.

And he was utterly heartless.

This Aiden was the master of his ship, in complete control at all times, and held no fear of anything—anything at all. A twinkle of madness danced in those bright green eyes as his blonde surfer boy hair shifted in the breeze.

"I watched you *die*," I rasped, torn between panic, fear, horror, and an overwhelming anxiety at the impossibility of what my lying eyes were showing me.

But it wasn't an illusion. He still wasn't holding his magic. I could sense his deep well of magical power, though, and he had to be at almost three times stronger than the Aiden I had let into Chateau Falco.

Aiden flashed me a truly appreciative grin from one side of his mouth, nodding. "And you wept like a little *bitch*, didn't you, Nate?" he chuckled softly. "Ever heard of the Doppelgänger Golem rune?" he asked, arching an eyebrow.

I felt my stomach writhe, instantly understanding the gist of the two terms when combined. "No, but it sounds pretty self-explanatory. It makes a clay body double?" I asked, frowning. Because golems were typically brute simulacrum made of clay, and neither this man nor the other Aiden had been made of clay. They were typically used as bodyguards with simple commands because they weren't too bright. They were brought to life by an enchanted strip of cloth placed in their mouths—and taking that cloth out of the homicidal monster's mouth was the only way to kill them. Something tickled at my thoughts, but I was too shaken to see Aiden walking and talking again to grasp the elusive thought.

Aiden held up a finger. "Close. But I'm talking about a completely authentic *flesh* golem that shares your *soul*. A spare body, if you will. And it works for *anyone*—Freak or not! Once you use it, you'll be half as strong and you'll die seven days later—or sooner if you're as ambitious as I was— but then your soul gets sent into your new ride," he said, waving a hand to indicate his own body, "which is *exactly* like the old ride but still oper- ational."

I stared at him, unable to speak. This was his body double after the original died. That was why he was so much stronger now. And Regulars could use it? Holy shit. My mind raced with potentials for abusing such magic, and it only took me a few seconds to realize how dangerous it really was. Suicide bombers working with impunity. Terrorists. Assassins. Dare- devils looking for a thrill. If something like that wound up on the internet, it would be chaos.

But...why had he gone to all this effort? What had he done in those seven days that he couldn't have done without the spell? I tried to remember everything we had done together, but I came up with nothing. He hadn't robbed me or done anything nefarious. We'd just spent a lot of time together. Talked a lot. Fought a lot of dangerous foes.

He crouched down in front of G-Ma so that he was level with her face. "Three people can keep a secret, old girl. If two of them are dead," he said, smiling.

She was unable to speak, only strong enough to lift a weak, bloody, pleading hand towards him.

He swatted it down with an amused chuckle. "Bad Grandmaster. Very, very *bad*. I invited you here so I could give you your golem spell back and then let you die with dignity, not so you could paw at me, you naughty minx!" He rose to his feet and brushed his hands together.

My mind was racing. He'd invited her here to...

"The artifact stolen from the Academy," I said in a hollow tone, staring at the scrap of leather in G-Ma's hand. If that was the Doppelgänger Golem rune, then there was no way I could have known it existed. It had been locked away, deemed too dangerous. According to Jasper Griffin, only two other people knew about it: Cyrilo and G-Ma. But...Aiden was the one who had told me that story of Jasper talking to Cyrilo. It...had all been a lie. "*You* stole it. *You* killed Jasper Griffin," I whispered. "So why give it back?" I demanded, utterly bewildered.

He glanced over at me and smiled, flashing his teeth. Then he stuck his tongue out at me like a crazy person. Except...the rune on his tongue was gone. His tongue tattoo...had made him a flesh golem.

That was what had been tickling my brain! Golems were powered by those enchanted strips of fabric in their mouths. Aiden's tattoo had been his enchantment!

No wonder we'd found nothing on the strange symbol. Long ago, Justice Jasper had killed anyone who knew about it, wrongly trusting Cyrilo, who had ultimately turned traitor to help Aiden in exchange for a suit. "I will share my toy with you, since I am now finished playing with it," he said, smiling.

I clenched my knuckles, and the bone spines sprouting out of my back quivered in a rattling staccato like I was a snake about to strike. The rune *had* been significant. And not even Tyr and Odin had known of it.

"My heartfelt childhood story about bullies and tattoos warned of the folly of gullibility," he said with an absent shrug. "Pay closer attention next time."

I stared at him, wondering what exactly we were doing here. I now knew how he had survived, but I didn't know why he'd expended all the energy to do it. If he'd merely wanted the armor, he could have found an easier way to go about it. Like having this current battle at Camelot. That would have been way easier to achieve, before I even knew he was coming.

It was like planning an elaborate heist to rob the Federal Reserve so you had the money to buy a pack of bubblegum at the gas station on the way home.

"I guess I should thank you for saving that little boy," I said, watching his reaction closely. "You spent your free death on him, at least."

I saw a darkness in his eyes, a momentary flicker of rage, and then it was gone. "I told my men to make it look convincing—you're Nate Temple, after all, so they couldn't underestimate you like everyone else always does —but they might have gone a little overboard with that axe. I have to admit, that *hurt*. A lot. But the dying hurt less than whispering those pitiful final words to you," he said with razor-sharp cruelty. "I don't know how I didn't burst out laughing as I said them."

"*Your* men," I repeated in a cold, distant tone, ignoring the cruel jab about his dying words—words that had inspired all of us to fight Summer's army. "The Justices at Camelot were yours. You made yourself a doppelgänger...so you could assassinate *yourself*?" I asked, confused.

He nodded delightedly. "Almost all of the wizards attacking us over the last few days were mine. She only just learned about that, too, so don't beat yourself up about it," he said with a malevolent grin, pointing his thumb at G-Ma. "Think of how foolish *she* feels. And this is really just the tip, Nate, so I'm going to need you to hold your shit together until the end."

He rolled his shoulders excitedly, as if eager to face the prospect of new opportunities as he glanced out at the battle raging across the cemetery. Then he let out a dejected sigh. "You didn't suffer a complete failure, you know," he said, jerking his chin towards the chaos. "I didn't know Kára wasn't with you when I picked up my replacement body and then left to inform Baldur that it was time to collect his suit. I presume she was watching either him or the Summer Queen," he said, glancing at me sidelong to discern an answer. I kept my face blank and he smirked, focusing back on the field. "I had hoped for at least one of them to get a suit of armor, but it looks like your Beast Master is about to kill the Summer Queen, and Baldur is having a pretty poor showing. Looks like they're both about to die. Ah, well. We can't have it all, can we?" He saw my grim look and patted me on the shoulder. "Oh, don't look so glum. I wasn't going to take *all* of the suits. Where's the fun in that? I was only going to take six. To be *fair*." I continued to stare at him and he frowned, looking mildly guilty.

"You're right. Do tell Kára that I truly don't think she's fat. I want to make sure I don't carry that on my conscience. I am a gentleman, after all—"

I flung a blast of fire at him, more out of frustration than anything else, but I apparently made it hot enough to melt rock, because when he casually deflected it with a peripheral wave of his hand, it struck the tombstones and they collapsed like fresh lava, burning through the snow and puddling on the cold ground beneath. Aiden sighed wearily. "Don't bother. It's a waste of energy. We can't kill each other. I made sure of *that*," he said, pointing a finger up at the dome around us. "Otherwise, we couldn't have our little chat."

And then he flicked his finger at me like he was 'kicking' a paper football in grade school. A ball of black flame slammed into me and...

It ricocheted off as if repelled by gravity. My eyes widened and I stared at the melting tombstones beside me. I turned back to see Aiden nodding absently. "Weird, right? It just rolls off like water on a duck's back."

I shook my head, stunned. "Why?" I finally asked, realizing there was nothing either of us could do to each other. He'd wanted *our little chat* to be undisturbed.

He shot me a disappointed look. "If I hadn't, you would have died here, walking up behind me like you did. And then no one would have gone to save the Elders from Cyrilo and my new Knightmares. It would have all been for nothing. We've only just opened our game board, Nate, and I want to *play*. It's your turn to roll the dice and make your move."

"You're a Master, aren't you?"

He scoffed. "If *that's* all you've figured out, then I am *terribly* disappointed in you." He motioned for me to join him, still staring out at the chaos of battle unfolding. "We should really watch this together, Nate. After all, we made this happen. This is our game," he said, holding his arms out with pride. "I know they're merely our game pieces, but I like to view them as our children, in a way." I hesitantly walked up and came to a halt beside him, staring out at the madness.

"*We* didn't make this happen," I finally said. "*You* turned everyone against each other. You caused chaos. I reacted," I said in a hollow tone.

He snorted. "Whataboutism is a straw man argument," he murmured. "I could argue that you forced me to do what I did. Then you would argue that someone forced you to do what you did. And on and on, the cycle continues," he said in a gentle, philosophical tone. "Do you think the first gods enjoyed watching their children fight as much as we do now?" he mused, curiously.

CHAPTER 62

I shook my head distastefully. "I am not enjoying this, because I am not a psychopath," I rasped.

He jolted as if slapped. "There is no need for name-calling, Nate. We are Gentlemen. Nobility. You are Master Nate," he said, and then he gave me a formal bow. "And I..." he trailed off, glancing back over his shoulder at G-Ma, who was now dead, "am now Grandmaster Aiden," he said, emphasizing the word *Grand* in a competitive tone.

We stared out at the battlefield, watching the bloodshed and carnage of men and women torn limb from limb by monstrous shifters. Wizards hurling lethal magic and severing arms and legs or catching Einherjar on fire, or Einherjar piling on top of wizards and hacking them apart with bloodthirsty eyes and passionate screams. From this vantage, watching it as a distant spectator...

It was...horrifying.

I saw Tory personally going against the Summer Queen, beating the living hell out of her as her shifters dealt with the giant ogres, bringing them to their knees. Baldur was having similar troubles with dozens of werewolves surrounding him and attacking from behind every time he turned around.

"Woo!" Aiden squealed with a surprised laugh, pointing at the

Chimera shifter as she picked up a Justice and physically ripped him in half with her bare hands. "Damn! Good move, Team Temple. That was one of mine," he explained, taking the loss like a good sport. He shook his head, awed by the scope. "Your allies truly are quite formidable. You should trust them more often—" he cut off abruptly and slapped a palm over his mouth as if embarrassed. "Whoops. I forgot how sore of a subject trust currently is. I will refrain with my sincerest apologies. I meant no disrespect." But he was grinning devilishly at me as he said it, and I wanted nothing more than to tear him apart with my bare hands.

"I get it. You won, and you get a sick and twisted pleasure from twisting the knife. But it is getting tiring, Aiden. I want to understand *why*. You don't want to kill me, so you obviously have something to tell me."

"Why, why, why," he said tiredly, shaking his head. "Nobody likes a why-ner," he said, chuckling at his own homonym pun. I stared at him with a level gaze, waiting. He sighed. "I guess this round *is* almost finished," he agreed, pursing his lips in disappointment as he surveyed the battlefield. "And you do have places to be, I imagine. I hope you can get there before Carl's family is horribly murdered. I do like the old bloke, you know, but we mustn't grow too attached to our toys. Security blankets are a crutch, and only hold you back later on in life. I learned that at a very young age."

That last comment had sounded surprisingly bitter and genuine, but I knew I could no longer read Aiden with any sense of objectivity. "Was any of it true?" I asked. "Your story."

"You mean if I was an Academy orphan?" he asked, glancing over at me like we were two old friends. I nodded. He turned back to the battlefield, considering the question. "I guess you could call her my foster mother. But she booted me from the Academy many, many years ago. Disciplinary issues. So, I added a small fib to my story about being Jasper's dutiful apprentice, but it was mostly true."

My mind raced, trying to connect all the dots. All the madness. All the lies.

"Where do we go from here?"

He grinned excitedly, his handsome features turning his charisma into a sinister weapon. "I have no *idea*, Nate! But imagine the possibilities! I can't wait to find out. Adventure calls and heroes answer," he said, holding out his arms like he was embracing the entire battle in one big group hug. He let out a parting sigh and lowered his hands. Then he turned to me, brushing them off. "Well, I'm off to make my next move." He glanced over my shoulder and smiled warmly. Then he pointed. "Look! It's Kára. She must have finally found my *gift*."

I spun to see Kára standing at the mouth of the Mausoleum, staring at the two of us with a stunned look on her face, looking like Aiden was the second ghost she'd seen in the past minute. Her shock soon faded to one of hurt confusion to see me standing beside the Boss Knightmare like we were old chums.

"What gift?" I asked Aiden with a hoarse rasp.

"That would ruin the surprise!" he said, clapping me on the back jovially. "I mean, look at how shocked *she* is. You expect me to deny *you* that same gift?" He chuckled, shaking his head. "Oh, no. I would never do that to you. Now, if you hurry, you should have more than enough time to do your thing in the Elder's Realm before the big...well, you'll see. It was so nice to see you again, Nate. Truly." He glanced back at G-Ma and frowned. "Wait! Not yet. You almost forgot this," he said, shuffling over to her and grabbing the leather scrap in her hand. He came back to me and pressed it into my palm before wrapping my fingers over it and patting it securely. "There. You should keep that safe," he said in a serious tone. "People died to get it to you. So. Many. People."

I stared at him, only inches away from me. He blinked at me with a compassionate smile.

And I slammed my Horseman's Blade into the side of his exposed neck. My blade careened off his flesh without actually touching it, and the force of my momentum sent me stumbling into him.

He caught me by the shoulders, steadying me with both arms. Then he lifted my chin with his thumb and fingers, staring into my eyes with sincere concern. "Are you okay?" he asked softly, pretending that I hadn't actually just tried to kill him.

"Yes. I slipped," I said, gritting my teeth.

"Ah. Gotta watch out for these *roots*, right?" he agreed, stomping a boot into the ground with a knowing wink. "Someone should really take better care of this place, and mind these dangerous things before they trip someone up and cause a real injury," he said, pointing at a few more exposed roots from a large tree nearby. He wrapped his arm around my shoulder. "Someone could get seriously hurt," he warned, tsking and shaking his head.

I clenched my jaw. "When will I be able to kill you?" I growled.

He hung his head. "I hope soon," he admitted, "for that would be a great game to watch. I love seeing the underdog pull off a win. Just know I'm rooting for you, Temple," he said, stepping away and bowing his head in farewell. "Until next time."

And then he abruptly Shadow Walked.

The purplish dome above us evaporated, and I felt my knees wobble and give out as my Horseman's Mask completely powered down. I caught myself on a tombstone, steadying myself as the world began to tilt and spin around me, my mind envisioning the moment Aiden had died in my arms in Camelot. Cold air caressed my skin as winter's breath danced through the land of death. I shuddered, struggling not to vomit.

Kára rushed over and hoisted me to my feet. "What the *fuck* is going on, Nate?" she whispered, sounding absolutely terrified and out of her mind, her eyes wild and panicked, darting in every direction as if expecting danger to come at her from any angle. She was sobbing but not even realizing it.

"What did he leave inside?" I asked in a hoarse tone as her fear and panic made tears of my own well up and roll down my cheeks. Tears of guilt for bringing her to such fear. I never wanted her to look like this again for as long as I lived, and it was breaking my heart, but I had to know.

The way he'd said it...

How sadistically and nonchalantly violent he was...

And Kára's mental breakdown upon seeing it was only serving to exacerbate my own imagined horrors on what *gift* he saw fit to give his new best friend. That I had plenty of time before...something happened.

I highly doubted that.

"I promise to explain what you just saw, Kára," I whispered, cupping her face in my palms, "but I have to know—right now—what he left inside. Is someone dead?" I whispered.

She shook her head firmly. "No. Nothing like that. No one is in danger...yet."

"Then why do you look so panicked? Just tell me," I begged.

She shook her head, glancing out at the battle in the near distance. The Shift students still had a wall blocking us and the Mausoleum off from the chaos, and had actually pushed forward, expanding the buffer area and condensing the fighting further away from the Mausoleum. That was smart. Better protection for the suits. The battle was definitely dying down as our overwhelming numbers continued snuffing out our foes.

"You have to see for yourself. I don't understand it," Kára whispered in a hollow voice. Then she turned to lead me to the Mausoleum, walking in stiff, shuffling steps of abject dread. "It will hurt, Nate. After what I just saw out here with you and...him, this is going to *really* hurt you. That is why I'm terrified," she whispered, glancing back at me. "I'm terrified of what you might become *after*. That I might not be able to *stop* you. That I might want to *help* you..."

She squeezed my hand, and then continued on.

"Nate Temple!" a man screamed from behind me. I halted, glancing over my shoulder and clenching my jaw to see Baldur standing five paces away. He had snuck around the Shift students somehow, but they spun upon hearing his shout. I waved a hand at them, stalling their attack. Thankfully, they obeyed, eyeing the god's back and licking their lips. As tough as they were, they could not kill a god.

The Aesir god was covered in blood and gripping a hatchet in each hand, trembling with fury.

"You survived," I said in a cold, dead growl. "Consider yourself lucky, Baldur."

"I am not leaving," Baldur growled.

Kára studied him and then looked back at the Mausoleum. "What I found...is not time-sensitive. It can wait until all of the fighting is resolved," she whispered, glancing back at the battle and then Baldur. "I would prefer you to let out as much aggression as possible before you see...what's inside," she whispered. Then she smiled faintly, wiping at her cheeks and taking a deep breath. "And...he won't die easily, so...win-win?"

I slowly turned back to Baldur. "Have it your way..." I growled, "foolish god."

CHAPTER 63

Baldur stared at me, seething. I shoved the leather scrap from G-Ma into my pocket, keeping my eyes on the god. I shifted the satchel behind my back and made sure the strap was tight. Baldur was covered in bites and scratches, and even wounds from blades, but they were slowly healing even as I faced him. This god could not feel pain. He wasn't tough, he just couldn't feel when to give up. I considered calling up my Horseman's Mask, but it had powered down abruptly, and it had done me a whole lot of nothing against Aiden. Granted, that was from the dome of power he'd kept over us, but putting on the Mask of Hope still didn't seem appropriate. Neither did using the mistletoe daggers in my satchel.

I...wanted to *feel* this. Anything to shut out the screaming thoughts of Aiden's epic betrayal.

Baldur was a god and I was a godkiller. Golden light slowly began to glow beneath my veins and I smiled at the instinctive hesitation on his face. He swiftly replaced it with a sneer, but we both knew the truth.

The battle was dying down fast, now. The last of the Justices had fled—those who hadn't died, and only a dozen Einherjar remained, duking it out with Tory's shifters. On that note, I saw Tory still beating the living hell out of the Summer Queen, although I caught a few reciprocated blows as they literally fought fist-to-fist, further proving my hypothesis that the Summer Queen couldn't get directly involved in matters of Fae.

Because...guess who was a brand-new resident of Fae after our war? Tory Marlin, the Beast Master.

And since all the queen's guards were dead or dying, Summer had nowhere left to run.

I turned back to Baldur and rolled my shoulders, loosening them up. "Why did you—a god who can't feel pain—let a human turn you into his little bitch? I'm being serious. I *really* don't fucking get it." I pointed a thumb over my shoulder where Aiden had been standing.

"Because you exposed me when you killed my brother, you son of a bitch. You opened us all up to his wrath, and I'm not afraid to say he fucking *terrifies* me," Baldur snarled as his eyes followed my gesture. "Then I tried to save my soul by working to catch the fucking wolf for him—but you fucked that up for me, too. And then tonight..." he snarled, and I realized he was actually crying. Panting with fear. "I fucked up for the last time. Three strikes are two more than anyone *ever* gets."

The fear on the god's face was especially chilling, given the juxtaposition of Aiden chuckling about Baldur's fear of him a few minutes ago. And Baldur's fear had been born and bred *before* Aiden got a suit of Knightmare armor. Aiden was rapidly becoming the Moriarty to my Sherlock. Especially with his mystery gift in the Mausoleum, and how it had almost given Kára a panic attack.

I shoved down my own instinctive fear and focused on the task at hand. Pummeling this god with my bare fists was going to feel positively orgasmic. In a non-weird way.

I stared at him, allowing a slow smile to stretch over my face as my peripheral vision noticed a flicker of movement in the background behind him, on the side of the Mausoleum where most of the statues decorated the exterior wall. He had no idea. I needed to get him over there.

I jutted my chin out. "Coward."

He laughed maniacally, shaking his head. "He has my fucking soul, Temple. If you knew him like I do, you would run as far and fast as you possibly could. And he would *still* find you." He laughed again, and I could tell that his fear of Aiden had quite literally fractured his mind. "I want you to know that I *hope* you kill me. Maybe death by Horseman will offer me a sliver of sanctuary before he finds me. A moment of peace. Screaming in Hel is a paradise compared to what he will do to me for failing tonight."

"Then just stand still for a second and I'll serve you up a piece of peace."

He clenched his knuckles. "Oh, no. I want to kill you so badly that I can taste it with every *breath*," he rasped, taking a deep, pointed breath to show me. "We will both die this night, Temple. You took my father. My mother. You took *everything* from me."

"Not everything, Baldur. Not yet." I gave him a very slow smile. "But that will soon be resolved."

"Do your worst. I can't feel a thing, Temple."

I nodded; my voice surprisingly calm. "You have no idea how pleased I am to hear that, Baldur," I said, slowly walking towards him. "Because this godkiller has had a very bad day, and I really, really want to enjoy this." I paused. "In fact, I think I *need* it."

"Please," he said in a surprisingly genuine tone, "do your worst." And I could tell that he meant it. He wanted a Horseman to execute him just a hair's width more than he wanted to kill me.

St. Louis, man. You meet the craziest people.

And shit just keeps getting weirder and weirder.

Baldur rushed, swinging down with the axe in his right hand. I rushed faster, straight at him. Right before his axe was about to strike me, I Shadow Walked behind him, taking a page from Aiden's Justices at Camelot. Baldur's axe slammed into the snow and he cursed, straightening back up.

Before he could turn around, my golden, glowing fist punched him in his exposed side hard enough to splinter his ribs, not just break them. Then, as he was curling in to protect the injury, my other fist came down in a haymaker and punched him in the opposite ear, sending him crashing down to the ground. I knew he couldn't feel pain, so I didn't bother giving him time to take a breather or get back up. My primary focus was to get him to the side of the Mausoleum, because I had an idea.

I grabbed him by both ankles and started swinging him in an increasingly faster spin, whipping him around and around like a discus. Then I let him go.

He flew into the side of the Temple Mausoleum, striking a statue of

Odin near the peak. Baldur hit Odin's groin face-first, and he struck so hard that he snapped the statue of his father in half. The two of them went tumbling down to the ground. I lashed out with my magic, catching the statue of Odin so that Baldur hit the ground first. As he was jumping back to his feet, I hit him with the statue of Odin like it was a hammer, pounding him back to the snow. I saw two sets of glowing eyes in the nearby shadows: green and red. I nodded at them, grinning.

I Shadow Walked over to Baldur right as he was scrambling to his feet —before he could turn to look where he had last seen me near the front of the Mausoleum.

But I was already behind him when he finally faced that direction. I grabbed the back of his pants and pulled them down to his ankles, pantsing him. Then I struck him in both kidneys with my fists. I swiftly shuffled back a few steps, clearing the runway. Baldur shrieked in horrified outrage and dropped his hatchets as he bent over at the waist to grab his pants.

"TIMBER, ASS-CLOWN!" Grinder bleated at the top of his lungs, barreling towards Baldur's exposed ass with his head angled low like a battering ram. I wasn't sure when he'd shrunk down to normal size and joined us, but I had seen his glowing green eyes lurking back here. I saw Baldur's eyes widen as he hung upside down, looking backwards from between his legs. He tried to straighten, but Grinder hit him right as the god's torso was parallel with the ground in his frantic rush to stand up straight.

Which probably made the next part worse.

Baldur flew forward like Superman, except his face struck the ground near the beginning of his trajectory, turning him into a godly field plow as he tore a twenty-foot-long trench through the cemetery, stopping only when his head slammed into a tombstone hard enough to crack it. The heavy marble slab crashed down onto his back and he grunted as the air was knocked from his lungs. The god stayed there for a few seconds, his bare ass sticking up in the air and the large hunk of marble pinning him down.

Then he shrugged off the marble slab, cursing and muttering as he dazedly struggled to all fours.

I heard a loud bleating from way up high and I dropped my jaw to see that Grinder had hopped and jumped his way up to the damned peak of the Temple Mausoleum's roof. Fucking goats, man.

"GRINDER IS THE GREATEST OF ALL TIME!" he screamed as he leapt out into the open air. Then he was falling, kicking his little hooves as he flew down through the air and landed with all four hooves on Baldur's lower back right as he was trying to get back up from his all fours yoga pose.

Grinder hopped off the god, flicked his tail up, and then let out a sneer before trotting my way. I glanced back over my shoulder at the pair of red eyes high overhead. "I'm finished—" I held up a finger. "Wait. One more thing."

I picked up a broken piece of statue and turned to watch Baldur struggling back to his feet. He gritted his teeth and lifted his head to glare at me and Grinder.

I lobbed the fist-sized brick at him, clobbering him in the nose right as he made eye contact.

He let out a shout, grasping his face as his nose broke and blood sprayed into the air. He began cursing up a storm and reaching down to finally tug up his pants.

"Okay. *Now*, I'm finished," I said over my shoulder. Then I started walking back to the front of the Mausoleum. Grinder joined me, trotting by my side happily. He sneered as we passed Baldur, who was finally tugging his pants back into place.

Baldur noticed us leaving and cursed, furiously. "What the fuck? Get back here, Temple. I'm not finished until I'm dead." He snarled at my back.

I turned to face him, watching as his wounds began healing in real time. Fenrir and Loki had silently stepped out of the shadows at his back and were slowly walking towards him. He had no idea.

"You know what, Baldur?" I asked, shaking my head. "For what you've done, you don't deserve a hope for peace. You're not worth a Horseman's time. But I will do my worst." He frowned, licking his lips in confusion at my conflicting comments. "I won't do a thing. I will leave you to suffer the consequences of your own actions, just like G-Ma did. Just like the Summer Queen is. You made your bed; now lie in it."

He sputtered, outraged. "You turn your back on me and I will hound you for the rest of my life. Until Aiden comes to take his due, I will destroy everything and everyone you've ever loved."

"Uh huh," I said, checking my fingernails absently. "That's nice," I said.

"Listen to me! Fight me!"

"Why?" I asked, pausing. "You haven't really done anything to *me*. Other than being an embarrassing opponent, I guess. And a feckless, cowardly, disgrace of a deity."

"I am not a coward! I faced your army tonight. I even worked with Mordred and Summer to trap that fool, Fenrir!" he argued, his face darkening.

"Oh?" the giant wolf in question growled from directly behind Baldur. "Is that so."

CHAPTER 64

He spun around, looking pale and shocked. "Fenrir!" he
squeaked. "It's so great—"
Fenrir lashed out with his jaws and chomped him in a
single bite, forever stealing the god's hope that I would grant him a clean
death that might help him escape Aiden's apparent reach. I wasn't sure
how true either part was—Aiden's reach or the benefits of me killing him
to prevent it. Fenrir's teeth impaled Baldur and the god screamed in fear at
his future prospects as he hung halfway out of the wolf's mouth. Fenrir
violently shook his head back and forth, wagging his tail playfully like a
dog with a new toy.

I reached into my satchel and grabbed Gleipnir, realizing it was the
most fitting use for the silk strand possible. Its rightful place. The rope that
had bound Fenrir would now bind the god who had abducted him.
Fenrir's bane would become his boon. I handed it to Loki, and Fenrir
slammed the god down onto the ground, pinning him in place with a giant
paw as the uncharacteristically quiet god of mischief tied up his son's new
friend.

Loki calmly slapped a Sensate bracelet on Baldur's wrist and my eyes
widened in surprise. "There. Now no one can *ever* find you," he said in a
chillingly calm voice. He drew two mistletoe daggers and waved them in

front of Baldur's terrified eyes. Loki's grin was horrifying. "You never should have taken my son."

Baldur sobbed dejectedly.

"We're going to get to know each other very well, Baldur. Very, *very* well..." Fenrir growled.

Loki made a Gateway into a desolate, snowy, mountainous place at the edge of nowhere, and I knew I wouldn't see the three of them for a very long time. They stepped through, pulling the sobbing god with them. It winked shut and I nodded, feeling much better about the conclusion.

He hadn't been mine to kill.

With a resigned sigh, I started walking towards the front entrance of the Mausoleum to find Kára. Grinder trotted along at my side, glancing left and right to make sure there were no dangers for me to worry about. He looked...tense, though. After our victory, I had expected some taunts or crude commentary.

I saw Tory peek her head around the corner and smile. "Oh, good. You're finished. Come here really quickly. I want to get your opinion on something."

I turned to Grinder. "Go make sure the kiddos are safe," I reminded him.

"Okay. They're inside with Gunnar and Ashley. Snarler is going to be so jealous. He missed everything!"

I nodded soberly. "That's what happens when you put Tiny Balls in your mouth," I said with a straight face. He shuddered and gave me a firm nod. Then he trotted past Tory and around the corner.

I made my way over, smiling weakly at Tory. She looked exhausted, dirty, and sported a few cuts on her face and an even a deeper one on her upper arm. I wondered if Summer had escaped, but I didn't have time to ask her about it—not with Aiden's gift and a traumatized Kára waiting for me. "I can't right now, Tory. I need to—"

Kára stepped out from behind Tory and shook her head. "It's okay, Nate. Tory has *good* news. The...other thing can wait a few more minutes." Kára gave me a reassuring smile, but it was half as bright as usual, still haunted by the gift she had found. I nodded; my own smile as hollow as hers.

She grabbed my hand as Tory grabbed my other, and the two of them pulled me towards a separate building that looked like a small work shed for the cemetery's caretaker. I frowned. "What—"

My question was cut off as Tory pulled open the door and forcefully ushered me inside the dim space. A single light bulb hung from the ceiling on a wire, casting the room in an eerie light. Kára stepped up beside me and rested her cheek on my shoulder with an affectionate sigh for a few seconds, as if desperately needing the human contact.

I squeezed her hand meaningfully and then turned back to the shed. Shovels, rakes, and other garden equipment hung on the walls.

A wheelbarrow sat in the center of the building.

And inside that wheelbarrow was the Summer Queen. She was tied to the wheelbarrow by thick, heavy iron chains that were burning her flesh with a low, crackling, hissing sound. She took one look at me, and her eyes suddenly bulged in horror as she tried to scream beneath the wad of dirty cloth that had been wrapped around her head, covering her mouth.

And behind that wheelbarrow was the Winter Queen.

And beside that Winter Queen was the King of Camelot.

Tory stepped up beside Winter and smiled at me. "Ta-da!" she said, holding out her hands to show me the kidnapped Summer Queen. "You missed her crying like a little bitch," she said smugly.

Alex cleared his throat, sensing my concern. "Don't worry, Nate. The Winter Queen and I are working together to guard the Summer Army. She brought her forces to the field to aid Camelot. We are allies."

I turned to the Winter Queen and nodded. "Thank you." My eyes flicked down to Summer and then back to her. "You were correct about your sister, if that's not apparent."

The Winter Queen grimaced at her sister. "For armor," she snarled. Then she spat on her sister's face. "You would betray a sister for armor. You vicious little twat!"

"Why are you all here?" I asked. I was fairly sure I knew the answer, but I didn't want to assume incorrectly.

Winter licked her lips. "She has earned death. Do any disagree?" No one spoke, so she turned back to me. "Killing a queen has major consequences. The power of her mantle would come to me, doubling my strength, and putting all of Fae at my command. Since none of you have doubts about my personal character and all here know me for my boundless grace and charity, I will gladly accept this new, immense power that will absolutely not corrupt me...maybe," she said, reaching for her sister's throat with long, icy fingernails.

I burst out laughing and Tory swatted her hand away with a scolding look. "Just tell him. He's busy."

The Winter Queen chuckled and shrugged. "There is a chance that I would not even survive such a transfer, resulting in the death of *two* queens," she told me, meaningfully.

Everyone was silent for a few beats. "So...we give her a leash and a food bowl?"

"She says I am strong enough to take her place, preventing the chaos of her death," Tory blurted, her green eyes flashing. "That's why Winter came. To see if I could defeat Summer—and I did!" she said, pointing at the bug-eyed proof, who had turned as white as a sheet.

I grunted, smiling. "I *knew* it! That was why you were selling Tory so hard on Fae," I said, smiling at Winter. "You knew she had to die but that someone had to replace her. That's why you abducted the kids."

Winter nodded. "I kidnapped the children because I care," she said, deadpan. "Oh. So. Much."

Tory rolled her eyes, grinning. "Oh, hush, Winnie. The kids told me you read them *bedtime stories*."

Winnie's cheeks blushed beet red. I was definitely going to use that nickname on her if it got this kind of reaction. She sputtered indignantly, unable to form words because she was so embarrassed by this evidence of her showing affection to someone of her own free will.

I turned to Tory. "Do you want this?" I asked her.

She nodded eagerly. "If it means I can better protect my students? Yes. St. Louis has nothing left for me. I don't ever speak to Regulars. I live at the school. The Reds are always gone, and Alucard is a Horseman now, so I hardly ever see my best friend," she said, sadly. "I don't *want* this...I think I *need* this."

Kára squeezed my hand and I smiled at Tory. "You don't need my permission, Tory. I know you want to do what's best for the kids, and if Winter is certain you can handle the mantle, then I think you would make an excellent queen."

I gave the Winter Queen a warning look that politely informed her of all the horrible things I would do to her if this was some sort of trick and Tory got hurt. She swallowed and nodded her commitment.

I knew I would need allies in the future, and it was better than giving the power to Winter—especially if it might kill her or turn her into a supervillain. Now I had King Alex and a Summer Queen in my pocket.

"Hey," I said, a sudden thought coming to mind. "There is a feathery ogre who was nice to me. No idea what his name is, but he was the only nice one I saw. He was carrying her palanquin. Maybe give him a second chance?" I remembered all the dead bodies outside and sighed. "If he's even alive."

Tory smiled sweetly. "That's very thoughtful of you, Nate. I did see one of them running away from the fighting," she said absently. "I will send some of my shifters to look for him."

Winter's nose was scrunched up as if she smelled something particularly foul—personally disgusted by our compassion. She was such a sweetheart.

As I gave Summer one last look, I remembered her telling me she'd been doing all of this to protect Fae from manlings. At the time, I'd assumed she was referring to me and Alex. But...maybe she'd been just as scared of Aiden. *More* scared of Aiden.

Winter cleared her throat. "You must have the conviction to kill her yourself, Tory. No one can do this for you. In Fae, we take what we want—" She cut off, turning to look at us shrewdly. "Slitting throats is queen business. Shoo."

Alex's eyes widened along with mine. Kára eagerly tugged me out of the shed, and Alex wisely followed suit, closing the door behind him. We left the sounds of the screaming, old summer queen behind us without a backward glance.

Alex must have picked up on our desire for privacy, because he jogged ahead of us without a word. He began directing shifters to start moving bodies and cleaning up the crime scene. I let out a sigh of relief, thankful that I wouldn't have to do it. We were halfway to the Mausoleum when there was a green flash behind us and the shed exploded, knocking the old wooden walls down and sending the wheelbarrow cartwheeling into the air.

We spun to see an explosion of Summer power. Trees suddenly

sprouted new offshoots, and grass exploded out from the snow, followed by rows and rows of vibrant, bright flowers. Tory stood in the center of the fresh growth, her eyes blazing with green light. She was laughing and her arms were spread wide. It slowly faded and she let out a deep breath, turning to Winter with a huge smile.

Winter stomped on a patch of flowers, grinding her heel into it with a growl. And then she walked over to Tory. I shook my head in surprise as she wrapped her arm around the Beast Master Queen's shoulders, guiding her away from the destruction for a leisurely walk with her new sister.

Flowers trailed in Tory's footsteps, and hoarfrost trailed in...Winnie's footsteps.

I saw two were-rhinos peel off from a tall obelisk they'd been leaning against. The two of them swept their gazes from left to right and followed their Beast Master, ever vigilant to keep her safe. I nodded approvingly. Now that she was queen, she would need it more than ever.

CHAPTER 65

We walked through the jagged hole that had replaced the door to the Mausoleum. Pockets of shifters huddled in alcoves, speaking in soft murmurs. Upon seeing us walk in, they immediately grew suddenly quiet. "Everybody out!" Yahn commanded, suddenly appearing a few feet away from me. The shifter dragon had the ability to turn invisible when he wanted to, and looked like a glass dragon when he wasn't blending in with his surroundings. He clapped his hands loudly. "Right *now!*"

They scattered like dried leaves in a storm, racing out the door as fast as they could. Alex dipped his chin at Yahn. "I want to talk to you about something later. No rush."

Yahn nodded. "I've got a few things to wrap up and then I'll find you."

Alex smiled and stepped outside, barking out commands to help the others with cleaning up the mess, like he'd been doing earlier. I heard him say something about transporting the bodies to Fae and I let out a sigh of relief. Yahn, rather than wrapping up a few things, turned invisible again, presumably guarding the entrance in stealth in case any more enemies arrived for a surprise attack.

Kára guided me deeper into the Mausoleum, and soon it was hauntingly quiet. I glanced over at her, but her lips were pursed, and her green and blue eyes were set dead ahead.

We walked past my Gateway to Fae and I saw Gunnar in his Horseman form guarding a pile of three sets of armor. Ashley was walking down the hall in her armor, checking behind each statue and tomb as if to make sure no enemies had snuck into the Mausoleum. A security check. Gunnar dipped his chin at me in silence, and it had a compassionate, empathetic feel to it.

I wondered whether I was the only one who didn't know what Aiden's gift was.

Or whether they even knew Aiden was behind all the insanity. Had everyone been gossiping about my long talk under the purple dome with the very man who had set all of this death in motion? Were they now afraid and wary of me?

I froze abruptly, glancing back at the armor. "There are supposed to be *five*," I growled, recounting in my head just to make sure. Gunnar's tail wilted and he nodded knowingly.

Kára grimaced. "Two more were missing when we collected the suits. No one has adopted them, but we only found three."

I gritted my teeth. "We need to get some bodies in those goddamned suits! This is fucking ridiculous. We're going to lose them all if we leave them empty!"

Gunnar nodded. "I agree. This is just asking for trouble."

Kára pulled me onward firmly, forcing me to walk or be dragged. "Come on."

I complied, but I was shaking my head angrily. Aiden had two more than I'd thought, but he had told me he intended to take six. "The smug fucking bastard," I growled. "Now we're even. Six for six."

Kára squeezed my arm consolingly as she continued guiding me on. "At least it's *even*," she said. "It could have been a lot worse."

"We don't have six Knights," I reminded her. "We have three. And three empty suits."

We came to a stop in front of the fountain and the family tree. My eyes instantly went down to the stairs hidden within the fountain, staring at the entrance to the Elder's Realm where Talon and Carl had gone to chase Cyrilo and the other two Knightmares working for Aiden.

Kára placed a finger under my chin and lifted it higher, pointing at the Temple Family Tree.

I frowned, opening my mouth to speak, when I abruptly froze.

A red line had been slashed across the wall, defacing the roots of the tree. I followed the red line to see a green gem had been affixed to the bottom corner of the wall, far removed from the tree and its rubies and sapphires that marked each Temple ancestor and their name on the extensive root system.

I leaned forward to get a better look. My heart thundered in my chest and I sucked in a breath.

Aiden, Mac's son had been painted in red below the green gem.

The other end of the red line stretched across to stop at another name.

Makayla Temple. Or *Mac*, as my father had called her.

I could hear my thumping heart in my ears as my knees grew weak.

Not Aiden *Maxon*...

Aiden, Mac's son.

I fell to my knees, panting desperately. Kára knelt down beside me, tears streaming down her cheeks. "It's a lie, right, Nate? He can't be your half-brother. It's a filthy lie," she said, sobbing. "He just wants to get in your head."

"I...have no idea," I whispered, blinking rapidly and hearing a sharp ringing in my ears. Aiden's insane infatuation with me suddenly made sense. Why he'd wanted to get close to me. This was what he'd done in the last seven days. He'd gotten close to...his half-brother. Why he'd shared his orphan story. It was for *this* moment.

So that I heard the story of his mother abandoning him. He had wanted me to show him empathy for his plight, and disdain for his mother's heartless act. He'd done that knowing that he would later show me that the horrible mother who'd abandoned him...

Had been *mine*.

Ours.

I'd walked him through Chateau Falco, showing him things and treating him like a friend, like a...

Brother.

I shook my head, replaying our conversations in a new light. If Aiden saw me as a brother, many of his strangely phrased or worded comments made much more sense. He'd joked about me stumbling over a root just outside. Roots—like my family tree.

And why he hadn't wanted to kill me. He did want to kill me, but part of him did not. I was family. His *only* family.

He'd wanted to play games with me. Share his toys. So many quotes from his lips over the past few days popped into my memory, all carefully orchestrated to deliver maximum damage.

He'd used the Doppelgänger Golem rune specifically so he could get close to me, make me feel compassion and friendship and concern for him, and then tragically die after we became friends—after I started to trust him.

But it had to be a lie, didn't it?

If not, my mother was the same mother who orphaned him, which would have been before I was born. Was that even possible? Before she met my father? Yet another lie?

Did my father even know?

And now I knew exactly why Aiden had chosen to save children to win me over. He had known everything about me. He'd studied me for years.

He'd crafted the perfect stranger for me to mistakenly trust. Only so he could die in my arms and make me feel sorry for him...to make me miss him.

And then to return and shove it all in my face.

I'd just been conned in the most complete way—not so he could lie, but so he could tell me a secret truth.

"Aiden will die," I swore, climbing to my feet and storming over to the wall. I grabbed the green stone and tore it off with a snarl, panting.

The gem puffed into dust and I was suddenly holding a black box with silver ribbons. It was about the dimensions of a greeting card, but deeper. I stared down at it in surprise. Kára stumbled to her feet with a sharp breath and leaned up against me, staring down at the box. I held my breath and opened it.

Inside was Aiden's little Moleskine journal. The same one I'd found in the delivery truck when I'd first discovered his unconscious body. Beneath that was a polaroid picture. I lifted both out, looking at the picture first. I sucked in a breath, seeing an image of Mordred, Baldur, and the Summer Queen smiling and posing in front of a bound Fenrir. Evidence of their crime. No wonder they'd been so terrified. Aiden had photo evidence. Blackmail.

I shook my head, setting the picture down and opening up the credit-card-sized notebook.

The first page had the same date as before, but below was a message.

Today, my brother and I started playing our first game together, but it's going to be a long one. I'm so lucky to have finally found him. We're going to have so much fun, but we have a lot of catching up to do. We will need each other now more than ever. Brothers always have each other's backs, even when they disagree on things.

Because family matters. Even half of a family. Take what you can get, right?

Aiden, Mac's son.

Postscript: Should I adopt the last name Temple? Nah...too pretentious. Nate would be furious, haha.

I'll think of something neat. Otherwise, how is history supposed to remember me?

I turned the page, feeling numb. Kára cursed up a storm, clenching her fists hard enough to crack her knuckles. The rest of the notebook was full of notes, dates, times, people, places, schemes, plans, and everything else he had done leading up to our first...game together.

"He...gave me all the answers," I whispered, staring down at the pages. "He had it all planned out. When the attacks would happen. Everything," I said, shaking my head. "He sent the wizards to Shift. He sent the wizards to Camelot to, and I quote, 'die so heroically that it breaks Nate's heart.'"

Kára swore.

And the pages continued in meticulous detail. On and on and on. I finally closed it, taking a calming breath. I couldn't read this all right now. I couldn't afford to break down. Talon and Carl needed me in the Elder's Realm.

The reason Aiden had done all this became perfectly clear. "He wanted revenge against the life he should have had," I breathed.

"But your mother wasn't a Temple," Kára said.

"No, but my dad stole her from Aiden—in his eyes, at least. The Temple family took his mother, and I am the last Temple. There is no one else to punish *but* me."

"Jesus," Kára breathed. "He's never going to stop unless we stop him. He has thirty years of jealousy to take out on you."

I nodded. "Let's hope my years in Fae count for my total, then," I said, rising to my feet. "Come. We need to focus. We can read this on our journey. I feel like killing some Knightmare wizards, Kára. I want the practice so I can get ready for him. He's a lot stronger than me, and Baldur was terrified of him—but not me. I have no idea why, but that's chilling."

"I want practice too." Her face was a storm cloud of fury as we made our way to Gunnar to organize the trip.

I looked up to see him still standing guard.

Two suits winked out behind him and I froze, skidding to a halt. "Gunnar!" I shouted, calling up my magic. Gunnar spun, staring down to see only one suit remaining.

Ashley came running down the hall, looking panicked. "Who the hell just took two—"

Calvin and Makayla abruptly shimmered into existence, staring down at the glossy, sleek armor covering their bodies. Calvin shifted into his wolf form and the armor shifted with him, turning into werewolf armor. He panted happily, wagging his Knightly tale as he turned to his mother and father.

Ashley's face turned white as her armor and she sputtered incredulously, unable to form words. Gunnar stared at his children with a baffled look.

Mac folded her armored arms and began tapping her foot. "We are doing what our Godfather requested. We want to protect people, and my friend is out there," she said, pointing towards the Elder Realm. "Carl needs me." Gunnar turned to check with his wife with a very cautious look on his face.

I smiled. "Well."

The other suit winked out of existence and I cursed. I opened my mouth to shout when Yahn winked into view, clad in the sleek white armor.

"What the hell?" Gunnar roared, realizing he'd completely failed at guarding the suits.

Yahn pointed at Calvin and Mac. "They did it, too." He smirked at his childish excuse. "Alex already asked me," he assured us. "Well, he implied it..."

Mac grinned, turning to me. "Now, all we need is the Dark Horse, Godfather. Are you ready to take us camping?" she said, pointing towards the Elder's Realm.

"Yes, Mac. I think I am." I wrapped my arm around Kára's shoulders and looked at Gunnar and Ashley. "Think about it this way. They're safer than they've ever been, and now you have something in common to bond over. Want to come with us on our camping trip?"

Gunnar growled happily, wagging his tail. "As long as it doesn't involve me guarding anything," he said drily. "I'm not too good at that."

Ashley nodded stiffly. "We will talk about this later, children. But I'm not letting you out of my sight, so let's go save our friends."

"Our family," Mac corrected, smiling at Yahn.

He shrugged. "Let's do it. You'll need a dragon to scout from above."

"Then let's go camping," I said, and our group turned around, stepping up beside me to face the Elder's Realm together. "We're coming, guys," I said under my breath.

"You're all grounded when we get back," Ashley snarled, drawing her two white axes.

Gunnar burst out laughing. "For at least a week."

"Years," Ashley corrected him. "But until then, Yahn is now their commanding officer, and I am *his* commanding officer."

"Worth it," Yahn chuckled. "Now, let's go kill those other Knightmares."

Grinder came galloping down the hall behind us. "Wait!"

We turned to face him and he skidded to a halt in front of us. "What's wrong?" I demanded, wondering what the hell else could ruin my day.

"You forgot your food," he said with a grin.

Nate Temple will return in 2021...

Turn the page to read a sample of <u>**UNCHAINED**</u> *- Feathers and Fire Series Book 1, or* **BUY ONLINE (FREE with Kindle Unlimited subscription).** *Callie Penrose is a wizard in Kansas City, MO who hunts monsters for the Vatican. She meets Nate Temple, and things devolve from there...*

(Note: Callie appears in the TempleVerse after Nate's book 6, TINY GODS...Full chronology of all books in the TempleVerse shown on the 'Books by Shayne Silvers' page)

TRY: UNCHAINED (FEATHERS AND FIRE #1)

The rain pelted my hair, plastering loose strands of it to my forehead as I panted, eyes darting from tree to tree, terrified of each shifting branch, splash of water, and whistle of wind slipping through the nightscape around us. But...I was somewhat *excited*, too.

Somewhat.

"Easy, girl. All will be well," the big man creeping just ahead of me, murmured.

"You said we were going to get ice cream!" I hissed at him, failing to compose myself, but careful to keep my voice low and my eyes alert. "I'm not ready for this!" I had been trained to fight, with my hands, with weapons, and with my magic. But I had never taken an active role in a hunt before. I'd always been the getaway driver for my mentor.

The man grunted, grey eyes scanning the trees as he slipped through the tall grass. "And did we not get ice cream before coming here? Because I think I see some in your hair."

"You know what I mean, Roland. You tricked me." I checked the tips of my loose hair, saw nothing, and scowled at his back.

"The Lord does not give us a greater burden than we can shoulder."

I muttered dark things under my breath, wiping the water from my eyes. Again. My new shirt was going to be ruined. Silk never fared well in the rain. My choice of shoes wasn't much better. Boots, yes, but distressed, *fashionable* boots. Not work boots designed for the rain and mud. Definitely not monster hunting boots for our evening excursion through one of Kansas City's wooded parks. I realized I was forcibly distracting myself, keeping my mind busy with mundane thoughts to avoid my very real anxiety. Because whenever I grew nervous, an imagined nightmare always—

A church looming before me. Rain pouring down. Night sky and a glowing moon overhead. I was all alone. Crying on the cold, stone steps, an infant in a cardboard box—

I forced the nightmare away, breathing heavily. "You know I hate it when you talk like that," I whispered to him, trying to regain my composure. I wasn't angry with him, but was growing increasingly uncomfortable with our situation after my brief flashback of fear.

"Doesn't mean it shouldn't be said," he said kindly. "I think we're close. Be alert. Remember your training. Banish your fears. I am here. And the Lord is here. He always is."

So, he had noticed my sudden anxiety. "Maybe I should just go back to the car. I know I've trained, but I really don't think—"

A shape of fur, fangs, and claws launched from the shadows towards me, cutting off my words as it snarled, thirsty for my blood.

And my nightmare slipped back into my thoughts like a veiled assassin, a wraith hoping to hold me still for the monster to eat. I froze, unable to move. Twin sticks of power abruptly erupted into being in my clenched fists, but my fear swamped me with that stupid nightmare, the sticks held at my side, useless to save me.

Right before the beast's claws reached me, it grunted as something batted it from the air, sending it flying sideways. It struck a tree with another grunt and an angry whine of pain.

I fell to my knees right into a puddle, arms shaking, breathing fast.

My sticks crackled in the rain like live cattle prods, except their entire length was the electrical section — at least to anyone other than me. I could hold them without pain.

Magic was a part of me, coursing through my veins whether I wanted it or not, and Roland had spent many years teaching me how to master it. But I had never been able to fully master the nightmare inside me, and in moments of fear, it always won, overriding my training.

The fact that I had resorted to weapons — like the ones he had trained me with — rather than a burst of flame, was startling. It was good in the fact that my body's reflexes knew enough to call up a defense even without my direct command, but bad in the fact that it was the worst form of defense for the situation presented. I could have very easily done as Roland did, and hurt it from a distance. But I hadn't. Because of my stupid block.

Roland placed a calloused palm on my shoulder, and I flinched. "Easy, see? I am here." But he did frown at my choice of weapons, the reprimand silent but loud in my mind. I let out a shaky breath, forcing my fear back down. It was all in my head, but still, it wasn't easy. Fear could be like that.

I focused on Roland's implied lesson. Close combat weapons — even magically-powered ones — were for last resorts. I averted my eyes in very real shame. I knew these things. He didn't even need to tell me them. But when that damned nightmare caught hold of me, all my training went out the window. It haunted me like a shadow, waiting for moments just like this, as if trying to kill me. A form of psychological suicide? But it was why I constantly refused to join Roland on his hunts. He knew about it. And although he was trying to help me overcome that fear, he never pressed too hard.

Rain continued to sizzle as it struck my batons. I didn't let them go, using them as a totem to build my confidence back up. I slowly lifted my eyes to nod at him as I climbed back to my feet.

That's when I saw the second set of eyes in the shadows, right before they flew out of the darkness towards Roland's back. I threw one of my batons and missed, but that pretty much let Roland know that an unfriendly was behind him. Either that or I had just failed to murder my mentor at point-blank range. He whirled to confront the monster, expecting another aerial assault as he unleashed a ball of fire that splashed over the tree at chest height, washing the trunk in blue flames. But this monster was tricky. It hadn't planned on tackling Roland, but had merely jumped out of the darkness to get closer, no doubt learning from its fallen comrade, who still lay unmoving against the tree behind me.

His coat shone like midnight clouds with hints of lightning flashing in the depths of thick, wiry fur. The coat of dew dotting his fur reflected the moonlight, giving him a faint sheen as if covered in fresh oil. He was tall, easily hip height at the shoulder, and barrel chested, his rump much leaner than the rest of his body. He — I assumed male from the long, thick mane around his neck — had a very long snout, much longer and wider than any werewolf I had ever seen. Amazingly, and beyond my control, I realized he was beautiful.

But most of the natural world's lethal hunters were beautiful.

He landed in a wet puddle a pace in front of Roland, juked to the right, and then to the left, racing past the big man, biting into his hamstrings on his way by.

A wash of anger rolled over me at seeing my mentor injured, dousing my fear, and I swung my baton down as hard as I could. It struck the beast in the rump as it tried to dart back to cover — a typical wolf tactic. My blow singed his hair and shattered bone. The creature collapsed into a puddle of mud with a yelp, instinctively snapping his jaws over his shoulder to bite whatever had hit him.

I let him. But mostly out of dumb luck as I heard Roland hiss in pain, falling to the ground.

The monster's jaws clamped around my baton, and there was an immediate explosion of teeth and blood that sent him flying several feet away into the tall brush, yipping, screaming, and staggering. Before he slipped out of sight, I noticed that his lower jaw was simply *gone*, from the contact of his saliva on my electrified magical batons. Then he managed to limp into the woods with more pitiful yowls, but I had no mind to chase him.

Roland — that titan of a man, my mentor — was hurt. I could smell copper in the air, and knew we had to get out of here. Fast. Because we had anticipated only one of the monsters. But there had been two of them, and they hadn't been the run-of-the-mill werewolves we had been warned about. If there were two, perhaps there were more. And they were evidently the prehistoric cousin of any werewolf I had ever seen or read about.

Roland hissed again as he stared down at his leg, growling with both pain and anger. My eyes darted back to the first monster, wary of another attack. It *almost* looked like a werewolf, but bigger. Much bigger. He didn't move, but I saw he was breathing. He had a notch in his right ear and a jagged scar on his long snout. Part of me wanted to go over to him and torture him. Slowly. Use his pain to finally drown my nightmare, my fear. The fear that had caused Roland's injury. My lack of inner-strength had not only put me in danger, but had hurt my mentor, my friend.

I shivered, forcing the thought away. That was *cold*. Not me. Sure, I was no stranger to fighting, but that had always been in a ring. Practicing. Sparring. Never life or death.

But I suddenly realized something very dark about myself in the chill, rainy night. Although I was terrified, I felt a deep ocean of anger manifest inside me, wanting only to dispense justice as I saw fit. To use that rage to battle my own demons. As if feeding one would starve the other, reminding me of the Cherokee Indian Legend Roland had once told me.

An old Cherokee man was teaching his grandson about life. "A fight is going on inside me," he told the boy. "It is a terrible fight between two wolves. One is evil — he is anger, envy, sorrow, regret, greed, arrogance, self-pity, guilt, resentment, inferiority, lies, false pride, superiority, and ego." After a few moments to make sure he had the boy's undivided attention, he continued.

"The other wolf is good — he is joy, peace, love, hope, serenity, humility, kindness, benevolence, empathy, generosity, truth, compassion, and faith. The same fight is going on inside of you, boy, and inside of every other person, too."

The grandson thought about this for a few minutes before replying. "Which wolf will win?"

The old Cherokee man simply said, "The one you feed, boy. The one you feed..."

And I felt like feeding one of my wolves today, by killing this one...

Get the full book ONLINE! http://www.shaynesilvers.com/l/38952

*Turn the page to read a sample of **WHISKEY GINGER** - Phantom Queen Diaries Book 1, or **BUY ONLINE**. Quinn MacKenna is a black magic arms dealer from Boston, and her bark is almost as bad as her bite.*

TRY: WHISKEY GINGER (PHANTOM QUEEN DIARIES # 1)

The pasty guitarist hunched forward, thrust a rolled-up wad of paper deep into one nostril, and snorted a line of blood crystals —frozen hemoglobin that I'd smuggled over in a refrigerated canister—with the uncanny grace of a drug addict. He sat back, fangs gleaming, and pawed at his nose. "That's some bodacious shit. Hey, bros," he said, glancing at his fellow band members, "come hit this shit before it melts."

He fetched one of the backstage passes hanging nearby, pried the plastic badge from its lanyard, and used it to split up the crystals, murmuring something in an accent that reminded me of California. Not *the* California, but you know, Cali-foh-nia—the land of beaches, babes, and bros. I retrieved a toothpick from my pocket and punched it through its thin wrapper. "So," I asked no one in particular, "now that ye have the product, who's payin'?"

Another band member stepped out of the shadows to my left, and I don't mean that figuratively, either—the fucker literally stepped out of the shadows. I scowled at him, but hid my surprise, nonchalantly rolling the toothpick from one side of my mouth to the other.

The rest of the band gathered around the dressing room table, following the guitarist's lead by preparing their own snorting utensils— tattered magazine covers, mostly. Typically, you'd do this sort of thing with a dollar-bill, maybe even a Benjamin if you were flush. But fangers like this lot couldn't touch cash directly—in God We Trust and all that. Of course, I didn't really understand why sucking blood the old-fashioned way had suddenly gone out of style. More of a rush, maybe?

"It lasts longer," the vampire next to me explained, catching my mildly curious expression. "It's especially good for shows and stuff. Makes us look, like, less—"

"Creepy?" I offered, my Irish brogue lilting just enough to make it a question.

"Pale," he finished, frowning.

I shrugged. "Listen, I've got places to be," I said, holding out my hand.

"I'm sure you do," he replied, smiling. "Tell you what, why don't you, like, hang around for a bit? Once that wears off," he dipped his head toward the bloody powder smeared across the table's surface, "we may need a pick-me-up." He rested his hand on my arm and our gazes locked.

I blinked, realized what he was trying to pull, and rolled my eyes. His widened in surprise, then shock as I yanked out my toothpick and shoved it through his hand.

"Motherfuck—"

"I want what we agreed on," I declared. "Now. No tricks."

The rest of the band saw what happened and rose faster than I could blink. They circled me, their grins feral...they might have even seemed intimidating if it weren't for the fact that they each had a case of the sniffles —I had to work extra hard not to think about what it felt like to have someone else's blood dripping down my nasal cavity.

I held up a hand.

"Can I ask ye gentlemen a question before we get started?" I asked. "Do ye even *have* what I asked for?"

Two of the band members exchanged looks and shrugged. The guitarist, however, glanced back towards the dressing room, where a brown paper bag sat next to a case full of makeup. He caught me looking and bared his teeth, his fangs stretching until it looked like it would be uncomfortable for him to close his mouth without piercing his own lip.

"Follow-up question," I said, eyeing the vampire I'd stabbed as he gingerly withdrew the toothpick from his hand and flung it across the room with a snarl. "Do ye do each other's make-up? Since, ye know, ye can't use mirrors?"

I was genuinely curious.

The guitarist grunted. "Mike, we have to go on soon."

"Wait a minute. Mike?" I turned to the snarling vampire with a frown. "What happened to *The Vampire Prospero*?" I glanced at the numerous fliers in the dressing room, most of which depicted the band members wading through blood, with Mike in the lead, each one titled *The Vampire Prospero* in *Rocky Horror Picture Show* font. Come to think of it…Mike did look a little like Tim Curry in all that leather and lace.

I was about to comment on the resemblance when Mike spoke up, "Alright, change of plans, bros. We're gonna drain this bitch before the show. We'll look totally—"

"Creepy?" I offered, again.

"Kill her."

Get the full book ONLINE! *http://www.shaynesilvers.com/l/206897*

(Note: Full chronology of all books in the TempleVerse shown on the 'BOOKS BY SHAYNE SILVERS' page.)

MAKE A DIFFERENCE

Reviews are the most powerful tools in my arsenal when it comes to getting attention for my books. Much as I'd like to, I don't have the financial muscle of a New York publisher.

But I do have something much more powerful and effective than that, and it's something that those publishers would kill to get their hands on.

A committed and loyal bunch of readers.

Honest reviews of my books help bring them to the attention of other readers.

If you've enjoyed this book, I would be very grateful if you could spend just five minutes leaving a review on my book's Amazon page.

Thank you very much in advance.

ACKNOWLEDGMENTS

Team Temple and the Den of Freaks on Facebook have become family to me. I couldn't do it without die-hard readers like them.

I would also like to thank you, the reader. I hope you enjoyed reading *SAVAGE* as much as I enjoyed writing it. Be sure to check out the two crossover series in the Temple Verse: The **Feathers and Fire Series** and the **Phantom Queen Diaries**.

And last, but definitely not least, I thank my wife, Lexy. Without your support, none of this would have been possible.

ABOUT SHAYNE SILVERS

Shayne is a man of mystery and power, whose power is exceeded only by his mystery...

He currently writes the Amazon Bestselling **Nate Temple** Series, which features a foul-mouthed wizard from St. Louis. He rides a blood-thirsty unicorn, drinks with Achilles, and is pals with the Four Horsemen.

He also writes the Amazon Bestselling **Feathers and Fire** Series—a second series in the TempleVerse. The story follows a rookie spell-slinger named Callie Penrose who works for the Vatican in Kansas City. Her problem? Hell seems to know more about her past than she does.

He coauthors **The Phantom Queen Diaries**—a third series set in The TempleVerse—with Cameron O'Connell. The story follows Quinn MacKenna, a mouthy black magic arms dealer in Boston. All she wants? A round-trip ticket to the Fae realm...and maybe a drink on the house.

He also writes the **Shade of Devil Series**, which tells the story of Sorin Ambrogio—the world's FIRST vampire. He was put into a magical slumber by a Native American Medicine Man when the Americas were first discovered by Europeans. Sorin wakes up after five-hundred years to learn that his protégé, Dracula, stole his reputation and that no one has ever even heard of Sorin Ambrogio. The streets of New York City will run with blood as Sorin reclaims his legend.

Shayne holds two high-ranking black belts, and can be found writing in a coffee shop, cackling madly into his computer screen while pounding shots of espresso. He's hard at work on the newest books in the TempleVerse—You can find updates on new releases or chronological reading order on the next page, his website, or any of his social media accounts. Follow him online for all sorts of groovy goodies, giveaways, and new release updates:

Get Down with Shayne Online
www.shaynesilvers.com
info@shaynesilvers.com

facebook.com/shaynesilversfanpage

amazon.com/author/shaynesilvers

bookbub.com/profile/shayne-silvers

instagram.com/shaynesilversofficial

twitter.com/shaynesilvers

goodreads.com/ShayneSilvers

BOOKS BY SHAYNE SILVERS

CHRONOLOGY: All stories in the TempleVerse are shown in chronological order on the following page

CHRONOLOGICAL ORDER: TEMPLE VERSE

FAIRY TALE (TEMPLE PREQUEL)

OBSIDIAN SON (TEMPLE 1)

BLOOD DEBTS (TEMPLE 2)

GRIMM (TEMPLE 3)

SILVER TONGUE (TEMPLE 4)

BEAST MASTER (TEMPLE 5)

BEERLYMPIAN (TEMPLE 5.5)

TINY GODS (TEMPLE 6)

DADDY DUTY (TEMPLE NOVELLA 6.5)

UNCHAINED (FEATHERS...1)

RAGE (FEATHERS...2)

WILD SIDE (TEMPLE 7)

WAR HAMMER (TEMPLE 8)

WHISPERS (FEATHERS...3)

COLLINS (PHANTOM 0)

WHISKEY GINGER (PHANTOM...1)

NINE SOULS (TEMPLE 9)

COSMOPOLITAN (PHANTOM...2)

ANGEL'S ROAR (FEATHERS...4)

MOTHERLUCKER (FEATHERS 4.5, PHANTOM 3.5)

OLD FASHIONED (PHANTOM...3)

HORSEMAN (TEMPLE 10)

DARK AND STORMY (PHANTOM...4)

MOSCOW MULE (PHANTOM...5)

SINNER (FEATHERS...5)

WITCHES BREW (PHANTOM...6)

LEGEND (TEMPLE...11)

SALTY DOG (PHANTOM...7)

BLACK SHEEP (FEATHERS...6)

GODLESS (FEATHERS...7)

SHADE OF DEVIL SERIES

(Not part of the TempleVerse)

by Shayne Silvers

Printed in Great Britain
by Amazon